E.V. Seymour is the author of ten novels and has had a number of short stories broadcast on BBC Radio Devon. Educated at an all girls' boarding school, which she detested, she spectacularly underachieved. Sixth form in Cheltenham proved a lot more interesting, enjoyable and productive.

After a short and successful career in PR in London and Birmingham, she married and disappeared to Devon. Five children later, she returned and began to write seriously. In a bid to make her work as authentic as possible, she has bent the ears of numerous police officers, firearms officers, scenes of crime, the odd lawyer and United Nations personnel. She also works by day as a freelance editorial consultant, specialising in crime fiction.

Eve lives with her second husband and often has a houseful of offspring, sons-in-law, partners, and a growing tribe of little ones. Nomadic by nature, she is planning another move very soon.

🐦 @EveSeymour
www.evseymour.co.uk

Her Sister's Secret

E.V. Seymour

OneMoreChapter

One More Chapter an imprint of
HarperCollins*Publishers*
The News Building
1 London Bridge Street
London SE1 9GF

www.harpercollins.co.uk

A Paperback Original 2019

First published in Great Britain in ebook format by
Harper*Impulse* 2019

A catalogue record for this book
is available from the British Library

ISBN: 9780008365806

Set in Birka by Palimpsest Book Production Ltd, Falkirk
Stirlingshire

Printed and bound in Great Britain by
CPI Group (UK) Ltd, Croydon CR0 4YY

For Fran and Jim

Chapter 1

I did the wrong thing. Just once. And there is a weary inevitability about what happens next; me in a stranger's car, sunshine tricking, morning heat ticking, with a throwaway look before I leave. Truth is, I slipped off the picture months ago, way before the terror set in.

Maybe it's connected to the heat, the dog days of summer inducing a kind of craziness but, no matter how hard I try, I can't catch a break. Can't. And four fingers of vodka don't change a thing.

I stare at the lonely road ahead. There's the odd worker bee but mostly traffic is quiet. Nobody to see or stop me. Checking the rear-view mirror, I take another sneaky swallow, not enough to dent my reactions, but enough to make me bold. Unaccustomed to the rip and burn of booze on an empty stomach, I love it —feels perfect in the circumstances.

Perfect.

And will Nate care? I don't know. Do I blame him for the sick chain reaction of events? Maybe. Will he feel guilty? Probably.

I'll be honest, half of me is terrified to tear a hole in an unimaginably beautiful day, the other sad, but it's the best I can do to keep those dirty little secrets shovelled back into the earth and buried deep. It's why something so wrong will be so right. You'll see.

A glance at my watch confirms it's time. Primed for speed, the four-by-four starts, its throaty engine snarling. Power thrills through my fingers, up my arms, and takes a spin around my brain. In that petrol-charged moment, I picture how it will play out after I'm gone. They will say I was drunk. They will say I was overworked and suffering from depression. Some will scream that I was mad and bad. Out of her mind, my mother will cry. Intoxicated maybe, but the rest is false. I could never feel more sorted. If someone threatens to topple the walls and bring them crashing down, you make damn sure they lie buried deep in the rubble beside you.

Sunshine smashes through the windscreen and briefly blinds me. I take one final slug of booze. For courage. For luck. For endings. Then, stamping on the gas, I drive.

Chapter 2

"How many men have you slept with?"

"What?"

I was less concerned with Lenny's intrusive question than with the fact I still stung from the furious argument I'd had with my sister three days ago. With bitter words and angry accusations, I'd blown my stack. And it hadn't ended there. The rest was a blur of emotion right outside any normal spectrum. At that moment in time I'd hated my sister for making me feel so bloody inadequate and unloved by my own mother.

"I'll tell you if you tell me."

"Lenny," I puffed, almost skinning my knuckles on the wall. "It's eight-thirty in the morning. It's bloody hot and I've not long had breakfast."

Sweat poured off me due to the weight of the hefty set of mahogany drawers we were manhandling down a flight of stairs. You need to be strong in the house clearance business and, although short in stature, I was, but this piece of old tat was proving a right bastard. "We have a full day of humping—'

She flashed a killer smile.

"Shifting furniture," I corrected, "and all you can think about is sex. What's wrong with you?" In my experience men who banged on (no pun intended) about getting their leg over weren't getting any. With Lenny, I simply didn't know. Wind-up merchant, or genuine enthusiast?

She bumped down another step with such force I thought my arms would pop out of their sockets.

"Ouch. Watch my hand." My biceps juddered and there was a faintly queasy sensation in my stomach. Motor-mouth didn't pause for breath.

"You haven't forgotten to return Mr Noble's call, have you? He needs us to clear his grandmother's house."

"No." I had forgotten actually. Mentally, I ran through my 'to do' list, which increased with each passing minute. The shop closed on Mondays, my time dedicated to admin and house clearance. I treated it as my weekly workout.

"Only he called again yesterday. You were supposed to get back to him a week ago."

I didn't dignify Lenny's criticism with a reply. Too busy manoeuvring around a tight corner. A knob came perilously close to lodging itself between two spindles. With a super-human effort, I altered the angle. Calamity averted.

With only a minor diversion in her train of thought, Lenny got expansive. "I reckon I've slept with thirty-three guys, give or take."

"Bloody hell. What are you trying to do? Set some kind of record?"

"It's not a lot for a healthy thirty-nine-year-old."

When did you lose your virginity, I nearly said. In my head I furiously did the maths. I once, memorably, had sex in a store cupboard in an underground tube station on the Bakerloo line, and my last fling had been in a client's home with Lenny's predecessor, a guy who got clingy. In general, I was discreet about what I got up to in my down time, whether drinking more than was good for me or choosing unsuitable men to hook up with – often one inextricably led to the other. Scarlet, my goody-two-shoes sister, with her perfect husband, worthy career and perfect bloody life, would never stoop so low, and certainly not without her clothes on. I think I still loved her although I wished, in a complicated, sisterly way, that her halo would slip, trip her up and send her flying.

"Would you sleep with a married man?"

At this, I practically screeched. "As taboo as doing drugs."

"A bit of blow never hurt anyone," Lenny chirruped.

One stern look from me took the tweet right out of her twitter. Pink zinged across her milk-white cheeks

"Sorry, Moll, I forgot about your brother."

"A *bit of blow*, as you put it, was what got Zach started." After that he snorted cocaine that made him over-excited and unpredictable, and heroin that turned him into an octogenarian overnight with memory problems and a tendency to fall asleep any time, any place and anywhere.

Lenny zipped it and, together, we flogged down the last two stairs, setting the drawers down with a mighty thump.

"Pit stop?" she said, suitably chastened, a rarity for Lenny.

About to answer, my phone rang.

The caller display indicated it was Dad. Some of my friends

disregarded calls from their parents when at work. My dad was different. A former senior police officer he'd taken early retirement and authority coursed through his DNA. Quietly spoken, quiet in every way, he was not an easy man to ignore, although my big brother, Zach, had managed it with ease for all his teenage years, most of his adult too.

"Where are you?" Dad said.

"Barnard's Green. House clearance."

"Can you come home?"

"Now?" I pulled a face at Lenny.

"Scarlet's been in an accident. An RTA."

I took a sharp intake of breath and translated the copper-speak; car crash.

"Is-?"

"It's bad," he said, a catch in his voice.

I spiked with alarm, not so much because of what he said, but how he said it. My softly spoken father sounded at least ten decibels louder than normal. "Dad—"

"I'm going to the hospital and I need you to stay with your mum."

"But—"

"Molly, she has one of her migraines and is definitely not fit to travel."

God, she'd be doing her pieces. "I'll be right there. You'll keep in touch?" The line went dead.

I gawped at Lenny who, from simply reading my expression, cottoned on that catastrophe had struck.

"Go, I'll deal with things here."

"But the van?"

6

"You take it. I'll shift as much as I can and pile it in the hall. I can load it later."

Knowing I could trust her, I flew.

Blood sprinting, guilt poking, I was consumed by the darkest of thoughts: was I the reason Scarlet had crashed?

Chapter 3

It took ten minutes to reach my parents' house in Malvern Wells.

Mr Lee's claws clattered across the hall the second he heard my key in the lock. Barely stopping to ruffle his soft Shih Tzu ears as he yapped and snuffled at my ankles, I headed straight upstairs and slipped into my parents' bedroom.

In darkness, light peeped through the curtains, leaving a golden criss-cross pattern on the sheets. My mum lay, starfish-style, in the middle. Absolutely still. Eyes closed. Skin deathly pale, blonde hair a storm on the pillow. Even though I was her daughter, even though she was unwell, I saw how beautiful she was. Exactly like Scarlet who, with her generous mouth and petite nose and elfin features, took after Mum.

"Molly, is that you?" At the sound of her voice, Mr Lee darted inside, hopped up and parked himself at the foot of the bed. He cast me a reproachful look and rested his chin on Mum's legs. Proprietorial. My mummy.

I kissed her forehead and sat down on dad's side of the bed. Mum took my hand and gave it a squeeze. Even my sister's fingers, long and fine, were like my mother's. Only the nails were different. Scarlet's were nurse short, mum's long and highly polished. Me, with my dark hair, scary eyebrows and olive colouring, took after Dad. I got my practicality from him too. Unfortunately, my shortness of stature – I'm a shade over five foot – belonged to a throwback somewhere down the family line.

"It's all right. It will be all right," I said, not really knowing if it would. Suddenly ashamed, I wondered whether Scarlet had confided in Mum about our argument just days earlier. The anger of our exchange suddenly swamping me:

"You what?" I blazed. "I'm not as pretty as you. I'm not as clever as you. I'm certainly not admired like you. Was that what you were going to say?"

"Don't be silly." Scarlet spoke quietly, hurt in her eyes. "All I was going to say is that you need to speak to Mum and Dad. This isn't my fault."

With a superhuman effort, Mum's eyes opened, tears pooling at the corners, bringing me out of my painful thoughts. "Oh Molly, it sounds so awful. They had to cut her from the wreckage."

An icy shiver tiptoed along my spine. "Mum, I'm sure it will—"

"Her beautiful face." While the situation seemed dire, I sensed that Scarlet's face would be the least of her problems. Oh God.

"My phone," Mum burst out, edging up onto the pillows, agitating. "What if your dad calls?" Her gaze darted in the direction of the window. "It's over on the dressing table."

I stood up, located her mobile and placed it in her hand. Meanwhile, Mr Lee snored softly, completely out of it. I wished I were dreaming too.

"Tell me exactly what happened," I said. "Was Nate with her?" Nate was Scarlet's husband. An architect, he worked with my father on his renovation projects. I jolted. Whatever must Nate be going through?

"*No*, Molly," Mum said, with icy patience. "Nate called your father."

"Sorry, yes. Any other vehicles?"

"A motorcyclist."

"God. Poor him. Or her," I added.

Mum's expression briefly darkened. Bad form to express pity for anyone other than my sister. "Pass my water, would you?" Her voice was tight and clipped. I passed her the glass from the side of the bed and she took a sip.

"Do you know where the accident happened?"

"Not really, but I'm guessing she was nearly home. She's working nights this week."

"Perhaps Scarlet was tired and took her eye off the road."

Mum's jaw stiffened. "Scarlet would never make a mistake. She's always so careful."

I considered this. A beautiful day, summer sun already up, and Scarlet travelling on a road with which she was familiar. "Do you know what time the crash happened?"

Mum hitched her shoulders. "Judging by Nate's phone call, between 7.30 and 8.00 a.m. Why, oh why, do I have to get one of my migraines now?" Mum placed the back of her hand against her forehead.

"Have you taken anything?"

"I'm trialling a new nasal spray. Scarlet suggested it." Her mouth creased with pain at the mention of my sister's name. Parents aren't supposed to have favourites, but I'd known for as long as I could remember that my mum adored my sister and cared for her more than me. Zach remained more difficult to categorise. Whenever Mum spoke about her firstborn and only son her voice would tremble with emotion, but it was Scarlet who remained the centre of her universe.

I nodded sympathetically. We didn't speak. "I wish your father would call," she said, fretting. "He promised he would."

"I'm sure he will."

"Do you think we should try Nate?"

Definitely not. "Honestly, Mum, I know it seems like an eternity, but I'm sure everything that can be done is being done. If anyone can sort things out, Dad can." My dad, in all our eyes, was the most capable of men, mentally, emotionally and physically too. He'd always been sporty, and now his building work kept him lean and healthy.

She forced a smile and sank back miserably into the pillows. "It was probably his fault."

"What?" I said, startled.

"That biker. Bloody speed merchants."

I took a breath, counted to ten, and told myself that my mum was understandably upset and already scratchy due to feeling unwell. "Probably too early to say."

"There are so many damned lunatics on the road."

"A bird could have flown out. It might be nobody's fault."

Or it might be mine. Oh My God. The room suddenly bloated with dry heat. Squirming, I stroked Mr Lee's head.

Don't let it be as bad as everyone thinks.

Let there be a mistake.

I promise I will never fight with my sister again. I will be nice. I will never blame her for anything.

"We should call Zach," I said. "Let him know."

She tensed. "Know what? At the moment there is nothing to tell."

I stifled a sigh. Contact with my brother was sporadic and difficult. To be fair, this was largely his choice and his fault. If we'd remained in Cheltenham, I could understand his aversion to possibly running into his druggie friends, but he had no connections in Worcestershire. That chaotic stage in his life was over, so I didn't really get it. Having put my parents through hell, he remained a touchy subject with Mum and Dad. Whatever the ancient history, I believed he should be told about the accident, although, admittedly, maybe not right now.

"Tea?" Despite the heat, it seemed the right beverage to drink. You couldn't drink vodka at quarter to nine in the morning even if Mum would not be averse to the idea.

"Please."

I padded out of the room, keen to escape, anxious to be doing something so that I didn't have to consider what might or might not be happening. Like a virus attacking my nervous central system, all I could think about was my sister, the crash, the fallout, the blame.

I put the kettle on and took the jolly cups and saucers –

my mum's favourite – from the cupboard and went through the motions. Spoonful of sugar for me. Light dash of milk for her. While it brewed, I tried my dad on his mobile. My call went straight to his messaging service, his voice sombre in a way I'd never noticed before. An omen? A scoot around local Gloucestershire news online revealed absolutely nothing. Before I got drawn into what was trending on Twitter, the kettle boiled.

Arranging everything on a tray, the way my mum liked, I took it upstairs.

"I've tried your father. No reply," she said, brittle with frustration.

"Maybe he can't respond. Could be driving, or at the hospital."

"Maybe." She didn't sound convinced.

We drank in silence. Her hands trembled. God knew what was travelling through her mind although none of it could be good. Eventually she eased back down the bed. Hid beneath the sheets.

I sat and stared off into the distance. For a second time I considered calling Zach. He and Scarlet had never been close, and it was always me who tried to maintain family ties.

"Can I get you anything else?"

She shook her head minutely. "The dog probably needs to go out."

Only if I scooped him up and forced him, which was precisely what I did. Picking up on the bad news vibe, Mr Lee's tongue darted out and licked my ear in a sort of 'sorry you're feeling sad' gesture. I gave him a squeeze and carted him downstairs, through the kitchen and conservatory and into heat resembling a fan assisted oven at 220 degrees centigrade. Too long outside and I'd be done to a turn.

I held back in the shade, watched as Mr Lee mooched across the lawn, skirted the vegetable patch and cocked his leg against one of the fruit trees. To the right, a teal-painted wooden bench where Scarlet and I once sat weeks before and prior to the row, the two of us gazing across the rooftops to the Severn valley, cold drinks in our hands after a blistering day at work. Peace between us. She'd seemed distant, I remembered now, not her usual smiley self. When I'd enquired if she was okay, she'd told me she was knackered. To be honest, I hadn't really bought her answer and wondered if there was something up between her and Nate. Looking back, I wished I'd pressed her because then I'd be able to make better sense of everything. But maybe exhaustion had led to the accident. Maybe it was nothing to do with me. Maybe.

The dog ambled back, cocked his leg again, this time against a flowering shrub on a patio bleached white with heat. I jagged in irritation because the weather felt all wrong. The sun wore a stupid happy-clappy grin on its face. It was way too lovely a day for unfolding events that I couldn't call, couldn't predict.

Retreating inside, I ran water into a bowl for Mr Lee.

The house seemed unsettled and empty, like a home in which a warring couple declare they are going their separate ways. Was it possible that we were all over-reacting? Might someone have got mixed up, identified the wrong driver? Was my sister really at home, sunning her rear and snoozing in the sun, while some other poor woman lay trapped in wreckage? Buoyed, I took out my mobile, punched in Scarlet's number. Nothing. Switched off. Dead.

Steeling myself, I went back upstairs.

"All right?" Mum asked in the way people do when they don't require a truthful answer.

"Yes."

"Dog had a drink?"

"Uh-huh."

"Sorry, you had to leave work."

"Doesn't matter. Lenny is managing fine without me."

"Even so—" She broke off, stirred, eyes flickering toward the doorway, to where Dad stood. Tall and solidly built, there suddenly seemed less of him in that moment. Purple shadows etched upon his face and underneath his eyes gave him the appearance of the gravely ill. As he walked silently towards us, I read all kinds of emotions in his brown eyes. That's when I knew. Indubitably. And so did my mother. Her hand gripping mine told me so.

My throat cramped. "Dad?"

In a voice stained with pain, he said, "Scarlet died this morning."

Chapter 4

Silence, like the split-second before an ancient tree, cut down, hits the earth.

Dad started forward, every step an exercise in agony. Mum, slack-jawed, let go of my hand, gripped and twisted the cotton top sheet through her fingers, a metaphor for a life irrevocably screwed. When Dad reached out and put his arms around her, she let out a deep-throated howl. I slipped off the bed, made way, excluded. Numbed, I couldn't really take it in.

There were tears. I'd never seen my big tough dad cry. Not when Zach got expelled from school – again – not when he'd OD'd, not when my brother went to rehab that would make most prisons look like recreational facilities, not when Dad walked my sister down the aisle. Not ever. But he cried now.

"There must be some mistake." Mum's sobs were dry. Excruciating.

"No, my darling."

"But—"

"I identified her."

Mum pulled away. "You did?" She spoke in a small, wondering, vulnerable voice. "Surely, Nate—"

"Too much for the boy. I offered."

"And you're sure? You're certain?"

"She's gone," he confirmed tearfully.

Mum wrenched back the sheet. "Then I must I go to her."

"No, Amanda."

"I have to see her, Rod."

Stricken, I held my breath, watched as Dad put his solid hands on Mum's shoulders, looked into her eyes. Firm. Back in control. All his ex-copper credentials showing through. "We can take flowers once the scene's secured and preserved."

Her mouth tightened, ugliness in her expression. "I don't want to take fucking flowers. I want to see my baby."

Dad glanced anxiously over his shoulder at me. I wasn't sure what he was thinking. Maybe he was embarrassed because my mum never swore, and he wasn't great with the drama. Maybe he feared the miasma of emotions about to break loose. Or maybe he was trying to protect me from what I already knew. My mother could live without any one of us, but not Scarlet.

"Amanda, listen to me. You have to be very brave."

"I can't," she gulped. "I just—"

"You can. You must. For Scarlet."

"Oh my Christ," she burst out. "She always said she wanted to donate her organs. We can't let that happen, Rod."

"That's not an issue at the moment."

I frowned. What did Dad mean?

"But there will be a post-mortem," he continued.

"No," she snapped. "You tell him, Molly. Tell him it can't happen."

I stared from one to the other, my breath staccato and shallow. "Mum, I wish I could but—"

"Oh, what's the use?" Ripping herself from dad, she tore out of bed and headed to the bathroom. Naked and unsteady feet crashed against polished wooden floorboards.

"I'm sorry," I stammered, but the accusing light in her eyes said it all. When she'd needed me most, I'd failed her.

Dad stood up, met my wounded gaze. "She doesn't mean it, Moll."

My expression told him that she did.

"Leave her. She'll —" He was going to say 'calm down' but, too late, realised the futility of it.

He sat. I stood. Lost. A hot ember of grief lodged so deep in my chest I thought it would never cool. I didn't know what to say, or how to feel, other than crashing grief and guilt. I'd never be able to make it up to my sister now.

"Come," he said, with a sad smile.

I went to him and threw my arms around his neck and rested my cheek against his big wide chest. As he stroked my head the years rolled back, except that Scarlet was no longer there to share them with me. Scarlet was a lonely shadow.

I pulled away, ran a knuckle underneath each eye. "How's Nate?"

"In bad shape. Went to pieces at the hospital. I left him with his parents. There's an FLO with him too." Family Liaison Officer. I was fluent in my dad's cop lingo.

"And now?"

18

"There will be an accident investigation followed by an inquest. Standard procedure."

"What did you mean about organ donation? Scarlet believed in it so much."

He let out a weary sigh. "I don't know the RP SIO but, as a former police officer, I might be able to extract some inside information." I dredged my brain. Dad meant Road Policing Investigating Officer. "It's a confused picture but I got the impression that the police were holding something back. The fact that they want to prioritise the post-mortem indicates as such."

I didn't like the sound of this at all. I understood that reports could take a week or so, although initial findings could be disclosed earlier.

Dad continued, as if on autopilot. "Every fatality on British roads is treated as a suspicious death and in this instance there's two. In the normal course of events, a Collision Officer will identify and preserve records and review witness evidence, and a Vehicle Examiner will check out the vehicles."

I didn't speak for a moment. I couldn't. I tried to absorb the news. Failed. "Dad," I said gingerly, "When will they find out what happened?" I had *to* know.

"Sounds like a high-speed collision."

"You think Scarlet was driving too quickly?"

"Maybe." He shook his head. "But don't tell your mother I said that."

I squeezed his arm; saw a flicker of fear in his eyes. We both knew that my mum would never recover from this. "It might or might not be a factor, but Scarlet wasn't driving her car."

"How come?" I said, puzzled.

"Remember that prang she had a month or so ago?"

"Hit a gate-post." Which was right out of character, I remembered with a twinge of anxiety. Scarlet was a good driver. Smooth. Fluid. Safe. Not like me with my tendency to curb it and poke my nose out too far at junctions.

"The Golf was in for bodywork repairs. She'd rented an off-roader for the week."

"Maybe she didn't know how to handle it."

"A possibility," he agreed.

"How long had she had it?"

"Three days." Yes, I remembered now. She was on her way to drop off her car and pick up the courtesy vehicle when I'd picked a fight.

"Surely, she'd take it steady simply because she wasn't used to driving the vehicle."

"I have to admit it does seem odd, especially as she was on the wide straight stretch on the Old Gloucester Road, after Hayden."

I knew my sister's regular route. The speed limit was 50 mph, but drivers often took it more quickly. Me included.

A hard lump swelled in my throat, making it virtually impossible to swallow. Still the tears wouldn't come. "Was it really awful, Dad? Seeing Scarlet?"

He glanced away, jaw bracing, his normal dark colouring a pale imitation. When he spoke his voice sounded raspy, dry and old. "I've seen many dead bodies, but nothing prepares you for—" He shook his head. Broken.

"Here," I said, clumsily handing him a tissue. He took it, dabbed his face and blew his nose. "We have to tell Zach."

"My job," he said, stoic and uncompromising. A pulse ticked in his neck, his expression reminding me of the bad old days when Zach was in thrall to his druggie friends. He hung out with crazies back then. Dad knew most of them in a professional capacity. It wasn't so much what Zach was doing to his body, destructive as it was, as what he was doing to our lives, Dad's especially.

He pulled out his mobile.

"Wouldn't it be better and kinder done in person?" In any case, Zach never answered his phone and, rarely, if ever returned a call.

Dad opened his mouth to speak then hesitated, whatever he was about to say was interrupted by the sound of a loo flushing and running water.

"Let me tell Zach," I murmured.

"No, I —'

"I want to, Dad." I needed to be alone, to think and work out whether I was condemned to a lifetime of guilt. I shuddered to think that Scarlet was so upset by our row that she'd not paid attention on the road. Had I argued with her when she was already at a low ebb? Jesus Christ.

His sad eyes met mine. "Are you sure? You've had one hell of a shock."

"Honestly, I want to help." And do something of practical use. "It won't be a problem. Promise."

He clutched my arm. "Are you okay to drive?"

"Yes."

"You're sure?" His grip on me tightened.

"I am."

Anxiously, his eyes darted to the en-suite. "I'll take care of Mum. You go to Zach."

Chapter 5

My brother lived a simple life in the arse-end of nowhere. It took me forty-five minutes to get there and then another fifteen through winding roads, flanked by high hedges hissing with heat, to reach the commune where Zach had lived for a decade. Thoughts fastened solely on my sister, my eyes clouded at the thought of never hearing her voice, never seeing her smile again. By the time I reached the potholed drive that led to Zach's home, I was shackled by grief.

Parking up on a patch of scrub, the ground rutted and dry from two months of hot weather without rain, a kaleidoscope of images clattered through my mind. Scarlet pale and clammy with shock. Scarlet bleeding. Scarlet dying.

Eventually, I forced myself to get out of the van towards what was effectively a scattering of ramshackle dwellings surrounded by vegetable patches, washing lines and pens with livestock.

Gareth, a skinny silent man from the Rhondda, was adjusting a halter on one of his horses. He supplemented his meagre living with woodcarvings and strange sculptures made from scrap metal. Nearby, two small children grubbed around in a makeshift sandpit. Think gypsy encampment meets Glastonbury on an unusually dry day and you get the picture. In front of the largest hovel, a raised piece of decking on which sat benches and old easy chairs with sagging bottoms, two semi-naked women sunbathed in the obliterating heat while Zach lay stretched out in a deckchair, legs apart, narrow feet bare. Clean for years and embracing abstinence with the same zeal with which he'd smoked crack cocaine, he looked reasonably healthy. If you didn't know it, you'd never cotton on that he'd once been a hair's breadth away from death.

He wore baggy shorts and a tie-dyed vest that exposed muscles rope-hard from manual labour. His weathered olive-skin looked as if it had been dipped in creosote. Like me, he had a wide brow, although his eyes were blue, like Scarlet's. A hybrid variety, he had Mum's pert nose and Dad's full mouth. Beneath his dreads, his eyes were shut tight against the sun; they popped open at my approach, a loose smile spreading across his face that vanished the second he caught my mangled expression.

"Sis," he said, climbing out of the chair. "Something wrong?"

"Is Tanya around?" Tanya was Zach's long-suffering girl-friend. I thought it best if she were there too. As much as anyone had a steadying influence on my brother, she did.

"Craft market in Ludlow," he said. "Selling cards and shit."

"Right," I said uncertainly.

"So, what is it? You look like someone tramped over your

grave." The smile attempted on his face, packed up and retreated.

"It's Scarlet," I said bleakly.

At the mention of her name, he started. "What's she done? Look, if she's said something—"

"Done?"

He blinked. "You're making me nervous. I meant what's happened?"

Whether it was the compressed heat or emotional overload, I caught that uniquely chilling vibe only a sibling can identify. Zach's was no ordinary slip of the tongue. I thought back to before the argument, sitting in the garden at Mum and Dad's, Scarlet preoccupied. Did Zach know something I didn't?

"Moll," he said. "For Chrissakes, tell me."

When I did, he made a sound, half groan and half exhalation. Brain fried a long time ago; his emotional responses were complex at the best of times.

A woman, with a flat nose and cracked lips, stirred. "Man," she said. "That's bad."

"Real bad," the other drawled, raising her head, turning over, in preparation to flash-fry her back.

Expecting a shedload of questions, I waited for Zach to fill in the gathering silence. But Zach wasn't like other people. Hands cupping his elbows, he stood mute, blinking rapidly from the sun or distress, or both.

Unsolicited, I gave him a précis of what Dad told me. "I want you to come home," I said.

"Nah," he said. "I'm all right."

"*You're* all right?" I was accustomed to my brother wittering on about his guilt, bad vibes and not wishing to further upset 'the folks', but what had started out as distance and separation, over the years had taken on the shape of a feud, the reason for its existence long forgotten by both parties. In the present tragic circumstances, it was pointless, ridiculous and a waste of energy, which is what I told him.

"I didn't mean it the way you twisted it," Zach said petulantly.

"They need you, Zach. Hell, I need you." Why couldn't he see it the way I saw it?

"Aw Molly, don't look at me like that."

"Like what? Jesus, Zach, this isn't about you."

"I never said it was."

"Fuck's sake, don't you care?"

"Of course, I fucking care. She was my sister too. And it's horrible what's happened."

"Well, then."

"Transport's a problem. I'm not exactly on the doorstep."

"I can take and drop you back. It wouldn't need to be for long." I was pleading with him.

"I have to be here." He tilted his chin in the direction of the nearest hedge, bullish, as if he had urgent business on the other side of the privet.

"For what exactly?"

"Don't you get it? They won't want me around. Especially now." His hands flew to his head, like he'd been caught in an explosion and was trying to protect himself.

I knew my brother and he was hiding something, all right.

26

And Zach's initial question, about what Scarlet had done, had given them both away. A victim in a tragic accident, Scarlet was dead. Nothing could change that fact. But my brother and sister had shared a secret. And I had to find out what it was.

Chapter 6

"When did you last see Scarlet?" We sat in the shade with homemade lemonade. The citrus tang hit the back of my throat like a blade.

Zach scratched his belly. "Last year, maybe."

"That long ago?"

"Christmas," he said emphatically.

"Not around her birthday?" Four months previously.

Zach tweaked his moustache, shook his head, dreads swinging. "She was going to come over at Easter but there was a change to her rota."

"Speak to her much on the phone?" I sounded like a Grand Inquisitor, but Zach had always been an impressive liar – rather came with the drug-ridden territory. Directness reduced his wriggle room.

"Now and then. Seemed okay."

"She didn't mention a disagreement?" I tried to sound casual. The root cause of my row with Scarlet was not about money, although to an outsider it might look that way, but about favouritism and the way she, according to me, sucked

28

up to our parents. If Scarlet had confided in Zach, he'd probably pass it off as a scrap between sisters. Cash, or the lack of it, had never featured heavily in Zach's life, because he was so adept at sponging off others.

Zach's brow furrowed. "Who with?"

"Doesn't matter. According to Dad, there's going to be an inquest," I said, not so skilfully deflecting.

Zach nodded thoughtfully. "How is he?"

I hiked an eyebrow. "Apart from being devastated?"

Colour spread across Zach's high cheekbones, shame and anger in his expression, most of it aimed at me. "I meant in general. No matter," he said. Waspish.

"He's doing his best to look after Mum." I kept my voice soft and conciliatory.

"God, yeah, how is she?"

"Taking it very hard."

Zach nodded, met my eye. Unlike me, he said it how it was. "Scarlet was always her favourite."

"Which is why it's important we rally round. It's what Scarlet would have wanted."

His answer to my lousy suggestion was to take a gulp of lemonade and top up his glass. "What happens next?"

"Post-mortem."

Zach visibly shivered, the hairs on his arms standing proud. There was an irony that Scarlet had danced with death every day in her professional life as a nurse, and would probably be matter of fact about lying on a slab and being pored over by a stranger, but the thought completely did me in.

"Dad wants to visit the scene to lay flowers," I said.

Zach gave a silent respectful nod. I could see that me trying to draw him out wasn't going to cut through or penetrate his lassitude.

"Zach, what did you mean earlier when you asked me what Scarlet had done?"

He let out a laugh, dry and arid. "Jesus, Molly, you're like a dog with a bone."

"Well, it was a peculiar—"

"Nothing. I meant nothing."

Odds on, from my set expression, Zach recognised my bullshit detector had flicked on. I might not have a degree, but I had an honorary in truth finding. I was like my dad in this regard.

We fell silent. I couldn't take any of it in. Not Scarlet. Not the surreal conversation I was having with my big brother.

Zach drummed his fingers on the table, searching around for something to say. When he spoke next, he was quick to change the subject and asked about business. He had as much interest in my shop as he had in earning a living. I read it as his cue for establishing that my time with him was up and gave a bland reply. Zach reciprocated with one of his own.

"Saw Chancer last week."

Chancer or Tristram Chancellor was Zach's oldest friend. They'd been at school together. Unlike the rest of Zach's mates, Chancer had stayed in touch, I suspected to keep a benevolent eye on my brother to ensure that he stayed on the straight and narrow. Weird really because Chancer was the opposite of my brother in every respect: successful, moneyed and happily married. The thought made me curdle inside. Long ago, I'd been smart enough to recognise that Chancer was way out of my league.

"He and Edie are having problems," Zach continued.

As surprised as I was, I couldn't give a damn. Exasperated, frustrated, I wished I could grab my brother and shake a normal emotional response out of him.

"Think the marriage is on the rocks, to be honest," Zach said. "Needy Edie certainly seems to think so."

"Don't be horrible." Edie was Chancer's wife. She wasn't simply in Chancer's league; she sat astride it. The daughter of a wealthy investment banker, she came from a stocks and shares, Ascot, Wimbo and a jet-setting lifestyle. "What about the kids?"

Zach pulled a face and shrugged. I drained my glass and stood up.

Zach stood too. I read everything in his expression: *Off the hook. She's going. Thank Christ.*

I could have asked him to reconsider his decision, to change his mind and come back with me right now, this minute, but knew it would only make us both angry. I had to face it. Even an event as momentous and monstrous as the sudden death of our sister was not going to drag Zach home, or turn him into the prodigal son.

He slung an arm around my shoulder, clumsily drew me close and kissed the top of my head and walked me to the van. "Give my love to Mum and Dad."

I gave it one last shot. "Think about coming home, Zach."
He looked down, scuffed the dry ground with a bare heel,
kicking up dust. Not a chance in hell, I thought, climbing
into the Transit and bumping back along the drive.

Chapter 7

Dispirited, I turned onto the main road and, after a few miles, pulled over into a lay-by from where I called Nate. My brother-in-law and me had always got on.

"Nate, I don't know what to say."

"There's nothing you can say. I can't believe it. I mean what the fuck? Straight road. Glorious day." There was a long pause. "Jesus," he said with a hollow laugh that battered the metal walls of the van, "me an atheist and I actually prayed and pleaded for her to pull through."

"I'm so terribly sorry."

He didn't speak for a moment. When he did his voice was all twisted up. "But Molly, how are *you* doing?"

To be fair, I didn't have the words to adequately and accurately answer his question. Most of me was in denial. I mumbled clichés about expecting this kind of thing to happen to other people. "Is there anything I can do for you, Nate, anything at all?"

"Be good to see you."

"What about your parents? I don't want to tread on anyone's toes."

"They'll go home. Mum, well, you know, her intentions are good, but what with the police updating me every five seconds, I need time to think and process and—" Nate broke off. At first, I thought he was crying, then realised that something was up. "Actually, I really need to talk. In confidence."

"How about I drive over after I've finished up here? About sixish?"

"That would be good. I'll see you then."

I strained every sinew to focus on the road. What did Nate want to tell me *in confidence*? Was he going to reveal how upset Scarlet had seemed a few days ago? Was he going to ask me why? A fresh wave of shame flamed my cheeks.

I reached Lenny a little over an hour later. Single-handedly, she'd shifted all the furniture from upstairs. Stacked. Packed. Ready to roll. Red-faced and done in, she stood with her back to the wall.

As I slid down from the van, she walked towards me, solemn faced, with open arms. "Your dad phoned. I'm so sorry, hon."

Solid, dependable, anarchic Lenny enveloped me in a sweaty embrace. A tight dry sob I'd bottled for hours escaped from the back of my throat.

I clung on, loss excavating a hole through my heart. I'd never dealt with this kind of news before. Scarlet gone. Scarlet dead. A moment longer and I'd start bawling and never stop. To head it off, I said, all business, "Could you run me home, then bring the van back to load up and take it to Flotsam?" This was my shop in Malvern Link. "I'll pay you extra, of course."

"No way," she said, as we clambered into the van. "And don't worry about the shop this week. I can handle it."

A day ago, it would be unthinkable for me to consider relinquishing control. Now it didn't matter.

I stared out of the window, remembering me and my big sister at my first pop concert; both of us poring over wedding dresses; a pub lunch when I'd shaken the ketchup and the top hadn't been screwed on properly and sauce flew all over Mum and we'd cackled with laughter until we were nearly sick. Happy days. Light days. Would I ever feel that carefree again? As stuffy and hot as the day was, I suddenly felt as cold as winter. Lost, I could make no sense of anything.

We pulled up outside my house. "Any particular jobs that need to be done this week?" Lenny said.

I shrugged my shoulders. I still had Mr Noble to contact, I vaguely remembered. He'd have to wait. I had one concern only and it wasn't to clear my conscience. I needed to understand what the hell happened on that road this morning.

Chapter 8

Glad to reach home, I escaped inside and closed the door on a world that I no longer recognised. Ugly. Dysfunctional. Desolate.

A wave of hunger grabbed my stomach and I realised I hadn't eaten all day. Not really fussed, I browned a thick slice of bread in the toaster, smothered it with peanut butter and ate standing up, mindlessly viewing my accrued possessions. A sucker for old things, the interior was really an extension of the contents of the shop. Most people didn't have a vaulting horse planted in their living room.

All set, my mobile rang from a number I didn't recognise. Normally, I'd reject calls like this, but these were strange times and I answered it.

"Molly Napier?"

"Yes?"

"Rocco Noble."

Rocco? The only other Rocco I'd heard of was Madonna and Guy Ritchie's son. Noble, oh yeah, the client I should have phoned. Scrabbling, I said, "I owe you a huge apology.

I should have got back sooner, but I've been overtaken by events." I winced, mortified. What would Scarlet think if she knew I'd referred to her death as an 'event'?

"All good, I hope," he said cheerily. He had a nice voice, rich and low. I pegged him about my age, maybe a bit older.

"Actually, not. My sister was killed in a road accident this morning." I cringed. How could I be so indiscreet and reveal something this personal to a stranger, in a business call, no less?

Judging by the stunned silence that followed, Mr Noble appeared to agree.

"Hello, you still there?" I said.

The unmistakable click that signals a caller hanging up asserted otherwise.

I stared long and hard at the screen. Screw you, I thought, weirdo.

"Your mother won't come out of the bedroom." Dad sat in the conservatory, hopeless and lonely. "How did Zach take it?"

"Upset. I'd hoped he'd come home but—" My voice died away.

"Zach is Zach. He'll be here when he's ready." He stared blindly out of the window at the garden.

"Have you talked to the police?"

"I've put calls through to Roger Stanton, the SIO in charge." Senior Investigating Officer. "Nothing yet. I phoned the garage where Scarlet rented the four-by-four and put them in the picture."

"How did they take the news?"

"Someone's death normally trumps business interests."

"Of course." I cleared my voice. "Will you be all right, only I thought I'd swing by Nate's." I couldn't mislead my father, although I mentioned nothing about confidences. Didn't breathe a word about my bad vibe concerning Zach either. Dad had more than enough to deal with.

"Tell Nate we plan to leave here about ten tomorrow."

To lay flowers, I remembered, the prospect unnerving. "I'll be there."

"And if there is anything I can do for him," he said, trailing off.

"I'll let him know." I kissed my dad's cool cheek and turned to leave.

"Molly?"

"Yes?"

He tore his gaze away from the garden and looked up at me with solemn eyes. "Any news from Nate, about what happened, I'd be grateful to hear."

I read disbelief and unease in his expression. While denial was entirely natural – I shared it too – Dad's instinct, sixth sense, whatever you wanted to call it, mirrored my own. A tragic accident it might have been, but there had to be more to why Scarlet came off that road. If I were wrong, I'd be the first to gladly embrace it.

I pushed a smile. My father had no idea how committed I was.

Scarlet lived – *had* lived – off the trendy Bath Road in Leckhampton. The road was more congested than usual and the side streets chock full of cars. A tricky place for parking, I found a spot outside an electrician's from where I walked around the corner.

As soon as I pushed open the gate, the front door cracked open. For a second, I imagined Scarlet standing there with a big warm smile and my heart caught in my rib cage.

"Hello, Nate."

A million miles away from the mousse and moisturiser guy I knew, he stood on the threshold like a man who'd emerged from a war zone. His hair was lank, jaw dark. Against prison pallor, deep shadows loitered underneath his hangdog eyes. He looked as if he needed a blood transfusion. He wore an old T-shirt over three-quarter length shorts. Both had seen better days. He grabbed hold of me, and we squeezed the life out of each other. Eventually, he pulled away. "Drink?" From the smell on his breath, I guessed he'd already started and was probably halfway through a bottle of neat spirit. Couldn't blame him.

"A small one. I'm driving, remember."

For a second, he blanched as though I'd made a joke in appalling taste, and then seemed to pull himself together.

I followed him down the short hall to the heart of the house, a stylish kitchen diner and family room with WOW factor; Nate's and dad's first project. Helplessly, my eyes zeroed in on the white and grey noticeboard that Scarlet told me had cost a small fortune. A mini home office, it paraded invitations, reminders and recipes, most of it written in my sister's organised handwriting. A sudden surge of tears threatened to catch me unawares. I bit down, choked it off.

"Wine or beer?" Nate said.

"Beer, please."

Pulling up a bar stool, all cream and Italian leather, I sat down at the counter while Nate fixed my drink and topped up his own glass with whisky.

"What's this?" I picked up a navy-blue folder with 'Brake' written on the front.

"A support pack. Someone dropped it off. As if that's going to help." Nate's tone was bitter.

I nodded sympathetically, glanced around the room which, usually so tidy, was a mess. My expression must have given me away because he said, "I've been searching for the bracelet I gave Scarlet for Christmas." Three carat diamonds set in gold; it had cost a small fortune. My sister had been knocked out when she discovered the price tag on-line. It had cost the thick end of four grand. As much as she loved it, she thought it too lavish, which was typical of her. Why the hell Nate was hunting for it at this precise moment beat me. For sentimental reasons, or something else? Except I couldn't think what the 'something else' was.

"Turned the whole house upside down," Nate complained.

I tried to mute any reaction to what seemed a strange obsession, given the circumstances. "Maybe she was wearing it."

He rolled his eyes. "Not at work."

"Want me to take a look?"

He hitched his shoulders in a 'knock yourself out' gesture.

I left Nate nursing his drink and stepped out into the narrow hall and up the tight staircase to the main bedroom.

It felt weird walking around Scarlet's home when she was no longer there in person, and there were reminders of her existence everywhere.

Nate had already searched Scarlet's jewellery box, judging by the lid flipped open, but I dived in anyway. The contents consisted of earrings, a couple of dress rings and a charm bracelet Mum had given her when she was twenty-one. Much luck had it brought her, I thought stonily, as I turned my attention to the drawer beside her bed that disclosed nothing of importance. A rummage through the wardrobe yielded a similar result. The only marvel was how neat and tidy everything looked. Not a shoe out of place. Best clothes contained in those fancy covers you pick up from the dry cleaners. Everything reflected my sister's ordered and tidy mind. If anyone was accident proof, she was. Or so I'd stupidly believed.

Back out on the short landing, I hung over the banister and called out to Nate.

"Did you check the spare bedroom?"

"Found nothing."

"Mind if take a look?"

"No, go ahead."

Small and sparsely furnished, a double bed consumed one wall. A lonely chair crouched in the corner. With no room for a wardrobe, a built-in cupboard provided storage. Inside, winter sweaters and boots and six handbags. I tore open each, turfed them upside down, unzipped the pockets and ran my fingers inside. Ostensibly, I was looking for a bracelet. In reality, I was searching for clues that would explain why the most sorted woman I knew had taken her eyes off the road and crashed in the sunshine and wound up dead. In truth, I also sought absolution.

I piled everything back in the cupboard and, dragging the chair across, stepped up onto the seat so that I could reach the top shelf. Two colourfully decorated storage boxes contained photographs, scarfs and hats. I smiled as I picked out the mad fascinator that Scarlet had worn for her hen night. I didn't bother with a plain box marked 'Nate's crap'. Of the bracelet, there was no sign. Nothing weird or out of place either.

Setting the chair back, and about to head out to the landing, I spotted a navy rucksack hanging loosely on the back of the door. It wasn't really Scarlet's style, but I lifted it off to take a look. There was no phone in the designated zip up section and the main compartment was empty apart from a small pack of unopened tissues. Plunging a hand into an interior section, I grazed something the size of a receipt or car parking ticket and fished it out. Torn from a lined jotter, a scrap of paper, with writing on it. I stared at a London address in a hand I didn't recognise, a name below read: 'Charlie Binns.' Neither meant anything to me.

With the note in my pocket, I returned to the kitchen and sat down next to Nate.

"No luck?" he said.

I shook my head.

"I'll need to close her social media accounts," he said randomly. "Have you seen the tributes?"

"God, so soon?" It seemed peculiar that death, a private

matter, should be made public when I hadn't even had a chance to grasp what had happened.

"People she worked with. Lots of lovely things said about her. Your sister was uniquely beautiful, inside and out."

A feather of guilt sneaked along my spine. I reached out, rested my hand over his.

"There's going to be so much shit to deal with." He was breathy, and his eyes were wild. "I'll have to cancel her credit cards and then there's the legal stuff."

"What legal stuff?"

"She died intestate."

I blinked in ignorance.

"Without a will," he explained.

"I'm sure Dad will know how to handle it."

Nate nodded sadly, put his glass down, scrubbed at his face with his hands. Again, the mad-eyed look. If I didn't handle this right, I'd lose him.

"Nate, what did you want to talk to me about?"

He looked at me with big soulful eyes. "You might need a stronger drink."

Chapter 9

"The motorcyclist was an off-duty copper with the Gloucestershire force."

My jaw slackened. Why it should make a difference was stupid and yet, somehow, it did.

"Coming back from a shift and heading towards Gloucester," Nate explained. Hence the head-on, I realised. "With both of them involved in challenging jobs, I reckon fatigue was the primary factor."

It would be the obvious conclusion. I shifted in my seat. The piece of paper in my pocket crackled. "What about the hire vehicle?"

"Jeep Cherokee four by four, beast of a motor. I teased her about it." His expression was wan. If speed was an issue, I realised that it would be in the accident report. Nate's shoulders slumped. "Took them half-an-hour to cut her out of the wreckage."

I baulked. Somehow, I'd thought she was killed instantly. "My God, she was conscious?" The thought appalled me. "And the police officer?"

44

"Never stood a chance," Nate said darkly. "Apparently he was thrown twenty feet in the air on impact."

Blood thundered in my ears. "Was he driving too fast? Maybe he swerved onto her side of the road." Guiltily, I remembered how I'd scoffed at my mum's speculations suggesting something similar.

Feeling grim at the prospect, we both fell silent. Nate was first to break. "Molly?"

"Yeah?"

"Scarlet was drunk."

If Nate had produced a hammer to thwack me over the head, I couldn't have felt more astonished. Scarlet was a classic teetotaller to the point of boring for Europe on the subject. I'd received enough lectures on what alcohol did to your physiology from her. Strangely, I don't ever remember Scarlet reprimanding our mum, a more worthy candidate. The thought of possible ramifications made my airways narrow and tighten. "That can't be right. She didn't drink."

"A smashed bottle of vodka was found in the wreckage."

"So what?"

"One of the firefighters cutting her free said he could smell alcohol on her breath."

"That's ludicrous."

"Exactly what I said."

"But —"

"Look," he said, abruptly testy, "I'll know more after the post-mortem. Promise you won't breathe a word?"

"Of course." It wouldn't be hard. I swallowed my beer to make the point that the allegation was ridiculous.

A cagey light entered his eyes. "When I was looking for Scarlet's bracelet, I found a note."

"Yeah?" I said, pretty cagey myself. Should I tell him I already had it in my pocket?

"From her to me. Here." He pulled out a sheet of writing paper from underneath a cookery book and planted it in my hand. With trembling fingers, I straightened it out. Definitely Scarlet's stylish, all loops and curls, writing. It read: *Nate, I'm so sorry. Forgive me. Love you, babe. S xxx*

I spiked with alarm. Did this imply suicide? "Forgiveness for what?"

"Search me." Nate took another pull of whisky. Quick and sharp and guaranteed to make me back off. He snatched the note off me and set it aside, out of reach.

Surely, our row couldn't have precipitated such a catastrophic turn of events. My blood chilled at the thought. That left another alternative: Scarlet had been in trouble somehow. But if she was, would I know? I thought we were close. Except — "Have you shown it to the police?"

"No."

"You're going to, aren't you?"

"Molly, the meaning isn't clear. There's nothing even faintly emotional about it."

"That's not really an answer. The fact she left a message at all could explain why she wasn't taking as much care on the road." Spectral fingers dug me in the back. "Maybe she meant to do it?"

Nate's expression darkened. "Suicide?"

I bit my bottom lip and nodded.

46

"It's not dated," Nate argued. "It could have been written any time."

"But it might not have been. Nate, you have to tell Mum and Dad and warn them about the booze," I hurried on.

"Are you kidding? Think what it would do to your folks."

"Mum and Dad will find out anyway if the toxicology results come back positive."

Nate looked into my eyes with a hunted expression. "Your dad was brilliant today," he slurred. "Identified her. Couldn't face it, see?"

"I know. He said."

"Did he?" Fat tears rolled down his cheeks. "The thought of her smashed up."

"Try not to think about it." Pain shot through me with fury, scorching my head. I had to concentrate on practicalities. I had to focus on the 'why' of it all. If I didn't, I'd fall apart and be no good to anyone. And Nate needed me strong, Mum and Dad too. "Have you eaten? I could fix you something."

He took a gulp of neat, obliterating booze, by way of an answer. "Sweet of you," he said with a crooked smile, "but this is fine."

"You must look after yourself, Nate. Scarlet wouldn't want to see you like this."

Eyes half-closed, heavy-lidded, he turned to me with a slow expression. "Like what?"

"Hurting. Drinking. Destroyed."

"Maybe, you're wrong," he said, with an ugly drunken expression. "Maybe she would."

What did Nate mean? Booze talk, I thought, and maybe

there were always odd little inconsistencies in the way people behaved in the wake of sudden death, but I couldn't ignore the remark from an experienced firefighter. I couldn't ignore the fact that Scarlet was the safest driver I knew.

Best to come clean.

"I didn't find Scarlet's bracelet, but I did find this." I showed Nate the scrap of paper with the name and address scrawled on it. "Mean anything to you?"

He stared, frowned at the name and address on the paper and made a sound similar to the half grunt half sigh Zach had issued earlier. "Charlie Binns? Never heard of him."

"You're sure?"

"Who the hell is he?" He sounded accusing. I spread my hands, couldn't say. "How much do you actually know?" The tone of his voice had that nasty 'bad news' ring to it – strange bearing in mind the morning's breaking headline.

My tongue tangled in my teeth and I bit down painfully on the inside of my cheek because I was right to be suspicious. There was definitely more going on underneath the surface. Nate's response pretty much confirmed it.

"How well did you really know your sister, Molly?"

Chapter 10

He didn't wait for a reply. "She'd been edgy and moody for a while. You must have noticed."

I flinched, forced myself to face the unthinkable: I'd been too obsessed by my own feelings of resentment to notice my sister's emotional state. Didn't make me feel good.

"Naturally, I asked her what was wrong," Nate continued, "but she never said. I thought it was the stress of work and suggested a weekend away. Then that conference in London came up."

On Critical Care, I remembered, about three weeks ago.

"I suggested I could go with her, we could make it a long weekend, but Scarlet wasn't keen," Nate continued. "Used that old excuse about not mixing business with pleasure."

"Seems perfectly reasonable to me."

"Except the conference takes place later this month."

"What? You mean —"

"Scarlet enjoyed a weekend away without me."

I stared at the writing in my hand. "She definitely went to London?"

"According to the hotel she phoned from, but I've no idea who she was with. Maybe now we know," he said, eyeing the piece of paper.

I pressed a hand tight to my forehead. For Scarlet to break her own moral code would be massive. It would have ripped her apart. And what about a lover? Was there some guy waiting for a phone call or a visit from her that would never happen? No, it wasn't possible, I thought firmly. No way could I believe that Scarlet would have an affair. It just wasn't in her DNA.

"To be charitable," Nate said in a tone adopted by those who have right on their side, "she might have gone to London alone."

Which still didn't explain what she might have been doing there. "How did she behave when she got back?"

"Sunny as hell. Said the conference had been good. *Informative*, was the exact word she used."

"And what did she say when you pointed out the lie?"

"I didn't."

I straightened up. "Your wife goes to a bogus conference and you don't challenge her, you don't breathe a word?"

"I wanted to wait it out, bide my time, see what happened."

In similar circumstances, I couldn't see me keeping my mouth shut. Maybe I was unsophisticated and impetuous.

"Certainly nothing on her phone or emails."

"You snooped on them?" I didn't hold with that.

Nate gave me a brazen look. *Who are you to judge me now?* His expression said. And he was right. I took a breath.

"What's the name of the hotel Scarlet stayed in?"

Irritation chased across Nate's features. "Leave it, Molly."

"Nate, all we have at the moment are wild guesses. I want facts. I want the truth. I need to understand why Scarlet died."

"There is no why. It was an accident."

Yes, it was. Or I thought it was. "Bu — t"

"It won't bring her back. It won't do any good."

"Nate, don't you want to know?"

He sidestepped my question. "Your dad has it all under control."

"If you don't tell me the name of the hotel, I'll ask Mum." The expression on my face assured Nate that I wasn't bluffing, and I wasn't giving up. With bad grace, he gave an address near Paddington train station.

"And the room number?"

"Molly —"

"It might help to put your mind at rest, give you closure."

"That, I doubt."

"Please, Nate."

"For God's sake, room number seventy-three."

The second I got home I grabbed a beer from the fridge, popped off the top and drank straight from the bottle. What seemed certain, the post-mortem would throw up the ethanol in Scarlet's bloodstream. It might not be lorry loads of the stuff but, for a committed non-drinker, even small measures could have Dutch courage effects. If Scarlet was guilty of causing the accident, the entire constabulary of Gloucestershire would be keen to blacken her name. With everything I believed in suddenly turned upside down and inside out, I wondered what other horrors lay in wait.

Rear on the sofa and feet parked on the coffee table, I fired up my laptop and switched to online local news in Gloucestershire. Sure enough, a factual report detailed that the police were investigating a fatal collision. The location was given, and an appeal made for witnesses to come forward with information. A later piece identified Detective Sergeant Richard Bowen as the motorcycle victim. Aged forty-two, he had an exemplary police service record and had received awards for heroism. An accompanying photograph of him dressed in uniform portrayed a sleek-looking man, not dissimilar from Nate in appearance, with a majestic smile, the picture of respectability. To my shame, it dismayed me. Already I could picture how the story would play out: courageous police officer and family man versus drunk driver. Didn't matter that Scarlet was a nurse with a glowing reputation. Her last inexplicable act was how she would be remembered, and it would sink her. Closing my eyes tight, I prayed the post-mortem the next day would prove she was sober. Maybe Bowen was in the wrong. Driving too quickly. Taking unnecessary risks.

Next, I tapped my way straight to Google and the name of the hotel Nate had given me. Shabby, with peeling window frames on the ground floor, the hotel in which Scarlet stayed for the non-existent conference charged less than fifty quid for a standard room. Unless the pictures were out of date, it didn't look the best location for seduction, but the type of place where unfortunate families were given temporary B&B accommodation by the council. What on earth was Scarlet doing there?

My phone rang. I picked up, saw it was Dad and braced

myself. My father could identify a liar at fifty paces. I'd have to box clever to conceal what I knew.

"I found out the name of the motor cyclist." Dad told me much of what I'd already discovered. "Poor bastard left a wife and two youngsters. One of my old contacts informed me this evening," he explained, verifying that the information came from a reliable source. "Thank God, the man wasn't working."

"Does it make a difference?"

"A world of. It's mandatory for the IPCC to be involved if one of their officers is on duty." Independent Police Complaints Commission, I registered.

"In case he was pursuing a suspect, or something?"

Dad went quiet.

"Dad?" I was sure I could hear the cogs in his brain in full motion.

"I should have thought of it." He spoke like he was kicking himself for being remiss.

"Thought of what?"

"Bowen was travelling home after a shift. If he was knackered, having worked excessive hours, the IPCC may still get involved and any investigation could take weeks."

And that would make a terrible situation worse, I thought in dismay.

"Either way, it won't be long before it hits the nationals."

"Really?" I was horrified. The thought of our private grief trawled through by strangers was hard to bear. That it might also provide some hack with a sensational story along the lines of 'Drunk Nurse Kills Police Officer' was intolerable.

I expected Dad to say something about the allegation that Scarlet was drunk. He didn't, and, from the clipped tone, I had the strong impression it wouldn't be wise to reveal it.

He didn't speak for a moment but, even on the other end of the line, I could tell he was thinking and trying to get a handle on the chain of events. "You weren't aware of any problems? Something she was upset about that might have made her distracted?"

I pushed every horrible thought away about the name of a mystery man scribbled on a piece of paper, the suggestion of suicide, a mysterious visit to a crappy hotel in London and the whopping lie Scarlet had told her husband. I told him I didn't know. "How's Mum?"

"Exhausted. I persuaded her to take a sedative. She's sleeping now."

"Dad?" I blurted out. "Do you mind if I don't come with you and mum tomorrow?"

"Oh," he said, obviously taken aback.

"Sorry. It's —"

"Of course, Molly, I understand." Except he didn't. Until seeing Nate, I'd been determined to go, wanted to, but now I had plans.

Chapter 11

First thing the next day, I texted Fliss Fiander, Scarlet's best friend, and asked if I could visit that morning. She replied: *Any time after ten. So very sorry, Molly.*

To reach my car, I routinely take the scenic route down the garden where I have a home office over a carport. This is where I park the vehicular love of my life, a flashy white Fiat 500.

Except that morning it was no longer white.

With a hand clamped to my mouth, I gaped at what I could see of the bonnet, which wasn't very much through a slurry of mashed flesh and bone. Reminiscent of a scene from *The Walking Dead* gore and shiny intestines spattered the windscreen. The smell, in the high temperature, was one of rotting meat and decay.

Heart in my throat, I took a pace nearer to try and identify exactly what I was looking at. Closer inspection revealed snarling fangs glinting in the sunshine. Curved claws attached to once powerful paws protruded from a coagulated mass of remains. The black and white marking would once have been striking. Tufts of thick black and white fur streaked with blood was all that signified that the roadkill belonged to a badger.

Anger flared inside me. I'd not accidentally run something over. I hadn't sleepwalked in the night, offed a creature and driven back to home turf. The tableau before my eyes was the worst kind of sick joke.

Shaking, I walked to the edge of the carport and onto the pavement to check the road both ways. Cars, pedestrians, school kids coming and going; everywhere perversely ordinary. The pub across the road had only closed down a couple of months before. Empty and boarded up, it had provided the perpetrator with the perfect cover to carry out their grisly mission undetected. It also suggested a planner and not an opportunist.

I ought to call the police but, with so many unanswered questions about Scarlet's death remaining, I didn't want it to detract from any investigation. Of one thing I was certain: the timing was significant. I had no enemies and no business rivals. Could this be a retaliatory act for Scarlet's actions? I resolved to call my dad.

Stepping back into the shade, I crouched down, staring hard at the floor, searching with my fingertips for anything that might have been left behind. Careful to avoid bird shit from a family of nesting house martins; grit, dirt and dust were the only items coating my nails. Disappointed, I straightened up, returned to the house where I dug out a dust-mask reserved for sanding down old furniture and clamped it on. Next, I grabbed a roll of thick black bin liners and a pair of rubber gloves from under the kitchen sink.

Back in the carport, I did what I had to do. The beast was heavier than I'd anticipated. Blood splashed my sandals and guts stained my clothes. The stink was indescribable and penetrated my face gear. Fortunately, I'd passed on breakfast that morning as bile filled my mouth.

Having got the worst off the car, and dumping the bags to one side, I hosed down the rest, flinching at the sight of tissue and animal fluids circling the drain. The smell would take longer to dissipate.

Locking the connecting door, I retreated to the house, where I peeled off my bloody clothes, tossed them into a plastic carrier bag and took another shower.

Dry and dressed, I called Dad and explained what happened. Whether it was the heat, or grief, it seemed to take him an age to process. "Are you all right?"

"Sort of." I wasn't.

"Some people are utter ghouls. I'm only sorry that you've been on the receiving end."

"It's just so extreme," I mumbled. Dad didn't know about the notes, didn't know about Scarlet's trip to London, the inconsistencies of her life.

"When people are upset, they sometimes do awful things. Unfortunately, I'm familiar with the species. It could have been a friend or family member close to Richard Bowen's."

Dad's suggestion opened up a valid possibility I'd not had time to fully consider.

"The best thing you can do, Molly, is to forget this ever happened."

"Forget?"

"Darling." I recognised that tone. It was specially reserved for telling me, in the nicest way, that I was excitable and gifted with an overactive imagination.

"I'm not making this up," I said crossly.

"Of course, you're not. Leave everything where it is, and I'll come and dispose of it later. Whatever you do, I don't want either Nate or your mother finding out. This remains between the two of us."

"I understand," I said reluctantly.

"Good girl, I knew you'd be strong enough. Now I really must go."

I had not forgotten my parents' pilgrimage to the scene of the accident. And despite what my Dad said, I would not forget the grisly gift delivered to my carport, or the messy message it sent.

Chapter 12

Dressed in T-shirt and joggers, sweatband banishing her long honey-coloured hair, and with top of the range trainers on her feet, Fliss Fiander had obviously returned from a run or the gym. I could see she was upset. Her make-up wasn't quite so immaculate or *au naturel* and her long dark lashes, which I suspected were permanently dyed, looked damp. Having never got the hang of applying foundation and lipstick, my look was more natural meets 'can't be arsed.' There was a difference.

Towering over me, she threw her arms wide, gave me a hug, and invited me in. "You look tired out, Molly."

"Didn't get much sleep last night." Correction: didn't get any sleep last night and that was before this morning's incident. On the drive over, self-doubt assailed me. Was I speculating too much about my sister's trip to London? Could there be a completely innocent reason? Was I making deductions without the evidence to back them up regarding the notes found? In a way, it would be more comforting because then I didn't need to be scared. Well, not much.

V. Seymour*

"Samuel's out with the au pair so we have the house to ourselves. Come on through."

I removed my flip-flops, my toes sinking into inches of thick oatmeal-coloured carpet and followed Fliss into a house that was the epitome of knockout design. The Fianders were 'hired help' folk, with staff for every aspect of their lives. I was as likely to watch Fliss Fiander with a mop and bucket in her hand as see her buy a sweater from the clothes section of the local supermarket. Designer girl. Designer house.

She appraised me in a way that I found faintly intrusive. Had Scarlet confided in her about our row? Did she know about Scarlet's trip to the Capital?

"I'm about to make tea. Camomile or fruit?"

"Fruit would be fine." I hated camomile. Like drinking distilled weeds.

From the kitchen, tri-fold doors led out onto a terrace with modernist furniture that matched the slate grey marble paving slabs and probably cost as much as the entire contents of my house. Beyond: a lush garden with ornamental paths, statues, arbours, exotic-looking plants and summerhouse. *Outdoor Grand Design* meets *Hanging Gardens of Babylon*.

"Pop outside, make yourself at home. I won't be a second."

I slid into a seat, stretched out in the sunshine, abruptly slain by the thought that it should be Scarlet sitting here with her best friend, not me.

"There you go." With a creamy smile, Fliss handed me a glass that came inside another, presumably to prevent condensation. I thanked her and she viewed me with a sombre expression. "Scarlet really was my very best friend, and me and Louis are totally devastated. I can't imagine how you must feel. It's such a shock. Your poor parents and Zach, poor Nate too."

Grim, I nodded, took a tentative sip, wished I hadn't. "You've spoken to Nate?"

"Briefly."

"Did he tell you that Scarlet lied about attending a conference and that he suspected her of having an affair?"

Fliss flushed and frowned. "Hang on a sec. I must grab my sunnies. Squinting into the sun is so ageing," she said. Needlessly, I thought. I stared off into the distance, listened to the birds, thought about a future I couldn't see, feeling awkward because I had one and my sister didn't. Feeling rotten because I wasn't only trawling through my sister's private life, I was about to trample on it too.

"That's better." Cartier sunglasses replaced the sweatband. She beamed an expansive, self-confident smile designed to recalibrate the conversation. Made no difference to me. I picked up right where I left off. "Was she?"

She threw me a 'mustn't speak ill of the dead' stare, although it was difficult to deduce much at all through the impenetrability of graded brown lenses. A slight flare of the nostrils was her only 'tell.'

I rephrased. "Would she confide in you if she were?" I tamed the jagging sensation underneath my skin.

"I'd like to think so." Which wasn't the same as 'Yes.' Fliss Fiander was choosing her answers with exquisite care. I needed to push her and I was shameless about it. "I really need you to be completely honest with me. And before you say a word, twenty-four hours ago, I didn't think my sister capable of drinking vodka neat from the bottle and driving under the influence."

"What?" she said with a jolt.

"Unconfirmed, but likely."

She snatched at her drink.

"Please, Fliss. What happened yesterday is so odd, so left-field, any scrap of information that can explain the tragedy, I'd be grateful if you'd tell me."

She rested her glass delicately on the low table in front of us, adjusted her sunglasses, and flicked both palms up in a defensive gesture. "There's a saying about not shooting the messenger."

Chapter 13

"I'm a lousy shot." It was supposed to put her at her ease. She responded with an imperious look that would take me years to perfect. "Sorry, please carry on."

"A rumour, nothing more, and definitely not the sort of thing for public consumption," she warned, "but Scarlet suspected Nate was the one having an affair."

"Nate?"

She flashed a worldly look. I felt like a child who'd found out about the birds and the bees – apt in the circumstances. Was this why he didn't want to show the police the note his wife had left? Was this why he didn't pursue my sister about her unscheduled stay in a London hotel?

I quickly regrouped. "You say she was suspicious, but she had no evidence."

"Apart from the bracelet he gave her at Christmas."

I frowned in confusion.

"Scarlet reckoned it was a guilt gift."

"Right," I said, scrabbling to process what I was hearing, "So Scarlet had had suspicions for a while?"

"Uh-huh."

"And it made her unhappy?"

"Of course."

"Enough to make her lose concentration on a bright summer day, enough to kill herself and to hell with whoever was driving on the opposite side of the road?"

"Good God, Molly, I really don't know anything for certain."

"Well, what are you sure about?" I'd briefly lost volume control. I coughed, flicked Fliss an apologetic smile.

"She spent most of last year moping about Nate," Fliss continued smoothly, "but then, this year, she was happy. Almost too happy."

"How can you be too happy?"

"Giddy then."

Giddy was not a word I'd use to describe my sister. And then it dawned on me. "Like she was having an affair as payback?"

"I'll be honest, I thought she'd met someone after we got back from holiday in Jamaica in February. She looked different. Radiant. I think I teased her about having a fling."

"Which she denied?"

"Fervently."

I cast my mind back. I didn't remember seeing much of Scarlet at the time. "Then what?"

"I didn't see her for a few months until we threw a party for Samuel's birthday at the beginning of June. Scarlet came, and she looked absolutely dreadful. Frankly, I was worried about her. She stayed on afterwards and I asked what was wrong." She gave me a long appraising look.

Was this what it was all about? Two people fucking other people and one getting upset enough to —No, no, no. She wouldn't. She couldn't.

My sister had only three boyfriends, tops, before meeting Nate, one of which never went beyond first base. And yes, we talked about things like that. When I ordered a hunky strip-a-gram for her hen night, she almost passed out. She was no prude, but she exuded decency and doing stuff by the book, in every aspect of her life. There had to be more to it. What Fliss described was like a cheap scene played out in a soap in order to push up ratings.

Fliss glanced down at her perfectly manicured nails, examined them and looked at me straight. "I got the impression Scarlet was in a jam. She didn't want anyone to know, Louis included, but she asked if she could borrow some money. Quite a lot, in fact."

I felt the air punch out of me. Scarlet was always so careful. She didn't earn a fortune, but Nate's job paid well, and they were doing fine —or so I'd thought. "For what?"

"She didn't say."

"How much?"

"Twenty-five thousand pounds."

"And you lent it?" I was aghast. What the hell would Scarlet need that kind of money for? Ironic, really, considering I'd had a go at her for accepting a free handout from Mum and Dad to buy their house in Cheltenham.

"I would have but, ten days later, she changed her mind. Said she'd found another way."

A way that meant money would never be a problem again?

My mind careered into overdrive. "How did she seem when she told you everything was okay?"

"Relieved. Good. Her mood lifted. She seemed better."

Isn't that how people who are about to commit suicide behave when they finally make up their minds?

It seemed important to understand the chronology. I had *to* understand. Mentally, I built a timeline of Scarlet's last weeks and months on earth. By my estimation, Scarlet's change of mind occurred after her trip to London. Fliss crashed through my thoughts.

"How's Zach taken the news?"

"Like Zach takes any news, as if he's impervious."

She tilted her chin. "Scarlet often talked about him, more so lately. I think she worried he was about to relapse."

It would be a miracle if Scarlet's death didn't tip him over the edge. I reflected on my visit to my brother yesterday. Subdued, a little odd, but no more weird than usual, yet there had been something. I'd neither forgotten his opening question: *What's she done?* Nor that sense he knew something I didn't.

Fliss angled her face at the sun, a light warm breeze lifting her long hair. "He was quite twitchy the last time she visited."

"When was this?"

Fliss frowned in concentration. "Must have been shortly before she told me she no longer needed the cash."

Fear tripped through me. That didn't fit with what Zach had told me. Which meant one of them was lying, and I didn't think it was Fliss Fiander.

Chapter 14

Dazed, I wondered what twenty-five thousand pounds would have bought my sister; freedom from her adulterous husband, or something else? And how did Charlie Binns figure? If he figured at all in this unravelling mess. As for Zach, was his inexplicable memory loss the residue of a druggie past, or because he was deliberately hiding something from me?

I climbed into my car and called the grotty hotel in which Scarlet had stayed. My enquiry was greeted with a yawned, *wish I was still in bed* "Can I help you?"

"I hope so," I said brightly. "My name's Molly Napier, and my sister Scarlet Jay stayed in room seventy-three." I gave the exact dates. "Thing is, her companion mislaid his sunglasses – they're rather expensive – and he's sure he last had them at your hotel. It's a long shot but I'm coming to London next week and wondered whether I could collect them."

"Hold one moment." A tinny rendition of the soundtrack from the *Titanic* cut in. Mercifully, on the second chorus, the guy on the desk returned. "No, nothing found."

"You've spoken to the housekeeper?"

"Yup."

"For Room seventy-three?"

"That's right."

"You're absolutely certain?"

"Miss, I already told you. We don't have a gentleman's sunglasses and, in fact, there was no gentleman registered to that room."

I thanked him and cut the call. It wasn't what you'd call hard evidence either way. For that I'd need to take a road trip. Next stop: Kensal Rise and the mysterious Charlie Binns.

It took me the wrong side of two hours to drive to Paddington, where I parked the car at a rate that made my eyes water. From there, I headed for the underground where I hopped onto a tube on the Bakerloo Line. Twelve minutes later, I was standing with my back to a big cemetery, squinting against the sun and looking at a map on my phone that told me I needed to walk via College Road and Leigh Gardens to Chamberlayne Road.

If I'd been less focused on locating Charlie Binns, I'd have noticed that this area of the borough of Brent was up and coming and lively, that there were plenty of pubs, restaurants and bars, and had a cultured, arty vibe. All of which appeared to escape Mr Binns, I thought, standing outside a door sandwiched between a tile shop and bookies. Big ugly picture windows with thick heavy curtains, which were drawn, loomed down from the maisonette above. Not a promising start. I rang the bell, inclined my face so that my mouth was close to the speaker. I hadn't rehearsed a speech. I'd have to blag my way in.

No reply.

I tried again, with the same result. Maybe the people in the tile shop would be able to help. I wandered inside and approached a middle-aged man at the counter. He had a pencil tucked up behind his ear and was avidly studying a holiday brochure. "Wonder if you could help me," I said, "I'm looking for Charlie Binns."

He licked the pad of his thumb and flicked over a page. "Funny, but you're the second punter to come knocking on his door recently."

My heart gave a little thump. "Did she give a name?" The thought of me following in Scarlet's footsteps excited and terrified me in equal measure.

"She did not."

"Was she tall, slender, pretty, in her thirties?"

"Barking up the wrong avenue, love. The she was a he."

"Oh," I said, crestfallen.

Settling on another page, he removed the pencil from behind his ear and made a mark against Tenerife.

"I do need to talk to Mr Binns and it's quite urgent."

Rattled by the interruption, he looked up, his deep-set gaze fixed on mine. "I'll tell you what I told him. Unless you have supernatural powers, you'll have a job. Charlie got offed a month or more ago. The only place you'll find him is at the cemetery."

I almost choked. "Murdered?"

"Shot dead, a few streets away."

As the shock of the revelation hit me, two thoughts swam to the surface. Why did Scarlet have the name of a murdered man in her bag, and who the hell was the guy asking exactly the same questions as me?

Chapter 15

"**Y**ES?" A lorry driver had just cut me up and boxed me in. I was so bloody strung out and exhausted, I'd failed to screen the call.

"I owe you a huge apology."

His voice was the equivalent of chucking a bucket of crushed ice over my head. I checked my rear-view, flicked on an indicator, shoved my foot down hard and pulled out. Fuck you. Let Mr Noble dig himself out of the hole he'd dug.

"It was unforgivable."

"I'm not in the business of granting absolution." To be fair, I had one too many sins of my own.

"I completely understand but I wanted to apologise for my rude behaviour and say how sorry I am for your loss." The sentiment sounded respectful and genuinely meant. Creep. "You caught me unawares, I'm afraid. I know what it's like to lose someone."

I only felt marginally less pissed off. I definitely didn't appreciate him doing an emotional number on me.

"Long time ago." And yet from the tone of his voice, I

71

reckoned it still felt like yesterday to him. Is this how I would feel in ten or twenty-years' time?

"Does it get better?" I wanted him to assure me that it did, that this raw, helpless feeling would one day disappear, that the guilt would shift too.

He paused, appeared to choose his words with care. "Don't believe anyone who tells you otherwise, but you never get over it. In time, it doesn't feel so powerful and overwhelming, but the pain is still with you. Always. Does that make sense?"

"Kind of." I had no idea.

"I'm calling about my grandmother's house clearance."

I pulled a face. What a selfish prick.

"It's pretty small but she had a lot of stuff."

Stuff was right up my street. A stranger's crap my bread and butter, I was the human equivalent of a magpie. Occasionally, I unearthed gems. But Holy Christ, what was I thinking? My sister was dead. My parents needed me. Nate needed me. *I* needed to fathom why Scarlet would have the name and address of a murdered man zipped inside her rucksack.

About to open my mouth to reject his business offer, he reeled off an address on the Wyche, a village and suburb of Malvern, the name derived from the fact that it was once part of an Iron Age salt route. "Drop by any time after five. Any day this week is fine." With which, he killed the call.

"How did it go, this morning?" I was with Mum, after driving straight to my parents, following my alarming trip to London.

"Grim. Painful. Horrible."

She looked so bereft, I felt bad for letting the side down. "I'm sorry I wasn't with you."

She made no comment, simply carried on as if she were talking to the dead. "We took her favourite roses from the garden. The verge was a sea of flowers. She was loved by so many. Such a bright, intelligent girl."

Mum was right about that. Out of the three of us, Scarlet had been the only one to go to university and get a degree. Zach, who was extremely bright, could have surpassed her academically, if only he'd applied himself, but drugs and taking the piss came before education. Me? I'd floundered. Briefly consumed by my own sense of inadequacy, I almost missed Mum's next remark.

"Most were for the police officer that died." A deep note of recrimination etched her voice. "And did they have to be so awful?"

"Who?"

"That man's colleagues. We felt like lepers."

Dad's words echoed in my ears. *It could have been a friend of Richard Bowen.* "Feelings are running high right now. It will pass." I said neutrally.

"Will it? I know how we were made to feel. I was there. You weren't."

Red-faced, I stammered an apology.

"Oh Molly," she said abruptly contrite. "It's me who should be sorry. We mustn't fall out with each other."

I blindly agreed. I had no such reservations about my brother.

"Truly, I'm glad you weren't with us this morning," she

continued, trying to make amends. "I still can't understand what happened."

A thought flickered in my temple. "Did you see tyre marks on the road?" I needed to know if Scarlet had tried to brake or swerve, basically to avoid what happened.

"None on Scarlet's side. It's odd, isn't it?"

Scarlet's death, or rather her life, had created questions with no slick answers for all of us. My sister wouldn't be the first person to die and leave a legacy of secrets behind, yet the questions that remained over a murdered man, a loan asked for and rejected, together with the carnage in my carport that morning elevated Scarlet's death to a whole new level. Neither a sick joke, nor retaliation for a life lost. Was the dumping of roadkill symbolic? A message to back off, a warning? It was small consolation that the individual responsible had made his first mistake. For who in their right mind would, a little less than twenty-four hours since Scarlet's death, act with such reckless and ruthless speed? It spoke of someone running scared and intent on issuing a warning, for reasons as yet unknown. That person banked on a blatant threat intimidating me. Who else knew that I had misgivings about the accident? What was it they feared? But that didn't quite make sense because only *I* knew what was going on inside my head. I'd expressed my reservations to nobody. As hard as it was to admit, my wild imagination was probably getting the better of me. Strung-out over Scarlet's death, I was thinking 'threat' rather than 'sick joke'.

Either way, as shaken and frightened as I was, it was the biggest come-on ever.

Chapter 16

I barely noticed the dawn as it crawled out of bed, or the birds bashing out a chorus, or even whether I was awake or asleep. I had so much stuff circling my mind, I couldn't tell the difference. When the first blade of sunshine stabbed a hole in the curtains, I sloped off to the bathroom.

After making a pot of builder's tea, I switched on my laptop and scoured for news of Charlie Binns' murder. I found it care of the local Brent newspaper. 'A murder investigation has been launched after the shooting of a sixty-eight-year-old man in Gladstone Mews, Brondesbury at 10.47 p.m. on 5 June. Armed police officers arrived at 11.00 p.m. after neighbours reported hearing several shots fired. The victim, who was shot at close range, was pronounced dead at the scene in what has been described as a 'professional hit.' Detective Inspector Neil Judd said, "Detectives are at the scene, working to build a clear picture of the circumstances of this attack. A contract killing is one of several lines of inquiry that police are pursuing. I want to appeal to anyone with information to contact the police as a matter of urgency. No arrests have been made." A

75

police spokeswoman later refused to confirm claims that Mr Binns was an informer.

A friend who did not wish to be named said that Mr Binns was a very private individual, a true gentleman and would be greatly missed.'

I sat back, wide-eyed. What was Scarlet's interest in this man? Was it sheer happenstance that Bowen was a police officer, or did he have a professional connection to Binns?

Reaching for my phone, I checked through my last texts from my sister. Anodyne and unrevealing, nothing leapt out. I had absolutely no inkling of what she was up to. If Scarlet had a wild, secretive side, she'd kept it hidden. Nothing conveniently explained the tragic turn of events. All I saw was difficulty and complication. All I remembered was bitter rivalry and angry words. Was this what was really driving me, a strong desire to relieve my guilt for accusations that I should never have made?

I made a brief call to the shop to check that everything was ticking along. If it weren't for Lenny, I'd have stuck a closed sign on the door and locked up for the week, the month, the year, however long it took to work things out.

Afterwards, and still trying to think the angles through, I scavenged the fridge for eggs and milk and knocked up an omelette. My mobile rang as I fished breakfast out of a frying pan. It was Nate.

Speaking in a dark, urgent tone, he didn't mention the potential booze in Scarlet's system, or the alleged affair, his or hers. He didn't muck about. "There was no note."

"But —"

"I burnt it."

I sat bolt upright. "You did what?"

"Had to be done."

"You destroyed potential evidence, Nate. You're interfering in a police investigation." Making me an accessory by default.

"Destroying it doesn't materially alter the enquiry." It sounded like my father speaking, except Dad would never condone Nate's action. "The cops will still do what they have to," he said, scratchy, heading off any argument from me. Damn right, my responding protest was loud and long.

"Do you want Scarlet's name to be dragged through the mud any more than it is already?" Nate demanded.

"Of course, I don't."

"What with drink driving and killing a police officer, it's intolerable."

Never mind Scarlet's interest in a man shot dead miles away. I went to interject but Nate beat me to it.

"It's best we never had this or any other conversation on the subject," he finished. Breathless. Furious. Desperate.

My jaw uncomfortably clenched. "Nate, tell me what the fuck is going on." The silence that ensued could penetrate reinforced steel. Time to brandish a diamond-cutter. "That man you thought Scarlet was having an affair with, Charlie Binns?"

"What of the bastard?"

"He was a pensioner."

"So is Mick Jagger."

"Binns was murdered."

I could almost feel Nate's brain revolve through 180 degrees.

"What, in God's name, are you suggesting? You surely don't think —"

"Are *you* playing away, Nate?"

"Molly, I —"

"What made her so miserable?" I want to know what *you* did to her, what drove her to do what she did and get mixed up in all kinds of mess. No way did I believe my brother-in-law had associations with a contract killer, but he obviously wasn't the innocent he portrayed himself to be.

"Bloody hell, Molly."

"You know I won't give up."

Another silence. I could practically hear Nate weighing up the odds. "It's difficult." I'll bet.

I sat still, feeling a bit sick, thinking and unthinking, everything inchoate and slippery and way out of reach.

"Shit happens, Moll."

"Don't call me that." I was cold, unmoved and threatening,

"All right, all right. Yes, I was having an affair. Things went a bit south between me and Scarlet."

"I'm coming straight over." My planned visit to Zach could wait.

"Might be awkward. My family liaison officer will be here in a couple of hours."

At this I smiled. FLO's existed to support victims. They also played an important role in chasing down any investigation. If dodgy stuff were going on with nearest and dearest, they were demons at unearthing it.

"Excellent," I said.

"Molly, for Chrissakes."

78

"Don't worry." My tone assured my brother-in-law that he should be very worried indeed. "See you in a bit."

Outside Nate's and Scarlet's home, two men and a woman hovered like buzzards preparing to consume carrion. Beady eyes swivelled in my direction. I had no doubt they were from the press, an observation confirmed when the woman stepped towards me and asked if I knew the family of the 'dead nurse'. Issuing my best 'fuck off' look, I swept past and rang the bell.

Someone, I presumed to be a police officer, answered the door. Sandy-haired, a little receding, not terribly tall, and with a flinty expression, he had that whole authoritative, commanding and suspicious vibe going on. One look and I felt guilty of nameless crimes.

"I'm Molly Napier, Scarlet's sister and Nate's sister-in-law," I said.

"Warren Childe, family liaison officer." His voice sounded as if it had a crack running down the middle of it. "Sorry for your loss. Best come in."

I glanced over my shoulder at the gathering ghouls. He nodded in sympathy and stepped aside. As I swept down the hall, I heard him direct all enquiries to the press office. "And guys, can you please respect the privacy of the family at this difficult time."

I found Nate seated on the sofa in the small sitting room with his face in his hands. He barely moved as I sat beside him. Seemed to be waiting for Childe.

"Tell her," he muttered, when Childe came in.

E. V. Seymour

I looked up questioningly as Childe cleared his throat. "The post-mortem threw up some anomalies."

Anomalies. Cold. Analytical. Factual. Full-on police mode. I knew what was coming next. Except I didn't. Not quite.

"Your sister had 240 milligrams per 100 millilitres of blood in her system – around three times the legal limit for driving," Childe explained.

"What about Bowen?" Nate said. "Had he been drinking?"

"No evidence of substance abuse of any kind," Childe said smoothly. "Preliminary enquiries suggest that the pre-collision mechanical condition of the vehicle was good. There were no tyre or skid marks on the road to suggest that Scarlet was forced to take evasive action." Childe looked with an 'are you with me so far' expression. I responded with a dull nod.

"Witness statements suggest that the driver of the jeep —"

"My sister," I protested.

"Deliberately," he said, raising his voice a decibel, "drove into the path of the oncoming motorcyclist."

I stared wide-eyed. Inside, a silent scream yelled No.

80

Chapter 17

My head felt as if a lump of lead was where my brain should be. Nate, next to me, physically jolted, his body lifting off the sofa by an inch. "What witnesses? Who are these bloody people?"

"The driver in the vehicle behind Bowen."

"How fast was *he* travelling?" I said irritably.

"Saw it all. Said that Bowen braked at the very last second but, by then, it was too late."

"You're suggesting that my sister used her vehicle like a weapon, a battering ram?"

"I wouldn't put it like that."

"Then how would you put it?" Nate interjected, cold with anger.

"I understand this is upsetting, but —"

"She could have blacked out, had a heart attack, or sneezed, for God's sake," I cut in. Throat raw and exposed, my voice was too loud. "There could have been oil on the road."

"There wasn't," Childe said.

"You said witness statements. You mean more than one?"

"There was a pedestrian."

"On that busy road?"

"A jogger," Childe clarified. "This corroborates an initial vehicle assessment of an absence of corresponding tyre and skid marks. Scarlet never braked. Quite the contrary; we think she actually sped up."

I nodded blindly. What else could I do?

"I've explained to Nathan that we need to talk about Scarlet's mental health."

"They think she was suicidal." Nate's tone was a mess of cynicism. Only I could detect the fake ring in it. The message left for Nate had been a suicide note, and he knew it.

Instantly, I thought about Fliss' observation, the way Scarlet seemed suddenly sorted, the relief she felt. I had to admit that suicide suddenly seemed a strong possibility. But I also knew my sister.

"If she'd wanted to kill herself, she wouldn't have hurt someone else. She was a nurse. She believed in saving lives, not taking them."

"I agree," Nate said.

"And, *if* that was her plan, which I definitely don't buy, she would have targeted something a great deal more solid. A brick wall, tunnel or bridge is more final, isn't it, more likely to do the job?" Articulating it made me go hot and cold and hot again.

Childe remained deadpan. "It's only one avenue of enquiry."

What other lines were they pursuing? Suspicion pinched my nerves.

Childe viewed the pair of us as if we were nobly defending my sister's honour, which we were. He returned to his favourite theme. "Were you aware of any difficulties your sister had?"

I swallowed, shook my head, glad that the scream inside, this time, was silent.

"No history of depression?"

"None."

"Never attempted to take her own life?"

"Of course not."

"Was she a heavy drinker?"

"I told you she didn't drink," Nate piped up, frustrated, simply not buying this particular piece of evidence. "She'd been on night duty, for God's sake. She drove home early morning."

Childe returned to the facts and, punch-drunk with information, I tuned out. Glancing through the window, I noticed people walking into town, heading off for appointments, some carrying bags of shopping. On the other side of the road: loud men with loud music erecting scaffolding. Life churning. Everything the same and yet nothing the same and wouldn't be again. Oh. My. God.

I noticed a woman marching along the pavement. Hair scraped off her face and manacled in a ponytail, her complexion spotty and slightly pitted beneath the tan, she had pale blue, luminous eyes and her full mouth curved down, carving deep lines from the corner of her lips to her chin. If anyone could be described as looking murderous, she did.

Childe followed my gaze. "Jesus," he cursed, and dived out of the room.

Taken aback, Nate also looked and we both watched, mysti-fied, as the woman flung open the gate, shot down the path, one hand diving into her handbag, the other clenched into a fist, ready to rap on the front door.

In strides, Childe got to it first. "Heather, we're all under-standably raw right now —"

"I'm not interested in what *you* feel," she exploded, "I want that bastard inside to know what his slag of a wife was up to."

Slag. Should I give her a mouthful? Nate tensed, turned to me and silently mouthed No.

"Heather," I heard Childe say sternly. "Go home. Your kids need you."

"Damn right they do, and whose fault is that?" Her eyes shot to the window. Automatically, Nate and I shrank back.

"You're not thinking straight, love. Sam Holland's your FLO, right? I'll give her a call." I had to hand it to Childe. He was the epitome of cool composure and warm compassion, yet no way was the woman setting foot over the threshold.

"I have Sam on speed dial," the woman spat back. "If I need her, I'll ring for her. Here," she said. "Give Mr Jay this. It's all I came for."

Next, fast footsteps followed by the gate smashing open and banging against its hinges.

Childe returned inside. He looked more shaken than he'd sounded seconds ago. "I'm sorry about that."

"Who was that bloody woman?" Nate said.

"Richard Bowen's widow."

I let out a groan, regretting my first instinct, which was to have laid into her verbally. Nate pitched forward, hands clasped over his head.

"I'm sorry but can either of you identify this?" Childe extended his arm. In the palm of his hand nestled a gold and diamond bracelet.

It belonged to my sister.

Chapter 18

"I've never seen it before." The conviction in Nate's voice blew me away.

Like me, he knew it was Scarlet's bracelet and yet he'd lied. The thought of how it had fallen into Mrs Bowen's hands made me queasy. *Slag,* she'd said. Christ, if Scarlet had been involved in a relationship with Richard Bowen, it changed the entire picture.

"And you?" Childe said, hawk-eyed.

"Me?" I said.

"Yes."

The muscles in Nate's thighs, inches from mine, tightened, the sofa complaining under his silent protest. "I can't be sure," I lied. Childe's eyes locked on mine. Buckling under his gaze, I mumbled, "She might have had something similar, but I'm not certain it's the same one." It was a pretty rubbish attempt to blur the truth.

"Okay," Childe said, in a way that assured me it was not okay at all. He got straight on his phone, all the while glaring at the pair of us. After reporting the incident with

Mrs Bowen, he mentioned the bracelet. When someone spoke back, he stepped out into the hallway. I heard him say something about 'escalating the investigation', which could only be bad. Nate turned to me, fury in his expression.

"Why, in God's name, did you admit it could be hers?"

"Don't have a go at me. Why did you lie?" I spat back.

"To protect my wife's reputation."

"Are you sure it's not *your* reputation?" I conveniently parked any suggestions about my sister's private life. "You're a hypocrite, Nate."

His jaw clenched. At that close proximity, I could almost hear his teeth grind his fillings to dust.

"According to Fliss Fiander, Scarlet suspected you were having an affair. Hell, she probably knew."

"She had no damn right to say such a terrible thing."

"Scarlet or Fliss?" I sniped back.

Nate tensed. Lines carved deep grooves in his forehead and his eyes became angry slits. "It's none of your business."

Given the circumstances, I strongly disagreed, and I was furious with Nate for making me his secret-keeper.

"How do you think Scarlet's bracelet wound up in Heather Bowen's hand —by teleportation?" Nate didn't wait for an answer. "The woman must have gone through her husband's things and found it."

As one picture smashed in my head, another ugly image revealed itself. The note now assumed new significance. Scarlet was apologising for what she was about to do, not something she had already done. She'd planned it. That note, damn it, demonstrated a degree of premeditation. And Nate had burnt it.

Tears sprung to his eyes. "Even if she were sleeping with Bowen or having sex with someone else, what the fuck does it matter? She's dead." He let out a weary ragged sigh. "Don't you see that I'm trying to protect her?"

The sincerity in Nate's expression made my pulse jive. He opened his mouth to say something else but stopped. Childe was back. Focused. Determined.

"We're going to need to conduct a search of the property, Nate."

"Why? I've done nothing wrong."

"We know that," Childe said, with a modicum of sympathy. "And I genuinely understand."

"Do you? Have you ever lost a wife?"

"No," he said plainly. "But I have plenty of experience of those who have."

"Not quite the same thing, is it?"

"Nate," I said, glancing at Childe, desperate to dial down Nate's bellicosity. "The guy is simply doing his job, trying to help." It's what Dad would say.

"Molly's right, Nate," Childe said, flashing me an appreciative look.

Nate glowered then let out an enormous sigh. "Yeah, yeah. Sorry."

"Good." Childe seemed glad the conversational dynamics had altered in his favour. "Did either of you have laptops or computers?"

Nate's pallor turned a shade lighter. "Well, yeah."

"We'll need those too."

Nate closed his eyes. "Jesus," he said, not angrily, as if he was cursed but as if the game was up. Was Nate worried a taste for porn would be disclosed, or concerned that emails to a woman he was sleeping with would be revealed? And what about Scarlet?

Everything seemed to be running away, notching up several gears. "Isn't this a little over the top? It's not a murder investigation." As my words broke loose, I sparked inside. If the police could prove beyond any reasonable doubt that Scarlet deliberately targeted Bowen, she would be branded a murderer.

"Standard procedure in the circumstances," Childe cut in. "Along with checking Scarlet's phone records and call log."

"Fuck's sake." A vein in Nate's temple stood out proud.

"Is that a problem for you, Nate?" Childe's tone was even, but his expression razor sharp.

Nate tilted his head, jutted out his chin. Guarded. I shot him a look. "Nope."

"Good," Childe said. "Is there somewhere close you can go for a few days?"

"He can stay with me." This time Nate shot *me* a look.

From the expression on Childe's face, he clearly favoured my suggestion. "We may need to ask further questions."

My thoughts entirely and the only reason I was about to take Nate captive.

"What sort of questions?" Nate said.

Clues to whether Scarlet had a prior relationship with Richard Bowen, whether or not she had a motive to harm him, I thought. I bet her bracelet would fall under the forensic microscope too. Whatever I believed or wanted to believe; I couldn't argue with the facts.

"Simply routine," Childe said, bouncing lightly on the balls of his feet.

"Ridiculous."

Forcing a breezy note into my voice and looking Childe directly in the eye, I said, "That's settled then." And before Nate could protest, I added. "I'll give you my address and contact number."

Chapter 19

Begrudgingly, Nate got his shit together. His words, not mine, and we set off. As if to taunt us, signs that said 'Think Bike' appeared at regular intervals along the route.

"Those witnesses should have their eyesight tested," he grumbled.

"Never mind them. I'm going to stop the car and you and me are going to have a chat."

"Christ, do you have air conditioning in this thing?"

Dutifully, I rotated the control on the air con. "Don't change the subject."

"I'm not. Pull over."

"So that you can do a runner? No chance."

"So we can talk."

I cast around, thinking I'd need to choose exactly the right spot, somewhere Nate would feel comfortable, but also not the kind of place he could easily make a break for it. Turning off the main road, I found a place a few miles on. Random. Surrounded by fields. Nearest house half a mile away. I pulled up next to a tree stump that resembled an animal carcass.

Blinking away unwanted memories, I killed the engine. Turning around to face my brother-in-law, I thought he resembled a man about to chuck himself off a multi-storey. His skin was pearly white, almost translucent. All I saw were his eyes, which were deep dark squirming pools.

"Did you know that Scarlet asked Fliss for a loan?"

Nate half-smiled, disbelieving. "That's rubbish. Fliss must be mistaken or she misunderstood."

I repeated what Fliss had said. Nate's body seemed to fold in on itself. "I don't understand."

"Maybe she wanted to start a new life."

"And leave me? Never. Not her style."

I was no longer sure what my sister's style was. Why else would Scarlet need £25k? If she'd changed her mind about taking a loan from Fliss because she'd found another source, it would show in her bank statements to which the police had access. She'd hardly be in receipt of £25k in used tenners. If anything of a financial nature was uncovered, the police were bound to follow the money trail. They always did. "Maybe she planned to take off with Bowen and got cold feet."

"You're suggesting that the accident was the result of a lover's tiff?" Nate scoffed. "A crime of passion?" Chill seized hold of my vertebrae. The scenario was believable, but would confirm my sister as a murderer, something I found hard to comprehend. Nate crossed his arms. "I don't believe it."

"It would explain the content of the note."

"What note?"

"Don't you damn well dare," I said, half-crazed with frustration. "The one you destroyed!"

Nate was becoming a specialist in moody looks, this one a variation on the resentful version he'd performed for Childe. "I should never have shown you."

"Well, you did, and you haven't answered my question."

Shoulders bunched up around his ears, he turned away and stared out of the window.

"What else could Scarlet's note mean?"

He turned back, flicked up the palms of his hands.

Getting somewhere. "You need to be as straightforward and honest with the police as possible." I wasn't thinking for Nate's sake. I was thinking of my parents.

"No way."

"If you say nothing and they discover she left a note, you'll get into trouble for not coming clean."

"But they aren't going to find out, are they Molly?" What he meant was that the only way they would was if I told them.

My stupefied expression got a lot more stupid.

"Are you going to tell them about the money?" I didn't like the challenge in his voice.

"Well, no, because —" I lost my train of thought. Money was my Achilles heel. Money was the spark that had lit the fuse for my fight with my sister.

I'd always had to struggle to be financially independent. Any money my parents gave me was always a loan. Whereas Scarlet only had to click her fingers and loot would be forthcoming, no strings, which was why it was so disturbing that she'd gone to Fliss for cash and not our parents. Unable to come clean and speak about my own resentments, I didn't finish.

"If we breathe a word it will be like trashing her memory." Nate's tone was a lot more dialled down. He briefly touched my arm in what was meant as a shared moment of understanding and complicity.

Grubby little fingers closed around my throat and gave it a good squeeze. Silence lengthened in the car. Now came the hard part. "I promise to keep your affair, fling, whatever, safe on one condition."

He looked incredulous and grateful.

"You're a gutless bastard, Nate, and the only reason you're making a big deal about Scarlet's affair is because you can't stand the heat and attention on your own."

"That's not —"

"Save it. I'm only doing this to protect Mum and Dad. If you have a shred of decency, as soon as the funeral is out of the way, you'll break your business partnership with Dad and clear off out of our lives."

Chapter 20

Despite Nate's protestation, I told Nate that he had a duty to drop in and see Mum and Dad before we went to mine. It's what they'd expect, and it would be unkind not to. We didn't speak for the rest of the journey. Noise from the car's squeaky brakes, the result of an extended period of hot, dry weather, bored through the silence. Gave me time to turn things over in my head. Murder and money, those incestuously connected twins. How the shooting of a man fitted into things I'd no idea, but it slotted in somehow.

The nearer we got to Malvern, the more the hills laid claim to the town. I'd always thought of them as quintessentially British. Today, they seemed like foreign invaders.

Pulling up outside Mum and Dad's, Nate grasped the thorny silence prickling between us. "Promise you won't say anything to your folks?"

I slammed on the handbrake. "It's bit late for that, isn't it?" He briefly closed his eyes, covered his mouth with his hand. He was sweating. A lot.

"You do realise that Dad could win super-sleuth of the year?" Which was a problem. If he found out half of what I knew so would Mum and it would kill her.

Nate issued a gale of a sigh in response. "He hasn't worked for the police for years."

As if this made a difference. "He still has connections. You want my advice?"

"Go on," he said, shrinking, as if trying to bury himself in the foot well.

"Be as honest as you can without destroying them."

Nate pitched forward, scrubbed at his face then his hair, and mumbled something indecipherable.

"And don't forget what I told you about the partnership," I added.

At the sound of the car doors opening and closing, Mr Lee went crazy and didn't quieten until we were inside. I bent down and was overwhelmed with a blast of slobbery doggy breath.

Dad appeared, visibly harassed. "Bloody newspaper hacks. Phone hasn't stopped. Nate," he said, softening, arms extended, pulling my brother-in-law close. Always tactile, it was one of the things I loved about my father. "How are you holding up, son?"

Nate glanced across, caught my eye, anxiety scribbled all over his face. "Okay, I guess."

Dad patted Nate on the back and pulled away. "Any updates from the police? Only my source appears to have dried up. Can't seem to get a word out of anyone."

I made a big play of stroking our dog. Close to Nate, I

could feel the friction coming off him in waves. Tense and perplexed, my dad looked from me to Nate. "Well, erm— my family liaison officer, a guy called Childe," Nate began in a strangled voice, "he visited this morning, confirming the results of the post-mortem."

Dad flicked an uneasy, expectant look.

I studied the floor as Nate revealed the toxicology results.

"Drunk?" Dad said, astounded.

"The vehicle examiner's report corroborated witness statements. They seem to think that Scarlet was unstable."

I could see Dad hanging on Nate's every word. His cheeks sagged in dismay. "I don't understand." I caught the distraction in his voice. For once, my father's sharp mind was slow to catch on.

"They believe she intended to commit suicide," Nate said in a low tone.

It was as if we'd all tumbled into a void. Pain that was almost physical accelerated through me. It was some time before my father recovered the power of speech.

"How could we have missed the signs?" He pressed a hand to his temple, as if trying to put pressure on the thinking part of his brain. "I don't get it," he said, shaking his head. "I have to ask you, son. Did Scarlet leave a note?"

Nate swallowed. His hands clenched tight, knuckles virtually bursting through his skin. I tried to catch his eye again, but he refused to make contact.

Dad viewed me in a way that told me he'd twigged he wasn't getting the full story. "Let's go into the study, Nate."

Ignoring Nate's cornered expression, I said, "Where's Mum?"

"In the sitting room. Had a few drinks." Code for she's drunk, which was hardly surprising if not exactly helpful.

"I'll keep her company," I said, as Dad turned on his heel, Nate gloomy, loping along behind him.

Dressed in an old tracksuit, Mum sat on the floor surrounded by boxes of old photographs. Engrossed, she didn't look up. Against the shuttered light, the smell of booze hung heavy. I slid onto the floor beside her.

"Remember this?" She glanced up, her face, without make-up, puffy with crying. She showed me Scarlet's graduation photograph. Goofing around, her mortarboard askew, you could see the happiness radiating out of her. The only person bursting with more pride than Scarlet on that day had been Mum. She touched the print tenderly, tracing the line around my sister's face, dropping a kiss onto it before planting it carefully next to a line of others. Method in her madness, the photographs were arranged in date order, from babyhood to childhood, adolescent and young adult. Millions of them, more even than Zach, her firstborn.

I wrapped an arm around her shoulders, giving her a squeeze. In the space of forty-eight hours, she'd lost weight, felt as fragile as spun glass. "And this," I smiled, picking out a photo of Scarlet and me on holiday in Cornwall. The weather had been atrocious, I remembered, although it hadn't deterred us from riding our bikes in full wet weather gear. Sodden and smiling for the camera, we couldn't have looked more pleased. A volatile explosion of grief took me unawares, hot tears unexpectedly surging down my cheeks. I checked them with the back of my hand.

Haunted, Mum reached for her drink, the sound of ice clinking against glass as familiar to me as her smile. "Did I hear Nate's voice?"

"He's with dad in the study." I wondered whether I should warn my mother of what was to come. I never expected drama and denials. This was not my father's way, but the effect of his displeasure was no less punishing. What I hadn't told Nate was that, as Scarlet's protector, Dad would demand to know why his eldest daughter was so unhappy and what part his son-in-law might have played in her distress. To Scarlet, family was all. My parents' commitment to her was no less strong. I imagined Dad listening quite reasonably then narrowing his eyes, getting Nate in his sights, speaking softly before he did the equivalent of pulling the trigger with a few well-chosen words. Dread dripped into my ear. "I expect they'll be out soon," I reassured Mum.

Mum selected another photograph: Scarlet in her nurse's uniform. "Her patients adored her." She slurred her words and took another deep swallow of gin. How I'd like to reach for the bottle and tip the contents down the sink, but I did what I always did and nodded blandly.

As if suddenly remembering Nate, she stood up, made for the door, unsteady on her feet. I called after her, scrabbling, about to give chase when Dad and Nate bowled in.

"Nate, darling." Mum flung her arms around him. "You poor poor man."

"He's going to stay with us for a few days, Amanda," Dad said.

E. V. Seymour

"Of course. Absolutely. You must, Nate."

Looking over her shoulder, Nate looked me straight in the eye. He didn't look flustered. He didn't look apologetic. He didn't look ashamed. I couldn't read him at all.

Chapter 21

Zach looked as if he hadn't moved since my last visit. Sitting down, shades on, thighs spread, soaking up the sun. The only difference: Tanya sat beside him cross-legged on the dry ground, as if someone had taken a pair of shears to her hair and tipped a pot of Dulux over what was left. 'Lady in Red' sprang to mind. As soon as she spotted me, she unfurled, lithe-limbed, and threw her arms around me in a hug. Sandalwood and sweat, incense and ingenuousness. Goodness knew what she saw in my brother. "Zach told me," she whispered in my ear. "So sorry." Drawing away, she asked after my parents even though she'd never met them. Probably never would.

I trotted out a neutral 'as well as can be expected' reply.

Much to my amazement, Zach had managed to prise himself out of his seat, stagger to his feet and engage in normal social niceties.

"Hi," he said watchfully. Sizing me up.

"Is there somewhere we can go and talk, Zach?"

Catching on, Tanya said she needed to check on an ailing chicken.

"Sure, I —"

"Darling Molly," a smooth educated voice, tidal in its delivery, one instantly recognisable, boomed over our heads. We did a collective turn and watched as Chancer bounded down the steps of what had once been a Romany caravan. He carried more weight than I remembered, the buttons of his white, open-neck shirt, which hung loose outside his jeans, competing with flesh and gravity. Fuller-faced too, a little dissolute around the eyes, he looked as though he'd returned from an all-night party. Before I knew it, I was grabbed and spun off my feet. Startled, I briefly forgot that I was in mourning. So had he, it seemed.

"Chancer, for God's sake," I struggled.

"Mad Molly," he said, quite delighted and squeezing hard enough to wind me. Nobody ever spoke to me the way Chancer did.

Inches from his sun-tanned face, I couldn't help but gaze at his extraordinary deep blue eyes, his jaw, not quite so sculpted and defined. Must have been several years, at least, since we'd last met. He'd acquired laughter lines that did nothing to detract from his good looks. My blood sprinted.

Placing me carefully down, he rested his hands on my shoulders, looked into my eyes. For a second it was simply he and I and nobody else. "I'm so very sorry about your sad news. Poor Scarlet."

"Thanks. It's appreciated."

"And poor Zach," he said, glancing over in my brother's direction to which Zach nodded dutifully back. "How are your Ma and Pa? Pretty broken up, I guess. Will you send my warmest best wishes and condolences?"

"I will." I realised that any chance I had of speaking to my brother in private had been ground into the dust under Chancer's size nine's.

"Did he tell you about me and Edie?" Chancer jerked his head in Zach's direction again.

I acknowledged my brother with a smile. "He did. It's a great shame."

"Yeah, well," he said, downcast, as though it wasn't his idea, but Edie's to split. "Bad business." Chancer dropped down onto the grass, my cue to sit next to him. Zach, meanwhile, had taken up his favourite position. All very Zen.

I had no intention of discussing Scarlet's death or the break-up of Chancer's marriage. Divorce is akin to suicide. The more couples bicker and bitch, the less likely they are to follow through. It's the ones that suddenly announce: 'It's over' who mean it. Similarly, successful suicides rarely leave a clue of intention until it's too late, which upped the odds of pre-meditated murder, I realised darkly. Was this Scarlet's legacy, that I would forever associate her with the taking of a man's life?

We sat in stony, gloomy silence. Conversation, when it broke through, was stilted and sporadic and, to me, meaningless. What did you talk about at a time like this? I lay back, closed my eyes. Sun-pennies danced in the sunlight. Stalking the silence, I willed for Chancer to go.

Maddeningly, the boys wound up discussing Chancer's job.

"My recent bonuses won't count for much, not after Edie has cleaned me out."

E. V. Seymour

"You could always transfer funds into my account," Zach said cheerily.

"You don't have an account," I said. I wouldn't be surprised if Zach reached his fiftieth birthday without ever having a payslip. Zach huffed loudly in protest, but that was all.

"Not a bad idea." The reflective way in which Chancer spoke briefly made me unsure whether or not he was serious. Silence kicked in once more. For God's sake, Chancer, leave.

"Mum and Dad okay?" Zach said eventually.

"They'd be better if you came home. Don't you think he should, Chancer?" Which I admit was low. In the absence of a response, I cocked an eye open. Zach's stare could melt a polar icecap.

Chancer wore a 'What do I know?' expression on his face. Male solidarity for you. We fell silent again, the heat having a soporific effect on everyone, bar me. I itched to get my brother alone.

"Anyone fancy a drink?" Chancer said.

"Tap water or tap water," Zach snorted.

"Nah, I've got a bottled of chilled wine in the car."

"Flip me, a car with a fridge. Didn't spot it," I said, casting about.

Chancer jerked his head in the direction of the entrance to the site. "Wouldn't dream of driving my beamer down that pot-holed piece of crap. Left it at the top of the road."

"Like the car, like the man. Go on, then." It was the moment I'd been waiting for.

The second Chancer was out of sight I jacked myself up on an elbow and twisted round to face my big brother.

"Why did you lie about Scarlet's visit?" While I was direct, my tone was neither accusing nor challenging. That approach wouldn't work. Nailing Zach was akin to taming smoke.

"Don't know what you mean."

"Last time we spoke you said you hadn't seen her for months. Fliss says Scarlet saw you weeks ago."

"Did I? Must have slipped my mind." His left leg fidgeted, and he itched both his arms below the elbows. Classic Zach under pressure. He used to do it all the time when he was wasted.

"Well, now it's slipped back in, why did she come?"

"To see me." His voice was heavy with sarcasm. "Or is that so surprising?"

I stuck my tongue out in response. "How was she?"

"Seemed fine."

"Nothing odd?" Nothing that indicated what she was about to do?

"Like I said, she was good."

"What did you talk about?"

"Don't really remember." He scratched his head, making a pretence of trying to recall.

"Did you know she was having an affair?"

"Ah," he drawled knowingly.

"You did?" I sat up straight. The air suddenly compressed with thick and poisonous heat. I swear my ears popped. "Did she mention a name?"

Zach's eyes thinned. His lips moved, like he was attempting to locate a piece of information from his brain and flush it out through his mouth.

"A guy called Charlie Binns?"

My brother is a proficient squiggler when it comes to telling the truth but even I could tell he hadn't a clue. "What about Richard Bowen?"

"Richard who?"

"The guy she killed."

Zach jumped to his feet. It would be fair to say I'd not seen my brother react with speed like that in the thick end of twenty years. "Why do you have to load everything?"

"Load?"

"Emotionally. You make it sound as if she murdered him."

"If she was having an affair with the guy, she might have meant to."

"That's complete crap." He was loud and agitated. At this rate Chancer would hear from several fields away.

"Zach, I didn't mean it to come out like that."

"Yes, you did." A bubble of spit balled at the side of his mouth.

"For goodness' sake, calm down."

"Then don't make such crazy allegations."

"The police are on to it. They're examining her phone and computer records. If you'd taken your head out of your backside and come home, it wouldn't come as such a shock."

He slung off his sunglasses and threw them onto the grass. Sparks of rage flashed behind his eyes. "Don't you dare," he growled.

Peripherally, I caught sight of Tanya strolling back. From the concerned expression, she'd heard the noise and loss of volume control. Zach couldn't care less.

"Why can't you stop meddling?"

"Now, you look here." My turn to jump to my feet and raise my voice.

"Fuck's sake, stop interfering in things you don't understand." Zach's full lips wrapped around and spat out every word. His eyes were everywhere but on me.

"All right, guys?" Tanya said with forced jollity, looking from me to Zach.

"I'm going to take a shower." He grunted something derogatory under his breath, then, kicking up dust with his bare feet, stalked off.

Chapter 22

In the silence of my own home all I could hear was Zach's warning words.

Dad always said, in homicide investigations, it was vital to study the victim. I didn't know whether or not Bowen was a murder victim, but I'd spent so much time looking at Scarlet, I'd neglected to fully check out the man she killed.

I grabbed my laptop, clicked my way to local online news. The accident remained riding high. This time there was a more personal interest article and I struck lucky. Frederick Allen, and next-door neighbour of the Bowens, talked of a family man tragically taken from his wife and children too soon. For security reasons, most police officers keep their addresses secret. But the neighbour had not been so circumspect. I knew Hales Road well, with its jowl by jaw terraced houses. Allen's unguarded remarks offered a couple of possibilities and it got me thinking.

Nate had said that Bowen was heading to Gloucester, but Bowen worked at the police HQ in Cheltenham, which was in Hester's Way. Why would Richard Bowen come off a night shift and head in the opposite direction to where he lived?

Amped, I threw open all the windows, kicked off my sandals, and changed into a loose-fitting silk dress that was a lot more comfortable than shorts and T-shirt. About to grab a beer from the fridge, my mobile rang. Rocco Noble.

"Hi," he said. "I hope you don't mind me calling."

I did. Perhaps he'd found someone else to do his house clearance.

"No pressure, but I have to go away for a few days."

In my experience, when people say 'no pressure,' they mean nothing but pressure. "Yeah?" So what? We haven't even met.

"We were going to schedule a meeting."

"At a mutually convenient time." Not after five, any day, as he'd instructed. I didn't say 'take a hike' but the tone of my voice suggested it.

"God, I knew I shouldn't have phoned." Agitated and cross with himself, he stumbled an apology.

My teeth grated. Everyone meant well but I really wished people, particularly those who didn't know Scarlet, would stop saying how sorry they were. I wondered what Scarlet would make of it and glanced around the room to check whether her ghost had taken up residence on the nearest easy chair. Before my damned imagination ran away with me, I cut sharply to the chase.

"Are you always this pushy?" Who else pursues a woman for a business arrangement when it's already been explained that there's been a death in the family? Someone used to getting his own way. Clearly, one of those thrusting ambitious 'Me, me, me' types.

"Oh my God," he laughed lightly. "Look, I'm so sorry. I hadn't meant to hound you. It's just—well—I'm leaving very soon, and I'd really like to get things sorted."

See him, quiz him and get rid of him, I thought. It would take me ten minutes to check him and his granny's stuff out before I offered to clear it for an exorbitant price that he was bound to decline. "I'll come round tomorrow. I could drop in after lunch, around 2 p.m."

"Won't work for me. Are you free now, by any chance?"

"No, I'm not."

"I'd be immensely grateful."

Did he have a neurological disorder, like Asperger's? I took a breath, mimed banging my head against the wall, then reached for my car keys and headed out. Right, Mr Noble, very soon you will be toast.

*

It was a genuine 'pinch me' moment. The first thing that struck me about Rocco Noble was his smile, and he looked like a guy who smiled a lot. Mr Sunshine. Cute creases at the sides of his alert, highly intelligent eyes told me so. His hair, which was short, was the colour of midnight. He had an olive complexion and probably needed to shave a couple of times a day. Stubble suited him. Tall and built, he wore a suit, the top button of his shirt undone, his tie loose and casual. In business mode, or because we were indeed doing business, he stuck out his hand, which was firm and smooth, not sweaty at all, a proper leader of men type handshake. He might be pushy, but I didn't detect anything off about him. When I addressed him as Mr Noble, he quickly corrected me.

"Rocco, please."

"Molly," I stammered in return. Standing in his gran's sitting room, a cavern crammed with dark Victorian furniture, ornaments and knick-knacks, I was acutely aware of a space brimming with neat testosterone. In danger of having a total mind-drain, I reckoned I could get pregnant from simply standing next to him.

I flicked a weak smile, which, when reciprocated, lit up the dark interior as if his personality alone could shape-shift the room.

"Right, my gran's gaff," he said, brightening the mood, "As much as I loved her, I'm not a fan of her furniture."

"It's a bit gruesome, isn't it?" I agreed with a tight smile. Glancing around, I made notes, my gaze finally resting on an ugly looking Chiffonier cupboard in darkest mahogany that ran along one wall. It would probably look okay painted.

"What's upstairs?"

"More of the same."

"Okay if I check it out?"

"Sure."

Clipboard in hand, I followed him up the quirkiest little staircase ever. You'd need to be a mountain goat to successfully navigate it and God alone knew how anyone had managed to get a bed, let alone a wardrobe into the upper storey. Already, I was making mental notes of ropes and ladders.

At the top, a landing the size of a sandwich, off which three doors with old-fashioned latches.

"In here," Rocco said.

Dusty light trickled through leaded windowpanes onto a magnificent Victorian brass bed that dominated the room. "My mother was born in that," Rocco said with pride.

It was fabulous. My only worry was how the shop would accommodate it. Since taking charge of a full-sized, non-PC stuffed grizzly bear, space was at a premium. "Don't you want to keep it?"

"I'd love to, but it's not very practical. Hell," he beamed, catching hold of my cautious expression, "Maybe I should."

"Is the cottage yours?"

"Bequeathed to me."

"Then definitely keep it." I flushed, hoping he didn't think I was suggesting I help him put it to good use. "You're planning to live here?"

"Eventually. I rent in Worcester at the moment." I wondered where, whether Rocco was the kind of man who lived in a modern purpose-built flat, or preferred older properties, whether he shared, had a girlfriend – not that it was any business of mine. "Obviously, it needs work," he said, glancing at the walls, nostrils briefly flaring as if detecting damp.

"Any designs to reconfigure the layout?"

"You think I could?"

"My dad's a property developer." Although I didn't think he'd be up for projects any time soon. Not after Scarlet. Not with Mum being the way she was. Not was going to figure a lot in all our lives.

112

"You on commission?" he said, raising a sexy eyebrow.

I laughed, shook my head, instantly guilty. I had no right to either solicit business or have fun at a time like this and yet I couldn't help myself. God knew what my parents would think if they found out I was pricing a job. They probably thought I was home mindlessly watching the tennis at Wimbledon.

"Are you in a commission-based profession?" I said, deflecting attention from me.

"Not personally. I work for ContraMed."

I was none the wiser and said so.

"Medical insurance, specialising in negligence cases."

"Sounds interesting." Not having a clue what it entailed, I mentally kicked myself for making such a crummy observation.

He smiled without expanding on the subject. "So, what do you reckon?"

"You say you want the lot cleared?"

"Apart from the bed, yes."

I made a big performance of looking down the list, crossing out the need for ropes and ladders now that the bed was staying, did a mental recce, gave him a price all in that was way over the top and should make his eyes water.

"Done," he said. "When's the earliest date you could do it?"

Breath stampeded out of me. I could hardly say I'd changed my mind, so I did that thing that plumbers do when they tell you a little job is in fact a big job. Pursing my lips, I blew out through my teeth, and shook my head. In my mind, I said, *Some time next year.* Mr Noble interpreted it as yesterday.

"I need to use up a day's holiday. Wondered whether you are free day after tomorrow?"

"To clear the cottage?" I didn't think he was asking me out on a date.

"Yes."

Fixated on clearing his gran's place to the point of obsession, my personal situation didn't seem to occur to him. I should have refused point-blank. The police had gone quiet but who knew when they'd come back with more confounding news?

I swallowed hard. "I can't manage this on my own and I'd have to pay my colleague time and a half, or double so it would increase the price for you. It would also mean closing the shop, which would —"

"I can help."

"But that's crazy. You're paying me."

"So? My time. My choice."

"Well, I —"

"As long as you feel up to it." His dark eyebrows drew together in a picture of concern, eyes melting into mine.

"Yes," I said weakly. "I can do it."

I kicked myself all the way home. Not the easiest person to grind down, I should have been more assertive. I should have told him to find someone else.

All this was drizzling through my mind as I drove into the carport. Dad had done a good job of cleaning up, the rotten smell replaced by the strong odour of Jeyes Fluid. Didn't stop me from looking around, or glancing over my shoulder, or asking myself why someone would take such a risk.

Relieved to be back in the safety of my own garden, I trogged off down the path and let myself in through the back door. Kicking off my sandals, the air whooshed out of my lungs. My thoughts blurred. Terror took a chisel to my brain. Embedded and jutting out of the kitchen table, a carving knife, its blade razor sharp. It belonged to me. But I hadn't put it there.

Chapter 23

I did not sleep.

After prising out the knife, I hung on to it while I investigated the rest of my home. Stupidly, I'd left a window open in the downstairs loo, which explained how someone had gained access. What I still couldn't explain: why would someone single me out for special treatment? Did someone know about my trip to London and my interest in a dead man, possibly an informer? Had someone rumbled that I wouldn't rest until I knew the truth about my sister's secrets? Together, Mr Blade and me waited for the dawn.

Early, the next morning, I drove straight to the scene of the accident. Aside from the 'serious incident' sign, announcing a collision, an appeal for witnesses, and a phone number to call, I couldn't miss it. Mum was right about the flowers. Bouquets, big and small, decorated the verge.

I pulled over a little way up the road, got out, walked back to where my sister had been cut out of the wreckage. Traffic was light and I could hear birdsong and the steady thrum of sunshine on hot telegraph wires. In my mind's eye, I saw the motorbike speeding along, Bowen without a care and no inkling of what was about to happen, next, both vehicles hurtling towards each other. I wondered what was on each of their minds in the game changing moment when death came calling. Blind surprise versus certain death and destruction? Then there'd be noise, like a bomb detonating followed by an eerie, inescapable nothingness. I pictured the arrival of the emergency vehicles, police redirecting traffic, erecting signs, closing off the road, a ravaged motorbike, blood on the road, the drama and action, something that Scarlet would have found detestable. She was never a centre of attention girl. "Come on, speak to me," I murmured. "Tell me whether you meant to do it. Tell me why. Tell me who the fuck is sending threats and upending my life." I swear I heard Scarlet's silvery laugh rippling through the trees, cut off only by the sound of approaching traffic.

A burst of anger flashed through me. It wasn't fate I wanted to stick a middle finger up to. It was Scarlet. How dare she cause so much pain and confusion and grief. As I cast a bitter smile to the sky, it seemed ironic that Heather Bowen's outrage should find a friend in me. Furious and shaken by the strength of my emotions, I stalked back to my car.

Hales Road is a narrow, congested thoroughfare, with vehicles slung up on pavements. I squeezed into a spot in between a people carrier and Mercedes. It took me ages before the traffic calmed enough for me to climb out without being run over. Barely 10 a.m. and blades of sun bounced off the pavement, white and blinding. You could taste the dirt, petrol fumes and heat.

I didn't know for certain which house, so I grabbed the railing of the nearest possibility, and climbed the steps to a black front door, and pressed the bell. From the other side, I heard the sound of machine-gun fire, mortars and explosions. For some reason I'd assumed that the Bowen kids were little. Judging by the noise coming from the computer game, I'd either gone to the wrong house, or there was a gap in my knowledge. Next, heavy tread on polished wooden floorboards.

Hair was no longer scraped off Heather Bowen's face but hung, lank and loose, like metal curtains in a butcher's shop. A heavy-set woman, with wide, open features, she filled most of the doorway.

"Yes?" Her full lips wrapped around the word, as though she'd not quite overcome a childhood lisp. Maybe it only emerged when she was on her guard.

"I wondered if I could have a word. My name's Molly Napier."

"Do I know you?"

"I'm Scarlet Jay's sister."

Her cheeks sagged, mouth tightened, and her skin turned chalky grey. The door began to close. I stuck my arm out. Stupid thing to do. "Ow," I let out.

"Take it away," she hissed.

"I only want to talk."

"I very much doubt that."

"Five minutes of your time, that's all I ask."

"This is harassment."

The blood in my chest raced. The pressure increased. She was going to smash my elbow.

"I'll call the police."

"Please. I only want to help," I gasped.

The door swung back with a mighty swoosh. I drew my arm back, rubbing it painfully. The volume on the game shot up several decibels. "Help? Your sister has destroyed my family." Her eyes narrowed to two venomous slits. "Now GET OUT."

"Mrs Bowen, I want to talk to you about my sister's bracelet."

Her wet mouth dropped open. Her breath came in short ragged gasps. She pressed a hand to her head. "What did you say?" she gasped, and I knew the police must have passed on Nate's denial about who the bracelet belonged to.

For a horrible moment, I thought she was going to lunge at me. "It definitely belonged to my sister, Mrs Bowen. Please can I come in?"

Chapter 24

Despite an average temperature of 29 degrees centigrade, we drank hot tea in a kitchen cluttered with trainers and football kit in front of a fan that redistributed warm air. Colour had returned to Heather Bowen's cheeks.

"I didn't mean to upset you."

"Bit late for that." She darted a look at the door. "Mind if I have a word with my boys? I'd prefer they didn't hear."

She disappeared. I picked up her phone, which lay on the table. It was unlocked and sneaking a look, I grabbed her number and entered it into my mobile.

Taking a guilty breath, I sat back, glanced around. Toast crumbs littered the work surface. A gloopy sauce had splashed from the gas hob down one of the units. The washing machine looked as if it couldn't make its mind up. Door open, half filled with clothes, the rest grubby and tumbling out onto a basket. The chaos of Heather Bowen's life reflected in domestic disorder. I'd once had a boyfriend who took apart his motorbike in the middle of the sitting room. No other artefacts or memorabilia. The Bowen's house felt like that.

I heard a door slam.

"I've sent them into town with money for a game. They'll probably return with something unsuitable, but it should buy us an hour or so."

"How old are your lads?"

"Dan's fourteen, Jed almost twelve. And before you enquire how they're doing, which is what everyone asks, they don't talk much, not to me at least." She placed the mug down firmly on the table. Her home. Her rules. "Do you know something I don't?"

"That depends."

She flashed a steady, 'cards on table' expression. "I was never under any illusions about my husband. Not long after we married, I discovered that Richard was unfaithful. I could have left. We hadn't had the children then."

"But you didn't."

"No."

"Must have taken guts."

She looked at me straight. "I never chose to stay because I loved him but because the alternative was too painful."

I didn't probe. Her reasons were none of my business. I took a sip of tea, scalded the roof of my mouth. "Did you discover anything else, apart from the bracelet?" I asked.

"Like what?"

"Text messages, emails, phone calls?"

Heather shook her head. My pulse skipped a beat. I was

hoping for something clear, substantial and tangible. Dad always said you had to look at the evidence. "Doesn't mean a thing," Heather said scornfully. "Wouldn't put it past him to have a second phone."

"Surely, the police will look into the possibility?"

"Good luck with that. Richard, God rest his soul, was sneaky."

I filed away the observation. "Richard's movements on the morning of the accident."

"What about them?"

"Wasn't he heading in the wrong direction from home?"

"Nothing odd about that. Richard would often go for a spin after work."

"After a night shift?" If I didn't get a straight eight hours, I was finished.

"He never needed much sleep. Me? I could sleep the clock around." Surely, he must have been knackered. And tiredness caused accidents. Heather continued with a thin and bitter smile. "Truth is, he had another life away from us. Another woman. Another child. Reckon that's where he was heading. Been penned up here with a bad dose of flu. Couldn't wait to escape."

Relief made me dizzy. If Scarlet had a mystery lover, it wasn't Bowen. He couldn't possibly have room in his life for a demanding job, a wife and sons, a mistress, and Scarlet? I put this to Mrs Bowen. My voice came out all weird, strangled by uncertainty. But then how did the blasted bracelet fit?

Heather regarded me with mild amusement. "He could handle it. My husband had a high sex drive."

I never believed all that highly sexed bullshit. When male celebs confess to a gullible public, usually via snazzy magazine articles, that they are being treated for sex addiction, I never think 'what a guy,' I always think 'poor, sad bastard.'

What she said next felled me.

"Never speak ill of the dead, but I'm afraid to say that Richard could be what you might describe as predatory when it came to the opposite sex."

"You mean he actively solicited female attention?"

"No money passed hands, if that's what you mean."

I didn't, but had Scarlet's vulnerability and unhappiness with Nate made her prey for a man like Bowen? I asked if he was ever violent.

"God no, never needed to be. Richard was only ever seductive and persuasive."

"Got what he wanted?"

"Always."

Most serial shaggers are saddos searching for love and security. The impression I got was that Bowen was not a man with a fragile ego. "No insecurities at all?"

"Richard insecure?" She briefly smiled. *Are you nuts?* Her expression said.

"No hang-ups?"

"I had enough for both of us."

"Did Richard ever mention a trip to London?" I recalled my conversation with the man in the tile shop. *Barking up the wrong avenue, love. The* she *was a* he.

The lines on her forehead contracted. "When would this be?"

"Roughly three weeks before the accident."

"Not unless he crawled out of bed when I wasn't looking."

Of course, he'd been laid low with the dreaded 'flu. Every time I came up with a possible lead, some unseen force slammed a door in my face.

I asked her if she worked.

"I've got a little part-time job in a shop selling artist's materials in town."

Perhaps Richard had snuck off, ill or not. I took the torn slip of paper from my bag with Charlie Binns' name and address on it and handed it to her.

She took it, looked at it and frowned. "That's Richard's writing."

"You're sure?"

"Certain. I can tell from the capital 'R' in 'Charlie.' Richard always wrote like that. Where did you find it?"

I ignored her question. "Does the name ring a bell?"

She shook her head, perplexed. "Never heard of the man. Who is he?"

"I'm not sure." Which was true in one way and a whopping lie in another.

"You've got an address. Why don't you ask him yourself?"

Because dead men don't talk. I smiled in seeming agreement, took a sip of tea, wondering how to couch my next question. "Richard, did he have a close circle of friends?"

"Why do you want to know?"

Time to turn up the heat. "Because someone left roadkill on the bonnet of my car and, last night, embedded a carving knife in my kitchen table."

Heather's expression contained a mixture of alarm and bewilderment.

"I think it was meant to send a message."

She greeted my remark with irritation. "No way. Richard's only friends, if you could call them that, were his colleagues at work."

"Police officers are not above the law."

"You've been watching too many crime dramas." Her old-fashioned look told me that I was out of my depth and drowning. "Like I said, he didn't have close friends, police or otherwise."

"Nobody he'd confide in?"

"Richard, confide?" She gave a half-laugh.

"He never had any problems?"

"None that he cared to discuss."

"Debts, drink, gambling?"

"Money was always an issue, which comes as no surprise with another woman and kid to support," Heather observed dryly. "He was always coming up with money-making schemes."

I flicked a smile to cover my physical response. Had Richard tried to inveigle Scarlet into one of them? Was this why she'd wanted £25k?

"Stable childhood?" I was shooting in the dark. Never had myself down for an amateur psychologist.

"Richard was adopted, but yes."

"That worked out for him?"

"He was lucky. Had lovely adoptive parents. His dad died some years ago, but he had a great relationship with his Mum, a smashing woman."

"She must be devastated."

Heather lowered her gaze, a minute movement, yet it told me I wasn't getting the whole picture.

"Did he ever search for his biological parents?"

Heather glanced up, scrutinised me. I didn't flinch. I needed her to trust me enough to tell the truth.

"He never stopped looking, actually. It became awkward. He didn't want to hurt the people who'd brought him up."

"And did he find them?"

"Only his dad. Pity really, the old boy was dying by the time Richard caught up with him. Passed away six months ago."

The timescale seemed significant, but I couldn't quite work out why. "How did Richard handle it?"

"Sad but resigned. And then you know the rest."

"Except we don't, do we?"

Heather leant back in her seat. "If you're looking for some deep meaning in all this, forget it. I didn't know your sister but the women he fucked all wanted to hang on to him. He could be very charming. I've lost count of the ones I told to piss off. Ringing him night and day, some of them. I suspect your sister met him at the hospital when their paths crossed at work, got snared into a relationship, found out about his other woman, couldn't stand the competition and cut up rough."

Unsurprisingly, Heather Bowen had given it a great deal of thought. It also had a ring of plausibility about it – apart from the fact that it didn't add up with the sister I knew. "You really think that?"

"What else is there to believe?"

I scratched my chin. "My sister was not prone to emotional decision making."

Heather frowned. "I was told that she was depressed, drunk, out of her mind."

"Drunk, yes. Out of her mind, no."

Chapter 25

Despite the oxygen-sapping heat, the brilliant sunshine, the buzz of insects, it felt as if storm clouds gathered directly over Mum and Dad's house. Mr Lee barely raised a flicker; too busy panting to keep cool as I let myself in. I gave his ears a stroke, told him he was a gorgeous boy, and wandered through to the living room where Mum was helping herself to the first drink of the day. I followed Dad's reproving yet helpless gaze. A pulse above his left eye flickered. I read the sign: say nothing. Nate sat in the corner, crumpled. You could slice through the atmosphere with a rusty spoon. Distinguishing one bad vibe from another, when all feels futile, is not simple. In my gut, I recognised something else was going down. It put me on high alert.

"Nate, can I interest you in a G&T?" Mum said.

"Why not."

Oh great, I thought. Dad must have glimpsed the irritation on my face and felt the need to explain. "Nate's received an email from Heather Bowen's solicitor, threatening to sue him."

Crafty cow. She never mentioned a word. "Surely, she can't do that."

"Apparently, she can," Nate said.

"We don't know for certain," Dad said evenly.

"On what grounds? Scarlet drove the car, not Nate."

"Why must you always blame her?" Mum's pale face and tight mouth gave the game away. She was pissed off all right. To my ears, the words ejected from her lips were like lit matches flung onto petrol.

"Amanda, I don't think that's what—"

"It's okay, Dad, I've got this. I really don't appreciate what you're implying, Mum." I ground my fingers into my palms to stop my hands from shaking. "I know you're grieving. We all are, but you can't escape the fact that Scarlet was responsible."

"That's not true," she shouted. "You've fallen for their lies. Tell her, Rod."

"Does she know about the booze in Scarlet's bloodstream?" I addressed the question to Dad, as if my mother were somewhere else. Unseen. Unheard.

"That's nonsense," Mum cried. "Preliminary findings can be wrong."

"So, what will you do when the toxicology report is finally written and it's there in black and white?" My frustration at my mother's refusal to face the truth unforgivably boiled over. In a few paragraphs, I could enlighten her about bloody offerings, threats and notes, and a stranger shot a few streets away from where he lived.

"We'll demand another, get a second opinion, won't we, Rod?"

"Well, I—" Dad began.

"Have the police found anything on the computers or phones?" I had images of laptops in evidence bags with descriptions of the exhibits; their data pored over and copied.

Nate's voice slammed into me. "What the hell do you expect them to find?"

I raised an eyebrow in reply, but I wasn't finished. "What about the absence of marks on the road, the deliberate act, the bloody—" I broke off, stared at Nate who looked as if I'd produced an axe.

"Let's calm down." Dad patted the air with the palms of his hands. "Understandably, we're all upset."

I focused on him, refused to look at my mother, whose penetrating gaze lasered a hole in the side of my head.

"Agreed," Nate said. "What are we going to do about the threat of legal action?" Dad virtually buckled with relief, grateful for a return to practical matters. Me? I was light-headed with fury and frustration.

"Talk to the blasted woman." Mum snatched at her drink. "Tell her to back off. Tell her if she doesn't, we'll sue the hell—"

"Mum, you can't."

Eyes sparking, she steamrollered right through me. "Your father will fix it."

"I can't fix everything, woman."

The sudden steep rise in emotional temperature took us all unawares. My mother could not have looked more stunned had my dad thumped her. Nate took an avid interest in his shoes. I didn't know where to look. Silence crawled through the room and hid in the corners.

"I'm sorry, Amanda, I —"

"Screw you, Rod." Slamming down her drink, she flew out into the hall, the furious beat of her shoes on the stairs as she fled to their bedroom. When Dad made to follow, I caught his arm.

"Think I'll go for a wander in the garden." Embarrassed, Nate shot out through the open French windows.

Demeaned and ashamed, Dad clasped the back of his neck. I felt for him. Scarlet's untimely death was smashing us all to pieces. And I was about to crush him some more.

131

Chapter 26

"When I got home, last night, I found a knife buried in my kitchen table."

Dad's mouth dropped open, like the aforementioned blade had stabbed him in the belly.

"I'd left the bathroom window open. I know it was stupid," I said, before he could remind me of the many times he'd impressed on me the importance of home security.

"Was anything stolen?"

"No."

"You're sure?"

"Yes."

"Have you fallen out with anyone?"

"Nothing that would warrant someone behaving in such a despicable way. Dad, don't you see, this is a clear threat?"

"I'm not denying it, Molly." He ran a hand under his jaw. "I'm trying to figure out why."

"Isn't it obvious? Someone doesn't want me looking into Scarlet's death."

A nerve near Dad's left eye pulsed. I knew that look. His

expression was not dissimilar to Heather Bowen's when she'd spelt out that I was out of my depth. Be that as it may, I wasn't finished.

"After the accident, I found something in Scarlet's bag." I took the note out of my pocket and handed it to him. He took his spectacles out of the top pocket of his shirt, studied it and handed it back. "It's the name and address of an elderly man killed in a suspected contract killing in London recently." I didn't dare admit that I'd seen Heather Bowen and she'd confirmed that the note was in Richard's writing. "You see, Dad. There has to be more to Scarlet's death."

"Enough." His anger was sudden, white and blinding. "Dear God, what are you playing at?" It wasn't the response I was expecting. "Scarlet's death was an unfortunate accident," he said. "Nothing more. Nothing less."

"But—"

"I haven't finished," he said with a glare. "Your mother and I have had our hearts broken. I appreciate why you might try to find sense in all of this, but you are mistaken. Sit down," he said. I did. "Now tell me calmly and logically what you've been up to so that we can put this nonsense to bed once and for all."

I took a breath and told him everything apart from the content of the note Scarlet left Nate. The more I told him, the calmer he became. When I finished, I couldn't tell whether he was impressed or horrified by my doggedness.

"You actually went to this man's address?"

"I did."

He looked at me in awe. "Christ, Molly, you were taking a risk."

I supposed I was, but I didn't know then what I knew now.

"Okay," he said bluntly. "Firstly, in the light of recent developments, the police will be looking at all of Scarlet's contacts. If this man was on her radar, you can be certain they will establish it."

I nodded in relieved agreement.

"Secondly, if you wish to take this further, I'll support you all the way. Realistically, however, the police don't have anything tangible to go on. I can vouch for the animal remains in your carport. We can report the knife you found but—"

"As it's mine, it makes it less eye-catching and, chances are, whoever did it wore gloves."

"I'm afraid so."

"So; unless someone smacks me over the head, I won't be taken seriously."

His expression told me that, regrettably, I was bang on. "Putting that aside," he continued briskly, "what exactly have you discovered about Binns?"

Like a pupil in front of a demanding, yet much admired, teacher, I wanted to slay him with the right answers. "It's claimed he was an informer."

"Odds on, the guy had criminal connections."

"Could you find out?"

He cast me a reproving look. "Let's not race ahead of ourselves. How did you obtain the information?"

"A newspaper report."

Dad half-smiled. I knew what my Dad was thinking.

According to him, newspapers turned opinion into Gospel. "And what do the police say?" he said.

He had me. I stalled. Everything about him suddenly softened. His tone. His body language. The way he looked at me. "To be scrupulously fair," Dad said, "if the man was an informer, sure as hell the police won't admit it."

"You see," I said, brightening.

"But even if he was, you still haven't explained why your sister would be interested in him. An old lag of pensionable age? It doesn't make sense." Dad rammed home the point with the force of a nail gun.

Put like that, it didn't.

He thought for a moment. I could see that, despite what he said, he had to admit it was all very strange. "What we don't know is why Scarlet had this man's name and address in her bag."

"I assumed she'd visited him."

"What have I taught you? Never assume."

He was right.

"Working theory then."

"Without evidence. Pity."

"But the trip?"

Dad spread his hands. "What about it? The capital is a popular venue."

"On her own, in a deadbeat hotel? You know that's not her style." Scarlet enjoyed weekends away in posh resorts with spas.

Dad drummed his fingers on the arm of the sofa. I looked out onto the garden and watched a crow strut threateningly across the lawn. I'd been hasty and foolish. I should have known I didn't have enough to persuade my procedurally bound by the book father.

"With your permission, I'll have a word with Stanton and explain about the break-in."

I tuned out. What was the point? The police could hardly give me a log number when nothing had been nicked. I must have looked as dejected as I felt.

"Molly," Dad said, leaning across and taking both my hands in his. "I understand what you're doing. If I learnt anything when I was a police officer, it's that when bad things happen to decent people they try to rationalise and explain them. It's the most natural human response. But sometimes there are no explanations. There are no answers. With so little to go on, you literally don't have a case. You'd need a lot more evidence than this. Not that I'm advocating you rush into a wild goose chase," he added with a sympathetic smile.

I nodded absently, thinking I'd simply have to find more. Taking my silence as acceptance, he continued, "From now on, pay particular attention to your personal security. You lock your doors. You don't go out alone at night. Make a list of anyone who could have something against you. You haven't had a tricky customer lately, have you?" He sounded wary.

Instantly, I remembered Rocco Noble. He was odd, for sure, but a threat? "This business with Heather Bowen," I began.

"It won't come to anything."

"You think?" I'd met the woman. Dad hadn't. Heather Bowen seemed pretty sorted and she had two teenage lads to support.

"I don't see how until after the inquest."

"When is that likely to happen?"

"Usually takes three weeks." He looked down. I got it. This wasn't usual. Anything but. "Depends if there's a criminal investigation, in which case the inquest will open and adjourn, with a verdict reached later."

He didn't expand, but I knew what he was thinking. If it were discovered that Scarlet deliberately targeted Richard Bowen, for whatever reason, our worst nightmare would come true and she would be officially labelled a murderer. I caught my breath, watched my Dad and tried to gauge his reaction.

He leant forward, squeezed my arm. "It's all right, Molly. Everything that needs to be done is being done. Now," he said, glancing up, "I'd better go and make my peace with your mother."

Good luck, I thought, not for him, but for me.

Chapter 27

I went straight to the shop, put a closed notice on the door and dragged Lenny out for a drink. Displacement therapy made me think more clearly.

We sat in a boozer where the food was hit and miss and, more often than not, 'unavailable'. Lenny drank high-octane cider, the petrol analogy no joke: not only did it rot guts, but dissolve teeth. This did nothing to dissuade a fruit fly intent on death by drowning while drunk. I was too preoccupied to drink the hard stuff so nursed a lime and soda. Probably explained why it took Lenny so long to prise more than a couple of sentences from me. What was the link between Scarlet and Charlie Binns, and Binns and Bowen? If Bowen didn't visit Binns, who did? Binns was the weak link. He held the key, but he was dead. I stayed silent; mind freefalling.

"Sure you don't want a proper drink?" Lenny eyed my glass as if I were drinking drain fluid.

"I'm all right."

"You're definitely not. You need to talk, Molly."

"Do I?" A dangerous, defiant note entered my voice. Not quite certain how it got there. I was done with talking.

If Lenny had taken a tight swig and looked offended, I couldn't have blamed her. She told me about a sale from the shop's website and we discussed delivery arrangements. It felt odd to talk about something normal and routine and grasp-able. Undeniably, a small part of me was desperate to cling to the things that gave meaning and form to my life despite Scarlet's death bending and bashing them out of shape.

We fell into awkward silence. I retreated into the shadows, the pub the kind of place where sunshine rarely penetrated. I doubted it had been refurbished since the smoking ban. A thick, claggy atmosphere heavy with dirt and sweat, and punctuated by the clatter of a fruit machine at full throttle. I welcomed it. Anything to drown out the chaos in my head. I never had Scarlet down for the suicidal type, if there were such a thing, let alone a person who would callously take the life of another in some crazy act of passion or revenge.

Lenny took a long swallow of cider with no visible ill effects. "You had a posh visitor at the shop this morning," she said brightly.

"Me?"

"His teeth were that white they nearly blinded me."

"Sounds like Chancer," I said puzzled. "Did he say what he wanted?"

"To check if you were all right."

"That's because I made a fast getaway from Zach's yesterday." Although why Chancer would want to track me all the way to Malvern seemed beyond the call of duty.

"And what does Mr Colgate do when not hanging out in clearance shops?"

"He's a banker." A profession I put on the same dizzy level as dark arts and magic. As a teenager, Chancer had shown a remarkable head for figures and percentages.

"Might have guessed. Typical ex-schoolboy with sociopathic tendencies."

I let out a nervous laugh. "You're not serious?"

"Deadly."

"Unlike you to go all chip on the shoulder. Considering his folks practically live in a stately home, I think he's incredibly grounded."

"Ever visited?"

"Several times." I remembered Chancer's dad, Stephen, a man possessed with a fierce, daunting intellect, which served him well at the bar. Apart from Dad, everyone else was terrified of the man, including Chancer. On the rare occasions I'd seen Stephen Chancellor laugh, it was always at someone else's expense, usually his sons. I didn't know how Stephen's wife, a gentle, kind-hearted woman, put up with him.

"Pretty easy to see why you've got the hots for Chancer," she teased.

"I have not."

"Minted, good looking, what's not to like?"

"The fact he's still married, for one."

"Still?"

From the mischievous way she spoke, Lenny scented blood. "He and his wife are having difficulties," I said, madly underplaying it.

"What's his missus like?"

"Beautiful, brilliant, bloody good at cricket. Played for county, once upon a time." Lenny made to stick her fingers down her throat. I pictured Edie: one of those delicate looking creatures that exuded vulnerability. Underneath the fragile exterior she was a demon cricketer.

"So you and Chancer—"

"Go back decades."

"How old is he?"

"Same age as Zach."

"I'd never have guessed."

I knew what she meant. Pushing forty, Chancer had already started on the slippery slope into middle age. Zach, with his washboard abs and simpler lifestyle, had largely kept his youthful appearance, despite his history of drugs.

"Why does he hang around with Zach?" She didn't say 'loser', although her tone implied as much.

"Like I said, underneath that brash exterior, Chancer is a decent, loyal individual."

"Yeah, right."

"It's true. He and Zach have been mates for years." I told Lenny about the day Chancer came to my rescue after Zach lured me into a tunnel in their grounds.

"Lost in the pitch-black, it frightened the crap out of me. I've been afraid of dark enclosed spaces ever since," I confessed.

"Nice brother you have there."

"Chancer seems to think so. Zach was best man at his wedding."

"Came out of rehab to do the honours, did he?"

Had anyone else said it, I'd have torn off several strips. But this was Lenny. I glanced around the bar, caught my breath. Lenny sat back and spread her legs astride. "Before I forget, did you call Mr Noble?"

I described the conversation, how off-beat he'd been and what we'd agreed.

Lenny jolted forward, fine eyebrows rushing up to meet her hairline. Seems she could be shocked after all.

"But, Molly, this is mad. You're in no fit state. Let me sort him out."

"What else am I going to do? Mope at home?" I had no intention of sitting around. "Anyway, I've agreed it with Rocco."

"Rocco?" she exclaimed.

"Not his fault his parents had weird taste. Bearing in mind some of the names foisted on kids today, it's not that peculiar."

"Might not be in L.A. but this is Worcestershire." She looked hugely amused. "And if he's paying, what else does he expect?"

"What are you implying?"

"Isn't it obvious? He fancies you."

"What's wrong with you? Me and Mr Noble have barely exchanged more than a few paragraphs."

"So back out."

"I can't." Except I knew I could. I knew I should.

Chapter 28

Rocco Noble, dressed down in a black Superdry T-shirt and skinny jeans, looked quite different. His easy on the eye physique belonged to a plasterer: strong arms, slim hips. Expensive sneakers too, with a crocodile embossed pattern on the leather, and zips up the side. Lenny's voice echoed through my head. *He fancies you.* I did my best not to gawp.

"You're keen," he said.

"I'm early. I'd like to get on with—"

"It's okay, I get it."

I looked in the direction of a fat mahogany sideboard glowering from behind a dining room table with thickset legs. "We'll start with the heavy pieces."

It's quite an intimate act to shift furniture with someone. There needs to be a level of synchronicity, give and take, an intuitive knowledge of whether someone can or can't manoeuvre a sideboard, for example, around a corner or through an exit or entrance. The doorways to the cottage were narrow and my spatial awareness that day was off. To get the right level of clearance, we were forced to upend a long refectory table with a stretcher base. God knew what it weighed. More than once, Rocco and I mirror-imaged each other's moves, in close quarters; breathing heavily, sweat pooling, fingertips grazing. Every time we connected it was like being struck with a cattle prod. And his eyes, bloody hell, they were the colour of bourbon and he never took them off mine. It wasn't only the heat that was hunting me down. When we went upstairs to clear the garret-like top, I thought I might vaporise.

Rocco had boxed his grandmother's less important items. The bed, thankfully, stayed put so we had the van packed in no time. I squatted on my haunches, knackered.

"Cold drink? I bought sparkling elderflower and Pepsi."

"I need a caffeine hit." I mopped my face with the sleeve of my T-shirt – not very ladylike and definitely not very sexy, yet he stared at me in way that was searching, haunting and intense. I flushed under his unnerving gaze. It was as if he knew every part of me: body and soul. Instinctively, I knew this man could mash me up inside. But that wasn't all. I was vulnerable and knew it. Images of dead creatures and knives in places they shouldn't be assailed me.

"You're allowed, you know."

"Allowed what?" I failed to rein in the shaky note in my voice.

Cool as you like, he answered my question with another: 'How many days has it been?" Rocco didn't need to spell it out.

"A little over a week."

"There's no right or wrong way to feel."

"Not sure others would agree." I should be at home in sackcloth and ashes and mourning. With me agitating, I only made things worse with my parents. And now there was the threat of litigation against my brother-in-law to add extra pressure.

I glanced up at Rocco. Maybe, he could be useful if I got him on a subject with which he was familiar. With his experience of medical insurance claims, he might be able to throw some light. I explained the threat of legal action.

"Outside my field, but a spouse, nearly always the wife will submit a claim of dependency. Was the dead man the sole breadwinner?"

"No idea. He had two children."

Rocco thought for a moment, eyes sparking with insight. "Is there any suggestion that your sister was driving dangerously?"

I told Rocco about the booze, to which he raised an eyebrow. "Don't ask."

"Were there witnesses?"

"Yes."

"And the police are actively investigating?"

I nodded.

He rubbed his jaw. "Technically, the widow could submit a claim against the estate of the negligent party, in this case, Scarlet's."

"On the grounds that she was culpable?"

"'Fraid so. You know there'll be an inquest?"

"Uh-huh." I wondered what the ruling would be and, clasping my knees, rested my face in my lap. I felt drained of every bit of energy.

Rocco disappeared and returned with drinks. He rested the

ice-cold glass against the side of my hand. It made me start, like he'd pressed a lighted cigarette to my skin. I took it, glanced up, met his eyes. "Shit situation," he said.

I agreed. No other way to describe it.

Feeling instantly disloyal for discussing family business, guilty for working, confused about my brother, anxious about connections I couldn't connect, fearful from when the next threat might come, I headed straight to my parents to see if peace had been restored. There was also a chance that the police had supplied more information. Like Dad said, they would dig up Scarlet's contacts.

The air, dense with thunder bugs and flies, clung to me as I stepped out of the car. A hum of voices drifted from behind the gate that separated the drive from the garden. At first, I thought it was Mum and Dad. The nearer I drew, the more identifiable one of the speakers became: Dad. The other male voice I didn't recognise. Something about the estuary accent, the pitch, not high but low and insistent, told me that the discussion was private. I wondered where Nate was. Was he the reason for the clandestine conversation? I edged forward, heart throbbing, pulse tripping, and the sound of gravel under my trainers give me away. I

"Molly."

Hand on chest, I spun round and came face to face with my mum's numb expression.

"What are you doing?"

Snooping. Eavesdropping. Earwigging. Take your pick; none of them put me in a flattering light. "I thought it was you and dad." Truth or lie, she'd be cross either way.

She let out an exhausted sigh. Fresh shadows had appeared under her eyes giving her the spectral appearance of one who never sleeps. Shoulders hunched, her once tall, lithe body looked shorter, reduced and stooped. My heart creased with pain because I could see how lost she was.

"Mum," I said, starting towards her. To my shock, she backed away.

"Your father is talking to an old colleague."

My stomach somersaulted. "What about?"

"A phone call made from a pay phone to Richard Bowen's mobile."

"So what?"

"It was from the hospital."

"You mean where Scarlet worked?"

Mum nodded, pale and sad.

I made a face. "It's a little tenuous, surely? Do the police know the content of the call?" Could they even do that? Mum hitched her shoulders. She didn't know either. "It could have been anyone calling," I insisted.

"It was made an hour before the accident."

"How long did it last?"

"Seconds."

Fear tripped through me as I imagined Scarlet's voice whisper in my ear. *Meet me.* Had she set Bowen up? I expected my mother to be bullish and stubborn and uncompromising in defence of my sister. Instead, she appeared ready to fold. I could read the expression in her eyes: weary, defeated and dismantled.

"What does it matter? Maybe Scarlet did call the man.

Maybe there was a relationship. Oh yes, I know what people are saying. I'm not stupid." Her voice climbed with hysteria and then abruptly came to a halt. Squinting against a sudden stab of sunshine, a single tear tracked down her cheek.

"Oh, Mum."

"Please don't." She raised a hand, warding me off.

I stared in consternation. I needed her to reach me as much as I longed to reach her, yet she was erecting all kinds of barriers. Her gaze concentrated on the ground; she spoke with neither malice nor anger. It would have been better if she had. "Why did you hate her so very much?"

I gasped. "Mum, how could—"

She looked up, questioning, still with the same quiet tone. "Scarlet told me about your row, what you said, how you accused her."

A shiver rolled down my spine, from the base of my neck to my sacrum. Denial was pointless. "It was stupid and nasty."

"Days before she took her own life."

"I didn't mean it. None of it." I was gasping. Memory burnt a hole in my head. Shame savaged me. "I'd had too much to drink and—"

"Envy is one of the deadly sins, Molly."

Speechless, I watched as she turned and walked away. The ground fled from underneath me. Mum had known all along and hadn't said a word. Worse, Scarlet had been devastated. And now she was dead. The fear I'd held back for days smashed right through me. What if this were the real reason she'd got drunk, took her eye off the road and died? What if all the other avenues I'd pursued were nothing more than white noise, irrelevancies and blind alleys?

I listened, really listened. As daft as it was, I hoped that Scarlet's voice would transcend time and space and somehow speak, reassure and convince me that I was *not* the cause of her distress. The only sound was my mother's brisk footsteps crunching across the gravel.

Half mad, I fled to my car, fired up the engine and pressed my foot flat to the floor. Gravel spitting. Blood pumping. Nerves aflame. In no time at all, I was back at the cottage I'd left only minutes before. Rocco Noble instantly opened the door, the 'nice surprise' smile on his face vanishing when he registered the stricken expression on mine.

"I've done something terrible," I cried, throwing myself at him. "It's all my fault. Oh my God, I killed my sister."

Chapter 29

O ne second, I was gabbling a confession, sobbing all over Rocco Noble, the next ripping off my clothes. Mutual and brutal. Want and take. A weird distillation of sex and death.

"Christ. Sorry."

"Don't be. I'm not."

Sleeping with strangers was outside my experience. Not on a first date and this definitely wasn't one of those. Not like that. Not ever.

I felt as if I'd been in a cage fight. My bottom lip was swollen. I had a graze on my knee and a bruise on the inside of my thigh. Rocco wasn't in much better shape. Any longer, we'd have eaten each other alive. Wondering what the hell had just happened, Scarlet streaked through my mind. Is this how she'd behaved with Bowen? With that overpowering desire to connect, forget, obliterate, at any cost? Passion like that could explain why she'd driven him off the road; one final 'fuck you'.

I rolled over and studied Rocco's face, the way his hair fell over his left eye, the smooth planes of his cheeks, the dimple on his chin, those lips that had searched my body. "So, what are you on the run from?" I knew why I was fleeing. But him?

He threw back his head and laughed. "Me?"

"Yeah," I said. "Takes two to tango." Or, in our case, fuck each other's brains out.

"I simply went with it." His top lip curved in a suggestion of a smile. Couldn't tell whether he was teasing, dissembling, or it was the truth. "You think too much." He ran an index finger delicately from the corner of my eye down my cheek, along my jawline. Part of me felt relief that there was no deep discussion of feelings, that sex was nothing more than a transaction based on physical attraction and desire. The other part felt leery.

"God, I have to go." I sat up, scrunching the covers up around my neck. My eyes searched the room for my clothes, which lay scattered, telling their own story.

"Why?"

"Because this is madness. I shouldn't be here, and you have places to be."

"Ah, change of plan."

I gave him a sharp look.

"It's cool. I didn't trick you, if that's what you're thinking. I took time off to see a good mate who broke off his engagement. Well, he had," Rocco said, as if his friend were several brain cells short of the full complement. "Seems they're all loved up and back together again, my services no longer required."

I wasn't sure I believed him.

"Honest," Rocco said, in response to my less than enthusiastic endorsement. "You don't think I'm that devious, do you? As I recall, you came to me last night." His smile was warm and trustworthy. When his fingers tiptoed up my naked arm and slipped the covers down, I couldn't resist.

Early sunshine spilled from the narrow lattice-window across the bed, illuminating the pair of us. To me, it felt like a searchlight.

"You were pretty upset last night," Rocco said. "Want to talk about it?"

"No." How could I tell him what I hadn't told anyone else?

I might have known, I raged. You always were the bloody blue-eyed girl –

Molly, that really isn't fair. Scarlet blanched, taken aback by the venom pouring out of me.

Not fair? What would Little Miss Perfect know about injustice? How come you get to have when I have to borrow?

Molly, I—

Sure, Mum and Dad helped me out, for which I'm genuinely grateful, but I have to pay it all back

"That's hardly my fault."

Yes, it is. You're always creeping round Mum. Makes me sick.

"Did you know that guilt is the most corrosive of emotions?"

I gave a start, unsettled that this man could read me so well. "Who do you think you are, my shrink?" The attack in my voice was unmistakable.

"I didn't mean to intrude."

"Yes, you did." I didn't know him. He didn't know me. End of.

"Molly, I—"

"If you must know, I laid into my sister a few days before she died."

"About what?"

"It's no longer important." So what if my parents gave her money to buy a house when I'd been forced to take out a loan?

"It clearly is."

"I was jealous, okay?" Monstrously so. The hitch in my voice gave me away. Quick to pick up on it, Rocco elevated an eyebrow, the intensity of his gaze enough to force false confessions from the innocent. No way could I lie to him, so I told him the truth about my parents' 'no strings' gift to my sister. "When they generously loaned me money for a deposit for my home and business, I'd always been expected to pay it back."

"And do you?"

"Religiously. Every month."

He shifted position. The butterfly tattoo on the top of his arm spread its wings. "Could the gift have been part of some sophisticated tax dodge? You said your dad works with your brother-in-law?" Only for now.

"My dad wouldn't dodge so much as a missing item on a bill. Used to be a police officer."

"You never discussed it with your parents?"

It would have been the honest thing to do. Scarlet had suggested it, but I didn't want honesty. I wanted retribution. In that one fatal moment all the jealousy I'd stored for the best part of twenty years came tumbling out and I was savage.

Throughout my tirade, Scarlet stood, white-faced and scared. Worse, I'd never apologised, and I'd never had the balls to talk to Mum and Dad. I could burrow under the covers on Rocco Noble's bed, but I couldn't hide from the guilt that cackled at me long and loud. Unsparingly, I described the rest of the argument – my argument –to Rocco. Shoot the messenger was my style because it suited me.

He didn't excuse the inexcusable, exonerate or let me off, which was pretty honest of him if rather alarming. He shook his head, disappointed, I'm sure. I wasn't fooled when he gave my shoulder an affectionate squeeze that utterly crushed me inside. "Had Scarlet lived, things would never have been the same afterwards and that's on me."

"You can't know that."

"I know how much I hurt her."

"Don't you think you're over-analysing because of the accident?"

It was a fair observation, but nothing could shift the blame. I'd half-expected him to throw me out once he'd digested how vile I could be.

Feeling as if I'd been hit by a summer cold, I lay exhausted, yet unable to sleep other than in brief snatched moments, Scarlet last on my mind as I dropped off and first as I came to. Staring into the shadows, I pictured her face staring back, haunting. Rocco, when not exploring every inch of my body, slept the way he lived: happy. Disinterested in words, he rarely talked. Me, I only needed to feel something other than the great deadweight of guilt and grief and fear that was weighing me down. Rocco seemed to get it and asked no questions.

I crooked myself up on an elbow. "You said you'd lost someone."

"My mum. Heart attack," he said sadly. "We were close, so it was tough."

Something behind his eyes briefly flared, shattered and drifted away. Is this how I looked to others? His long fingers smoothed the sheet as if to wipe away the past.

"What about your dad?" I said.

"Don't really see much of him."

"I can't imagine what that must be like." And I couldn't. Love them or loathe them, we were family, 'brand Napier' Scarlet would often joke, that huge source of strength and human weakness. Except one of us was now missing.

And I still didn't know why.

Chapter 30

"As lovely as this is, I have to go home." I'd been there for most of the weekend. Here, I could physically and mentally regroup and nobody with malicious intent could reach me.

"Trying to get rid of me?"

"Don't be silly."

"Good," he whispered, sliding his warm hand down my flank, drawing me close, making me tingle, "patch things up with your mother later."

My body tensed beneath him. I'd deliberately switched off my phone and my parents would be worried sick. Conceivably.

I made to move. Rocco pinned me down. Playful. A languid smile spread slowly across his mouth. When he pressed first his lips and then his skin against mine, I thought I could stay that way forever.

Afterwards, we lay together, his lips a feather's touch on my neck. Tender. Gentle.

"Hey," he said. "What's up?"

"Isn't it obvious?"

"Sorry, of course, Scarlet. What was she like?"

I took a moment. I hadn't done right by my sister when she was alive. I had a chance to set the record straight now.

"Quite simply, she was brilliant. With Zach, with Mum, who isn't the easiest woman on the planet, brilliant with everyone. For Scarlet, family was all."

"The kind of woman with everything to live for," Rocco observed.

Except Rocco didn't know the half of it.

"Tell me about Richard Bowen."

"You ask a lot of questions."

"That wasn't a question. It was a request."

"Had an interesting private life with a mistress and child."

"Anything else?"

"Isn't that enough?"

He hitched a shoulder. Why did I feel that Rocco was trying to pull a dressing off a badly healed wound?

There were dozens of messages on my phone, via Messenger, on Facebook and Twitter, and through my emails. And numerous missed calls, four from Lenny, two from Chancer. "Molly, darling, are you all right? You left in such a tearing hurry the other day. Gather from Zach you had a bit of a spat, which comes as no wonder as your brother is a lovable pillock. Anyway, hope you're okay. See you soon and come and talk to me, otherwise I'll come and find you, ha-ha!"

I returned dad's first.

"Molly, thank God."

"I'm very sorry. It was wrong of me to worry you."

"Nobody has seen you for the best part of thirty-six hours." He lowered his voice. "You haven't had any more trouble, have you?"

I glanced over my shoulder in Rocco's direction. "No, nothing like that." I cursed the false note in my voice.

"Thank God. Where have you been?"

"Staying with a friend." I pulled a face at Rocco who flashed a grin and zipped up his fly.

"I went to the house, then phoned Lenny, spoke to Zach."

Zach. I wondered how that had played out. "I should have told you I wanted some space." I winced as I piled on cliché after cliché. Typically, Dad cut to the chase.

"Mum told me you'd had words."

There was no defence. Without anything to say, I said nothing.

"Come home, Molly. We need you."

"Did Mum say that?" My voice was thick and heavy. How could I face either of them?

"She did."

I pretty much buckled with relief.

"Dinner at six?"

"I'll be there."

"Stay over?"

"Yes." It would give me a chance to have a proper talk with my dad.

I smiled weakly at Rocco as I finished the call.

"See, that wasn't so bad?" He slipped his arms around my waist. A good fit, mine snaked around his neck. He smelt of old-fashioned soap and something more astringent.

"Thank you," I said, meaning it.

"For what?"

"For not judging me too harshly."

He grinned, nuzzled my neck and dropped a soft lingering kiss upon my lips. "So, shall we–" He grimaced, cut off by the sound of rapping at the door.

"Expecting someone?"

A gleam of irritation sparked behind his eyes at the intrusion. Maybe he'd hoped for a crazy action replay. "Stay right where you are." He sprinted towards the door, closing it firmly behind him.

Voices drifted up the stairs. I plumped down on the bed and listened.

"Are you decent?" a voice called from the landing.

Astonished, I opened the door to find Lenny's solid frame occupying the doorway.

"How on earth?"

"The question you should be asking is what took you so long?"

"You mean you knew where I was?" I stepped aside.

"Credit me with some intelligence." She swished in, the large canvas bag on her shoulder almost knocking me off my feet. "After a frantic phone call from your dad, which I handled as if your little disappearing act were no big deal, I retrieved Mr Noble's name and address from the diary. Thought I'd give it a bit for you to come to your senses. Looks like that might take time." The way her eyes scoped the room you'd think she was hunting down criminals.

"I didn't feel well." I winced at my cowardly and pathetic lie.

Lenny plumped down in the place I'd recently vacated. Disapproval tightened her mouth. Didn't suit her. She stared at me for several seconds.

"It's complicated," I said.

"A mercy fuck is not complicated."

"That's not what it was."

"Look," she said in a gentler tone, "your parents are going through hell, Molly. I know you are too but shagging a client and disappearing without trace isn't going to remove the pain."

Ouch. Lenny knew how to land a blow. I opened my mouth to reply then thought better of it.

"You need to go home."

"I am."

"Good." Pleased with getting a result, she reached out, patted my hand. "What made you run?"

Blown away by her doggedness, I told her about the row with my mother. "So, call a truce."

"Are you done?"

"Not quite. I brought you this. Thought it would help you see the light - in more ways than one." She rummaged in her bag and handed me a small cardboard box that weighed heavy. Puzzled, I took it. As I opened the container, Lenny's face cracked into a wide forgiving smile. Inside was a torch. But not any torch: a BYBLIGHT. I looked up, truly touched. She'd remembered my story about Zach, my fear of the dark and Chancer coming to my rescue.

I felt the weight of it in my hand. "It's very fancy."

"Be careful where you point. It's powerful enough to rip out retinas."

"What's that?" Rocco said.

"Lenny bought me a present in case I get stuck in a tunnel." I exchanged a grin with her. "I guess you two have met?"

"Briefly." Lenny gave Rocco the big look treatment although her smile seemed genuine enough. I think she wanted to prove that she didn't disapprove of Rocco Noble, only what I was doing with him.

Lenny got up and made for the door. "Remember what I said, Molly." Turning to Rocco, "Nice to meet you," and then she thundered down the stairs and was gone.

Chapter 31

Standing outside, bracing myself to go in, it felt like someone had bashed six-inch nails into my flesh. Back on intimately familiar terrain, all those things that didn't make sense oppressed me.

In the space of days, the house and garden had fallen into decline. Paintwork looked faded, bleached by the sun, and worn. The grass was too long. The drive sprouted weeds, flowers wilting and shrivelled in the fierce heat. The Malverns didn't so much as stand majestic as loom over Mum and Dad's home like the backdrop to a horror movie.

Mr Lee was first to greet me. Shiny-eyed, he jumped up, glad to have someone take an interest. The smell of barbeque wafted in from the garden and I followed my nose, with Mr Lee in hot pursuit.

Dad had his back to me. Of Nate there was no sign.

"Hi," I called. "Where's Mum?"

Dad turned. He wore a stripy butcher's apron, a long fork clasped in his hand. To the casual observer, nothing appeared wrong and yet nothing felt right. What the hell were we doing having a barbeque? Shouldn't we be indoors, out of the sun, in the shade? "Showing your aunt to her room," he said with a heavy sigh.

"Dusty?" Christened Jean, everyone called my aunt by her nickname. I had no idea why. Loud and over the top, my mum's sister, whom my mother hardly mentioned, was not the kind of woman you wanted in your house at a time like this. I think I'd probably seen her on half a dozen occasions during the course of my life. Unmarried, and retired from running a high-end dress shop that had been her life, she travelled around sightseeing, and sometimes took off for long stints abroad. The last time I'd clapped eyes on her I'd been a teenager. For some reason that escaped me, she'd never made it to Nate and Scarlet's wedding.

Dad, obviously unnerved by the prospect, stared back at the grid. Chicken legs, steaks and sausages spat and sizzled through a haze of white smoke. Looked as if he were feeding an army.

"Nate around?" I asked casually.

"Somewhere." Vague, lost in his own thoughts, Dad was a man going through the motions without understanding why. I couldn't imagine how difficult this must be.

It didn't take long to find my brother-in-law. He was in the kitchen, helping himself to a drink. Expecting my mother, the smile briefly vanished when he saw who it was. "Hey, you gave your folks quite a scare. You okay?"

"Yes." As okay as can be expected.

Nate looked down, fished a lemon pip out of his drink. "Want one?" he said, gesturing with his glass.

"G&T would be nice."

He took his time fixing it. We didn't say 'Cheers' or anything like that. I didn't fill in the gaps with small talk, but that didn't stop Nate. "Journalists still call despite our pleas for privacy and refusal to comment. Your dad has grown an obsession with tidying his garage. Your mum spends much of the day upstairs. Sometimes I hear her crying."

Focus, I thought, on what you *can* do instead of what you know you can't. "Any fresh developments?"

"If there are, the police aren't sharing them with me."

"But aren't they supposed to? Isn't that Childe's job?"

"I've no idea."

"What happened in the study?"

Nate's expression tightened. "Wondered when you'd get round to it." He eyed me over the rim of his glass. "Your dad is a lot smarter than you give him credit."

"I've never underestimated my father. And I think I told you that."

He flicked a smile in a weak attempt to take the edge off. "Following the letter from Heather Bowen's solicitor, Rod's been making a few enquiries." He spoke in a giving me the lowdown, 'know what I mean' tone. "It seems our Mr Bowen is not as squeaky clean as he's portrayed. He had what you could call a colourful private life."

I could hardly tell him this wasn't breaking headline news, so I sat down and took a long swallow of gin. It tasted bitter. In the absence of a riveted response, Nate elaborated. "While playing happy families, his mistress and child were tucked up in Dorset."

How could Bowen afford a mistress and child on a sergeant's salary? Was this the reason for Scarlet's request for a loan? Had Bowen manipulated his 'other woman' in order to fund his alternative lifestyle?

"The police aren't going to muck-rake over one of their own, are they? Don't you see," Nate continued, "Bowen's unconventional lifestyle is enough to discredit him and put the police right off."

"The point is to prove Scarlet's innocence, not Bowen's guilt. What about the bracelet – any prints found?"

"It was clean."

It could only be clean if it had been wiped, surely? This didn't seem to occur to Nate. So, I told him.

Nate shrugged. "Belonged to the mistress."

"We both know that's not true."

"We don't," Nate sniped back. "You'd better go and join them in the garden," he said pointedly.

"Don't you think you should show your face?"

He shook his head.

I got it. Barbeques were for fun, not funerals.

Chapter 32

Dusty did that *mwah mwah* actressy thing on either side of my nose. Apart from looking as if she'd been left out in a desert to bake, she was still very much the woman I remembered from way back. Taller, older and with a rangy build, quite dissimilar to my mother, she wore a navy knee-length cocktail dress with sleeves. Her matching sandals revealed a highly polished pedicure. A gold anklet teased a millimetre below a gaudy piece of body art that trailed up the side of her leg to her knee. She had suspiciously thick bright blonde hair – could it be a wig, or hair extensions? Beneath the fringe, surrounded by tons of eyeliner and mascara, she had sharp blue eyes that could leave you blind if you stared into them for long enough; amazing she could jack them open with that lot clinging to her lashes. The lines on her face suggested that she'd spent her entire life laughing. She wasn't laughing now.

"I came as soon as I heard." She tilted her head in Mum's direction. Mum, wan and gaunt, a listless, 'not there', look in her eyes, glanced back, distracted. She must have dropped a stone in weight. Utterly lost. On the edge. Lights out. I tried to catch her attention, but she was too spaced to notice. "Scarlet was such a lovely girl," Dusty murmured.

"Yes," I said, my turn to avoid my mother's gaze.

"Nate not coming?" Dad asked.

"He wants to be on his own."

Privately, I thought we could all have done with being on our own. I was right about the barbeque: a bad idea. Sure, we had to eat, but this?

"No Zach?" Dusty glanced over my shoulder as if he might suddenly materialise.

"Not coping too well," Dad explained. "Better off where he is."

Was this the conclusion my dad came to after his most recent conversation with Zach, or was this my brother's idea and my dad was going along with it?

A deadly silence cast a shadow over the lawn. Even the birds seemed to have packed it in for the evening. We stood, each of us fixed on the grass, eyes squinting against the curling smoke from the barbecue.

"Mand, are you all right?" Dusty said. *Mand?* I'd never heard anyone call my mother anything but Amanda. A difficult smile flashed across my Mum's lips. "Darling, don't be like that."

"Like what?" Mum's voice was metallic.

"Like you don't know who I'm talking about. Everyone called her that," Dusty told me with a chuckle.

"Long time ago," Dad said, shooting a look at Mum, one part warning; two parts concern.

I pictured Scarlet sitting on the bench near the water feature, watching proceedings, thinking what stupid twats we all were.

The next two hours were incongruous, awful, and exhausting. The terrace filled with smoke. While Dad obsessed about the food, whether or not it was cooked properly, whether he'd got the charcoal at the right temperature, whether he was going to kill us all with food poisoning, my mother, glassy-eyed with booze and bellicosity raised the tension in the garden to seismic proportions by uttering not a single word. Seriously wondering whether Mum might lump Dusty one, I was glad when she excused herself and went to bed.

"How long is she staying?" I asked Dad when Dusty tottered off to the loo some time later. In the sipping stakes, she could rival my mother. Must have shifted at least half a litre of gin before necking into wine.

"Christ knows." Exhaustion chiselled deep grooves along his forehead and either side of his mouth. My youthful-looking dad looked old.

I reached up, gave his shoulder a squeeze and followed his gaze. He was looking up longingly at his and Mum's room. "Mind, if turn in?"

I patted his arm. "You go ahead."

He cast a doubtful look in the direction of the French windows, from which Dusty would, no doubt, emerge at any second, torn, it seemed about leaving me with my aunt. I knew what he was thinking. "How much does she actually know?"

168

"Only the bare bones."

"Shall I keep it that way?" Instinctively, I knew this was what he wanted.

He was unequivocal. "Most definitely."

Chapter 33

"Talking to your mother is like engaging with a terrorist about to kill a hostage," Dusty said.

We were sitting on the bench in the same spot Scarlet and I had shared weeks before.

"That's a little strong."

"You think me unkind?"

"I do."

"What a lovely young woman you are," she said with a beam. "Not afraid to tell it straight." She linked her arm through mine in a 'part of the sisterhood' gesture, which I didn't much care for. "Bit of a black sheep, aren't you?"

"I think Zach was awarded that particular title."

"Of course, yes," she said, as though she'd only just remembered I had a brother. "How is he? Still on the straight and narrow?"

"As far as I know." Which wasn't much at all.

"Your mother was extremely distressed at the time, I recall."

Which time, I wanted to ask. The trouble with relatives who flitted in and out was that, understandably, they had a poor grasp of the main narrative.

"Naturally, I appreciate how dreadful things are for your parents right now, truly I do," she continued, "but your mother lives as if in a perpetual state of atonement. People like that take tragedy to heart."

"Is there any other way to take it?"

"I don't see you falling apart."

"Everybody grieves in a different way. Scarlet wasn't my daughter." I wondered how my mum would have reacted had it been me in the crash. Would she have been stricken? I kicked the malodorous thought into the rockery where it shattered into a gazillion pieces.

"You know, Molly, you're so like your dad. Strong, stoic, silent. Always admired him. Typical Gemini. Considered quite a catch back in the day when he worked in Vice."

"They still call it that? Sounds very old-fashioned."

"Talking of which—" She gave a little snort of laughter, reached for her bag and slipped out a pack of cigarettes. "Would you mind? Only I've been dying to light up since I got here. Your mother hates me smoking."

"She hates anyone smoking."

"Want one?" Dusty shook out two cigarettes.

"No, I'm good."

"I won't tell. Our secret."

I'd had quite enough of those. Secrets confer power. Give it away and it loses its vitality, and the secret-keeper is forever feared and despised. In an offbeat second, it occurred to me then that too many people were asking me to keep my mouth shut about various things.

I shook my head and watched as Dusty took out a fancy gold lighter and went through the ritual. Tilting her head back, she narrowed her eyes and exhaled a sigh of deep pleasure. "You know they're burying that poor man day after tomorrow?"

I didn't know. How did she? Suspicious, I asked her. "Your dad mentioned it," Dusty said. "Someone from inside the police keeps him in the loop."

Odd, I thought. Dad had intimated that his source had dried up, unless it was Stanton, which would be incredibly indiscreet of him if not plain wrong. It also told me something. Any investigation by the coroner and police must have been concluded. Surely, that wasn't remotely possible in the time-scale?

"So?" she said.

"So what?"

"Molly, darling, I'm not daft. Whatever is going on?"

"I don't know what you mean." Which was true.

"Nate, poor boy, told me Scarlet was drunk."

"Yes."

"Do we know why?"

"No."

Her crafty gaze fell on me. With Rocco, I'd almost crumbled. Dusty stood no chance. "You have no idea?" I spread my hands. "Always seemed such a together young woman."

"Mmm."

"Quite the little princess when she was little."

"Uh-huh."

"Your mother idolised her."

I did not need my aunt to tell me what I already knew. My mother's mantra was that pretty gets you a long way in life. In this regard I fell massively short. It occurred to me that, as much as I'd envied my sister, I didn't covet the weight of expectation on her shoulders, the degree of smothering she'd endured from Mum. It seemed to me then that Scarlet was always destined to tumble from the pedestal on which she'd been placed.

Smoke snatched from the corner of my aunt's mouth and drifted skywards. "Obviously something was very wrong." I gave her my best clueless look and, slipping my arm from hers, said goodnight and went to bed.

The next morning, I rose early and so did Mum. I found her outside in her dressing gown, deadheading roses. Barefoot, the polish on her toenails was chipped and flaking. She didn't look up as I approached.

"Scarlet loved these," she said dreamily.

"I know."

"Wonderful fragrance." She burrowed her face into a spray of yellow blooms.

"Mum—" I began.

"Every second of every minute of every hour reminds me she's not here." She spoke slowly, softly, painfully, as if every word cost her dear. How I wished I could shift her sorrow.

"It will get better."

"Will it?" She looked at me then, like a small child seeking reassurance from a parent. I saw Scarlet in her expression, the hurt and the fear and blind hope. "I wish I had your certainty." She picked up a pair of secateurs. Snip. Snip.

"Mum, about the other day—"

"It's forgotten," she said. "All rather silly."

This was not how I remembered it. "The man in the garden," I began. "Dad's old colleague."

The light behind her eyes flickered. "Yes?"

"What's his name?"

She frowned. "Why do you want to know?"

"I'm interested."

Indecision shadowed her features. I faked my biggest smile. She cleared her throat. "Clive Mallis."

I'd never heard the name before and said so.

"They don't see each other that often. Clive came to pay his respects."

"And Stanton? I mean did he and Dad ever work together?"

"Never."

She carried on with what she was doing, as unanchored and lost as a guest stumbling around a country pile after a late-night party.

"Are we all right, Mum?" I blurted out. "You and me?" I didn't bother to tame the desperation in my voice. I didn't want to be a black sheep, as my aunt had suggested, as though being an outsider was glamorous and exciting. I wanted to belong; now more than ever. It's all I'd ever wanted.

Mum stopped, straightened up and looked me dead in the eye. Then, unpredictably, a smile, big enough to rival the morning sun, broke out across her face. "Of course, Molly."

I didn't believe her. Not when she opened her arms. Not when she held me too tight. Not when she dropped a kiss on top of my head.

Chapter 34

If the police hadn't phoned on the dot of 9 a.m., I'd have made a break for it.

We assembled in the living room. Light poured in. I couldn't help but think there was no smile in the sunshine, that it wanted to shrivel and burn, and consume the sky.

Roger Stanton was short, whey-faced and had a voice that could put you into a coma. Not that this was particularly relevant right now. All we were interested in was what came out of Stanton's thin-lipped mouth. Was Scarlet condemned, or not? What else had the police unearthed during the course of their investigation? Were they going to slay us with a revelation and connection to a dead Charlie Binns, and an anonymous contract killer? A shiver travelled all the way up my spine and shot out at the base of my neck.

I glanced around the room. Dad and Mum huddled close together on one sofa; Stanton and Childe sat on the other. Nate and I opted for a couple of wingback chairs.

I understood why Dusty had fled. The atmosphere was as taut as cheese wire. It made me feel faintly dizzy and there was a weird knocking sensation in the middle of my chest. Both officers were impossible to read. Stupidly, I thought how smart they looked – like villains who scrub up well for the court appearance.

Childe glanced at Nate. "Are you happy to discuss Scarlet in front of your in-laws?"

"You're talking about my daughter." Mum's face was thunderous, her voice pregnant with outrage.

"I appreciate that, Mrs Napier, but Nate is Scarlet's next of kin."

Mum stiffened. Fat tears swelled up into her eyes. I tensed. Any second it could all kick off. Dad took her hand. "Come on, Roger," he intervened, ignoring Childe and addressing the senior officer, "we're in this together. We're all family. No secrets to hide. Isn't that right, Nate?"

"It's fine. No secrets here." Nate twitched a smile. Stanton twitched too. Didn't look as if he appreciated my father's assumed familiarity. I looked straight ahead.

Peeved at being upstaged, Childe shut up and Stanton did the talking. Wisely, he was inclusive and addressed his remarks to each of us. Not at all appeased, Mum sat ruler straight, blue eyes intent, watching every twist and slant of Stanton's mouth, like she was lip reading.

"Had Mrs Jay lived, she would be charged with one count of causing death by dangerous driving and another of driving while over the prescribed limit."

"I understand," Nate said gravely.

"This, as you know, would have likely resulted in a custodial sentence." I caught my breath. Stanton didn't need to spell it out. We weren't stupid. We knew this. I dared not look at Mum and Dad. "Having carried out a thorough technical audit, we've found nothing on either Mrs Jay's phone or laptop to suggest that she had a connection to Richard Bowen."

Tension in the room eased. I clamped my mouth shut and studied the carpet. Stanton cleared his throat. "Pornography was discovered on Mr Jay's computer, but this fell within the parameters of the law and we regard this as a side issue."

I stayed focussed on the floor.

"To conclude," Stanton droned on, "and as far as we've been able to establish, Nate, we have no reason to believe that there was any prior or existing relationship between your wife and Richard Bowen."

I was floored. Fear threw a thick, stifling sack over my head. This couldn't be right. Astonished by the speed with which the investigation had been carried out and wrapped up, I almost asked Stanton to repeat it. Nate caught my eye, looked at me deadpan. Don't. Mum sat, still and stony. Only Dad reacted with open relief. If he could have taken Stanton's hand in both his and shaken it, I think he would have done. I wondered how many corners were cut to reach such a speedy conclusion. Without a connection, it would be impossible to prove that there was intent to kill. While I welcomed the outcome, I wasn't sure about its veracity.

On firmer ground, Childe picked up the conversation and ran with it. "Now the criminal investigation has been concluded, the inquest will go ahead in due course."

"So, I can bury my wife?" Nate said.

"You can."

A defining moment, I should have felt pleased. I didn't. I couldn't shake off the feeling that something was badly wrong. Wasn't helped by the prospect of Scarlet's remains lying in the ground.

Stanton glanced at Childe, his cue to bring down the final curtain on their performance.

"I understand that Mrs Bowen threatened to sue you, Nate."

"She lodged a claim against Scarlet's estate, yes."

Stanton did that thing people do when they hold all the cards. He took his time, flicked a non-existent speck off his neatly pressed trousers. A company man, he appeared to be enjoying the show, the power he wielded. "Mrs Bowen has been under enormous strain."

"So have I," Nate said darkly.

"Appreciated. You'll be relieved to know that all proceedings are to be dropped."

Nate's jaw slackened. "That's marvellous news. Whatever made her change her mind?"

"Does it matter?" Dad said with a tight smile.

I can't fix everything, woman, he'd said. But had Dad tried?

"Let's say, it was a pragmatic decision, based on self-protection." Stanton stared straight ahead, for Nate's attention only. Theatrically, I leant forward, elbows on my knees, my chin cupped in my hands in an attempt to break Stanton's concentration. Didn't work. I might as well have been a sideboard.

"Is there anything else we can help with, Nate?" Stanton said.

"I don't think so. You've covered everything."

"Very thorough," Dad chipped in.

Childe stuffed his notes into his briefcase. All four men stood and shook hands.

"I'd like to ask a question."

Four sets of eyes fixed on me. Obscured by Dad, I couldn't see Mum.

"What happened out there?" I was taking a big risk. At any moment my parents could remind me of my argument with my sister and damn me. As guilty as I was, I was not so bent by grief or challenged by authority that I couldn't recognise a piece of window-dressing designed to pretty up an ugly picture. I knew other things were in play.

Stanton frowned. Wasn't nice. "I beg your pardon?"

"Road was clear. Beautiful day. No rubber on the road. Nothing found in the post-mortem suggesting that Scarlet blacked out." I held my breath, wondering if either Mum or Dad would launch in, take the opportunity to tell everyone what nobody else appeared to know. To my surprise, Dad remained silent, muscles in his jaw clenched. When he shifted his stance, I caught a glimpse of Mum looking down, not really listening, her fingers screwing up the fabric of her skirt, tighter and tighter as if she wanted to rip it to pieces.

"I think we made this perfectly clear," Childe said, appealing to my father to help him out, which he did, but not in the way I thought he would.

"She was drunk, darling, suffering from depression."

"Was she, Nate?" My boldest move, and still Mum and Dad didn't kill me off with a few well-chosen words.

"I didn't spot it. Who knows?" He sounded calm. His mouth was resolute. Only his eyes flashed fear. Seemed we all knew things —apart from the real story behind Scarlet's decision to drive off the road. I held his gaze.

Stanton's voice cut through the foetid atmosphere like sharpened glass. "Suicide rates among young women are definitely on the up, regrettably."

"Scarlet was the most grounded person I knew."

"Molly," Dad said sternly. "Sometimes there are no neat answers." I opened my mouth to speak, to tell them everything.

Dad's expression darkened, suggesting that if I knew what was good for me, I would shut up and there would be a reckoning later. My cheeks burnt with humiliation. It was enough to make me lose my bottle.

Silence as deadly as carbon monoxide enveloped the room.

"I'll be in touch," Childe said awkwardly, speeding towards the door, Stanton in pursuit, Dad following close behind.

Nate looked through me as if I were sheet glass and turned to Mum. "You don't mind me going home, do you, Amanda?"

She glanced up. Distant. Loose. Not connecting. "As you wish." A fake smile stuttered across her lips.

"I'll go and pack." After he made a break for it, I got up to leave.

"Scarlet didn't kill herself because of your row."

Amazed, I turned and looked at my mum. "You're right, Molly. She was too sensible."

Thank you. Thank you. Thank you. Tears of relief pricked my eyes, not because I was absolved but because Mum had, for once, agreed with me on something that really mattered. "So why did she?"

Mum shook her head sadly. "It's a mystery. We'll probably never know. Best left."

No, no, no. This wasn't what I wanted to hear.

"It was a good outcome, better than expected. I suppose that's it," she said, almost in a trance. "No more police. No more waiting. The end."

I shivered at the thought. She was so wrong. This was only the beginning.

The slow burr of male voices drifted in from the hall followed by the sound of the front door opening and the crunch of gravel under boots. Mum dropped her head. "How do I go on?" She spoke quietly, more to herself than to me, her face pinched and wretched.

"Mum, I need you; we all do."

She flicked a vacant smile, patted my hand, as if I'd uttered a nice speech using words I neither meant nor understood, which was so far from the truth, it made my heart ache. Deep down, I'd hoped that somehow, she could love me like she'd loved Scarlet. I wanted to tell her that I could never be as pretty as my sister, or witty, or as smart, that I was no substitute for the daughter she adored, but I'd do my best if only she'd give me a chance.

She got up, went to the kitchen. I followed. Couldn't leave things as they were. "About Zach," I began.

"Yes?" It was as if a light switched on behind her eyes. She seemed suddenly with it, alert, in the present, in the moment.

"Will you talk to him? Tell him what the police said?"

"Naturally."

The door flew open. "They've gone," Dad said. "Time for a drink. Want one, Amanda?"

"My usual."

Mum might help herself to gin at coffee time. My father never did. I watched as he avoided my eye and meticulously prepared gin and tonics. Cool blue Bombay gin. Ice and slice.

"Where's Nate?" Dad asked. There was an odd jaunty ring in his voice as if the news from the police was cause for celebration. I supposed it was.

"Packing." Mum lifted the glass to her lips, taking a long deep swallow.

"Good God, no need for him to go."

"He wants to," I cut in, thinking the silent treatment really didn't suit my father. "Don't I get offered a drink?"

He focused on me as if he were looking down the barrel of a gun. "I assumed you were driving."

I forced a smile. "You're right." Couldn't have two daughters screwing things up. Before I was tempted to say something I'd regret, my mobile bleeped. A text from Rocco: 'Meet at mine. I have a surprise.'

I made my excuses and left. Their sigh of relief was as great as my own.

Chapter 35

I'd have done anything to escape the distorted dynamics at home. When Rocco bundled me into his car and said we were going out, I didn't argue.

"Any news on the investigation?" We were in his Mini, hurtling to God knew where.

"What investigation? Case closed."

"Do these coppers have names?" he said with an amused grin.

I cast him a look that told him, if he knew what was good for him, he should back the fuck off. His expression instantly changed.

"I want to understand, Molly. That's all."

The warmth in his voice *sounded* genuine enough. Without disclosing anything that didn't compute, I gave him a potted version of the police visit: facts without fiction. His eyes flared when I told him that Scarlet had been cleared of deliberately targeting Bowen. "The police found no pre-existing relationship between Richard Bowen and my sister."

"But that's fantastic. It must come as a huge relief."

"I'm pleased. Yes."

Rocco glanced across, uncertain how to measure my response. "But isn't that great news?"

I forced a reassuring smile.

He changed down a gear as we headed up hill. "Your dad was a copper, wasn't he? Sorry," Rocco said with a grin. "I mean police officer."

I smiled back. "Even Dad talks about coppers. He retired ten years ago."

"Any particular reason?"

"Burn out."

"Comes with the job description, I guess."

"My older brother, Zach, didn't exactly help. He was a drug addict at the time."

"Whoa," Rocco said theatrically. "On your father's patch?"

"'Fraid so, a nightmare for my parents. Every time there was a drugs raid, Dad expected my brother to be under arrest."

"Must have been upsetting for you too."

"I developed a knack of detaching myself from the daily drama."

"What about Scarlet?"

"She took a medical interest, which made her more objective than Mum and Dad."

"And how is Zach now?"

"He's good."

"Does he live at home?"

"I don't think Zach ever lived at home," I said with a dry laugh.

"Bit of a rolling stone?"

"You could say. Lives in a commune." I looked out at the road and speeding countryside. It must have been the heat, but I was tired of answering endless questions. Put me on my guard, too. "Where are we going exactly?"

"It's a surprise."

"Clues?"

"You like ancient things, don't you?"

"A tour around antique shops?"

"Busman's holiday. Definitely not."

"Castle?"

"Not quite."

"Getting warm?"

"Little bit."

I smiled. It seemed a long time since I'd had someone take this level of interest in me. Then, with a jolt, I remembered the weirdo who'd broken into my home.

"You okay?" Rocco seemed adept at picking up on my fast changes of mood.

"I'm like a weather forecast," I said, making light of it. "Sunny periods followed by a big depression coming in from the East."

He rested his hand on my thigh. "We can turn back, if you prefer."

"It's okay. There is no turning back, is there?"

*

"That was amazing." I gazed back up at eight hundred years of history, Hereford Cathedral.

"Best bit?"

"You first."

"Well, the Mappa Mundi was pretty cool but, for sheer impact, the SAS Memorial. You?"

"The Chained Library. I've never seen so many medieval manuscripts in one place. And what a neat security system – all those rods and locks."

"Read but can't nick."

"Maybe I should adopt something similar for the shop." I squeezed his hand. "Best first date ever."

Rocco turned with a suggestive smile, drew me close. "Bit late for a first date, isn't it?" Taking my face in his hands, he kissed me on the lips in full view of a bunch of Japanese tourists.

"That was nice," I said. "Fancy something to eat or coffee?"

"I know exactly the right place."

We headed out of cathedral yard and down aptly named Church Street, a narrow-pedestrianised area with quirky independent craft, art, food and coffee shops.

"I love it here," Rocco enthused. "When I'm old and grey, this is where I'm going to settle."

"That's some pre-planning. Seriously?" I teased.

He turned, dark eyes fastening on mine. No smile. An emotion I couldn't gauge travelled behind his eyes. The intensity freaked me out. Despite the easy-going veneer, Rocco had an iron will. Something about that didn't stack with the rest of him.

"Easy," I said, squeezing his hand, "I get it."

He snapped on a smile and we headed into a cafe.

In seconds, we were sitting in a walled courtyard amongst lavender-scented rockery, Cappuccinos and chocolate muffins ordered.

I leant back, tipped my sunglasses onto my head and turned my face to a blaze of sunshine. Mellow, beautiful, at odds with the ugliness of another summer day. A simple moment in time, I longed to let go and enjoy it. If only.

When I opened my eyes, Rocco was watching me. He did it a lot, I'd noticed, funny boy. "What?" I said.

"I like looking at you."

He tipped forward, kissing me lightly. "I'll have to ruin your view for a few seconds. Does this place have a loo?"

"Bottom of the garden, I believe."

"Watch my bag?"

"Won't take my eyes off it."

So off I toddled, feeling warm and fuzzy with happiness however fleeting it might be.

The loo was more potting shed than bathroom. I had to search around for loo roll. It took me an age to turn on the tap, and when I did, it gushed boiling water. Soap was a dried up sliver. There was no towel. None of this dented my mood, which was absurdly buoyant, bordering on rapturous. Halfway up the path, back to our table, cold fear settled in the centre of my chest. I stopped, blinked, looked again. *What the hell?*

"Hey, what do you think you're doing?"

Rocco paused, looked up with a puzzled smile and broke off from his conversation. "Your phone rang."

"*My* phone."

"I thought it might be important."

"I asked you to watch my bag, not dive into it." My voice was uncomfortably raised. Several people turned around.

"But—"

"You had no right."

"It's Zach."

"What?" I could count on one hand the number of times my brother had phoned in the last ten years. Most occasions had been thinly disguised requests for money.

"Your brother."

"I damn well know who he is." I snatched my mobile out of Rocco's hand, marched back down the path, out of earshot and into the shade.

"Yes?"

"Did I ring at a bad time?"

Was there ever a good time? "No."

"Sounds as if you're having a bundle."

"A misunderstanding." *Liar.*

"Nice guy, whoever he is."

I cast a long look back up the garden, my cold stare enough to drill holes in Rocco's face. "How would you know?"

"Because we just had a conversation." He spoke in a 'duh' tone, vaguely reminiscent of my mother. In a bid to calm down, I attempted to count to ten. I managed five.

"Zach, the last time we met you told me not to meddle in things I don't understand."

"Ah, well, that's why I'm calling. To apologise."

"Really." Two tones underpin that word. The WOW, surprised 'tell me more' version and the cold sarcastic 'you can't be serious' version. Mine fell into the latter category.

E. V. Seymour

"Honest." An attribute I don't normally associate with my brother. "Am I forgiven?" he asked, wheedling.

Obviously, in an attempt to broker peace, Mum had put him up to it. "Easy, isn't it? Shooting shit and then expecting one word to make it all better." To be fair, Zach rarely said sorry because he considered it a weakness. It must have cost him, but my mood had swung to north of foul and I refused to cut him slack.

"Molly, please don't be cross."

I pictured him hopping from one foot to the other; sweat gathering underneath his arms, exploding across his brow, fingernails scratching at itchy druggie skin. "I'm not cross. I'm confused. What did you mean when you told me to back off?"

"I didn't mean anything. Angry words. Heat of the moment. Jesus, after what happened to Scarlet, what do you expect?"

"Don't use Scarlet as an excuse for your behaviour. You threatened me."

"I didn't, but if you think I did then I'm sorry." After that, he shut up.

"Okay," I said finally. "Let's draw a line underneath it." Mine was extremely squiggly.

Off the hook, Zach became almost chatty. "Dad told me they have a house guest."

"Unfortunately."

"How long is Dusty staying?"

"'Till the funeral, whenever that is. You will be there, won't you?"

"Yeah. Course."

"Only—"

"Gotta go. Tanya needs me. Emergency."

I stared at the phone for several seconds then returned to cold coffee and what I thought would be chilly conversation. Wrong. Rocco's face was a picture of contrition.

The second my rear hit the seat, he said, "I shouldn't have picked up your phone."

I felt my spine stiffen despite him looking genuine enough. I barely knew Rocco and already he was asking a ton of questions and helping himself to the contents of my handbag. "Privacy is something I treasure."

"I know. It won't happen again." He reached across, placed a warm hand over mine. "Are we good?" A smile broke across his face so mesmerising it could give the sun a run for its money.

"Okay," I said, relenting. "We're good."

Chapter 36

Maybe Scarlet's sudden violent death had made me paranoid. Maybe I was thin-skinned, yet I was consumed with the fact that Rocco had answered a call on my phone, which had been tucked into my bag, and spoken to my brother. At some length, it would seem. After our date, Rocco dropped me back to my place, I hadn't asked him in for a late lunch or anything else.

Still bruised by the incident the next morning, I went to the shop.

'Flotsam' is a labyrinth of landings, staircases and dead ends. Oh, and a dirty, dank cellar, barely ventured into. You couldn't pay enough to get me down there. Big pieces of furniture and large paintings are on display downstairs. Upstairs: vintage clothing, china, chairs, cutlery, occasional tables and what could only be described as bric-a-brac. Locked display cabinets contain vintage toy cars, medals, jewellery, knives and swords.

Lenny eyed me over the rim of her Royal Doulton coffee cup – no point in having classy stuff if you're not going to use it. "How did it go with your Mum and Dad?"

"Fine."

They were all looking at a picture from the wrong angle and I couldn't find the focus. I shrugged and clammed up, further conversation not up for grabs. Shrewd enough to catch on, Lenny steered the conversation onto a different footing.

"Seen anything of Mr Noble?"

"Spent the morning with him yesterday."

"And?"

"It was nice."

"Nice?" Lenny uttered it in the same way she says 'Fuck'.

"You need to stocktake the china upstairs."

"Don't change the subject."

"I'm not. It's long overdue."

"Lover's tiff already?"

"Shut up, Lenny." Spying a customer, who'd taken an obvious liking to a French cherry wood set of drawers with bowed legs, I headed off in her direction.

"Would you do a deal on this?" the woman asked.

"Could let you have it for eighty-five."

"Seventy-five?"

"Eighty."

"I'll take it."

"Will you need help to your car?"

I looked pointedly at Lenny. "Hand Lenny your car keys, while I take the payment."

Diversionary tactics lasted as long as it took for Lenny to step out and back in. "Rocco not quite so rocking?"

Heat flooded my chest, and sprayed up my neck, collecting on both cheeks. I swear 'Boris' the stuffed bear smirked at my obvious concern and, yes, disappointment. "Drop it, Lenny. Please."

Lenny's soft blonde eyebrows drew together in dismay. "Sorry, didn't mean to snap."

"You look as if you're going to cry."

"I'm not."

"Don't tell me, you thought he was caring and compassionate. And now you think he's sketchy."

I think he's suspicious, but I could hardly tell Lenny this. I forced a smile. "My own fault. I should never have tumbled into bed with him."

"Your timing could have been better."

"Serves me right for sleeping with a stranger." I swear the shop filled with the scent of Scarlet's perfume, one of the Dior's. I dragged myself back to the here and now, the visible, as opposed to the invisible, the unknown and unseen. "Things are moving way too quickly." It sounded like a confession because it *was* a confession.

"So, slow them down."

"You don't understand." I told her about the phone incident.

Lenny crooked a knuckle under her chin and for once didn't interrupt or pull an extravagant facial expression.

"Is it such a big deal?"

"You think what he did was okay?"

"Not really but, if as Rocco says, he thought he was doing you a favour, maybe that's all it was. Taking a liberty, granted."

"And talking to Zach?"

Lenny shrugged. "Rocco's personable and socially at ease. He likes to gas."

"You think I'm overreacting?"

"Molly, I don't blame you. I'd be fuming, but don't let it stress you out. If Rocco Noble is what you need right now, who am I to argue?"

"You've changed your tune."

"People do," she said, with a wink designed to cheer me.

"You're a good pal."

"Why don't you give him a ring?"

"No way."

"From what you said, you were pretty frosty."

"We left things on an awkward note. I'm sure he'll get over it."

I retreated to the back room, which doubled as a place to make drinks and sat down at the desk, a lovely nineteenth century twin pedestal number with a green leather top. With the intention of gathering my thoughts, I reached for a pad and pen and drew a diagram, in which Scarlet sat at the centre, the other names and players circling her like planets around the sun. I hadn't got very far when I heard voices, one louder than the other.

"Molly," Dusty said, her greeting carrying over Lenny's shoulder as if she were speaking via Tannoy. I flipped the pad face down, shoved it in a drawer, and returned to the show-room. "What a lovely shop, darling. I could spend a fortune in here."

"We've no problem with that, have we?" Lenny said.

"Not at all, although you might need a home first. My aunt is always on the move," I explained to Lenny.

"And that's part of the reason I'm here."

"Oh?"

"I'm booking into a hotel in town for the foreseeable future. Understandably, the atmosphere at home is highly charged. This way I can be on hand without—" She petered out, fluttering her fingers as if the right words were waiting to be snatched out of the ether. I felt for her. There were no right words for a time like this, only wrong ones. "Anyway," she said, brightening. "Aren't you going to introduce us, Molly?"

"Lenny meet Dusty, Dusty, Lenny," I said mechanically.

"Be a sweetheart, Lenny, and give me a guided tour. Oh Molly," Dusty said as she sashayed past. "A good-looking man dropped by first thing this morning with flowers for you." Straight out of the Chancer school of charm, I thought with warmth. "He said his name was Noble."

Lenny caught my eye. "Peace offering," she said with a grin.

Chapter 37

"STOP".

I'd never read *Fifty Shades of Grey*, or seen the film, but I felt sure that Rocco Noble had. From the second I walked through the door; I was in thrall. Every cell in my body wanted him.

You're weak and pathetic, Molly Napier, I told myself.

In the past I'd had bad sex, fast sex, cheap sex, drunken sex, good, maybe even thrilling, sex. Not in huge quantities like Lenny, with numerous partners, but I generally thought I recognised what pleased me and turned guys on. I knew my way around a man's body. But I'd never felt such abandon, such intensity, never ever surrendered myself in that way. But I had my limits. After we disappeared into the void together, I wondered, not for the first time, who the hell Rocco Noble was. What was he trying to prove? What was his game? Why were we going at each other as though we wanted to kill? I understood where I was coming from, but the oddball guy with clever eyes and dazzling smile defied me.

"Hell," Rocco said, throwing himself off me stoked and slick with sweat. We both were. "Got carried away."

"Is that what it was?" My voice rasped. I was spent and there was a dull ache between my legs. I'm sure I had a love bite on my neck. I reached over, grabbed a glass of water from the bedside table. My hand was shaking so much it nearly slipped through my fingers. Taking a greedy gulp, most of the liquid dribbled down my chin. At least we'd made it to bed. Eventually. The room looked like it had been trashed. Christ knows what the rest of the cottage looked like. My knickers were torn and the remnants clung for dear life to the bedpost. Rocco's shirt lay ripped on the floor. Several buttons had popped off my shirt and littered the carpet. If we kept this up, we'd both need new wardrobes.

He stretched out, hands above his head, hair damp at the temples, muscles in his torso rippling. Gym-bunny, I thought and said so.

"Weights when I can be arsed. I'm not one of those guys who's religious about it."

'Religious' was not a word I'd associate with Rocco Noble. Despite his superficially clean-cut persona, there was something strange going on underneath, some of it positively Heathen. What demon drove him? Instinctively, my thoughts returned to Scarlet and to a contract killing in the mean streets of the capital.

Familiar with the hollows and flat planes of his body, the fine line of hair running from his navel, I was surprised I'd missed a small tattoo high up, on his inner left arm.

"That must have hurt."

"Yup."

I studied it inquisitively. Looked like a Japanese style temple. Inside, in classic script, the letter 'D'. Intrigued, I asked Rocco what it signified.

"Someone I knew."

The closed expression on his face gave him away. "Who was she?" I teased.

Unclasping his hands, his arms dropped back to his sides. Not amused.

"Must have been special." I felt awkward, like I sometimes did when I said the wrong thing to Mum.

Rocco turned towards me, smoothed a lock of hair away from my face. I looked at him intently. "Cute move to bring me flowers."

"It was meant as a genuine apology."

"I'm astounded by your detective skills."

Rocco tapped the side of his nose.

"Why not go to the shop? It would have been simpler."

"Your parents and where you come from are part of you." He didn't smile. It wasn't said to flatter. He appeared to be serious about me. Muscles in my stomach contracted. "I like your mum. She isn't what I expected."

"Funny observation." And distraction.

"She seemed quite a character—"

"Tall, blonde, big eyes?"

Rocco nodded.

"That's my aunt Dusty, my mum's sister."

"Right," he said, eyes alive, as if putting together my family tree. He ran an index finger along my ribs, tracing the hollows and curves of my body. "You're very tense."

"It's nothing." I rolled away, reached for my underwear.

"It clearly isn't."

He crooked himself up on one elbow. Interest sparking.

"I did something ridiculous," I said, "and I wished I hadn't because now I don't believe the police. I don't believe my brother. I don't damn well believe anyone or anything."

"Do you believe me?" he said.

I didn't answer.

Chapter 38

Rocco leant back on the pillows; hands tucked behind his head. "There's one thing you have faith in."

"What's that?" I said, hooking up my bra. I was annoyed at being put on the spot.

"You. Every instinct tells you that Scarlet was not depressed. Perversely, you also believe that she meant to do what she did. Except you don't understand why and, sure as hell, you can't understand why the police have wrapped it all up. In fact, you think it's a whitewash."

I stopped getting dressed. How had he intuited that much from the little I'd said, or had I revealed more than I thought? Pillow talk was a dangerous activity.

"I follow the news, Molly," he said, rolling his eyes, pretending to be exasperated.

Did this explain how he could read me so well?

He reached up and pulled me back down on the bed with a thump. When he reached for and gathered me close, I felt the rhythmic beat of his heart beneath my ear. "So, what's this ridiculous crime you've committed?"

I pulled away a little. "I haven't broken the law."

"Well, that's a relief." He gave my arm a playful squeeze.

No way would I tell him about Charlie Binns. "I visited Heather Bowen," I said, fudging it.

He looked genuinely impressed. "Was this before you found out about the lawsuit against your brother-in-law, or after?"

"Before. She's no longer going after Scarlet's estate."

"That's quite a turnaround." Suspicion narrowed his eyes, but I wasn't going there. "Even so, doesn't talking to the opposing side complicate things?"

"Maybe. I'd hoped she'd tell me something new."

"And did she?"

I revealed highly edited highlights of the conversation. "What do you think?" I finished, shamelessly fishing.

He didn't speak for a moment.

"Heather might be right about how they met, in a professional capacity."

"Might have started that way."

"But you think it developed into something more. Like this. Us. Naked. Having sex." Rocco's eyes locked onto mine. Searching. Urging. "And that's why she—"

"I've been through this a hundred times. The lovers' scenario doesn't stack."

"No?"

"Scarlet wasn't sentimental. She wasn't dramatic."

"Wasn't it Sherlock Holmes who said, once you eliminate the impossible, whatever remains, no matter how improbable, must be the truth?"

I twisted round, pinned down by Rocco's searching gaze. "Huh?"

"Conan Doyle," he said, with a 'where have you been all your life' expression.

As I thought about the quotation, a blade of fear shot along my spine, making me gasp with sudden knowledge. "She acted in cold blood." Isn't that what contract killers did? I sat up straight.

"To shut him up."

There was a lot of shutting up going on. Someone had wanted to shut Binns up, me too. "She hired the Jeep days before the accident."

"For the job."

Coming from Rocco's mouth, it gave it more weight somehow. I baulked at his uncanny ability to say out loud what I most dreaded. "If she'd driven her own car, Bowen would have seen her coming. He would have recognised her. A surgical strike," I murmured, ignoring the obvious medical pun.

"Still comes back to the same question," Rocco said.

"Yeah," I said, wide-eyed and not a little excited.

He pressed a knuckle under my chin and tilted my head. "Have you spoken to Zach?"

"*Zach?*" I shook my head. "My brother isn't into conspiracy theories."

Rocco's expression sharpened. His mouth twisted, as if I'd insulted him. "You think that's what it is?"

"I don't know." I spoke quietly. Why was Rocco narky? This

wasn't his problem, wasn't his brother. "As yet, I don't have a shred of evidence to support any particular theory." I realised that I was parroting my father's words.

"Then find it."

I glared at him. He made something difficult sound easy. I was mourning. I was confused. "Heather said there were no texts, no emails, no phone conversations between my sister and her husband so how did they communicate?"

"Maybe they used dead drops."

"Dead what?"

"Spies use them."

I jumped up. "For goodness' sake, Rocco. This isn't a game or an intellectual exercise. I can't think straight with all your crazy suggestions."

"Please don't get angry, Molly."

"Well, shut up then." I was too rattled to cut him slack.

Cool and composed, he pulled me back again, ran his fingers lightly down my arm. "Dead drops are messages in hidden places."

Like hotels in London? "Next, you'll be talking about secret codes—"

"And cut-outs?"

"As in cardboard?' I was bewildered. A big grin broke out on his face. It took all the heat out of me. "I haven't the faintest clue what you're talking about." I settled back into him, the shadow of a forgiving smile in my expression. He sneaked an arm around my shoulder.

"Third parties. So-and-so gives a message to someone who then gives a message to someone else."

I had a little think about it, tried the messenger idea out for size, wasn't sure either way. "Do you really work for MI5?"

"I wish; simply an interest in espionage. It's a boy thing."

I didn't know any men like that. Zach wouldn't— Oh goodness, had Zach acted as a go-between? Is that why Scarlet saw him before she died? "Even if I could establish that they were actively communicating, how am I supposed to find out what Scarlet was allegedly protecting?"

He flicked a smile. "Allegedly – I use that word all the time at work." I wasn't sure what he meant or whether he was taking the piss. He waited a beat. "From what you've told me," Rocco said, "seems the cops are doing a good job of whitewashing. You should talk to your father."

Caught up in Zach, I blinked. I already had. It hadn't ended well. My laugh was as dry as it was cynical.

Chapter 39

"What's that?"

"Huh?" Consumed by my conversation with Rocco the night before, I'd mentally gone off the reservation. How could I find out more? Wasn't as if I could give the SIO in charge of the Binns murder case a ring.

"On you neck?" Lenny said. "Looks like someone tried to throttle you."

"It's nothing." I'd attempted to disguise the bruising with make-up, obviously not very well.

"MOL-LY." Lenny dragged out each syllable. "You're such a crap liar."

"We got a bit frisky."

"Frisky?" Lenny's top lip curled. "Looks more like armed combat. I hope you gave as good as you got."

"Yeah. Probably. How did you get on with my aunt?"

Lenny shot me a 'we'll return to this later' look. "She's a laugh and drinks like a witch. Travelled to so many interesting places. I hope when I'm her age I can look back on a life like hers."

"Glad she has a fan. She's been driving my parents insane." To be fair, I had a sneaky admiration for my aunt with her wayward ways and outspoken words.

"Dusty told me how relieved your parents are now the police have concluded the criminal side of the investigation."

I made a non-committal sound.

"Is it me or do I sense you're not satisfied?"

"It's not you."

Lenny frowned big time. "But isn't this what you wanted? Scarlet in the clear?"

"What I want and what I need are two very different things." I told her what Rocco suggested about the police whitewashing.

"He said what?" Anger lifted off her in lots of tiny sparks.

"Don't be like that. He has a point."

"He has an opinion and one he is not entitled to have."

"Lenny, the police enquiry was rushed as hell."

"This guy rocked up like yesterday and now he's putting a warped spin on a family tragedy. He might be magnificent in the sack, but it doesn't make him an authority. He didn't know Scarlet. He hardly knows you."

"I get it, but I really—"

"And you don't know the first thing about him."

"His mother's dead. I know that much."

"Only because he told you."

"Oh, so now he's a liar?"

"He's trying to win your trust."

"Lenny, that's paranoid garbage." Even as I said it, I recognised the several grains of truth in what she said. Did Rocco have a borderline mental disorder, or an unhealthy interest?

"Is it?" She looked very pissed off indeed. Hurt, too.

I glanced anxiously towards the front of the shop, noticed a man studying a rather fine clock through the window. I prayed he wouldn't come in.

"You're vulnerable, Molly. It makes me mad to think of him taking advantage of you." Her eyes locked on to my neck. Automatically, my hand shot up to shield it. Lenny wasn't done. "It's despicable."

I stood mute. Lenny shook. The door clanged open. The clock-seeking customer. Underneath slicked back hair; acne scars covered his forehead and cheeks. He had a short blocky, powerful build and a flat head you could land a helicopter on. Grey-blue eyes, the colour of wet Welsh slate met mine. Although I didn't know him, I nodded back. Somehow it seemed important. He didn't speak. He wasn't a browser. The way he picked up one item and then another spoke of someone that understood what he was doing and was possibly involved in the trade. Normally, I'd have ventured over and made nice, but a force field of aggression surrounded him and a deep dark part of me registered that an approach was not advisable. Fortunately, he didn't stay long, and I was relieved to see the back of him.

Lenny and I didn't talk for two hours. No sooner than the shop emptied, it filled back up. Irony of ironies, Lenny sold a couple of pieces from Rocco's collection, a small side table and jardinière. I racked up an old school trunk, a music stand and 'Boris' the bear; a middle-aged man wanted to put him in the foyer of a restaurant.

"Sad to see him go," Lenny said as Boris was carted unceremoniously out on a sack truck.

"Yeah."

She pulled at a thread on her T-shirt. "About earlier."

"It's forgotten."

"It's only—"

"You don't need to spell it out or apologise." My smile was feeble. "You're not telling me anything I don't already know, Lenny."

Chapter 40

Both Mum and Dad's cars were in the drive, together with a black BMW I didn't recognise. It had black tinted windows, seemingly impenetrable. Steeling myself to go inside, I called Zach.

"Hi, Molls." Typically, he'd forgotten our spectacular fallout.

"You sound up."

"Yeah, well, it's a lovely evening and I've spent a nice day with Chancer." Music with a grinding beat pummelled through the phone line.

"Hellooo," Chancer boomed. "Or rather goodbye. Kiss. Kiss."

"Daft fucker," Zach said.

"Is he drunk?"

"Hang on, Moll."

There were lots of muffled noises, which I equated to manly hugs, back slapping and 'See you laters.'

"That's better," Zach said. "He's gone."

Good. This wasn't the kind of conversation I wanted to

have with Chancer earwigging. "Are you up to speed with the police investigation?"

"Spoke to Mum last night. Sounded a bit tiddly." Did she sound anything else after 8 p.m.? "Seems the pigs have called a halt."

"Don't refer to the police like that, especially not in front of Dad."

"But I'm not talking to Dad. I'm talking to you."

I scratched my chin. Zach could be so maddening. "What else did she say?"

"That it was all over and the funeral is planned for end of next week."

I blinked. It was rare for Zach to have the drop on me when it came to family information. I took a huge breath, as if wading out into a cold sea. "What if it's not all over?

"I don't follow."

"What if the police got it wrong?"

"Molly," Zach snorted.

"What if Scarlet knew Bowen."

"We've been through all this." He gave an irritated sigh.

"Please, Zach, listen."

He paused for a few moments, thinking how to slide out of the conversation. I pounced before he had the chance.

"What if Bowen had something on her? What if she wanted to shut him up?" Stealing a line straight from the Rocco Noble school of vocabulary.

"Are you cracked?"

This was good coming from my brother. "Hear me out."

"I don't want to."

"You don't want to understand what made our sister do what she did?"

"If she did. And if you're right, I definitely don't want to know."

"Coward."

"Drama Queen."

"Talking to you is like talking to a pile of bricks."

"Ditto."

I glanced across, caught sight of Mum, standing close to the window. She looked angry and was jabbing the air with a finger, mouthing words I couldn't read to someone I couldn't see. When she turned on her heel, a man's hand, not my Dad's, caught her arm, which she wrenched away.

"Are you still there, Molly?"

"Sorry, yeah. Aren't you the least bit curious?"

"Curiosity killed the moggy."

Everywhere I turned I came up against invisible walls. The only person who took me seriously at the moment was Rocco Noble. And Lenny was right. That was worrying.

"Speak to you later." I hung up, my gaze fused to the window and whoever was in the room with my mother, but out of view. Concerned, I opened the car door, my eyes never leaving the curious story unfolding in front of me. That's when I saw Dad. He was patting the air with his palms in a calming gesture. He didn't seem angry and I got the impression that Mum was standing in between him and someone else. I wondered if it was a police officer.

Dad said something over Mum's head to whoever was in the room and then addressed her directly. I blinked, stared harder. Dad seemed to be remonstrating with my mother. I didn't know what to make of it, other than it was nothing good.

The prickly exchange with my father remained fresh in my mind. I wasn't sure I could take any more family drama. Although I longed to discover the identity of the mystery man and the reason for the row, cowardice got the better of me.

Feeling exposed and as if I shouldn't be there, I slunk back into the car, switched on the engine, turned around and drove back down the drive before anyone would notice. I needed my own space, where nobody could touch me, not even my own family and friends.

Chapter 41

"Will you do a Bible reading?"

"No way."

"Please."

"Nate, I can't."

"Why not?"

"I don't believe in God."

"You don't have to."

I was in the car, on speakerphone, turning off the motorway at junction ten for Cheltenham. I glanced out of the window. Someone had messed with the sign again at 'Uckington'.

Last thing I needed was Nate cajoling me into doing something I shouldn't. That slot was already bagged.

"I'm not sure I'll be able to hold it together. Ask Fliss. She'd be much better at that sort of thing." More polished, more sorted, Fliss would do a brilliant job. I pictured her dressed in dramatic black, her dress designed to flatter her figure, long hair tied back, beautifully made up to achieve that no make-up, natural effect, a fine portrait of dignified and contained distress. I'd be lucky to get through the ceremony without bawling my eyes out, a shuddering red-eyed snivelling heap of humanity.

He brightened considerably. "Not a bad idea. It's been a nightmare to organise."

I understood what he meant but he sounded like a guy planning a team-building day. Bastard.

"I've asked Zach to sort the music."

"Are you out of your tiny mind?"

"I thought it would be nice to involve everyone."

Bringing along your mistress too? "As long as you don't mind *Babyshambles* or, God help us, rap, I guess it will be fine."

"Hmm. Maybe I should have a word."

"Where's the funeral to be held?"

"I want it here. Your mum prefers Malvern." Perhaps that explained the source of aggro last night, although it didn't explain the presence of the BMW driver. "In fact, she wants to organise the whole thing. What do you think?"

I crashed the gears and juddered from third to second instead of moving up to fourth. My nerves felt on fire. "You're seriously asking me?"

"Well, yeah."

"Let Mum have her wish and, don't forget, the second this is over you're toast."

"Molly, for Chrissakes—"

I hung up and drove through town, skirting the college and hospital and out towards Hales Road.

"You, again."

It wasn't the warmest of welcomes and I couldn't really

blame her. This time, Heather Bowen kept me standing on the threshold. With all the traffic whizzing past, it was difficult to speak and hear.

"Why did you change your mind about suing my sister's estate?"

"Why do you think?" Her smile was thin. She glanced over my head at the houses opposite.

"Someone warned you off?" My blood froze at the possible implications.

"Not in so many words."

"Who?"

"My family liaison officer and, off the record, your brother-in-law's."

"Warren Childe?"

"Correct."

"Not Roger Stanton?"

"Stanton is Childe's boss, but, no. I mean have you met the man?" she said with the faintest suggestion of a smile. "Never say never, but Stanton is a pedantic sod. Incorruptible," she said, as if breathing new life into the word. A clammy hand of fear pressed against the lower part of my back. Whitewash was one thing, corruption another. Is this what we were talking about? I listened hard, waited for Scarlet's ghostly breath on my face but there was nothing.

"I was also told again categorically that the bracelet didn't belong to your sister."

"Then who did they say it belonged to?" Without doubt, it was Scarlet's. I'd recognise it anywhere.

"I'm not sure they looked that hard."

Could the police have found a more compelling reason to act in this way, I wondered, one they were hiding from both families?

"You said that Richard didn't have close friends."

"Correct."

"But he got on fine with colleagues."

Heather shifted her stance. Her eyelids fluttered with impatience.

"Did he have any contacts in the MET?"

"One."

"Yeah?"

"The best man at our wedding, but we haven't seen him in years."

"His name wasn't Neil Judd by any chance?" The officer and SIO handling the Charlie Binns murder investigation.

"It was not. Now if you've quite finished, I've got work to go to." And with that she slammed the door in my face.

Chapter 42

With bad thoughts rattling through my head, and wondering what else might break loose, I drove straight down the M5 to Worcester, missing gear changes the most notable features of my journey.

Coming up for noon, I hoped to catch Rocco on his lunch break.

My Satnav told me that ContraMed was close to the cathedral. I parked in a nearby multi-storey, bunged three hours on the car, and crossed over the busy dual carriageway to College Road. Historic three storey buildings swept around College Green like wise old owls. Among the solicitors and accountants, the offices of ContraMed.

I stood outside, took out my phone and dialled Rocco's number. He answered, sounding bright and pleased to hear from me.

"Are you free for lunch?" Stunned by the revelation that Heather Bowen had been leant on, my voice contained a strained, shaky note.

"Erm— not really."

"That's a pity."

"Sorry, Thursday madness. Cock-up after cock-up."

I glanced skywards, wondering which office he worked in. It was too much to hope that he'd glance out of the window and see me standing there. "Never mind. Another time." I wanted to sound cool, not brave and disappointed.

"Molly, has something happened?"

"I have to talk to you."

"Where are you?"

"In the street, outside. Look."

A head popped up, startled and wide-eyed. "Bloody hell. Be with you in a minute."

I love surprises. Rocco didn't. I could tell straightaway that I'd struck a bum note. His jollity was too forced, the smile too stretched. A quick peck on the cheek and then, with one hand crooked under my elbow, he propelled me away from the office and back in the direction of the main road and Edward Elgar's statue.

"What's happened then?"

I looked at him, wondering exactly the same. Were we only in tune when we were sharing a bed, talking about the dead? Would it be impossible for us to go on a date, to have dinner, shop together, share friends? The visit to Hereford cathedral seemed an age ago and look how that had ended?

"I'll tell you the details later. If you're not too busy." I loathed the snarky vibe in my tone.

"Sure," he said, returning to his laid back, 'no offence taken' persona.

"At mine."

"I'm honoured." He really looked it. His eyes lit up with pleasure.

"I'll cook."

"I'll bring a bottle. Apologies, but I really have to go." He dropped a kiss on the top of my head and walked swiftly back. I watched him all the way, right up to the second he bounded up the steps and disappeared from view.

At least he worked where he said he did.

With three hours on the clock, and nothing in the fridge, I walked straight to the nearest food shop in the centre of town. It was so hot outside and so cool inside, I fancied climbing into the nearest freezer.

Unable to get the vision of Childe having a quietly firm word in Heather's ear, I drifted down the aisles, not really thinking what I was doing or what Rocco would enjoy eating. I scooped prawns into my basket and put them back. I picked up a ready meal and put that back too. Playing it safe, I collected lots of different salads, bread, chicken, expensive butter, and fresh coriander because I liked it. For no reason at all, I added a pot of cream. For every reason in the world, I selected a bottle of white wine and one of red. I didn't know whether or not Rocco drank wine. I had a bottle of vodka at home and some beer so he could have them if he preferred. It never occurred to me that he would drive home. Tonight, he was mine. I needed him.

Staggering out of the shop, I heard a voice shout my name. I turned in surprise.

"Edie?" I barely recognised Chancer's wife. Rail thin, big-eyed, the elusive vulnerability that had made her so attractive was now replaced by tragic fragility. At any second, she looked as if she might shatter before my eyes. Dust to dust and ashes to ashes.

"Yes," she said shyly, grateful almost. "I'm so sorry to hear your terrible news."

"Thank you." I touched her bare arm, trying not recoil. She was all pale bone and sinew and I wondered if she were ill. If this was what marriage break-up did to people, I was glad to be unattached. "Where are the children?"

"With Mum and Dad." She leant in close. There was a sour odour on her breath. "You've heard about me and Tris?"

"I have. I'm sad for you."

"Oh Molly," she said, big eyes swimming with tears. "I don't suppose you have time for a coffee."

"Actually, I do."

Chapter 43

"So you see, he doesn't mean to be unkind. I think he gets it from his father."

The type of man who'd cut your throat over dinner and continue eating, I'd always thought. "Stephen scared the hell out of me, but Tris?" I pulled a face. "A prankster who sometimes takes things too far but—"

Her eyes welled with tears again. "You don't believe me."

"Oh, Edie, of course, I believe you. I'm—well, taken aback."

"It was only the once he hit me."

We were sitting in an Italian eatery off the Crowngate, where they don't mind if you take five years to drink a coffee.

I put a hand on either side of my temples. What went on behind closed doors was anyone's guess, but this was so far from left field, I couldn't take it in. The Chancer I knew was a laugh, could be a little bit cruel verbally, but never in the way Edie described. Besides, I was still digesting the events of the morning.

"He was drunk." She said it as if this were a mitigating factor.

I swallowed, thought of my sister, nodded as if I understood. What was strange, Edie didn't slag him off. I would have run out of expletives by now. "Last time I saw Chancer, he—"

"When?" Edie bolted forward, salivating for news.

She doesn't want to split up, I realised. No way. If someone hit me: THAT. WOULD. BE. IT. "I don't remember exactly. Not long ago. At Zach's."

Her eyebrows drew together in concern. "How is he?"

Terrific question. Evasive, shifty and detached would make the perfect answer. "He's dealing with it. Obviously, Nate, too, feels a terrible sense of loss." In his very own special way, I thought cynically. "We all do."

"Sorry," she flashed an embarrassed smile. "I meant Tris."

"Oh, um—" Confounded, I said, "Would you like another Americano?"

"Can't. Makes me dizzy."

I was feeling fairly dizzy myself. Had I stumbled through a time warp into soap opera land? She was so bloody self-obsessed, I could scream. Edie's wet eyes stared at me, in anticipation.

"Chancer was his usual effervescent self." Mean of me but it was, at least, the truth.

Dejected, Edie ran long fingers through her hair, twisting and turning, pulling and tugging, the very picture of a wronged woman. "No offence," she said, but I think he always cared more about Zach than me."

"That's silly."

"Is it? Zach came first, I suppose."

"They've known each for a very long time and, as you know, Chancer always stood by Zach, which was really good of him. My brother has been through a lot, Edie."

"And so have I." She snivelled, stifling a dry sob.

I forced my best sympathetic smile. I had coffee breath and the beginnings of a headache. When couples split it was usually a fifty-fifty affair. I didn't want to be dragged into this.

"Edie, I have to ask you."

"Yes?"

"Who called time on the marriage?" I knew what Chancer told me, but I wanted to hear what Edie had to say.

She bit her lip. The tip of her nose glowed red. Equally weak and vulnerable, she reminded me of a newborn bunny.

"It's none of my business. I shouldn't have asked."

"No," she said, with a level look. "You have every right. Tris filed for a divorce."

"Right," I said, perplexed.

Her face twisted in sudden anger. "Said I was a needy bitch."

Had Chancer stolen the epithet from my brother? 'Needy Edie.' It seemed unnecessarily cruel.

"Problem is," she said, blowing her nose. "I'd take him back in a heartbeat. Despite everything, I love him, Molly."

"Can't you go to counselling, or something?"

I was stumbling around, out of my depth. I was also mindful of the clock ticking, the need to pick up my car, get home and cook a fabulous dinner for Rocco.

"That's what Zach suggested." Really? I didn't think my

brother would be that perceptive. "Mediation forms the initial part of proceedings," Edie continued. "I thought it would help but Tris views it as a formality."

"Surely, it's not a done deal?" Although why she would want to stay with a man who thumped her escaped me, and that forced a big question: could Edie be lying?

"You really think so?" Her eyes swam with hope and gratitude. If I wasn't careful, she'd latch on to me and never let go.

I made my excuses to leave. Edie scraped back her chair. "We'll stay in touch, yeah?"

"Great," I lied.

Walking back up through town and past the Guildhall, I wondered if Scarlet had fought to save her marriage to Nate.

Driving home, my mobile rang: Mum. Immediately, I thought of the previous evening.

"Hi," I said warily. "I'm on the road."

She caught her breath. "Hands free?"

"Yup."

Her sigh of relief was audible. "Everything all right?"

Nothing was all right. I pushed the sun visor down.

"You still there?"

"I am."

"Were you at ours last night?"

So I'd been spotted. Had to be my dad. He never missed a thing. "Briefly."

"Why didn't you come in?"

I was thinking how to lie and got the distinct impression that my mother was thinking how to tell the truth. "You had company. Who was it, incidentally?" I'd aimed for a breezy tone and missed it by a mile.

"The man I told you about."

"Dad's old colleague, Mallis?"

"He didn't stay long."

"Right."

"You'd have been welcome."

Impenetrable silence filled the car. I could hardly make out that my visit was fleeting if I expressed concern for what I'd witnessed.

"As long as you're coping." My mother tailed off clumsily.

I assured her I was. When I said goodbye, I knew that enquiring about the state of my health wasn't the reason she'd called.

I was in strange waters and it frightened me.

Chapter 44

"**Y**ou have to go."
   "I don't do funerals."
   "Neither do I but I'm not going to miss our sister's. For God's sake, Zach."

I was trying to prepare a fancy salad with couscous and glazed chicken, well outside my range of culinary expertise. At this rate we'd be eating at midnight.

"I suppose I could hang around outside."

"Skulking in the graveyard isn't going to cut it. Think of Mum and Dad's feelings." So little dinged on Zach's emotional database, I doubted anything I said would persuade him.

"Churches creep me out. Couldn't I just come to the wake?"

I gave a cross sigh. Zach hadn't suddenly decided not to attend the funeral. He never intended to go. Just the mention of family gathering, and he was off. "And get pissed? I don't think so. Look, I have to go. I'll speak to you tomorrow."

Fortunately, Rocco turned up later than expected. "Got caught up in a meeting." He set a bottle of red down on the kitchen table. It had a distinguished-looking label and a silver medal award from a proper wine club.

"Would you mind opening it?"

"Not at all, but first—" He wrapped his arms around me, tilted my chin and kissed me long and softly on the lips. "Better." He smiled warmly. We stayed like that for a little bit, which was lovely. All the tetchy feelings I'd harboured care of Edie and Zach vanished. He drew away. "Where's the corkscrew?"

I pointed to a drawer, watched as he deftly uncorked the wine and poured out two glasses. He handed me mine and we chinked and sipped. It tasted glorious, at least as good as some of the stuff Dad served up. Dad, I thought, my mood clouding. I hadn't heard from him since our last frosty exchange. I began to tell Rocco about my morning.

"Shall we eat first?" He seemed to want to extend the moment, to engage in something uncomplicated that didn't require answers that inevitably led to more questions. It frustrated the hell out of me. I'd made a vital discovery. It felt like a disservice to Scarlet to put food before justice.

We talked about books he'd read – I wasn't much of a reader – and films, which, for me, was safer ground. It turned out that Rocco was a blues fan, which wasn't really my thing. I was more of a *Florence and the Machine* and *Adele* kind of gal, although Scarlet and me had been crazy about *Dido* in her heyday.

"That was great," Rocco said, leaning back. We'd moved through to the sitting room and the sofa. "Seriously good." He took a long swallow of wine, looked around the room. Feet firmly planted apart. Friendly. Open. Expansive. I didn't care for the way he took control, occupied the space and set the pace. "You can tell you're in the antiques business."

"Makes it sound grander than it is. Posh up-cycling is closer to the truth."

"You do yourself down. Why is that?"

The hairs along my arms collectively stood erect. I took a gigantic swig and almost missed my mouth. I quickly wiped a dribble of wine from my chin. "Habit," I said.

He viewed me with such focused concentration I dropped my gaze, keen to escape. Rocco would make a damn fine interrogator.

"What did you want to tell me?"

I wasn't sure I did anymore.

"You don't have to say anything if you don't want to." He rested his hand lightly on my thigh, waited a beat.

Oldest trick in the book: no pressure, no sweat, open your mouth. The gleam in his eyes gave him away. He wanted to know all right. "Heather Bowen was leant on."

"By whom?"

"The police."

"Seriously?"

I told him what she told me.

"That's pretty bloody awful. Poor woman."

I agreed, although I suspected that Heather Bowen, a strong individual, would be all right in the end. She'd recover and build a new life. The same could not be said for the rest of us.

"Not sure how to say this," Rocco said, "but is it remotely possible that your dad had a hand in it? I mean I could understand him wanting your sister to come out of this with dignity and her reputation intact."

A lick of fear, like flame, scorched my skin. I had to admit that the thought had crossed my mind, not that I cared to openly admit it.

"Rocco," I said sternly, "it's not his way to influence an investigation. His integrity wouldn't allow it. Besides, even if he wanted to, he no longer has that type of leverage." *I can't fix everything, woman.*

"Yes, I see," he said, although he didn't particularly sound as if he did. "Do you have access to Scarlet's stuff? You might find answers there."

"Already done," I said crisply.

"Seems you've looked at all the angles." He flicked an apologetic smile. "Sorry, I'm not really helping. This is all way above my head." Reaching across, he placed a hand on my arm, his touch solid, dependable and reassuring, only I wasn't entirely reassured.

*

"Here," Rocco said, "Let me."

Eyes fixed on mine; he unbuttoned my shirt, slipped it off slowly, his lips gliding along my shoulders up my neck, kissing the side of my mouth, my face, my lips, reverently. He talked so low it was almost a whisper. Every move measured. Tender. Every touch weighed. Light. Intense. I felt shy, like this was the first time between us, the first time ever.

Afterwards, we lay in the dark, arms circling each other,

the moment so perfect, I wept. For this. For me. For Scarlet. And he let me.

With stars twinkling through the Velux window above our heads, I drifted off; fell into the deepest sleep I'd known since Scarlet's death. I don't know how long I'd been out for the count. When I woke, bright moonlight shone like a spotlight, illuminating the room. I reached out for Rocco, fingers grasping empty space. My hand dropped to the sheet and pillow, both cold as ice.

Puzzled, I slipped out of bed, crossed the landing and looked out of the front bedroom window to the gravelled parking space. Rocco's Mini was still there.

Dragging on a robe, I checked the bathroom then went downstairs, through the sitting room and the kitchen. The back door ajar, a sliver of light crept in and onto the kitchen floor.

I slipped outside, tried to focus. The night was warm and sticky, bearing down, moonlight encircling the garden in a passionate embrace. I strained my eyes to see, pulse racing, primed for something unholy to strike from the shadows.

"Rocco," I called. From down the path, he emerged, naked apart from his boxers. "What are you doing?" What the fuck?

"Getting some air."

"Without clothes on?"

"I'm decent. Nobody can see me."

I inclined my head, looked up at the houses on either side. Mercifully, windows open, curtains closed. "Half the town's population can see you."

"Lucky them." He flashed a grin, slid his arm around my waist and gave it a squeeze. "You coming in, or what?"

Chapter 45

Back to his ridiculously sunny self, the eccentricity of the night before forgotten, Rocco left for work, no more said about his nocturnal adventure.

He stooped over the bed, took my face in his hands, kissed me. "Have a good day."

"See you tonight?"

"Can't, babe. Got some work to catch up on. I'll give you a ring, yeah?"

I huddled under the sheets, fully intending to go back to sleep. Thick headed from drinking wine, scratchy and out of sorts, I gave up, got up and cleared up. As soon as it hit 8 a.m. I called home.

Dad answered. Difficult to ascertain his mood, there was no mention of our disagreement. Ill at ease, I asked how things were, more specifically how Mum was.

"Up and down. You know how it is. She's busy with funeral arrangements after Nate phoned last night, out of the blue, and asked if your mother could take over. He's finding it all extremely difficult. I'm worried about him, to be honest."

Don't be. "Oh?"

"He talked about dissolving the partnership."

Good. "Understandable in the circumstances." I bit down hard on my teeth, briefly endangering the enamel. "There are plenty of other decent architects you can work with, Dad."

"Won't be the same." He sounded properly cast down. "It feels like another link to Scarlet broken." I felt bad for my dad, but I'd have to be flayed alive before I whispered a word of Nate's affair. It would break his trust and his heart. "Nate's got it into his head that he needs to go travelling." From Dad's tone, I could tell he thought it a daft idea. To my mind, nowhere could be far enough away. "Which reminds me, could you collect Zach for the funeral?"

"He's coming?"

"Of course, he's coming," Dad said, put out. "I spoke to him late last night." I pinched myself. Two slippery individuals had actually taken my advice seriously or, in Nate's case, threat. I told Dad I'd gladly chauffeur my brother. He gave me the details: funeral at a local crematorium, wake at the house. Mum had got her way. Cremation not burial; I wondered how Scarlet would feel about that.

"Hang on a second, I think Mum wants a word."

I briefly closed my eyes and braced myself for a conversation I didn't wish to have.

"Molly, darling, how are you doing?"

It was the best I'd heard her since Scarlet's death. "So-so."

We discussed flowers and readings. I chose a hymn, *The Day Thou Gavest*' because we'd sung it at school, and it was Scarlet's favourite.

"Do you think we should have something more uplifting on the way out?" Mum said, which took me by surprise. "I was thinking *Morning Has Broken.*"

"Great idea. What about dress code? I don't have anything in black that's really suitable."

"How about that rather nice navy wrap-over with the short sleeves?"

"Not too informal?"

"I don't think so. Scarlet always liked you in it."

Then it was good enough for me. We chatted some more, mostly about the caterers she'd hired.

"Have you any idea of numbers?"

"A lot," she said, without quantifying it.

After the rotten press Scarlet had received, I wasn't so certain Mum's expectations of a large turnout would be met.

I drifted around the house, took a shower to cool down and instantly wanted to take another. The second time, I had a little cry as cool water cascaded down my face.

Adrift. Lethargic. Gloomy. It felt as if something were brewing, like a low front coming in, or a seasonal 'flu epidemic that would put me in bed for a month. Sadness swamped me, and I worried obsessively about what to write on the card to accompany my flowers for Scarlet. A couple of efforts on rough paper were screwed up and dropped in the bin.

Scarlet's death might be driving me potty, but it didn't affect my ability to function. I spent the rest of the morning mentally copying and pasting pieces of information, including short calls sent from payphones from the hospital to Richard Bowen's mobile an hour before his death, Scarlet's reason to shut up Bowen, the various police connections that seemed to run everywhere and nowhere. Finally, I asked myself whether steering a grieving widow down a particular path amounted to corruption.

Unable to make headway, I poured myself a glass of fruit juice, and padded outside, walking barefoot across the grass and, thinking I should get the mower out and give it a trim and water the plants, most of which were already frizzled by the sun. With no fixed idea in mind, I stepped onto the old fire escape and staircase that connected to my home office. The treads felt cold, almost damp, beneath my feet. By contrast, the office was stuffy with heat, oppressively so. I chucked open a window, let out a number of half-dead flies.

I never left my laptop in the office, which was great for security, but bad for order. Way too tempting to throw every piece of paper I possessed on top of the desk instead of filing it neatly away. To the untrained eye, it looked like chaos. To me, there was an unwritten symmetry, which was why I knew in an instant that someone had been through my stuff. A sharp blast of fear chilled my skin. It could be the individual who had already invaded my personal space. It could also be someone close. Maybe they were one and the same.

Rocco.

Chapter 46

Truth can be cruel. Rocco Noble didn't want to get inside my knickers because he fancied me. He'd had an agenda from the start.

Anger consumed me. Hurt would come later. I'd never entirely trusted him. Why would someone as alarmingly good-looking as Rocco Noble be interested in plain old me?

At teatime, I was outside Worcester Cathedral, pretending to be a tourist. From the yard I had a good view of ContraMed. Who went in and, more importantly, who went out. I was taking a punt: Rocco could be one of those guys that worked at his desk long into the night.

He'd mentioned an apartment in town. I'd no idea where. I didn't know if he flat shared, had another woman in his life, or lived alone. I'd guessed he was a singleton; too solitary to be anything else, but what did I know? Did he travel to work by car or bike? Please God, he walked.

The front door swung open. Two young women tripped down the steps, spilling out onto the street, laughing and joking, followed by a middle-aged guy in a suit. The second he hit the pavement he reached up and, with an exasperated expression, loosened his tie, obviously glad to see the back of the office for a couple of days. Minutes passed. I wondered whether Rocco had taken the afternoon off to work at home.

I tried to soak up the sun and achieve a sense of calm and control when purposeful footsteps, instantly recognisable, clicked against the pavement. I sharpened my gaze, caught a snatch of Rocco striding to the end of the street, turning left, pausing by an antique shop next to a pedestrian crossing.

Sliding into a group of office workers, far enough away not to be noticed, near enough to keep Rocco in my sights, I followed as he crossed the road and over the square, and belted, head down, along the main road leading out of town.

Ducking down a side street, towards the Shambles, he quickened his step. Fewer cars. More people. I had to be careful. What I would say if he twisted round and caught me snooping, I hadn't the faintest. He walked so quickly; I was jolted along like a trailer towed across rough ground.

We were in Old Worcester. Fifteenth and sixteenth-century half-timbered houses and hostelries clamoured drunkenly together. There were pubs and clubs, cafes and restaurants.

A car horn made me start. Didn't so much as flicker on Rocco's emotional spectrum. Just kept walking. No deviation. Heading – he had to be – for the place he called home.

The road widened, cobbles under foot, a car park on the left, shops on the right. Suddenly, Rocco jinked right and disappeared. I waited several beats then followed. In between a barber's and wine bar, a tall wrought-iron gate with spikes on top that opened out onto a short yard and red front door, which was ajar. On the adjoining wall, an intercom with two names and numbers revealed that Rocco Noble lived in number three.

Giving him enough time to sling off his jacket, maybe change out of his work clothes, and settle down for the evening, I pushed open the door and found myself at the bottom of a grand staircase that smelt of old polish, dead flowers and ancient lives. Sunlight drifted through the dust from stained glass windows. Flattening my back against the wall, crab-like, taking tiny steps, I crept upstairs, crossing one small landing and then up again, slowly, and within sight of another vertiginous flight to go. Pulse jackhammering in time with my knees I hung back.

Rocco was smart. When confronted he'd have a ready answer. I pictured him all sympathetic, saying that grief had made me hallucinate. Why on earth would he go through my things, he'd cry? And I'd come across like needy Edie and feel an idiot.

But I wasn't delusional. I was no fool, though it hurt to confess I'd become a fool for him.

At the top I reached a wide corridor. Two doors opposite, both open. Snatches of conversation. Male. Rocco and another man. Voices drifting from the apartment on the right like smoke on water.

"It's really no problem, man. Anytime … No, can't, not tonight, mate. Hope you feel better soon … Sorry, what was that?"

Before my mind gave way, I shot up the last step and, instinctively, sped into Rocco Noble's apartment on the left and into what, I assumed, would be a sitting room, which turned out to be a spacious open plan kitchen and living area with a view of the street below. I planted myself in front of an old fireplace over which hung a large limited edition print of some woman called Esther. She wore a purple dress, hitched up invitingly to reveal bare legs and feet, her face obscured by thick dark hair. Mysterious. Sexy.

I paid no attention to the furnishings. Couldn't tell you whether the decor was beige, neutral or screaming red. Didn't register whether the kitchen was a mess with piles of washing-up, or it was clean and tidy. Every blood vessel in my body focused on the doorway. At any second Rocco would enter, full of swagger and confidence and lies.

I stood up straight. Tried to arrange my face into a picture of cold composure. My fingers clenched. My knees, defiant, refused to stay still and steady. Tension held my head in a vice.

Any moment now ...

Noise. Not of Rocco's return, but the door to the apartment slamming shut.

I started forward. Was Rocco playing games, or what?

I tore back to the window and looked down to the street below. Rocco, with his long stride, crossed over to the opposite side, heading nonchalantly towards the centre of town, oblivious. With a sports bag slung over one shoulder, he wore sweats and trainers. One thing was certain: he wasn't working late.

I slid down onto the sofa, a slab-sided leather thing and viewed the room for clues. Widescreen TV, modest and not too imposing; small pine dining table and two chairs underneath the window; the main cooking section barely used. No dirty plates waiting to be done or put away. There were no photographs, no visible clues about who Rocco was, or where he came from. Apart from the sexy painting, no other art adorned the crooked walls.

I stood up. On a hunch, I felt around the seat and found the mechanism to release it into a bed, which, when extended, could comfortably sleep two. Either Rocco regularly entertained guests or, for some reason, chose to sleep there. A quick feel around told me that there were no coins, slips of paper or objects hiding in the upholstery.

I opened drawers and cupboards; I went through the rubbish bin, recently emptied by the look of it, and found an old shopping list detailing coffee, milk, pizza, loo rolls and fruit. Assuming it was Rocco's handwriting, the letters were small and stylish and sloped to the right. I imagined him writing with a lazy flourish.

The fridge contained a half empty carton of milk, two energy drinks, a slab of Cheddar, real butter, half a Pork pie, wilting lettuce, a pack of tomatoes and a cucumber that had gone squishy. The freezer section contained oven chips and frozen peas and two loaves of white sliced bread.

A trawl through a wastepaper basket unearthed a sales voucher for a sweatshirt from Animal, an invoice for a dental check-up in Worcester, a receipt for the bottle of wine he'd brought with him to my house and a balance enquiry from an ATM machine that proved he had two hundred and sixty-four pounds and twenty-three pence in a bank account. A drawer full of information told me that he paid council tax, his energy supplier was SSE, water care of Severn Trent, and he had a phone contract with Vodaphone. Viewing the evidence, he came across as a regular guy. So what was he doing in my garden, in my office, in my handbag? It took me seconds to open his laptop. It took me another couple to work out that, without a password, access was barred.

Back out in the corridor, I opened the door to a bathroom that housed a loo, sink and shower – no bath. Rocco, I noticed, squeezed toothpaste from the middle. He used an electric toothbrush to accentuate his dazzling smile. A mirror-fronted cabinet revealed shaving foam, razor, painkillers, plasters, deodorant, after-shave, condoms and Calvin Klein's eau de parfum, Eternity. I flipped the lid off his current shower gel, held it to my nose, the fragrance whacking my olfactory nerves instantaneously. A dark blue towelling robe hung on the back of the door. No signs of another occupant, still less a female presence. Everything, so far, shrieked blatant masculinity.

Another door off the corridor revealed a small room consumed by a wardrobe and set of drawers. Quick examination told me that he had two suits, work affairs, three pairs of jeans, loads of T-shirts and six smart shirts, one recently purchased and still in the bag from 'Next.' He had one pair of smart black shoes, the rest were trainers and pumps. Underwear: Jack Wills – I already knew this but looked anyway. There were no real surprises.

About to enter the last room, I let my hand dance above the doorknob. What might I find? What good would come of it? Shouldn't I leave while I could? And wouldn't *I* be furious at such a personal invasion? Then I remembered my office, the way the papers had been rearranged. Someone sneaking. Someone spying. Someone like Rocco with his blasted dead drops, his blatant curiosity, offbeat manner and scary imagination. Tightening my resolve and my grip, I twisted and threw the door open wide.

The pause button in my brain flicked on and I stood frozen.

Chapter 47

Iknew about incident rooms following major investigations, how they became the hub, the visual memorial of a victim's life. To be honest, most of my knowledge on this score came from television dramas and documentaries, usually connected to murder cases. If I had to mock-up a scene, this would be it.

A large whiteboard covered one wall. On it were maps, location shots, photographs and names. Arrows, drawn heavily in black marker pen, connected these to addresses and phone numbers. Resembled the work of a mad mathematician. Blitzed with thoughts I was unable to process; I was drawn to a picture of a woman in her mid to late twenties with laughing green eyes. Wild dark hair framed a strong-featured face that told me she knew her own mind. Her lips were sensuous. You could imagine playful words dancing out of her mouth. She wore studs in her nose and above her right eyebrow. Her clothes were layered, peacock bright, mad and adventurous. Bohemian. Vibrant. The pose was unstudied, spontaneous, as though she was unaware of being snapped. But here she was

243

in Rocco Noble's bedroom. No, not in it, *stalking* it. Who is she?

My mind raced in a ton of different and wildly divergent directions. I'd held my breath for so long, firecrackers showered before my eyes. Breathing deeply, I tore my gaze from the mysterious woman to the maps. One featured Winchcombe, an Anglo-Saxon market town seven or so miles from Cheltenham, another: Box, in Wiltshire, not far from Bath. How the disparate pieces of information fitted together, I couldn't fathom. In shock, vision working independently of my mind, my brain locked onto a name written that stood out beyond all others. Written in the same hand as had appeared on Rocco's shopping list: *Scarlet Jay.*

Terror took a pot shot at me, caught me smack between the eyes. Sweat exploded from every pore in my skin. If only my sister could speak to me from the space between the living and the dead and give me a steer in the right direction.

I dragged my eyes back to the other names: Rod Napier, Zach Napier and;

Me.

Swallowing hard, I turned to a mess of newspaper cuttings pinned to a corkboard. Only the headlines made it to my brain: YOUNG WOMAN VANISHES ON NEW YEAR'S EVE. MISSING WOMAN FROM GLOUCESTER FOUND DEAD. MYSTERY WOMAN IDENTIFIED AS MISSING DREA TEMPLE. WOMAN IN DISUSED MINE DROWNED.

The tattoo on Rocco's arm. The special girl. Feeing faint, I shot out a hand, placed it flat against the adjoining wall to steady myself. How did Drea Temple fit into his life? And how come my family were included in his macabre wall of fame?

Whole paragraphs of newsprint blurred before my eyes. Why her? Why Scarlet? Why me? Three women and two of them dead. Was I standing in the lair of a fantasist, or something worse?

Inescapably, I saw how I'd been chosen, groomed and seduced. All those questions and suggestions he'd tried to persuade me to read as concern and interest. When Rocco had delivered flowers to my parents' home, he'd been checking them out. Immediately, Lenny's warning boxed my ears. Rage coursed through my veins at how I'd defended him and all the while he'd been screwing me – and for what? Did everything come back to Scarlet? Was she pivotal? Move over Charlie Binns. Drea Temple now appeared central to the reason Scarlet had died.

I straightened up, reached for my phone, held it as steady as I could, and snapped everything on both walls. Then I did what I wished I'd done the second I stepped inside Rocco's flat: I got the hell out.

Chapter 48

I reached home, locked the doors, closed the curtains and downloaded the images from my phone to my laptop. The hot evening choked me. To sharpen up, I selected Grey Goose from a set of miniatures and drank it neat from the bottle. Ice-burn, blood and fire.

The first image contained photographs and newspaper cuttings. According to the Gloucester Echo, Drea Temple had gone missing from Cheltenham on New Year's Eve, ten years previously, and was found in a disused mine near Bath six months later. She'd last been sighted in Winchcombe. I knew the market town well because we'd visited often to go to the pubs and visit Sudeley Castle. A tourist destination, it was also popular with walkers travelling along the Cotswold Way.

A more detailed account revealed that Drea and friends had rented a cottage. This tallied with a photograph of a stone terraced dwelling in Vineyard Street, a popular place for rentals and steeped in history with ancient links to the vineyards belonging to the monks of Winchcombe Abbey. The only other picture: The White Hart, an old coaching inn. Recently tarted up, it bore little resemblance to the place it was a decade or more before. Beside it, Rocco had simply inscribed three question marks. Next to the photograph of the cottage, Rocco had written: *where Drea was last seen.* He'd also dated it and scribbled *New Year's Eve,* Drea's body had been found in June. She'd gone off the radar for months, which, to my mind, didn't necessarily mean that she'd been dead all that time. Rocco didn't seem to think so either. He wrote: *Where did she go? Who with?*

I turned to a later article in the Bath Chronicle, which reported that Drea's last resting place was the largest stone mine in the country. It consisted of a sixty- mile network of tunnels, parts of which were so unstable that it was illegal to enter. Despite this, there were numerous entrances, which could be accessed from Box Hill. And people did; from curious cavers to naïve youngsters wanting to party. Ownership belonged primarily to a building materials company and the MOD. In short, only idiots would enter. Initial reports made no mention of cause of death. I recognised that this was standard procedure, at least until a post-mortem was carried out. Dad had also told me that sometimes, with murder cases, for example, police kept their cards close and withheld information in the initial stages because that one vital clue could be a game-changer when nailing a culprit.

With the place shut to all personnel, including the employees of the owners of the site, only government environmental advisers were allowed in to monitor the progress of two species of protected bats. It was on one such visit that Drea's body was found, by chance. What were the odds of making such a discovery?

More perplexing, a later article in a national newspaper reported that cause of death had been drowning. Nowhere was there mention of water in the mine. I was chewing this over when my eyes snagged first on Rocco's writing: *Cranial injuries cause of death?* Secondly, the name of the Senior Investigating Officer: Detective Chief Inspector Clive Mallis, my dad's old colleague.

A flicker of fear lit me up inside.

Feverishly, I returned to the earlier newspaper cuttings, read more slowly, looked more carefully. Phones apparently didn't work at such depths, which made descent into the mine even more precarious. Abundantly clear, the company who owned most of the site had done everything in their power to warn people off and block up a number of entrances while ensuring that rescue teams could enter so that people had a fighting chance of making their way out.

Unable to draw conclusions that didn't scare the life out of me, I got up, went in search of more booze, fished out the half bottle of vodka that had loitered underneath the sink for a year or more. Needing to dull the shock, without clouding my judgement, I poured a healthy measure and topped it up with fresh orange juice. One big brainstorming gulp later, I forced myself to return to the screen. With creeping dread, my finger hovered over the second attachment. Click click, I was in.

The names read like a cast list in a popular television series.

I read, as if in a trance, until my eyes shot to Scarlet's name. Below it was newspaper pieces, some of them printed from the internet, that I recognised only too well. Why would Rocco Noble be this interested in Scarlet's life and, more importantly, her death?

In a sort of inverted family tree, there were photographs of me. No snaps of Zach or Dad, but below my brother's name, Rocco had written: *former drug addict, lives in a commune. 38 years old. Son of Roderick Napier, police officer and disinterested bastard.* I practically swayed off my seat. Either Rocco had asked me questions about my family, already knowing the answers and seeking to corroborate them, his interest entirely fake, or he had actively pumped me for information. Noted beside Zach's name, his mobile phone number with three questions: *Did he know Drea? Was he the mystery man? Was he the last to see her alive?*

Now I understood why Rocco had snatched up my phone, why he'd gone through my stuff, why he'd spoken to Zach. He was digging for dirt.

I sat back, tried and failed to tame the sick sensation in the pit of my stomach. Ten years ago, I was travelling, and Scarlet was working at a hospital in Edinburgh. That year, Dad pretty much had a nervous breakdown and Zach went into rehab after one narcotic trip too many. A case of clean up or check out. Forever. He'd appealed to Mum – Dad was too unwell – to give him one last chance. She had and, at their insistence, he'd embarked on a brutal regime of supervised withdrawal. Blood pulsed through my brain at the implication. Had Zach and Drea shared a common passion:

drugs? Is this how their paths had crossed? But what was Rocco's game? Why the tableau, the drama, the deception?

Snatches of conversation rippled through my mind. Too smart to question me openly, Rocco had sneaked into my bed and into my life. Tricked me. Duped me. Used me. Seduction and honey trap sounded soft and lovely and sexy. It was nothing like that. Rocco had betrayed me. A shameless opportunist, he'd exploited Scarlet's death and taken advantage of my vulnerability. Shame flamed my cheeks at my own stupidity for falling for it.

The third attachment contained location shots that included the interior of the mine. Dark, brooding, with sheer walls, some reaching up for what looked like hundreds of feet. I scoured each photograph for underground lakes and pools and saw none. As if to confirm this, Rocco had written: *No water visible. Body moved?*

I thought about that. It implied that Drea had been murdered. As a place to conceal a body, it was a clever choice and that meant the killer was smart too. But I was running ahead of myself.

I logged out, reached for mental footholds that were as slippery and ungraspable as the sides of the mine.

A glance at my watch confirmed it was late. Scarlet's funeral was in three days. No way could I keep this to myself until it was over, and a respectable period of mourning had passed. Without hesitation, I reached for my phone.

"Dad," I said as soon as he answered.

"Molly, sweetheart, how are you?"

"I need your help." My words came out all thick and shaky

as if someone had filled my mouth with glue and sand. "Can I come over?"

"Have you been drinking?"

"No, well not much, yes, a bit."

"Stay where you are."

"But—"

"I'll come to you. See you in a minute. And Molly—"

"Yeah?"

"Make yourself some coffee. Make it strong."

Chapter 49

"Who the hell is this man?" My dad's voice was dead-weight.

We sat side-by-side on my sofa, the coffee table with two mugs and my laptop in front of us. I was purple with embarrassment. My father had every right to disapprove of me starting a sexual relationship in the wake of Scarlet's death.

I'd never seen him look so furious and we hadn't started on the heavy stuff I'd downloaded to my computer.

I gave him a verbal account of how I'd met Rocco and when; his fixation on some random woman's death and forced connections to our family, including Scarlet. The warning signs were plain to see. Dad's skin drained to the colour of sour milk. Thin blue veins in his neck pulsed, but it was his eyes that did me in. They were narrow and sharp and accusing. I felt condemned.

"Did he hurt you?"

I was insistent that he hadn't.

"Where does he live?"

"In Worcester but his grandmother left him a house here in Malvern, up on the Wyche."

Something unknowable passed behind his eyes and his jaw tensed. I guess he felt threatened. His patch. His daughter. His family. My eyes widened as a creepy thought took shape in my head. Dad caught the vibe. "We've found the culprit responsible for breaking into your house."

I pressed a hand to my mouth. Oh my God.

"Write down both addresses – and where this creep works." It wasn't an ask, but an order. I wrote on a notepad, ripped out the page, handed it to him. Without a glance, he shoved it in the back pocket of his jeans. "The stuff you found in his flat," he said quietly, slipping out his spectacles. "Let's see it."

I took a breath, leaned across, opened one attachment, and got up, walked off a little, gave him space. He sat, fused to the screen, without a flicker of visible emotion in his expression.

"Next," he said. Deadpan.

I closed one attachment, opened the second, and when he'd read that, the third. I studied his face, waiting and primed for a strong reaction at seeing his old colleague's name there in black and white. Not a flicker. When he finished, he took off his glasses, rubbed his eyes and leaned back, staring ahead. Silence, as suffocating as a bonfire on a hot summer's day, enveloped us.

"Dad?"

He leant forward, steepling his fingers over his nose and mouth, and briefly closed his eyes. Confusion rampaged through me. My insides curdled, blood thickened. Eventually, he let his hands fall.

"Right." He spoke as if he'd come to a massive decision, like he was about to tell me something that would explain absolutely everything, including the reason for Scarlet's death. I realised I was holding my breath.

"This is all my fault," he said.

No, no, no. A fresh current of fear jolted through me. I couldn't comprehend and, in that moment,, I wasn't sure I wanted to.

"Drea Temple, the missing woman. She was my case. My last case, as it turned out, the one that broke me."

Okay, I thought shakily. That's not so bad. "But how does Rocco Noble fit?"

"Noble is her half-brother."

I was glad to be sitting down. So that explained his obsession – sort of. "And is this how your path crossed with your old colleague, Clive Mallis?"

He nodded. "I picked up the first half of the investigation, Clive, sadly, the second."

"Is Clive still with the police?"

Dad shook his head. "Got out, like me. Works in the antiques trade in Gloucestershire. I never imagined that, ten years later, he'd be offering me his condolences." His eyes were no less hard but this time there were tears in them.

"So, Rocco bore a grudge?"

Dad took his time answering. "Nothing excuses his behaviour."

"But?"

He let out a long sigh. "I didn't take Drea's missing status as seriously as I should have."

Hence Rocco's phrase: *disinterested bastard*. "Doesn't sound like you." My dad was assiduous in all that he did. Ask him to give a hundred per cent and he would, body and soul.

He smiled sadly. "I'd been under a lot of pressure, heading up a number of serious investigations. Ironically, that Christmas—"

"The one before Drea disappeared?"

"Uh-huh, I was given leave, first time in I don't know how long."

I sipped my coffee. "And New Year?"

He flicked a wry smile. "Your mum likened my behaviour at the time to diver's decompression."

I thought back. I had still been travelling through Eastern Europe.

"Anyway," he said, serious again, "I went back to work on 3 January and no sooner than I'm at my desk when I get wind of a missing status report. I didn't exactly jump on it."

"Surely, it wouldn't be unusual to suppose Drea was still enjoying the festivities? I mean if she'd gone to Scotland, New Year there is taken a lot more seriously."

"The thought had crossed my mind."

"But?"

"Even as the days passed and turned into weeks, I'm ashamed to say that I regarded her as a woman who could have gone anywhere with anyone at any time."

"Presumably, based on evidence."

"Based on what I'd established – yes."

"So you made a judgement." Was that such a crime? Isn't that what you were paid to do? As a police officer's daughter, I understood better than most the pressures and fine distinctions that came with running major investigations.

"I did. And I was wrong."

"And if you'd taken it seriously, would she be alive today?"

"Maybe not," he conceded. "I don't know. I'll never know. Put it this way, the family blamed me and so did others."

So that's what had led to his breakdown and retirement. It all dropped snugly into place and I was aghast. This was the first time I'd heard the precise reason why my dad had left the job he loved. I was so wrapped up in my own little world it had passed me by.

"Drea was found on 23 June. I handed in my resignation the week after."

He stared ahead, numb and unreachable and detached. As uncomfortable as I found it, I had more questions.

"Why would Rocco suggest that Zach knew Drea?"

Dad hitched a shoulder. "Drea was a drug-user."

"Could their paths have crossed?"

"Theoretically, but it's tenuous. Zach wasn't the only young man off his face on drugs in Gloucestershire."

It sounded to me as if Rocco was cobbling together evidence to fit his own narrative. I put this to Dad.

"It's not uncommon for a victim's relatives to fixate on a particular line of enquiry or, indeed, on someone they regard as a potential perpetrator." I pinched inside. Wasn't this exactly what I was doing since Scarlet's death? Strain tugged my father's face into a mask.

"What about Rocco's suggestion that Zach was the last person to see her alive?"

"Where's his evidence? Zach was at home with us."

Thank God. "I'm so sorry, Dad, that I wasn't more supportive with Zach."

"You had your own life."

"It must have been hard."

"If I'd been in any other job, it wouldn't have been so bad, but as a copper —" He shook his head in dismay. "There were all sorts of rumours flying around."

"Like what?"

"That I'd turned a blind eye. The best one," he said with a short laugh, "I'd helped myself to confiscated drug supplies and handed them to Zach."

Was this what Heather had alluded to when she talked about digging up the dirt? "God, Dad, how didn't I know this? You never breathed a word."

"About rumours that were lies? What was the point? Anyway, I had your mum to lean on. She was my rock." I'd heard that expression so many times it seemed a phrase devoid of meaning. Out of my dad's mouth, it assumed its original status. I realised what my mother had been forced to put up with. In a flash, I saw her with fresh eyes. Again, I lurched inside for getting things so wrong.

"Should we talk to Zach?"

"About what?"

"About this," I said, gesturing at my laptop.

"No. Zach is still fragile. Always will be."

I hadn't forgotten the way Zach had got antsy with me when I'd pushed him about the reason Scarlet took her own life.

"You don't look happy, Molly."

I wasn't. I wanted to have a grown-up conversation with my brother, but Dad was probably right.

He rested his hand on my knee. "There's nothing more for you to worry about. I'll handle Rocco Noble."

"How?" I said anxiously.

"I'll speak to Stanton again."

"Right," I said, unsettled.

"Promise you won't have anything else to do with Noble?"

"You have my word." The thought of running into him made me queasy.

"And delete those files."

I wasn't at all happy about this. It felt too much like getting rid of the evidence. How else could I confront Rocco if I didn't have the files? I nodded emptily.

"Now." Again, his tone demanded total obedience.

Reluctantly, I did as he said. Neither of us spoke. A thought still tugged at the back of my mind. "Why would Rocco be interested in Scarlet?"

"He wasn't. His interest was simply a means to get to me."

I tiptoed up to my next question as if walking a high wire strung across a canyon. "About Drea."

"Yes?" His eyes were steady.

"Were there any sightings of her between the time she went missing and when she was found?"

"Two. One in Birmingham and another in London."

"Not exactly helpful."

"We followed up but there was no trace of her."

"The newspaper report stated that she'd drowned."

"That's true."

"Wouldn't her lungs have decomposed?"

"Obviously, but the pathologist found the presence of diatoms, or micro-algae in her bone marrow. The only way these could enter would be via the respiratory system."

"Is there water in the mine?"

"No."

"So she'd drowned some place and her body moved?"

"That's the working theory."

"She was murdered then?"

"Not necessarily."

"What about the cranial injuries?"

"Abrasions on the skeleton were identified. Obviously, variables in such cases are immense, but the pathologist concluded that cause of death was drowning."

"Someone drowned her?"

"No evidence to suggest it."

I let out a frustrated sigh. Was he driven solely by what he could prove? I guess, as a former policeman, he was.

"What's inescapable," Dad conceded, "is that someone moved her body, a crime in itself."

"Why would they do that if not for the obvious reason that they'd also killed her?"

Dad broke into a smile at my tenacity. "There was a full investigation, Molly, if that's what's troubling you. We never really got very far and, with the coroner declaring it an open verdict, a decision was made to call it a day." The stress of that dark time was, without doubt still etched upon his face. I knew what he was thinking. My dad, a perfectionist in all things, believed he'd failed Drea's family.

I put my hand over his. "If I hadn't chanced upon Rocco Noble, we wouldn't be having this conversation."

My dad looked at me straight. "Nothing chance about it. That little bastard targeted you deliberately."

Chapter 50

I switched on the TV, watched programmes without listening or understanding. Betrayal, on top of sudden violent loss, had robbed me of my faculties. The oppressive heat of the night didn't help.

I woke with a hangover. I was feverish and queasy and unutterably cold. My legs ached and the inside of my mouth felt sore. A check in the mirror told me my tongue was a mess of mouth ulcers. Unable to develop any thought that was vaguely coherent, I dropped into the shop at lunchtime. Lenny picked up on my sombre mood. No jokes. No gossip. "I'd like to pay my respects on Monday," she said.

"Put a notice in the window before you leave tonight. Say we're closed for the day. Actually, make it two." Could make it a week for all I cared.

"You're sure?"

"Look at the place," I said bitterly. "It's like a morgue." Normally, she'd laugh. We both would. Trade had taken a nosedive since Scarlet. In a small town like this, word got round. Death, however it came calling, was bad for business.

"Molly?"

"Yeah?"

"You look terrible. How are you sleeping?"

"So-so."

Lenny ducked down behind the counter, pulled out her bag, rummaged through it like a Springer Spaniel digging up sand. She fished out a blister pack of pills, offered them to me. I viewed them with suspicion.

"Diazepam," she said.

"Valium?" I took a step back. "No way."

"They're a tiny dose, two milligrams."

"How come you take them?" Lenny didn't seem a likely candidate.

"I'm a tooth-grinder. See?" She tilted her head back and opened her mouth wide, pointing vaguely to a molar. I peered in reluctantly. Caverns and mines sprang to mind. "My dentist prescribed them. Relaxes the jaw, helps you sleep."

I looked at her doubtfully.

"Go on. Big day on Monday."

"I *am* exhausted," I admitted.

"Take them with you," she said, pressing them into my hand.

I drifted around the house for the rest of Saturday, expecting Rocco to call. I'd prepared a show-closer of a speech should he be foolish enough to contact me. He didn't call. He didn't text. He didn't email.

Used, frustrated and abused, I thought about Dad's big revelation. As for Clive Mallis, I'd been looking for sinister goings-on that didn't exist. Nothing Dad had said threw any light at all on Scarlet's death. Binns was literally a dead end. The only potential lead: the money.

I didn't have a key to Scarlet's home. In any case, if there were any incriminating evidence, the police would have unearthed it already. Fact is, Scarlet was too smart. She hadn't left a trail because she didn't want anyone to follow. Unless—

I drove to my parents and was surprised to find them out. I let myself in and received an effusive welcome from Mr Lee. After assuring him that he was the best dog in the world, he padded into the living room where I knew he'd take advantage and hop up onto the nearest sofa.

Wandering into the hall, I noticed the door to Dad's study open. Glancing over my shoulder, listening hard for the sound of tyres on gravel, I shot inside. The room smelt of wood smoke, old books, aftershave and leather. It was a good room, a sanctuary, and the kind of place you went to when things weren't right.

Sunlight tumbled from the window, splashing onto Dad's desk, and shining onto a notepad beside the phone. My eyes slid automatically to Dad's handwriting, a collection of inde-cipherable squiggles. Among the lower-case script, a name in capital letters: ROGER STANTON, followed by a mobile number, both heavily underlined three times. Dad had acted quickly, like I knew he would, and yet something in the heavy script made me twitchy.

I'd never been through my dad's belongings and private papers before and, although it was terribly wrong, I couldn't help myself. It was as if an unseen force had taken hold of my mind against my will and I was powerless to resist.

Was it possible that Dad knew more about Scarlet than, so far, he'd been prepared to reveal?

Nerves shredded by such an unwelcome thought, I tried and failed to contain a tidal wave of panic surging up inside. Stress, I told myself. Getting myself in a state, Mum would say.

Still, I looked.

The deepest drawer in my father's desk contained files, which ranged from household bills and bank statements to invoices and quotations for jobs. A separate file contained drawings for current projects. Typically, and as expected, everything was arranged with meticulous care. Two drawers above held no shocks or surprises. Aside from a copy of a Home Office publication, entitled 'Police and Criminal Evidence Act 1984,' there wasn't a single reference to Dad's former occupation or the case that had finished his career. Relief trickled over me. It wasn't long before it puddled at my feet.

On dad's desk, a half empty mug of coffee obscured a pocket-sized notebook, which he used as a coaster. I slipped it out and was surprised to find that it was an 'Internet Address and Password Logbook.' How anyone involved in law enforcement could be so lax, I'd no idea. All my passwords were safely stowed inside my brain. I guess it flagged up the difference between the older and younger generation.

Armed with his password, which was pants from a security point of view, I switched on and logged in. With another password, I had access to his emails. In Scarlet's name, I convinced myself that I had the right to do whatever was necessary.

With a fast glance over my shoulder to check the drive was still empty, I took a breath and hacked in. Aside from dense work-related email traffic between him and Nate, my dad was clearly one of those people who didn't send but received. There were tons of communications from building suppliers, most of which hung around his inbox like a bad smell. The only personal emails were those to me after I'd drawn his attention to something of interest, like articles on construction and design. Not a thing from or to friends, or ex-colleagues, including Clive Mallis.

Ditching his email correspondence, I cruised through folders, which again were work-related, including details of planning applications sent to councils with their responses. Dad kept all his insurance documents in one folder, legal and accountant stuff in a couple of others. About to log off, I stumbled across a file named 'Operation Jericho.' With its association with walls tumbling down, it felt stupidly significant.

I double-clicked it and found access blocked, as if someone said, 'Not so fast'.

With damp fingers, I flicked through Dad's notebook, searching for the code to the only password-protected file.

It didn't take me long to discover it. By comparison to his other passwords, this was relatively complicated, including lower and upper case letters, numerals and a dollar sign. Standing solo on a page, near the back, this had to be it.

The silence of the room stuck to me like tar. I could log out, switch off, replace the notebook under the mug and walk away, never to return. Maybe I should. Scarlet wouldn't have snooped on Dad or invaded his privacy like this.

But I was not my sister.

As the file opened, I blinked at the volume of information. Dating back thirty years, to when my dad worked for the MET, there were lists of names, including police officers by rank, dates and details of police activities. Scrolling down, and to my untrained and unprofessional eye, it seemed like a diary of events that, perhaps, any police officer might keep. Nothing dinged my alarm bells. The only anomaly were two names and addresses itemised at the end of the document: Cecil Vernon and—oh my Christ, Charlie Binns.

Chapter 51

I thought I would throw up. Couldn't concentrate, couldn't focus. I didn't know how to feel. What was normal? Is this what happens when life takes you by the throat and gives you a damn good shake?

Had Dad lied to me or had the passage of time made him so forgetful that one name among many failed to register? And what about Cecil Vernon? Who the hell was he? I took out my phone, snapped Vernon's details, logged off and left everything as I found it.

Another glance out of the window to check the coast was clear, I shot out of the room and out of the house, feet scrabbling on the gravel. Nervously casting my eyes down the drive and, with nobody in sight, I chose a key from my key ring.

The up-and-over garage door cranked open with a horrible wrenching sound. Fortunately, Dad hadn't locked the ladder. Dragging it over to the wall, I switched on the overhead light and clambered up.

The aperture gave me enough room to stand upright.

Sandwiched in between the floor and rafters, heat hung dense and heavy, as thick as smog. It was difficult to breathe and within seconds, my hair was plastered to my face.

Like tramps in an all-night shelter, souvenirs, unwanted gifts and keepsakes stared back at me. My gaze fastened on a couple of old TV's, defunct electrical equipment, lampshades, ornaments and household items. Most of the clutter near the front belonged to my mother and included two massive plastic boxes containing old school reports, including an end of yearbook belonging to Zach that told its own tale of a popular boy who messed around too much. Among the contents, Scarlet's swimming commendations and family photographs, which I forced myself to look at. Another box marked 'Scarlet's Stuff' revealed nothing of interest.

The back of the loft space told a different story. End of year accounts, going back seven years, cozied up to old paint-ings, prints and DVD's that cracked and warped in the heat. A mini-shredder loitered next to an old suitcase filled with plugs, adaptors and extensions. Dad, by his own admission, was a hoarder so I wasn't surprised. Red-faced and drenched in perspiration, I made to descend into cooler air when I spotted a bland cardboard box held together with gaffer tape, no markings to suggest what was inside. A methodical man, my dad labelled everything. I sat back on my haunches, wiped my brow with the back of my hand.

What are you waiting for? I muttered aloud. What could be worse: knowing or not knowing? I scoped the area, the blood in my veins clotting in the soaring temperature.

Half-crazed, I ripped open the lid to discover a pile of old car magazines. I fished out several glossy numbers, flicking through pictures of Aston Martin's and Bentleys, before setting these aside. Below, another layer of magazines that encompassed homes interiors and gardens, more my mum's reading matter. I thought I'd keel over if I didn't get out. One last ferret around proved fruitless and, throwing everything back into the box, I decided to make a move. Straightening up, I reached out for one of the rafters to steady myself. That's when my hand bumped up against something solid strapped to the wood. Puzzled, I pulled at the bindings and levered out a small notebook, my fingers leaving sweat marks on the moleskin cover.

Aside from the opening and closing pages, most were blank. Written in Biro and in a hand I didn't recognise, a list of restaurants, clubs and businesses with London addresses. One stood out from the crowd: the name of the hotel that Scarlet had visited before her death. My breath turned rapid and I felt mildly ill and blurry around the edges.

Beside each entry, there was a gold, silver or bronze star. If it was some kind of rating system, whoever made the awards had eaten in an awful lot of establishments, but that didn't gel with businesses that included bookies, pawnshops and jewellers. Information on the back page was more cryptic, with codes I didn't understand.

Deep inside, I realised that the box was a marker and what I held in my hands dynamite. The notebook was deliberately hidden, never meant for nosy people like me.

Fearing my parents' return, I hurried across the loft boards and slid back down the ladder with the speed of a fireman shooting down a pole. The garage locked, I took off with the notebook in my hand, leapt inside my car, fired the ignition and slammed the air con on full blast. Tyres spitting and hissing against the gravel, I drove away and hoped nobody would discover what I'd been up to, least of all my father.

Chapter 52

Horrible suspicions took hold like weeds and I caught the first train out from Worcester, Shrub Hill the next morning to London.

Paddington Station was same as ever: busy, noisy and no grubbier than the average train station. Swinging my rucksack up onto my back, I headed out of the exit and towards Norfolk Square, a haven for budget hotels. It took me two minutes to find the hotel flagged in the notebook and where Scarlet had stayed, five minutes to find someone manning reception. Gave me plenty of time to observe the tired-looking furniture, narrow dark corridors that threatened a cellar and basement, and threadbare carpets.

"I'd like a room," I said to a man who looked as if he'd been up all night. Dark hair stuck out at right angles above eyes that could have been brown but were mostly red. His tie was askew, and the cuffs of his shirt were grubby.

He turned his bleary-eyed gaze towards a computer manufactured in the early days of the technological revolution.

"Would it be possible to have room seventy-three?" I said.

Surprise flashed across his features. I wasn't sure whether his animation was due to the unlikelihood of any guest paying a return visit, or because this particular room was used for nefarious purposes. I projected my best winning smile.

"Sorry," he said. "It's already taken. I can offer a similar room on the same side."

"No, thank you," I said, feeling awkward. 'Thanks for your trouble,' I added needlessly.

I headed back to the train station. Praying I'd have more luck at my next stop, I retraced my steps and caught the first tube that would take me further down the line, to Harlesden.

The urban high street was like any other on a summer Sunday. Goods spilled out of shops, market style, and onto pavements. From an upstairs window, the sound of reggae lightened the mood, and the aroma of jerk chicken, coconut and sweet potato hung heavy in the heat. The only suggestion of criminality was the unmistakable pong of weed drifting across the pavement as two guys, in low-slung jeans and tattoos on steroid-fuelled biceps, walked past.

Rounding a corner, a police car sped by, siren wailing. Reminded me of Richard Bowen. Had he, as Rocco had done, used Scarlet for other purposes?

What if—

A fuse caught light inside my mind.

Cecil Vernon lived in an eight-storey high-rise block, a confection of seventies architecture and fifties-style facilities, with balconies across which gaily coloured washing hung, and the occasional bike lurched against railings. Out of my comfort zone, my white, comfortably off middle-class persona jarred with the surroundings.

The lift was out of order and I made my way up a stairwell that stank of urine. I kept my head down, avoided eye contact and hoped that others would not cotton on to the fear raging inside me.

I reached the top floor, rang the bell, immediately heard a dog barking, a female voice shushing it and a door opening and closing.

Next, a woman my height and build, with a hard expression, looked me dead in the eye. Her hair was scrunched back into a ponytail. Grey and de-oxygenated, her skin was a classic smoker's. Lines snapped at the corners of her eyes and there was a Georgian fanlight of wrinkles above her top lip. She wore a tight top in a shade of Guantanamo orange over pale blue jeans. On her bare feet, toe-rings.

"Hi," I said, forcing my best smile. "Is Mr Vernon at home?"

"You from the social?"

"No. I—"

"A copper?"

I let out a nervous laugh. "No way."

"Then who the fuck are you?"

"My name's Molly. I think my sister visited Mr Vernon some weeks ago."

The woman crossed her arms. "I don't remember."

"Her name's Scarlet, Scarlet Jay."

I watched her eyes. The way they flickered from dull to something approaching a gleam, like she was thinking and scheming. I smiled encouragement.

"Pretty, nice manners, respectful?" She stared at me in a way that suggested I was a very different kind of animal.

"That's her. Is your father in?" I shifted my stance, did my best to peer into the space behind her.

"Away on holiday. Spain. Had a bit of good fortune, lucky sod."

I felt my face fall, along with every hope. I'd come all this way for absolutely nothing, unless; "Do you know what they talked about?"

"Why don't you ask her?"

I bit my lip, tears of frustration and grief sparking at the corners of my eyes. "She died."

"Sorry about that." There was no fluctuation in her facial expression.

"Please, can you help me?" I said in desperation. "It's important."

She shifted her weight from one foot to the other, tilted her head, sizing me up. "Your sister paid Dad for the information she had off of him."

My mind reeled. For Scarlet to do such a thing, she must have been as certain, as she was desperate. I had no choice but to follow her lead. "I can give you money."

"What are you like?" She rolled her eyes. "Should have said so before. There's a cosy little boozer down the road. You're buying."

Chapter 53

For cosy, read cramped.

Next to a vape shop, the pub was a haunt for regulars. Most looked as if they'd sloped off the set of *Pirates of the Caribbean*. QPR regalia decorated the walls and I got the impression that if you were a Spurs fan you'd be dead meat.

"My name's Tina," she said, sinking the first half of her pint of Guinness in a couple of swallows. A foamy layer of froth coated her top lip. She pinched it away with a grubby thumb and forefinger. Nervous, I nursed an orange juice.

I had no idea of the etiquette for paying for information. I imagined Scarlet had faced the same dilemma. It wasn't comforting. Any coherent thought about what to do next was obliterated by noise from the vast Sky TV screen behind my head. Spotting my cluelessness, Tina said, "A ton for starters." I blinked in confusion. "Right toff, aren't you?' she sneered. "A hundred quid." She stuck out her hand, palm up.

Out of habit, I carried cash on me for the business – easier to persuade someone to part with an item if you put the readies on the table. With a heavy heart, I took out my purse, counted out five twenties, which Tina spirited away. "So, what do you want to know?"

"Tell me about your dad."

She pulled a face in mystification. "Like what?"

"Like what he was doing thirty years ago."

"S'easy. Ran a painting and decorating business."

"Is that all?"

Tina's smile was wide enough for me to notice a missing tooth. "Thing about getting into people's houses, you can see what they've got."

She didn't say 'burglary' or aiding and abetting others in the act, but it's what I believed she meant. "He made money on the side, right?"

"Nicely put." Tina took another swig.

"Does your dad talk a lot about the old days?"

"Talks about nothing else." Her tone approached something like fond regard. "Got plenty of tales to tell and all. Knew a lot of faces. Decent men with codes of honour." The way she said it made clear that it was not an opinion up for discussion.

"Did he know a man called Charlie Binns?"

Tina's eyes thinned. "What's it to you?"

I interpreted Tina's response as an affirmative.

"You know he was murdered?"

"Poor old Charlie got popped, yeah. Bang out of order."

"Any idea why he was shot?"

She tipped her head back and laughed, giving me a damn fine view of her tonsils. "Doncha read the news? Place has become like the Wild West. Wrong place, wrong time."

"That's not what happened. Someone got to him."

"Is that right?" She sniffed, took another healthy slug of Guinness.

I didn't dare mention claims that Binns had been a snitch. If I so much as mentioned the word in a place like this, Tina would be first in line to scratch my eyes out. I kept it zipped and reached for my rucksack, slipped out the notebook.

"What you got there?"

As tempted as I was to charge her a hundred quid for the answer, I pushed it towards her. She swooped, thumbed through, stopped on the page with the star system. Her face came alive and her eyes darted across the print like a city trader reading the market.

"Fuck me," she kept repeating. Eventually, she glanced up. "A right little encyclopaedia of dodgy stuff. You know what this is?"

I took an educated guess. "Details of a protection racket. I bet money is regularly extorted from the businesses on the list." Why it was sitting in my dad's garage I hated to think.

"Not bad for a posh girl." She ran a nail-bitten finger down a list of establishments. I craned over to get a better view. "See this, the star rating tells you the amount of money someone is good for."

When we were done, she closed it and handed it over. "So, what's your game?" The hard expression was back.

"I need to find out who it belongs to."

Tina's face cracked into a wide smile. Reminded me of fork lightning in a dark and threatening sky. "Now that is going to cost you."

I met her eye. "You actually know?"

"I have a pretty good idea."

Was a pretty good idea good enough? "But you were only a kid at the time."

"Very nice of you to say so. Thirty years ago, I was eighteen. More than old enough to know what was what. I knew the 'faces' and all."

I wanted to get it over with and get out of there. Before I lost my nerve, I blurted out, "Was Detective Chief Inspector Roderick Napier running a protection racket?"

A sly smile lifted the corners of Tina's lips. "Your sister had that same tone of voice, too." My heart rate accelerated. She drained her glass. "I'll have the same again. Get us a packet of crisps while you're at it," she said with a loose grin. "Cheese and onion."

Pissed off, I went to the bar, ordered refills, paid and returned with drinks and Tina's snack. She took a slurp, offered me a crisp, which I declined, took one, crunched it and rear-ranged her bony rear on the seat. Probably took no more than forty seconds. Felt like forty years.

"Another ton for starters, cash."

"Sixty," I said, bullish.

"Seventy-five. Your sister didn't have a problem."

Obediently, I handed over four twenties. Tina swiped the lot. "I don't do change, not a bleeding vending machine."

"You were saying," I said, grimly gritting my teeth.

"'No need to get bolshie. Course the notebook wasn't his. Your old man's a legend in these parts. Absolute gent. Kind as the day's long. My dad said he was the most genuine

278

community-minded copper he knew. Met him once. I'd be in my twenties."

After the build-up, it wasn't what I expected. *Thank you, thank you, God.*

"Your sister reacted like that, proper brightened up, she did." Tina posted another crisp into her mouth. Crunch. Crunch. Tongue darted out and licked her fingers. Tina was on a roll. "Back in the day, kids could play in the street, walk down the road without having a knife in their gut or bullet in their backs. Never had no trouble when Mr Napier was on the beat."

Glad to hear although I wasn't sure I bought Tina's 'we never had it so good' routine. "How did my dad pull it off?"

"How do you think? He worked with us, not against us, not like some of the hard-arsed bastards in the filth back then."

I thought about what that could mean. Had Cecil Vernon given my dad tip offs? Had Vernon been taking money and playing both sides? Tina interrupted my thoughts. "Your dad was one of the good guys."

"Good guys," I repeated, my relief obvious.

"One of us."

"So, who's the owner of the notebook?"

"Like I said, it will cost."

"I don't have any more cash on me."

Tina shrugged. "Cashpoint's outside."

"Don't you think you've had enough?" It felt like a mugging.

"Fucking joking. This bloke ruled the fucking roost. Got arms like tentacles."

Arms long enough to reach Charlie Binns, long enough to reach Bowen and Scarlet? Is that what she means? Fear echoed through me. "All right. How much?"

"A grand."

I took a sharp intake of breath. What she was demanding was huge with no guarantee that she would tell me the truth and not spin me a load of lies. But I'd come this far and, whether I liked it or not, the book was the only solid, tangible piece of evidence I had. I needed to find out who it belonged to. With a premier account for the business, I'd have to take it out of the shop's account. I stood up, stepped outside, found the hole in the wall, pushed in my black debit card, extracted the loot and headed back.

"Here," I said.

"Tidy," she said, pushing it into her bag.

I waited, perched on the edge of my seat. Tough as titanium, Tina looked at me straight. No loose grin. No smart remarks. A gleam of anxiety in her eyes.

"Detective Inspector Clive Mallis," she said.

Chapter 54

"That's not possible. Mallis worked for the police in Wiltshire as a D.C.I."

"Not thirty years ago, he didn't."

And this was Dad's friend. Or was he? I was too stunned to think about it with any degree of clarity. Friend or colleague, neither sounded right.

"You okay?" Tina said.

No, I wasn't. "Did my sister mention Mallis?"

"No."

"Binns?"

"Might have done. Don't remember," she said, with a furtive glance.

I took a sip of orange juice. Once an informer, always an informer so chances were Binns supplied info to Mallis when he worked at the MET all those years ago. The fact Mallis's name never crossed my sister's lips suggested that she hadn't found out about our dad's association with him.

If Tina is telling the truth.

I thought about my last conversation with Heather. Richard

Bowen's best man had been a serving police officer in the MET. If Richard had somehow elicited information about Binns's informer status, he might have made a connection between Binns and Mallis. Although how it was relevant and how all the interconnecting pieces locked with Scarlet, I wasn't certain.

"Anyway," Tina said, "you got what you come for." Pleased with her morning's work, she turned towards a man at the bar, her signal that I'd had my money's worth and our conversation was over.

I slung my rucksack on. Before I left, I handed Tina a business card I used for the shop. "When your dad gets back, ask him to give me a call."

"As long as there's some cash in it, my old man won't give a flying fuck."

With everything I'd previously believed now in doubt, I checked out Clive Mallis on my laptop during the two-and-a-half-hour journey home. After a scroll through antique emporiums in Gloucestershire, it was a simple enough exercise to unearth the shop belonging to Mallis, 'specialist in vintage firearms,' mostly imported from the USA. I carried a stock of weapons at 'Flotsam,' but nothing on the same scale. It surprised me because the market was niche; my best customer a guy who made fantastic sculptures that incorporated decommissioned weapons. He once told me that a decommissioned Colt Frontiersman could be reactivated in a little over two hours. I thought about the manner of Charlie Binns's death and swallowed hard.

I read on and discovered that Mallis's home address was

situated in the newly gentrified Gloucester docks. He had a two-bedroom penthouse apartment, with two balconies from which he'd have a decent view of the boats, and secure allocated parking. I roughly valued it at around £250k; business premises around £400k and the stock anything up to three quarters of a million. Not bad for an ex-copper. And now I knew how.

I looked out of the window, watched fields speeding by. *One of us.* How had Scarlet interpreted Tina's sentiment? Were her questions more direct than mine? Were Cecil Vernon's answers more illuminating? I found it difficult to keep my wilder suspicions at arm's length.

Sunday evening passed with the grinding gait of a motorway traffic jam. Each time I looked at my watch, it seemed stubbornly stuck at the same point. I expected something to happen. Nothing did. Every part of me was primed for the unpredictable, the unforeseen and dangerous. Rocco hung around the fringes of my mind like a dirty cobweb. Only Scarlet eclipsed him. I saw her in the sun in the evening. I saw her in the moon at night.

Too wired to sleep, I seriously contemplated taking Lenny's advice. What the hell? One little pill was not going to turn me into an addict. If it helped me rest, I'd see things more clearly and feel less jumpy. I showered, dosed myself up and went to bed with a warm drink. I'd already laid out my clothes ready for the funeral the next day.

Heavy and airless, the night clung like a shroud. I made a conscious effort to relax. Let my limbs go slow. Let the drugs do their work. Finally, sleep overtook me. In a void of nothingness, I didn't dream.

On stirring, I'd expected to drift back up slowly through several layers of consciousness. I thought I'd wake feeling great for at least ten seconds before reality kicked in. I did none of those things. I awoke with a bump.

Panic scissored through me. My eyes narrowed against the darkness. I glanced at the bedroom window. I'd left it open to grab some air. My brain sluggishly made deductions. Someone was in the room. I heard before I saw.

"Molly, don't be afraid."

Bright terror screeched through me and I leapt out of bed. "Get out." I did not scream. I snarled.

"You're angry."

"Of course, I'm angry. You betrayed me. You used me." Now my night vision kicked in, I could see Rocco sitting over by the wardrobe. Nothing threatening about him apart from the small fact he'd broken into my house. Again.

"I never used you. What I felt and feel is real."

"Don't insult my intelligence."

"It's the truth."

"What would you know about that?"

"Okay, in the beginning, I had an agenda."

"You dumped a dead animal in my carport. You stuck a knife in my own kitchen table."

"No Molly, that's not true." He looked shaken.

"You stalked and seduced me."

"I know how it seems, but I need you to understand."

"I understand plenty. I was a means to an end in your doomed and deluded quest to find out what happened to your half-sister. Now get out before I call the police."

284

Rocco gave a dry laugh. "Didn't you do that already? The police came to my gym, Molly. I was marched out in front of my friends and work colleagues. I'll probably lose my job."

"Not my problem."

"They threatened to do me for harassment."

"Well, what would you call it?"

"Pursuing the truth."

At least we shared something in common, although my truth was connected to Scarlet, not Rocco's half-sister, Drea. I didn't tell him this. "Who cautioned you?" I wanted to be certain.

"Two detectives, Stanton and Childe. They cut up pretty rough."

"I know, Rocco. I know about the investigation, about everything."

"And Mallis?" He was back with the intense look again.

The corrupt copper, the extortionist and my father's friend. That was the inescapable bit that rattled and twisted inside.

"Look, I'm sorry about your sister," I said.

"Drea. Her name's Drea."

I repeated it slavishly. "But you have to get real. Her death has nothing to do with my family other than the fact my dad didn't take her disappearance seriously, for which he is sorry. It cost him his job, too." And his mental health.

"I should have guessed you'd stick together." He didn't say it spitefully. He was resigned and disappointed, as if he'd always known it would be this way.

"What did you expect? That I'd accept the crazy words of someone I met five minutes ago, someone who deceived me,

285

against the people I've known and loved for a lifetime?" My voice wavered. I felt sad and sorry and miserable, and, damn it, uncertain.

"Please sit down, Molly. I'm not going to hurt you."

"More than you already have?"

His expression was beseeching. Rocco knew he'd crossed the line and that nothing he could say would make things better between us.

"It's Scarlet's funeral tomorrow, isn't it?"

"Yes, it is."

"I should leave you to sleep." He leant forward, making to go.

"Wait," I said. "Your mum. She died. That's real, right?"

"Drea's death broke her heart and that's the truth."

I didn't know how to respond. What could I say that hadn't already been said?

"Funny, but if I close my eyes, I can still hear her voice," Rocco said. "She's like the angel on my shoulder."

If I shut mine, would I hear Scarlet's voice too? "It's pretend though, isn't it?" It came out rough and unsympathetic.

"Probably, although nice to imagine. Someone told me it's not uncommon for white feathers to appear following the death of someone we love. Supposed to signify that angels are near."

"Well, I haven't seen any." Sceptical, my voice was flat.

An awkward silence cast a net over the room. I sat down gingerly on the edge of the bed.

"Has it occurred to you that we both want the same thing?" he said. "We both want answers to why our sisters died."

That much, I guessed, was true. "What was she like?"

His eyes warmed with nostalgia. "Mad, a little bad, and a free spirit. Her problem was that she thought everyone was lovely."

"She trusted too much?"

"It's what got her killed."

I thought about that. "Can I ask you something?"

"Fire away."

"Why now? Why not sooner? It's been ten years since she died."

Rocco flicked a smile. "But only months since Gran passed on. It was something she said when she was ill." He hesitated, reluctant to share and stood up. "I've cleared out of the house and the flat. If you need me, you know where to find me."

"I don't need you."

He seemed to falter, hurt in his eyes. "I'll be at our special place if you do." I looked dead ahead. I didn't know what he meant. I didn't care enough to find out. "Could I leave through the front?" He angled his head towards the open window. "It's a long drop down there."

"I'll see you out," I said stiffly, getting up. This really was goodbye.

I followed him downstairs. Sliding back the chain, I opened the door. Dawn was breaking, stippling the sky with red and gold. I pulled my robe tight around me. "Why did you really come?"

"To talk, to tell you that, if I had to do it all again, in different circumstances, I'd still choose you." The sincerity in his voice was unmistakable. He looked at me with a steady gaze, no tricks, no dissembling, like he'd caught me one-handed as I dangled over the side of a huge drop. It was probably the single moment of truth between us and an unwritten part of me wanted him still.

Serious and anxious, he paused on the threshold. One last thought, one last declaration.

"Be careful, Molly."

"Careful?" Fear tiptoed down my spine.

"It's not a threat," he said with a quick smile. "There's a killer out there. Somewhere." Then he turned and vanished into the early morning light.

Chapter 55

I looked in the mirror and felt older than my years. It was plain in my eyes. Loss and fear did that to people. If I could be anywhere else without disrespecting my sister, I would have been. I felt no sense of goodbye or celebration of her life. Mum and Dad might have closure. I did not.

I drove to Zach's in a dismal mood. Revelations clattered through my head. Scarier still, Rocco's parting remark.

Tanya came out to greet me.

"You okay?" She looked shy, danced from one bare foot to the other. Her silk dress spun and swirled, catching the sun and dazzling like a firework, yet her face was pinched, her naked arms crossed tight, hands clutching her elbows as if she were frozen with cold, odd in the twenty-eight degree heat.

"I've been better," I said honestly. "How's Zach?"

"Oh, you know. Tuned out a little bit."

"He's not using, is he?" Alarm shot through my question. Tentatively, she smiled. "I think he's frightened of seeing your folks."

"It's been a long time," I admitted. "But today is about Scarlet. I don't think Zach need worry."

"Yeah," she said with another clunky little smile.

Zach appeared on the steps.

"Blimey, where did you find that?"

Warily, Zach looked down, touched the cuffs of his shirt. "The suit is one of Chancer's cast-offs. Doesn't fit him anymore. Is it okay?"

"It looks great. You look so smart." My gaze dropped to his feet. Thank God, he'd washed them. "Shame about the flip flops."

"You're a funny woman." There was no smile. I met his eye, sad to think that it took the day of our sister's funeral to bring about such a transformation in his appearance and in his heart. As he climbed into my car, Zach's return felt like that of the prodigal son.

We were halfway to the church when I broached the subject of Scarlet's trip to London.

"Jesus, can't you leave it?" Zach's hand shot to the door and I had a horrible vision of him opening it and tumbling out.

"Okay," I said quickly. "Sorry." Choosing less contentious ground, I told Zach about my random cup of coffee with Edie. "Did you know Chancer hit her?"

"Who told you that?"

"Edie."

"She's a liar."

"She was very convincing."

"Convincing is part of the deal," he said without rancour. "Takes one to know one."

Occasionally, my brother's self-awareness took me by surprise. "But why would she spread such a terrible rumour?"

Zach shrugged one shoulder. "People do."

"She also said that Chancer called time on the divorce. I thought it was the other way around."

Zach stared out of the window at the countryside whizzing by. "Does it matter?"

It didn't require a reply.

The vicar was a jolly-faced woman with a scrubbed appearance and gap-teeth. She looked better suited to serving sausages than dispensing comfort. I had a dark suspicion that we'd be handed tambourines, encouraged to wave our hands in the air and bellow 'Hallelujahs'.

Mourners were notable by their absence, which only went to prove that having over three hundred followers on Facebook was no guarantee of a good turnout. Lenny would be proud of me for my admission.

Childe and Stanton sat at the back on the right-hand side. Glancing to my left, I was drawn to the face of a man I recognised yet couldn't place. As I walked past, he nodded imperceptibly. The man in the shop, I realised with a jolt. Too shocked to speak, I didn't react, kept walking, frozen, staying as close to Zach as possible.

Sleek and polished and dignified, the Fianders sat mid-way down the church. I acknowledged Fliss and Louis, Samuel nowhere to be seen and probably parked with grandparents. A few of Scarlet's nursing colleagues were present, scattered among the aisles but, as for those who knew and admired her, there were many absentees.

I caught Dusty and Lenny's eye. Some of my parents' friends were in attendance. Poor Mum, I thought, as we slipped into the pew at the front, Zach next to her and me next to Zach. Dad and Mum murmured something to my brother and my mother slipped her arm through his. Pale and empty-eyed, she looked terrible. Nate sat on Dad's left. He leant forward a little. I did not greet my brother-in-law.

As the service was about to start, a disturbance at the back heralded a wave of people entering the church. I twisted round and watched the entire Chancellor family proceed down the aisle. Stephen, granite-faced, pushed his wife's wheelchair, Edmund, his eldest son, behind them, followed by Chancer. Behind him, several paces back, Edie too. She nodded at me, grave and big-eyed. She'd done something weird with her hair, which was the colour of arterial red. Dad turned in the same direction and smiled vaguely, pleased that they'd all turned out in a show of solidarity.

The service passed in a blur. Cold gripped my chest, crushing my heart and lungs. Fliss' fluting voice, reciting a poem I'd never heard of, the only bit I remembered. While Louis delivered a eulogy, my mind hooked on Binns and Vernon, and Mallis and my dad, connections and circles within circles, with Scarlet at the centre. Somehow, I needed to grab hold of the cold and analytical traits inherited from my father, and suppress the hot, crazed, grief-stricken part of me. I need to cut through the crap and think straight and true and clear.

When the coffin was wheeled forward for cremation and

the curtain closed behind it, my mother let out a howl that would pierce the soul of a psychopath. Zach braced and I cringed inside with despair.

Back at the house, after the service, and about to go inside, Zach grabbed my elbow, "Don't leave me." He trembled and his eyes shot wide with panic. The nagging sensation that Zach's fear was unconnected to sobriety or large gatherings would not go away.

"Please, Molly," he said, his grip stronger.

"I won't. I promise."

"We don't need to stay long, do we?"

"Zach, we really can't—"

"They'll understand."

"They won't. It's unthinkable, you idiot."

"But, Molly, you know how it is. All those people. I can't. Just can't." He scratched an imaginary itch under his arms, and was so agitated and jumpy, I wondered if he'd slipped illicit pills into his mouth when I wasn't looking. I asked him.

"NO." We were eyeball to eyeball, and a fleck of spittle landed on my cheek. I exhaled, wiped it away.

"Good. Fine. Now don't be wet." Like escorting a prisoner to a cell, I half-dragged him and propelled him inside. "Get a drink and go and talk to Chancer. Look, he's over there, with Dusty." I pointed to one of the sofas in the sitting room. "And look, there's Edie." She cut a lonely figure, standing over by the French windows. Against her pale complexion, her freshly dyed hair made her look vaguely vampiric. Catching my gaze, she smiled hopefully. I gave her a little 'see you in a moment' wave. Zach looked across but didn't move. "I need to speak to Mum," I insisted in irritation. "Fuck's sake, Zach, go."

I watched as he trotted off, obedient. The strange thing about my brother was that, like a little boy lost, he responded to firm instruction. I was searching out Mum when Stephen Chancellor cornered me in the hall. In a beautifully tailored linen suit, with a pale blue shirt that matched his eyes, he looked as though he'd stepped off a big game reserve.

"Molly, my dear, I'm so very sorry for your loss."

I looked up, felt the heat of his gaze on my cheeks. The man exuded power and authority; there was no escape. "Thank you."

"How long has it been since we last spoke? Several years, I should think."

"Must be." Stephen had changed very little. His fine shock of hair was greyer than blonde and contributed to his distinguished appearance. His eyes were the same, slightly more hooded maybe, and his expression, penetrating and inescapable. I'd hate to be up against him in court. In common with my dad, Stephen Chancellor could reduce a man to mush with one rapier-like look. Perhaps that's why they hit it off. It struck me that they both recognised the effect they had on others.

"I must say you've positively blossomed. You used to be such a shy little thing." His lips twisted into a full smile. Gave me the creeps.

"I noticed Lavinia earlier," I said.

"Ah, the wheelchair."

"Nothing serious, I hope."

"Sudden onset MS, I'm afraid."

"Very sorry to hear it."

"It's life. Nothing much to be done other than to endure." He turned on his heel and walked away. I watched for longer than was necessary, remembered Edie's words. They were all fucking nuts.

I found Mum in the kitchen. She poured two glasses of wine and handed me one. "To Scarlet." She swayed a little unsteadily and I realised that she'd already sunk a few. We chinked glasses. I couldn't think of anything to say that didn't sound stupid. I think she felt the same. We simply viewed each other, hollow-eyed.

"If there's anything I can do," I began.

She shook her head slowly then did something really odd and out of character. She leant towards me, cupped my chin in her hands and gazed at me with such a sad smile. "Sweet of you, my love, but no. You're a good daughter. All I want is for you to grab life and live it. Don't look back, Molly. Ever."

"Mum, I—"

"Promise me."

"I promise." Two promises to my parents in less than a couple of days. Strange times. Then she kissed me on the cheek and slipped away to join the other mourners.

Chapter 56

But I broke my promise to Mum immediately: I did look back. I looked back on two little girls dressing up in our mother's clothes and shoes. I looked back on a smoke-filled kitchen, burnt pizzas and buns. I looked back on mud on our faces and salt sea wind in our hair. I looked back on sulky tears and scraps like only sisters have. I looked back on laughter that made our ribs ache and tummies hurt. And then I looked back to a string of newspaper cuttings about my sister and another dead woman and thought that, no matter what my lovely Dad told me, there was a connection – there had to be a connection.

Exhausted, I staggered out of bed early. The view from the bedroom window revealed a sky bloody with red. Fiery light caught the tops of volcanic-looking hills, making fools of them

I took out my phone. No messages. One flick of the camera setting took me to images from Rocco's room. Undeleted from my phone. Dad would be furious if he knew.

I stared until my eyes popped. Words and pictures and questions, but where was the angle? Rocco had sprung into action shortly after his grandmother's death, something she'd told him the trigger. I wished I'd pursued it. As I stared at the players in Rocco's hall of fame, I realised that one of them was missing.

Despite the unrespectable hour, I called Heather Bowen. It was a long time before she answered. When she did, she sounded muzzy, thick with sleep. Suited me. I wasn't looking for intellect. I wanted truth.

"Did Richard know a man called Rocco Noble?"

"No. Why? And Christ, do you know what time it is?"

I apologised unreservedly.

"It's bloody inconsiderate," she barked. "Wait a minute, how the fuck did you get my number?"

"I ... um—must have been in the papers from your solicitor to my brother-in-law." I squeezed my eyes tight at the stupidity of the lie and my own hypocrisy. I'd gone mental at Rocco for snooping on my phone. Either Heather was too dozy to see through my obvious deception or she didn't care.

"What's this Noble character got to do with anything?"

I couldn't say because I didn't know. "His half-sister went missing ten years ago from Gloucestershire and was found dead in a mine in Wiltshire."

"Now you've lost me."

"Her name was Drea Temple."

"Doesn't ring any bells."

"Richard never referred to it?"

"I've just told you."

"Never mentioned Clive Mallis, a police officer last operational ten years ago?"

"No."

I stifled a sigh. Like trudging through a bog, I was sinking.

"Heather, when you talked about Richard, you described a man who always got what he wanted."

"What's your point?"

Whether it was the hour, or she'd had second thoughts about me, she was a lot more guarded. "Did you see a different side of him in the weeks and months before he went down with 'flu?"

"For goodness' sake."

"Did you?"

There was a long pause. "He was agitated."

"In what way?"

"Excited. As if he were on to something. Happens all the time with coppers."

"Connected to a personal relationship, do you think?"

"No, I can spot the difference. This was professional."

A police matter involving police officers, one of whom was bent? Sure as hell, Bowen wouldn't breathe a word of it to his wife.

If Bowen's interest was sparked by Mallis, maybe Binns' name came up during Bowen's investigation and private chat with his mate in the MET. Binns became a figure to pump for information, simply to get the lowdown on Mallis. Similarly, Bowen's motivation for taking up with Scarlet was because my father had an association with Mallis.

Empowered, it put a fresh idea in my head. "What did Richard's real father do for a living before he became sick?" I wondered if he too was a police officer, someone connected to old unexplained cases.

"Cab driver."

"And his adopted dad?"

"Engineer."

I chewed my lip in frustration. "Did his biological dad have a wife?"

"No he never married. Lived with his sister, Jacqui. She took care of him during his last illness. Richard used to go and visit them."

"Do you have her address?"

"I do, but—"

"Please, I'd like to talk to her."

"It won't help."

"Please, Heather."

"Okay, but on one condition."

"I agree."

"You don't know what it is yet."

"I'll agree to whatever you want." I winced at the pathetic plea in my voice.

She relented and gave me an address in Whaddon, a suburb of Cheltenham.

"Thank you, and your condition?"

"I never want to hear from you again." The line went dead.

Chapter 57

Jacqueline Bevan lived in a dull looking house identical to the dull looking house next to it. Everything was bland and plastic, including the window-frames and door, the latter the colour of an inflamed gum. Brilliant sunshine highlighted its drab appearance.

Hovering outside, I spotted a notice that displayed 'No Cold Callers.' It wasn't a great start. What would I say? Would she talk to me, a stranger? Before I had time to get my story straight, a morbidly obese woman filled the entire doorway. I should have come bearing cakes. Strangely, her face didn't match her physique. It was as if someone had stuck her head on the wrong body. She had short, cropped grey hair, kind brown eyes and remarkably unlined skin. Her mouth was a small perfect rosebud. It was hard to imagine her putting anything into it.

Before she had time to tell me to clear off, I launched in with a whopping lie. "Hello, I'm a friend of Richard Bowen. I wondered if we could have a chat?"

Her face clouded and she went very pale. Her lips turned

down, the rosebud mouth blooming, overblown and then dying. This was it. She was going to slam the door in my face.

"Any friend of my nephew is welcome here," she said, inviting me in.

We drank milky coffee.

"Have a flapjack. They're homemade." Jacqueline Bevan pushed a plate towards me. I wasn't hungry but took one. We'd done the pleasantries and I'd told the lies. As far as she was concerned, I was Amy Pearson, (a bully I'd loathed at school) worked in the wine trade, travelled far and wide, and lived in Cirencester.

"I didn't see you at the funeral." It didn't feel like a statement designed to catch me out.

"I was abroad unfortunately, on business. That's why I'm here now."

She nodded and sipped her drink tentatively. "So very sad. And to die like that," she said with a shudder that made the tops of her arms wobble. "He was a lovely man. Oh, I know what people said about him having an eye for the ladies," she said, heading off any possible criticism, "what with his mistress and child, but I speak as I find. He was an attentive and loyal son. Came every week to visit until Barry passed on." She lapsed into a respectful silence.

"Richard loved to see your brother." True, according to Heather.

A big girlish smile illuminated Jacqueline's smooth face. She leant forward. The chair creaked in protest. "We don't get many visitors and he was so made up when Richard made contact. Such a wonderful surprise. And him a police officer, too." Her eyes widened with awe and delight. "Barry was really proud of that. 'Who'd have thought it?' He kept saying. Restored his faith a little bit."

"Oh?" I said in a tell me more tone.

"It's nothing really." She lowered her gaze, removed an oat flake from the corner of her mouth. "These are rather good, aren't they? The last lot were a little chewy. Do you cook?"

I shook my head, desperately thought how I could shift the conversation back to Barry's distrust of the police. Had he somehow come up against Clive Mallis, the man everyone loathed? Apart from my dad, that is, I thought grimly.

"No time, what with your busy job, I expect." She gave a sad sigh, giving the impression that she'd missed out on work, relationships too, on life in general.

I looked around the room. Uncluttered. Sterile. Photographs on a sideboard displayed a younger Jacqueline standing beside a man half her size. I could tell at once they were brother and sister.

I tilted my head. "Is that Barry?"

"It is. Taken a long time ago on holiday in Brighton."

"You were close?"

"Like peas in a pod."

"You must miss him."

"I do." Crestfallen, her small white teeth rested on her bottom lip. A tear welled at the corner of her eye and trickled down her cheek. I touched her arm in sympathy. I was in her living room under a false pretext, but my reaction was true and honest. She patted my hand. I fished out a clean tissue, gave it to her and waited for her to recover. "We became especially close after Bethany left him."

"Bethany?"

"Richard's mother. She and Barry were never married. Far too flighty, that one," she said, shaking her head in disapproval. "She wasn't nearly good enough for my brother."

"What became of her?"

"No idea."

And didn't much care, judging by the terseness in her voice. "Richard mentioned that Barry drove taxis for a living."

"He worked for a cab company here in Cheltenham."

I sparked with interest. "When was this?"

"Worked for Randalls for almost twenty years. Mind, he left a decade ago, had enough by then. More coffee?"

I declined. My brain hissed and fizzed. It came back to the same window of time: ten years ago. Happenstance or connection? I'd never find out unless I took a gamble.

"You mentioned Barry's distrust of the police."

"Did I? Would you like another flapjack?"

"No, thank you."

"Think I'll have one," she said with glee. "They're so moreish and irresistible, aren't they?"

"What made Barry lose faith with the police, Jacqueline?" No way was I going to be fobbed off with a pastry diversion.

Jacqueline's eyes swivelled from me to the walls to the door. She lowered her voice. "I can't really say. Barry made me promise." She took a bite. Chewed mechanically. Like it was something to do in a crisis. If you eat, you can't speak.

"My father's a police officer. He'd hate it if someone brought the force into disrepute." Although Clive Mallis was the glaring exception to my father's rule. By contrast, Jacqueline Bevan was a nice woman, a loyal sister, trusting and without a friend. Wasn't I exploiting her in the same way Rocco had exploited me? I might have been working with what I had but it didn't feel good.

She swallowed, almost choked, took a big glug of coffee. "I suppose now he's gone, there's no harm, although I'd rather you kept this to yourself."

I smiled, did my best to look confidential instead of eager.

"Bank Holiday, Christmas, New Year, Barry worked every one of them. The pay wasn't better, but he'd get decent tips. He wasn't a wealthy man. Between you and I," she said, dropping her voice a tone, "he liked a flutter on the horses."

"He was in the right place," I said with a jolly smile.

She looked perplexed for a second and then broke into a laugh. "Cheltenham. The Races. Oh yes."

"You were saying," I said, fearing I'd destroyed her train of thought.

"The last New Year's Eve he worked, he picked up a fare from Cheltenham to Winchcombe. A young man. Bit scruffy. Long hair, all braided. You know the type?" She didn't wait for an answer. "Barry was very particular about his vehicle. Didn't like taking youngsters he thought might pass out or be sick over the upholstery."

"What was the man like?"

"Well spoken, but I don't know, Barry said he thought he might be on drugs, or something. He was very chatty, talkative, nervous with it. Kept scratching at his arms." She leant forward theatrically. "It's the drugs, poor things."

Blood swelled in my head and I had that curdled feeling that warns of impending disaster. I stared blindly.

"Twenty-four hours later, Barry gets a knock at his door."

"New Year's Day?"

"That's right?"

"Where was this?"

"Barry lived in Swindon Road." I knew it. Zach's old stamping ground in St. Paul's, grotty back then. He'd always favoured the seamy, uncut side.

"Anyway, it's the police. Well, I say the police. It was one officer. He put pressure on Barry."

"How? Why?" My voice was hoarse, rasping, and then, with relief, I remembered. Dad returned to work on 3 January. He knew nothing about Drea Temple. The timing was off. It had to be Mallis.

"He told Barry that he was to forget ever picking up the young man with the long hair. You won't remember it, but there was a lass reported missing a few days later. Barry always wondered if there was a connection."

My mind spun out at the implication. I described Mallis.

"I wouldn't know. Barry didn't say what he looked like."

"Did Barry ask to see the officer's warrant card?"

Jacqueline wrinkled up her nose. "Don't think so."

"He asked his name?" Must have done.

"If he did, Barry never told me."

"He was afraid?"

"Very."

I suppressed a shiver. "How old was the officer?"

"Hard to say. Middle-aged, maybe?"

My throat dried. I took a drink and wound up with milk skin on my teeth and lips. "Where did Barry drop off his fare?" I thought back to the newspaper cuttings. Odds on The White Hart, or Drea's rental.

"Dropped him outside Winchcombe, about a mile away."

I racked my brains. Why outside? Nothing there apart from fields of sheep. Didn't make sense.

"Did the officer say anything else?"

Jacqueline's expression stiffened. "He threatened Barry. Said that, if he opened his mouth, there would be consequences." She glanced from me to the door and back again. "Promised to fit him up for something he didn't do."

I rocked back in my chair so hard I was in danger of doing a back flip. Jacqueline's smooth features creased with concern. "I expect your dear dad would be appalled."

I snatched a smile in agreement. Confused and churned up, I had one last question. "Did he talk to Richard about it?" I held my breath. Everything depended on the answer.

Her eyes widened. She nodded slowly, then murmured, "I think he did."

Chapter 58

It was as if I stood on the edge of a massive forest fire, with the wind changing direction, and forcing the flames towards me. The second Jacqueline described the young man I knew instinctively she was talking about my brother.

The drive should have calmed me down. It didn't. I was wired and fired, and murderous. Zach was weak. Given enough pressure, he would spill his guts.

Flooring it, I clung on tight as the little car flew down the motorway. Every bit of my body tensed, my focus dead ahead, eyes braced against a sun doing its best to penetrate my shades and sear my eyeballs. If I hadn't glanced in my rear-view mirror before overtaking, I wouldn't have noticed the BMW dropping in behind and remaining close. When I overtook, it overtook. *Mallis.*

Sweaty fingers slipping on the steering wheel, I changed down and dropped speed, straining to steal a look at the driver. The paintwork of the Beamer dazzled, and, with its tinted windows, it was impossible for me to get a fix without risking crashing the car. Designed to intimidate, I was intimidated.

Desperately trying to regain control of my body as well as my mind, I took a deep breath, accelerated and changed up to top gear. Consumed by staying on the road, I didn't even notice when the vehicle turned off and disappeared.

*

The curtains of Zach's trailer were drawn, the door unlocked. I slipped inside. It looked as if it had been looted. Mounds of washing up. Screwed-up dirty laundry. No sign of anyone. I stepped back out into rising heat.

My gaze searching the orchard, I spied my brother. He had his back to me, "Zach," I yelled.

His head jerked up and, as he twisted round, his ready smile tightened and vanished, replaced by slack features, flaky around the edges, and a fuzzy expression in his eyes.

He wandered over, idly scratching his arse, taking his time, treading carefully like he was avoiding broken glass strewn beneath his bare feet. I knew my brother. Could read how he ticked. If shoved in a corner, he would manoeuvre like crazy, dodge and blindside, and take me down dark, empty, meaningless alleys. I waited for him to reach me and then, with an expression that would snap steel, I socked it to him. "Is Drea Temple the reason Scarlet's dead?"

His mouth jacked open. His hands balled into fists that shot to his temple, as if I'd produced a twelve-bore. And there was fear. Lots of it. It leaked out of his every pore, dripping off him and puddling around his bare, dirty toes. I was afraid too. My brother and Mallis. My brother and—

"Oh Zach. Oh shit. What have you done?"

He rounded on me angrily. "I've done nothing. I warned you not to meddle. Now look what you've done?"

"Me?"

"I told you. I told you. I told you." Each time he spoke, he delivered blow after blow to his head. I stared in horror, utterly sickened that, after my all my digging, it had come to this. If I needed proof of guilt, I had it. Outwardly, I was unmoved. Inside, nausea gripped me, and my pulse raced.

"Fine. See this," I said, raising my phone. "One call. That's all it takes, and I'll tell the police everything."

He gasped. His eyes rolled in panic. At any moment he would take to his heels and run and run and never come back.

"I can't help you if you don't tell me the truth." The word 'help' did not have the desired effect. I expected his face to soften. Less flight or fight. My big brother stood, big and lumbering, wringing his hands, in tears.

"You don't get it. You don't know what you've started, what you've unleashed." The more he spoke, the greater my desire to throttle him.

"Zach, for Chrissakes. Where's Tanya?" I thought this would snap him back to his senses.

"Away. At her parents."

"Good," I said, not knowing whether it was or wasn't. He was shaking and so was I, but I'd get nowhere out here on open ground with the sun shooting death-rays at us. "Let's talk back at yours. Somewhere," I muttered under my breath, "where no one can hear."

He nodded vigorously.

Somehow, we stumbled back to his place together. I cleared a space for him to sit down, rinsed out a couple of mugs, found some vile herbal tea bags and made us drinks. Zach, still trembling, reached for tobacco and rizlas. He could have smoked weed for all I cared. I didn't even bother to ask what he'd dropped, smoked or ingested.

"How can you live like this?" I angrily pushed a chipped mug towards him. "It's a shit heap."

He shrugged, too busy thinking and rolling, and trying to assemble thoughts that could not be herded together. I waited for him to light up, watched his shaky fingers.

"It's true, isn't it?" I spoke without judgement.

"Do Mum and Dad know you're here?" The sly note in his voice put me back on my guard. I should have been afraid of him, but I wasn't. I was only frightened of what Zach would reveal. My knee jackhammered at the prospect.

He ran the tip of his tongue along the paper, tamped the tobacco down and plugged the roll-up into his mouth. He took a deep drag, then another. The fight and bullishness vanished as swiftly as smoke from his rolly. His head bowed; shoulders slumped. "It was an accident."

"Drea Temple?" An accident was good. An accident I could cope with. Except Scarlet's death was no accident. I didn't point out the distinction.

He looked up, questioning, the slippery expression back in his eye. "How much do you know?" Not nearly enough. He was trying to gauge how much I'd found out, how much he could edit the highlights. "I'm not pissing about, Zach." I waved my phone in front of his face.

"All right. All right." He took an enormous drag, held a breath in and exhaled. "There was a group of us."

"Who?"

A crafty look entered his eyes. Zach hiked a bony shoulder. "Doesn't matter. People you don't know. Most of them probably dead now."

"Your druggie mates."

"Don't say it like that."

How else was I supposed to say it? I flicked my palms up: *sorry.*

"We'd hang out together. I met Drea in one of the pubs."

"In Winchcombe?"

He frowned. "How do you know that?"

"Doesn't matter," I said, imitating him.

He took a petulant puff, ignored me. "I liked Drea immediately. She was funny, off the wall."

"Fancied her?"

"You'd have to be blind not to. Yeah, I would have shagged her."

"But you didn't?"

He shook his head, fierce with it.

"Go on."

"We arranged to meet."

"The two of you?"

"Uh huh."

I narrowed my eyes. Zach caught on quickly. "The two of us," he repeated.

"At her place?"

Zach shook his head. "She hadn't paid the rent in weeks and her house mates had thrown her out. She moved around, dossed down all over bu—t" He trailed off, losing his thread.

"So, she had no place to go."

He reached over, caught my wrist, his grip tighter than seemed possible. The acrid smell of tobacco was on his tongue, on his skin, poisoning the air. "You know how I was back then?"

His face was in my face. I didn't flinch. "Off your tits. Wasted. Out of it." Zach was catholic in his tastes. If you could smoke, snort or inject it, he'd take it. I remembered days when he'd howl with stomach pain after he'd checked out with ketamine or 'K', as Zach called it.

His wet eyes bored into mine, grip loosening. I picked up my mug, took a drink that made me heave. "Was Drea under the influence?"

"Nothing hard core, but yeah."

"And you'd got your mitts on a supply?" Of what didn't really matter. It all had a similarly lobotomising effect.

He nodded, eyes a gleam in the shadow of the interior. "Quality, really quality."

He said it without the 't', in imitation of gangster slang. By *qualiie*, he meant pure. Probably something that screwed with his brain and made it work harder, spiking body temperature, a killer on a cold night. I could see how this was rolling.

I flicked my hair as if I had a fly land on my ear. "Where did you go?"

"The home in a home, we called it."

I looked at him quizzically.

"Some jerk decided to use the site of an old house and build a new one around it. I suppose he was going to knock down the old walls once he'd finished."

Clearly, didn't understand a thing about the building process. I watched Zach's face. Ghost-pale, he was sweaty with unease.

"Where exactly is this place?"

I listened to his answer, a property outside Winchcombe, situated up an unmade drive, set back from the road, easy to miss. A perfect place for murder, I realised, hardly daring to breathe.

Roll-up extinguished; Zach started on another; a ploy to buy him time that he was fast running out of. "For some reason it never got finished."

"And became a home for squatters?"

Zach shook his head. "Too dangerous."

"How dangerous?"

He stiffened. His savage gaze pierced mine. "Extremely."

Chapter 59

"Let me get this straight, you don't know what happened?" I was incredulous. Zach had told me a tale where he'd wandered outside and found Drea dead inside.

"I'd taken enough shit to kill an elephant." Zach said, mighty defensive, pupils shrinking to pinpricks.

"What about Drea?"

"Yeah."

"Yeah what?"

"I don't understand the question."

"What did she take?"

"Why do you want to know?"

Because now it matters; now it's important. "Fuck's sake, Zach, tell me."

"K." He lowered his eyes. "Other stuff too. She liked White Russian."

Cocaine. "Enough to kill her?"

"No, no," Zach said. "She knew what she was doing. We both did."

To me, taking drugs was like roulette. How did any addict know what was safe and wasn't?

"And then you wandered outside?"

"To take a piss, yes."

"But you don't remember how long you were gone for?"

"I already told you." Agitated all over again, in between smokes, he smacked his palms on his thigh, as if he were playing bongos. "It was dark. The place was a death trap. I had to find my way out and then back in."

Search me why he didn't drop his fly in the next door room. Wouldn't someone off his face on crack, or whatever Zach was on at the time, take the simplest course of action?

I adopted my best humouring tone. "Right, so then you came back."

He stood up. Dark patches of sweat stained his T-shirt. Every part of him shook. His eyes were wild. Had he dropped acid in front of me and I'd been too spun out to notice?

"Sit down."

"Molly, if I tell you what happened, my life is over. Please, I'm begging you. I could go to prison." His pleading expression turned me inside out.

"Zach, you're already there." In a prison of your own making, with walls constructed of lies.

Slumping down, he put his face in his hands. I reached across and gently touched his arm. "You said it was an accident."

"She fell," he sobbed.

"Fell? Where?"

I prised his fingers apart. He stared at me with dull eyes. Snot trickled out of one nostril. "I swear I didn't know about it."

"Didn't know what, Zach?"

"About the well."

I stared at him for what felt a full minute. God.

"It had been partially filled in but the boards above were rotten." He gaped at me, praying I could fill in the gaps so that he wouldn't have to relive that night, except I think he'd done nothing else but relive that night ever since.

"So Drea fell through the floor?" Dad's words echoed through my head: *the pathologist found the presence of diatoms, or micro-algae in her bone marrow. The only way these could enter would be via the respiratory system.*

He nodded crazily. "I came back in. Couldn't find her. It was quiet. Too quiet. Like a snowflake drifting through space," he said, madly extemporising. "Then I saw. Oh fuck." He wrung his hands.

"How did you see? Wasn't it dark?"

"We had torches."

"Then what?" I nodded for him to continue.

"I inched over. Didn't want to get too close, and—" He let out a slow moan.

"Come on, Zach," I urged him. "Tell me."

"I saw blood. There was blood," he repeated, agonised.

"She hadn't gone to the bottom, right?"

"It was worse. She'd got wedged somehow."

I briefly closed my eyes, tried to visualise. Bloody hell. "Upside down?"

"No, no. She plunged straight through backwards and then got stuck below the water line." Zach's shoulders heaved up and down in despair. It sounded plausible. It did. But;

"If the stupid owner hadn't tried to block it up, she would have stood a chance."

"The blood, where did you say it was?" *Cranial injuries,* Rocco had written.

"What do you mean?"

"Was it on her or—"

"Christ, Molly, on her head, on the wall, on the beam. Jesus, Molly, I don't know. Head, face, building what does it matter?"

It mattered. It made the difference. Bile filled my mouth. "Are you sure you're telling me the truth?"

"I am. I swear I did not hurt her."

I locked eyes with his. Would Zach even know? "It was only the two of you? Nobody else?"

"Yeah. Course."

"Okay, then what?"

"I panicked. I mean I really lost it."

"And?"

"I got the fuck out of there."

"Was she dead?"

His face contorted in anguish. "I don't know," he whined, obviously haunted by the possibility that she wasn't. "I couldn't tell. I had no phone, so I went to get help."

"Good," I said weakly. I wanted to find something in this that would redeem my brother in my eyes, but I was running on empty, running on fumes. "Then what?"

His eyes darted to the door. "There's a phone box down

the road. I reversed the charges." His shoulders rounded, eyes looking everywhere but at me. A terrible thought broke loose, and fear marched straight at me, grabbed hold of my throat with its greedy fingers, and would not let go. Oh God, couldn't be, but if it did, everything made sense. And Scarlet, poor Scarlet, had paid for them all.

"You phoned Dad, didn't you?"

Zach looked up. "I'm sorry," he said, "so sorry."

Chapter 60

"Where are you going?"
             "Where do you think?"
"Don't, Molly. You can't. Dad will kill me."

"You think I won't bust the lot of you?" Beside myself, my breath came in sharp bursts. I had a pain in the middle of my chest, like you get from running in bitterly cold weather. "You involved Dad and he covered for you. And," I said, red-faced with fury, "he threatened the only person who could verify that you were in the same place as Drea that night."

"He said he would fix it. That was all."

Like my father fixed everything. "He sold out for you. Now I know why you got clean. I know why you never show your face at the house. You're a constant reminder of what you and he did. Does Mum know?"

Zach looked straight ahead. I had my answer.

I'd run out of words, out of energy, out of belief and hope and faith. The thought that they had all been in on a bloody awful conspiracy did me in. I felt crushed under the weight of it, physically, mentally and spiritually. I let out a howl. Zach's arms slid around me.

"Get the fuck away," I shouted, shaking him off. "Scarlet found out, didn't she? That's why she came to see you."

Zach hung his head. "Molly, I—"

"You destroyed her every belief in the people she loved." I wasn't like my sister. I didn't believe in family, the way Scarlet did. She bought into it; heart, body and soul.

"It wasn't my fault. It was Richard Bowen's. He had a thing for her when she and Nate weren't getting along. She liked him a lot, but then Bowen somehow found out about what happened and threatened to expose Dad and me if she didn't pay up."

I lunged towards him. "You knew, and you said and did nothing?"

Zach cowered, put his hands up to protect his face. "We thought it would be okay. She paid him, but he wanted more, said there was plenty of family money she could tap into. She even gave him that bracelet Nate bought for Christmas."

"He was blackmailing her, for Chrissakes. And you let him?"

He tapped the side of his head. "I'm not strong like you. She said she'd found a way to take care of it, so he'd never bother her again."

"Fuck's sake, Zach, instead of coughing up, or having it out with Dad, or going to the police, she drove into him."

"I swear I never knew what she planned. You have to believe me, Molly."

Oh. My. God.

Scarlet saw sacrifice as the simplest way out. That way,

Zach and Dad didn't go to prison. Mum wouldn't be destroyed. Nobody got hurt. Nobody got crucified.

And she was so wrong.

I shook my head in a bid to tame my messed up mind. Angrily wiping away my tears, I stood up. Zach eyed me nervously. "What are you going to do?"

"Speak to the man who lied."

*

Confronting my father was as risky as drinking with a chainsaw in my hand. I'd once respected him and now I feared him. How betrayed and disappointed Scarlet must have felt.

Dad was in the conservatory eating a late lunch: cheese and pickle, with crackers. He looked up, glad to see me. I'd almost forgotten that the day before we'd buried my sister. Seemed a lifetime ago.

I drew up a chair, scraped it across the floor as hard as I could and, strung-out, sat down opposite with a thump. "Where's Mum?"

"Shopping. She'll be back soon. Wants to talk to you about Scarlet's ashes. Can I get you something to eat?" I didn't answer. He caught my mood. "Is everything all right? That boy hasn't been bothering you again, has he?"

"That boy? Do you mean the one you lied about?"

His eyes became suddenly alert, on guard. "Is this about Stanton?" Dad was so earnest it almost made me doubt myself. Almost.

"Was Mallis in on it from the beginning?" My father had

used the notebook, with its dodgy references and associations, to ensure that Mallis played along.

He screwed his face into a mystified frown. "Molly, I really don't—"

"You played me. Don't pretend you don't know."

He pushed his plate away and gave a puzzled smile. "Molly, I assure you I have no idea."

"You assure me?" My laugh was arid. I fastened my gaze on a pulse in his jaw. The more I stared the more it ticked. "You sat in my living room and spun me lie after lie. You didn't investigate Drea Temple's missing status because you didn't need to. You knew where she was. Dead at the bottom of a mine because you took her there."

"Molly, you're not making sense." The smile went cold, congealing on his face.

"Which bit don't you understand, Mr Back in the Day? You moved her body from a well. You knew exactly how Drea Temple died and you covered it up. Hiding her body miles away was a genius idea."

He pitched forward as if he were hard of hearing, did that thing when somebody talks to you in a language you don't understand. Then he made a fatal mistake. He reached out his hand, in a 'take mine, trust me,' gesture.

I didn't move. Birds sang. Someone in a next door garden mowed a lawn. A dog barked. Normal everyday noises, yet the only sound I heard was shallow breath and the thrum of stone-cold panic. I was first to drop my gaze. It took every part of me for my body not to fold and crumple. This was my dad, the person I'd loved forever, the one I'd believed in and trusted and looked up to, whatever the hell that meant, and now it was all gone. Maybe he understood that. Maybe he knew that there was no going back, that nothing could ever undo his betrayal and would ever be the same. Couldn't be.

"You would understand if you were a parent." He spoke while my eyes fixed on the table in between us. "I did what was for the best. I couldn't let your Mum endure her only son in prison. It would have broken her."

I looked up, smashed it to him with a dead-eyed stare. "And what about Drea's parents, her grandmother? What about Rocco Noble?"

"Fair point."

"There's nothing fair about any of this." Or just. "And you had the bloody brass neck to unleash Stanton on Rocco when, all along, you knew that he was onto the truth."

"Molly," he said, trying to break through to me, "I did it to save my son. He wouldn't have lasted a day in prison."

"You put a family through hell."

"I did and I'm sorry, but Drea Temple was only another dead junkie." I gasped at his callousness, but he carried on, his warning stare enough to melt steel. "She had no proper home. She'd chosen a way of life away from her family. She was an addict that was never going to get any better. She was one of life's losers."

"You can't mean that. Damn it, you can't say that." And yet he did. He had. Did I even know this man? "You contaminated a crime scene. You covered for a murderer. Those injuries weren't caused by the fall, were they? Oh my God," I gasped. "You think Zach killed her, don't you?"

Dad flinched. "Zach did not murder Drea Temple."

"How do you know? On drugs, he was capable of anything. What about the blood?"

"How did—"

"He told me."

Dad's cheeks sagged. A heavy sigh wooshed from between his lips. "Drea Temple died as a result of drowning. It was unfortunate but there was nothing odd about it. It was a simple accident."

"Did she sustain defence injuries?"

"Of course not."

"No signs of a struggle?"

"No."

Cold silence consumed the conservatory. I stood up, kicked back the chair. "She was standing and fell through backwards," I said, acting it out. "So injuries would have been to the back of her head, maybe her face as she hit the sides."

"Precisely," he said as if I were a slow learner that had finally grasped the basics of arithmetic. "And as you know very well, head wounds bleed a lot."

"Enough to spatter the walls and beams? Sounds more like blunt force trauma." I spat out the words in terms my dad would definitely understand. "What was it, a brick, piece of wood, lead piping?"

Anger flashed across his face, pinching and tightening the muscles in his jaw.

"Don't be ridiculous. I know my son," he repeated.

"But you didn't know your daughter. None of us did. Scarlet died to protect your vicious little secret."

His head jerked up; nostrils dilated. Streaks of red flashed across his cheekbones and his eyes shrank to two tiny pinpricks of rage. I thought he might hit me and, despite my own hot sense of justice and truth finally prevailing, I cowered.

"That's a monstrous thing to say." Dad struggled to contain his fury. "How dare—"

"How dare I? How dare you! You put the fear of God into Barry Bevan."

At the mention of the cabbie's name, Dad's jaw jacked open. The red in his cheeks fled to white. Time to go in for the kill.

"Bevan was Richard Bowen's biological father."

I waited a beat, watched Dad's face, merciless.

"But how did —how?" His expression was one of stunned confusion.

"You're the detective. You figure it out."

Chapter 61

"All right. All right. Keep your pants on." Lenny threw open the door, took one look. "What's wrong?"

Agitated, I bowled in, almost colliding with the console table in the hall. I'd tried to phone Rocco en route but the line registered as being discontinued. When Rocco said he'd cleared out, I thought it was temporary. I didn't think he meant excommunication, rip and run. Sending an email from my phone to his work address resulted in a failure notice.

"Through to the lounge," she said. "It's cooler in there."

"Did I get you out of bed?" The way her robe hung off one shoulder, she'd clearly slung it on. I glanced at my watch: 3.05 p.m.

She wrinkled her nose. "It's not a crime. You gave me the day off, remember?"

"'Course." I looked up at the ceiling gingerly. "I haven't disturbed you, have I?"

"I wish." Lenny's laugh was genuine. "Do I need to put the kettle on?"

I looked at her soulfully.

"Booze?"

"Can I leave my car here?"

"Sure." She gave me a shrewd look. "Does Rocco Noble have anything to do with your unexpected visit?"

If only it were that simple.

While she fixed drinks, Lenny indicated I sit down. "Gin," she declared. "The only drink in a crisis." I sat down on a mauve coloured Chesterfield in a room that resembled an abstract painting knocked up by a four-year-old. The walls were painted in alternating raspberry and Grecian blue, the contents mostly identifiable purchases from the shop, the exception a high-tech sound system.

Lenny returned, deposited an ice-cold glass in my hand and sat down beside me. She swung her legs up onto my lap, rather like a cat stakes its territory. Normally, I'd protest, but normal counted for nothing these days.

"Now I'm sitting comfortably, you'd best begin."

So, I did. It took me fifteen minutes to blurt out the whole sorry tale, from my refusal to believe that Scarlet's alleged depression led to the accident, her involvement with Richard Bowen, his attempt to blackmail her, the terrible revelations about Zach and my father and his connection to Rocco Noble, to Scarlet's final desperate act.

"Christ, that's awful," Lenny said, visibly shocked. "Poor Scarlet." Sombre, I took a big gulp of gin. "And poor you," Lenny said. "There's no easy way to put this but most addicts are liars." She spoke without judgement, simply a statement of fact. "Did Zach have anything to do with Drea Temple's death?"

"My heart says no."

"What about your instinct?"

"Is there a difference?"

"Your heart is what you want to believe. Your instinct tells the truth."

"Then no."

"But she was murdered?"

I met Lenny's eye. Rocco thought so. Why else would my father behave in such a reckless way? And the blood spatter – how had that happened? "Which means that, if Zach didn't do it, the killer is in the wind." I told Lenny about Rocco's warning.

Lenny pulled a face. "I feel bad for saying what I did about him."

I smiled weakly.

"I need more booze," Lenny announced, swinging off the sofa. "You?"

"Please." I handed her my glass. While she was gone, I took out my phone and spotted a text from Chancer: 'Need to talk. Are you free?' His timing was terrible.

Lenny plonked a tray of drinks in front of me. "Brought the bottle and there's ice in the bucket. Thought it could be a long afternoon. You can stay if you want. The bed's made up in the spare room."

"Thanks, Lenny, but I'd like to sleep in my own home. I'll grab a cab."

"Well, the offer's there if you change your mind."

She viewed me with a hawkish expression. "What are you going to do?"

I ran my fingers through my hair. "About my father?" My family resembled a cheap film set; nothing solid behind us except fake computer-generated images. Would I dismantle it all? I honestly didn't know.

"About everything. Rocco? Zach? Dear God, was your mum in on it?"

"Not sure." Was that what their argument was about the evening I dropped by? And did my father somehow steer Nate away from attracting any more attention when he spoke to him in the study?

Lenny waited a respectful beat. "Whatever you decide, there will be consequences."

Out of my depth, I nodded in dismay.

"Do you think Dusty could help?"

"Can't see how."

"She's family. Older, wiser, she might be good in a crisis."

My aunt was not an obvious choice, although she had known my father for a very long time. I let out a sigh. "I guess a phone call wouldn't hurt."

Chapter 62

Dusty took a big swallow of gin. "I'm not going to defend my sister. If she knew about Drea Temple, she's as guilty as your father in my book, but it's important that you understand the dynamics that govern their relationship."

I baulked inside. How important?

"You remember our conversation at the barbeque?" Dusty said.

"Some of it."

"There's a reason your mother is not the easiest individual."

I wondered what else might be revealed. My questioning look said as much.

"When we were kids growing up, we weren't very well off. Actually," Dusty said, ejecting a lemon pip, "we were bloody hard up."

I had no idea. Us children had had next to nothing to do with either of our grandparents. In fact, it felt positively discouraged. My father's parents were both now dead and I believed only my grandfather on my mother's side was alive.

"Our father was a gambler," she continued, "and when he

wasn't gambling, he was drinking. It was quite a wretched upbringing. I lost count of how many places we moved from, each one a little smaller and cheaper than the previous home.

"Your mother, like me, wanted nice things in life. Nothing wrong with that," Dusty said firmly.

Things started to make sense. My mother needed stability and then she met my father. "Dad was her saviour."

"He rescued her. She owes him a great deal."

Lenny eyed me nervously. "See, that's not so bad."

"They are very much a couple," Dusty continued. "Your father is a daffodil when it comes to your mother. She views him as the really dependable type of man you go to when you're in a hole."

This was not a hole. It was a chasm.

"They truly love each other, Molly," Dusty continued. "Always have and always will. Your father would do anything for her, and she for him. Do you understand?"

I did. After all the years spent together, they still acted like a couple of lovebirds. Family was important to both of them, but I'd always sensed that they could have survived without having us kids. My mum, who wasn't exactly a pushover, deferred to Dad on everything. He'd always have the last word. She admired his dependability, loved all that Alpha male, macho crap. White anger swept through me.

"But we're talking about covering up murder."

"Alleged murder and your mother played no part in it, from what you say."

"She maintained the lie."

"And look how much it's cost her, Molly."

Not something that my sister had factored in, it had been her greatest miscalculation and mistake. She must have been out of her mind to act in the way she did. "Are you saying that I should keep quiet too?"

"That, my darling, only you can decide."

I drained my glass. How could I make that kind of choice?

"You have to tell Rocco," Lenny said, a sentiment with which Dusty agreed.

I explained about him losing his job, clearing out of his home, and cutting off all communications.

"Maybe, he'll come to you."

"Not after the way I treated him." I ran my fingers madly through my hair. "Maybe I should go straight to the police."

"And say what?" Lenny spiked with alarm. "You do realise the consequences?"

"At the moment I'm living with the consequences," I said bitterly. And I hadn't forgotten Charlie Binns and the fact someone, possibly Mallis, had had him bumped off. I asked Dusty if she'd ever heard my father talk about him.

"Ah." She clinked the ice in her glass and took a long swallow. Insides contracting, I asked her to explain.

"Mallis and your dad served together in the MET."

"What are you implying?"

"Nothing, my sweetheart."

"There were rumours. Is that what you mean?" What was it Dad had said? I screwed my brain up tight, trying to recall. Oh yeah, rumours about him supplying Zach, rumours about tipping him off. But the notebook wasn't rumour. That was real.

"What I mean is that there were rumours about Mallis."

"Not about Dad?"

"None of which I'm aware." Dusty chinked the ice in her glass and took a long, thoughtful swallow that made me jag inside. Fascination sharpened Lenny's features. For her, this was an afternoon's titillating entertainment. For me, it was life and death.

I took another swig of gin. The astringent taste sharpened my thinking. What the fuck, I told them about Charlie Binns and the subsequent conversation with Tina Vernon.

Dusty listened hard. When I finished, she said, "I appreciate you might not wish to go directly to the police, but I have a dear friend who might be able to help."

"A police officer?" Surely, that was against the rules. All police officers, retired or not, were bound by the Official Secrets Act; to discuss inside information was a serious offence. "Would this person talk to me?"

"I can't promise. Possibly."

"And?"

"Come on, Dusty," Lenny said, "Stop playing cat and mouse and tell us who it is."

Dusty flashed Lenny a warm smile. "Patience, darling. My source is a senior police officer. Ex-Met, retired to the Cotswolds."

"And he talked to you?" I was astounded.

"Oh for goodness' sake, Molly. Don't be so dramatic. She mentioned that she knew your father."

"And Mallis?"

"She knew him too."

My mind teemed with possibilities.

"Want me to give her a call and grab you an audience?"

Lenny gaped from Dusty to me. "Is this a good idea? Who knows what she might say and if it's bad, there won't be any going back."

"It's fine. It's what I want. I need to hear it. All of it."

Chapter 63

Dusty called a cab for both of us and, after brief discussion, I handed the full running of the shop to Lenny, with my aunt's help.

"What about the alarm system in the shop?" Lenny said.

"Haven't got round to sorting the remote package yet. Look, don't worry, I'll continue to take responsibility."

"You sure?" Dusty said with a rare frown.

"Yup, I'm closer than you. Make sure you arm it each night before you leave."

"Okay, between us we'll drop your car back tomorrow," Lenny said, "push the keys through the door."

"What would I do without you?"

"Manage." My aunt laughed, squeezing my shoulder.

I couldn't imagine anything getting Dusty down. It didn't have the elevating effect I'd hoped for. Dazed and with a terrible sense of foreboding, I asked the driver to drop us both at Dusty's hotel, in town. After paying the fare, she asked if I'd be okay.

"I feel a lot better for talking."

"Good girl. Want to come inside?" She looked up at the grand façade.

"No, thanks. I need to think."

"Not too hard, I hope."

She clip-clopped away on high heels and I walked up the steps to Belle Vue Terrace, a promenade with shops and galleries, set high up on the apex of two roads, and towards Rose Bank Gardens, with its impressive metal sculpture of fighting buzzards. On the steep path leading to one of the hillside walks, I heard my name called. Twisting round, I gaped at the extended hand. The man in the shop. The guy with the BMW. I wasn't sure which appalled me most, the fake grin, rancid breath, or the threat of his touch. I dug my palms into the pockets of my shorts.

"Clive Mallis." A smile lifted the edges of his mouth.

"I know who you are."

His lips stretched thinner. I was in no doubt that he was possessed of a cold and ruthless intelligence. "Sounds like you've already made your mind up about me."

"What do you want, Mr Mallis?" I took a step back.

"Clive, please," he said, with a snicker. "I'm one of your dad's oldest mates. No need for formalities."

Breathing hard, I thought my pounding heart would detonate inside my chest.

"I know what kind of police officer you were," I said with less emphasis than I'd intended, mainly because fear was oozing out of my every pore. Straightaway, he picked up on it.

"Some of it bad, if you believe what you're told, which wouldn't be wise at all. I only wanted to tell you that your father is a good man. Loves his kids," he said, rolling his tongue around the words. "It would be a pity for a family, already broken, to be smashed apart over a silly misunderstanding."

"Is that so?"

He continued to grin, although any warmth evaporated when it reached his cold and empty eyes.

"Did my dad put you up to this?"

"Molly," he said, feigning shock. "How could you think such a thing?"

"I'm not Charlie Binns or someone you can extort loyalty from or threaten with knives and dead animals.'

'I have absolutely no idea what you're talking about.'

My breath briefly snagged in the back of my throat. Mallis looked genuinely perplexed. No matter, I thought, furiously recalibrating. "Did you shut Binns up, or did you get someone else to do it for you?" Probably not my wisest move. The fixed grin faltered. His jaw tensed. Eyes narrowed to two thin slits. I was quite pleased to see a line of sweat break out across his brow. "Not sure I know what you mean."

Attempting to push past him, I felt Mallis's hand clamp on my arm, pinching the skin beneath my elbow. His grip was surprisingly dry – like a snake's.

"Let go of me."

"Calm down."

"If you don't, I'll scream the town down."

His lips hitched into a half-smile. "Okay," he said, releasing me. "Sorry," he added without conviction.

Peeling away, I retreated the way I'd come, the only physical legacy of the conversation a red mark on my skin where Mallis had gripped me. More worrying, was his strong emotional reaction to my question about Charlie Binns.

Out of the gardens, I shot back onto the pavement. At any second, I expected him to catch up and drag me to some place he could kill me. I liked to think I'd landed a fatal blow. Sixth sense told me he'd be back.

Jumping on a bus signed for Malvern Link, I got off at my stop and ran the short journey home. No sooner than I'd stumbled through the front door, Chancer called me again.

"Now's not a good time." Pain creased my temple, the makings of a cracking booze-in-the-day fuelled hangover.

"Tell me when is."

I parked my phone between my left ear and shoulder and slumped onto the nearest chair. "What is it, Chancer?" One part irritation, two parts resignation.

"Firstly, how are you?"

You don't want to know. "I'm all right. Early days. Sorry, I didn't get to speak to you at the funeral."

"That's fine. I completely understand."

"Nice to see you and Edie showing a united front."

"Oh that," he scoffed. "All show. Edie's idea."

"It was a kind thought."

"Nothing kind about it. She couldn't resist tagging along with me – manipulative cow."

"Don't be so vile."

"Yeah, well," he blustered. "Thing is, I wanted to invite you out for a walk."

I scratched my chin. "You've never once asked me out for a walk."

"Well, it's high time I did. And," he said pointedly, "I want your advice."

"Is this connected to Zach?" I said warily.

"Zach? Not sure I follow." I listened hard for any deceit in Chancer's voice. "It's about Edie."

"Oh God, Chancer, I'm no good at relationships."

"On this we can agree." I was supposed to find it funny. I didn't. "Please, Molly. I need to talk to someone. She's driving me crazy."

I took a bold breath. "Is that why you hit her?"

"Who on earth told you that?"

"Edie."

"That frigging little bitch is the limit. Surely, you know me better than that?"

I didn't know. From where I was sitting, anything was possible.

"Molly? Are you still there?"

"Sorry, yeah. Okay."

"You'll see me?" His voice soared several octaves, peculiarly overjoyed by the prospect. You'd think I'd agreed to hook him up with royalty.

"I meant I believe you."

"Aw, Molly."

"All right, all right, I give in." If only to prove to Mallis that if he had any malign designs on me, I had a sturdy male companion.

"Great. Tomorrow afternoon. Got any walking boots?"

"Of course." It was practically a requirement of living in Malvern, although I drew the line at walking sticks and the rest of the kit beloved by serious ramblers.

"We'll have a smashing trudge across the hills in the sunshine and then I'll treat you to dinner at The Swan."

"Chancer, I don't need to be treated."

"Nonsense. I'll pick you up at 3.30 p.m. See you then."

With a splitting head, I fell into bed and pretty much slept the clock round, only waking to drink water, take painkillers and totter off to the bathroom. Magically, the next morning, I woke exceptionally early but with a clear head. That was the problem.

And then there was Rocco. I had to find him.

Chapter 64

I showered and ate breakfast. About to leave, my phone rang. As if by some weird kind of telepathy, it was Mum.

"Molly, can I come round?"

"I'm just on my way out, Mum."

"Could you hang on for a few moments?"

"Sorry, I have a hellish schedule." Not the real reason for my reluctance to see her.

"Please, Molly. We're all upset."

I bet.

"This is important."

"Then say it now."

"No, sweetheart, not like this."

I blinked back sudden tears. My mother rarely applied terms of endearment. I don't think she'd ever called me 'sweetheart' in her life.

"Please, Molly. Don't shut us out."

Shut me out, more like. Grappling with my temper, I said, "If you've come to plead on behalf of Dad or say you didn't know, forget it."

"This is between you and me, Molly. Your father has no idea I'm making this call."

Had to rate as a first in Napier history. Everything they did, they did together. No secrets between them; only secrets between them and me. "Did you cover for him?"

"Molly, it's complicated."

I took a deep breath, looked at the wall. I'd spent so long wanting to know and now I did, I couldn't bear any more lies. And I was wary. I didn't want my mother knowing to what extent I could ruin them. "I'll be here for the next twenty minutes."

She must have been virtually on my doorstep because, by the time I'd popped to the loo, she was in my kitchen. I stood with my back to the sink, arms crossed, as defensive as I felt. Mum stared at me with haggard eyes. Dusty was right. My father's actions and Scarlet's death had cost her everything.

"I'm not apologising for what your father did."

"Good."

"I had no idea until after it was done."

"I believe you."

The lines around her eyes relaxed a little. "But I was in a difficult position. If I'd told the truth, my husband and my son would have gone to prison. You know how badly police officers are treated behind bars."

Which was why I felt so torn. "Did it ever occur to you that Zach could have killed Drea Temple?"

"Never. It's not in his nature." Her voice was strong, unwavering. I believed her, or at least I believed that she had no doubt. Mother love is as powerful as dragon glass.

"Your silence protected a murderer."

She flushed angrily. "I was told it was an accident. As soon as your father told me what he'd done, I asked for a divorce." I blinked in surprise. "He begged me to stay. It took him a while to get me to change my mind. We paid for Zach to go away, making it clear that, although we still loved him, he was no longer welcome at home." She glanced down so that I wouldn't see the tear of frustration and distress beading down her cheek.

"And Mallis? Why does my father stay friends with a corrupt police officer? He's a thug and he threatened me."

"He did what?"

I described my recent encounter. I'd like to say she looked surprised. She didn't. "Clive will do anything to protect his interests."

"His interests meaning himself." I repeated my question.

"Have you ever heard the saying about keeping your enemies close? Your father saw a greater advantage in controlling Clive than making an adversary of him."

"He's afraid of him?"

"Mallis is not a man to cross, Molly."

And I'd made a big mistake in being so loose mouthed around him. The sooner I could speak to Dusty's contact, the better. "That night Mallis visited, what was that all about?"

"I wanted to come clean with you. I thought if I explained, we could work something out, but your dad and Clive were dead set against."

And they were right, her expression said. At least we could agree on something. "What made you change your mind about leaving Dad?"

"You and Scarlet."

I expressed disbelief. "We'd already left home by then."

"It was still important to keep the family together." It seemed like a lame, badly rehearsed response. Recalling my aunt's words, I believed that my mother's strong sense of self-preservation was a more compelling reason. I think she read the cynicism in my eyes because she said, "You were always such a daddy's girl. It would have broken your heart."

"And yet he broke it anyway." The sad truth: it would take me more than a lifetime from which to recover from his betrayal.

"He's not a bad man, Molly."

"How can you say that?" Except I knew; because he'd rescued her.

"Your father didn't set out to deliberately hurt. He was only protecting his family."

"Well, sometimes that's not possible." My voice was uncomfortably on the rise. "Sometimes you have to let people take the rap for their mistakes and pay for them."

My mother spread her hands, eyes glistening, fingers trembling. "Don't you think that's exactly what we're doing?"

I couldn't argue with that.

Chapter 65

Rocco would know what to do. His decision whether or not to go straight to the police and tell them the whole sorry tale trumped any that I might take.

It took me a few minutes to reach his cottage on the Wyche. As I thumped on the door, a man, climbing into a van outside, looked across. "Nobody there, love. Must be on holiday, or something." Next, I hammered it to Worcester, taking bends too fast and overtaking blind. Breathlessly, I parked opposite the cathedral. Despite the early hour, sunshine bleached the pavement, the walls, and every building in between, the city of Worcester gasping in its thrall. The insane heat felt like another obstacle in a trail of others and I staggered up to the crescent near the cathedral and hurried into ContraMed. Blissfully cool inside, it exuded professionalism and respectability. It felt safe.

A middle-aged woman with heavy features sat in reception, pecking intently at a keyboard with short powerful fingers. She did not look up. I waited, feeling invisible. When she eventually glanced up, I plastered on my best people-pleasing smile.

"I was wondering if I could leave a message for Rocco Noble."

"He no longer works here." The way she said it you'd think I'd asked to speak to a celebrity convicted of indecent behaviour.

"I don't suppose you know where he's gone."

"Even if I did that information is entirely confidential." End of.

I thanked her and slunk out. Now what? The chance of Rocco actually being in his flat seemed remote. I tried it anyway. Pressed the buzzer. No reply. 'You'll know where to find me,' he'd said, except I didn't. So, I had a better idea.

From Worcester, via the M5, I drove to Winchcombe and the location of a crime scene known to at least three of us. The house could have been done up and sold. In fact, it was likely, and I was hardly going to ask its new owner whether I could poke about in a fruitless attempt to look for the remains of an old well. Yet I couldn't turn my back on where it had all started. I owed it to Scarlet and to Drea.

I parked in a gateway not far from the phone box Zach had used that night and from which he'd sent his SOS. It was still there and in working order. I walked a little way up and turned onto an unmade drive on my left that veered off from the main road. Long and winding, up a steep incline, it almost appeared to reach back on itself. The higher I climbed, the more the noise of traffic receded.

The drive petered out, squirming into a narrow track with high hedges. Instinctively, I looked about, my blood running a little too quickly, my breath too slow. Seemed I was alone.

346

Squatting down, I examined the ground for human activity, like tyre tracks from a quad bike or small tractor, but the earth was too dry and difficult to read.

Rounding a bend, the house appeared. A construction of brick and timber made invisible by woodland. Regarding it through Zach's eyes, I instantly saw the appeal. Secluded, secret, out of sight, it was the perfect place for illicit and illegal activity. Strangely, I felt as if Scarlet was with me in spirit. Maybe that's why I felt as if someone was watching. Would Mallis' halitosis give him away if he were near? I craned my head to see if anyone lurked in the undergrowth then swivelled my gaze from the building to the surrounding web of trees. There was no wind, but I swore the leaves rustled.

A sign, not very recent from its dog-eared appearance, warned me that demolition was in progress and to keep out. I drew near and skirted cigarette butts, used condoms, crisp packets and empty cans.

Traditionally built, with timber weatherboarding, the front of the house had a lean-to entrance with a single window beneath an oak lintel. The door had been replaced with sheet metal, impossible to penetrate. I peered through the broken glass. Aside from a rank smell of damp, mildew and dead flies, there wasn't much to deduce because stone walls obscured my vision and mirrored the weird Tardis effect of a house within a house that Zach had described. Even if I could climb in, I wasn't sure what, if anything, I'd find after so much time had elapsed. Like most people, I knew the value of DNA and the fact that every contact left a trace, but criminals still got away with murder. If anyone could cover his tracks, or rather Zach's, my father could.

I slipped round the back, my footsteps loud against dry air that hummed with insects. The back door had also been replaced with sheet metal. Every window in the back elevation was boarded up, but on the ground floor, below a stretch of guttering suspended mostly in thin air, the planks across one aperture had crumbled from damp and woodworm.

With a couple of tugs at the rotten section, it came away quickly, yet there still wasn't enough space for me to climb through. Banking on the fact that when wood rots, it quickly spreads, I grasped hold and, digging my heels in, used all my body weight as leverage. Sawing back and forth, two more boards came away and made a big enough opening for me to burrow through. I put my hands flat against the window-ledge and clambered up and through on my tummy, arms extended, landing headfirst.

The gap between the new and old house spread to about three feet. Whoever had made the site secure hadn't bargained on or allowed for the first line of defence being breached. With little room to manoeuvre, I entered the original building through the first available entrance, which happened to be the front door.

Inside was dark and musty, and the damp organic smell increased to suffocating proportions. Fumbling in my rucksack, I took out the torch Lenny gave me, switched it on, letting the light play on the walls. I'd expected bare stone, brick and silence. Instead, the house whispered. Its walls were covered in wallpaper mottled with black mould. Holes in the fabric told me that there had once been wall lights, but these were ripped out, only wires remaining. Beneath my feet, quarry tiles, old newspapers, mail and litter.

Doors off to the left and right were open. Mindful that the place was a death trap, I shone the torch around from the safety of the corridor. Mahogany furniture, too heavy to nick easily, glared back. In one room: chairs without seats and a sofa sprouting horsehair. An ornate gilded mirror, that must have been wonderful once, now cracked in three places, hung off the wall. Gingerly, I ignored the stairs and edged my way towards a door at the end. When I pushed it open, with a loud creak, fear zapped my spine. I had the sensation of being entombed.

Chapter 66

Flashing the torch across the floor revealed that it was cobbled. Taking tiny steps, I inched further into the jaws of the house. On the far right: an old range cooker and what looked like a bread oven. Hooks, presumably for pots and pans, hung from low beams over a static central unit with drawers and cupboards. Away, to the left, the room disappeared into nothingness, without shadow or form. Spooked, I focused ahead, on another door. At what I suspected was the sound of trickling water I took an insane look over my shoulder. In this house, with its shifting walls and fathomless spaces, it was hard to tell what was real and what imagined. At every step, I saw stuff that goes bump in the night. Thankfully, I did not see the ghosts of my sister or Drea Temple. Perhaps I wasn't as far gone as I'd feared.

Forcing myself forward, I crossed the kitchen. Darkness clawed at me, digging in its talons, hooking me by my toenails, dragging me forward. Heart thumping, I flashed the torch, saw a door and two windows ahead at what would have been the back of the original building. Guiding the light down to the floor, I could see why. The ground on this side of the house was boarded. Right in the middle, a metal mesh grille covered a hole that gaped like an open wound. This was where Drea had died and where my brother and father conspired to cover up a crime.

A sour taste flooded my mouth. I wondered how my father had prised her out. It would have been difficult with the floorboards already unstable. Looking up, I noticed a rafter that hung about two feet from the ceiling, the same rafter that would have been spattered with blood. It looked solid enough to take extra pressure. When shifting bulky furniture up through or out of windows, I'd devised a system of ropes and pulleys. It was conceivable that Dad had applied a similar method. It would have been a painstaking task, which only told me how committed he was to covering Zach's tracks.

Standing still, I begged the house to give up its secrets. With fresh eyes, I pictured Drea standing before me with a lazy smile and drugged-up expression. She wouldn't be expecting danger. So easy for me to reach out and touch her. Or strike her. Or smash something against her face, or over her head, and send her flying backwards. Droplets of blood would be bigger than a gunshot wound, smaller than a punch. How had Drea's blood wound up on the beam and up the wall?

I threw my right arm out in front of me, swinging it forward; registering that any blood could be cast off a weapon while in motion. Potentially, an assailant would also be spattered with blood.

I backed away. Every muscle in my body constricted as I

retreated, fearing that the house could suck me in forever. When I dived back into the light, I gasped with overwhelming relief.

Knackered and nauseous, I pitched forward, resting my hands on my knees, taking deep breaths, my nose level with a wasteland that once would have been a garden. A weed-riddled brick path carved a route through chest high grass to apple and pear trees that stood dejected and choked by thistles and brambles. I imagined Zach stumbling out in the dark, walking a little way off to relieve himself against a tree. He said he didn't know how long he spent. Under the influence, he could be forgiven for not knowing his own name. As I straightened up, a spark of knowledge ignited inside me, confirming what I'd already suspected. With Zach off his head, it would be easy for someone else to approach and sneak in. With two exits and entrances, maybe whoever it was entered through the back door, while Zach and Drea had entered from the front. Yes, that would work. And Drea, in her drugged-up state, would have been fair game for a murderer. Period.

Fear washed over me as an alternative scenario assumed greater credence. Nerves grinding, aware that in this strange and hostile place I was as vulnerable as Drea Temple, I took to my heels and ran and didn't stop running until, out of breath with a stitch in my side, I reached my car.

Mind teeming with images, I didn't let up until I was safely back in Malvern. I needed light and colour and shops and familiarity, and drove into town, parked near the Winter Gardens.

Dusty's call came through while I was debating whether I had the bottle to climb out of my car.

"How are you fixed for tomorrow?"

"No problem." Can't come soon enough. Mallis lurked at the forefront of my mind like a demonic presence.

"Rachel was keen to stress that she can only talk to you in general terms. She can't give you specifics due to confidentiality."

Disappointment racked me. If she couldn't do that, why bother?

"Still want to go ahead?" Dusty said, reacting to my lacklustre response.

I said I did.

"Her name's Rachel Haran." Dusty gave me an address in Moreton in Marsh. "10.30 a.m."

"I'll be there."

"Don't be late. She detests unpunctuality."

Chapter 67

"I'm devastated."

I'd parked the car in the garage and was preparing to close the door when Edie door stepped me. I could tell straight-away that I was the cause of Edie's devastation. It didn't take a neurosurgeon to work out why. I'd opened my mouth to Chancer, and he'd had a go at his estranged wife. Shit.

"I thought I could trust you. I thought you were my friend." Very few women manage to pull off crying their lungs out without ending up with a red nose, red eyes and mascara down their cheeks. Edie wept with abandon and savage grace, like it was an art form, yet she did not have so much as an eyelash out of place. In her flowing sleeveless dress, all pinks and muted greens, she resembled a damsel in distress from a hundred-year-old old fairy-tale.

"I am your friend, but I'm Chancer's too." And I was Chancer's first, although I didn't spell this out.

"You accused him," she sobbed.

"I didn't accuse him. I asked him. Anyway, if it's true—"

"If?"

I took a smart step back. "What I meant is that you're a victim, so you don't need to take any garbage from Chancer."

"I told you in confidence," she wailed.

"Then I'm very sorry you think I broke it." Which was a mealy-mouthed way of saying I apologise for nothing. "Look, why don't you come in?"

Although she did a mean line in hurt and dejection, mercifully the tears magically stopped.

"I was so touched you came to Scarlet's funeral," I said with genuine warmth.

Edie dithered, plunging her hands into the pockets of her dress, weakening. "If you're sure."

"I'd like it." Because an idea, that had hovered on the edges of my consciousness, with Edie's help, I could net.

"All right," she said.

I led Edie through the garden and up the lavender scented path. She admired my best effort at a cottage garden, a rebellious patch of phlox and old-fashioned plants like foxgloves and hollyhocks. Subconsciously, it was my response to the ordered borders at my parents. I thought again about my conversation with Mum. What could she say that would change a thing? How could she defend the indefensible?

I opened the back door and Edie followed me inside.

"I love the way you've done your kitchen. It's modern but still cosy." Edie, it seemed, had gone from injured starlet to gushing sycophant in the time it took me to boil an egg.

"Elderflower or Cranberry?" I didn't have Edie down for a Coca-Cola sort of girl – too much caffeine.

She plumped for Elderflower and I poured two glasses. We

sat across from each other and Edie took a nervous sip. She really was very pretty. I let her settle and set the pace.

"I'm sorry about earlier. I didn't mean to have a go."

"I take it divorce proceedings aren't going well?"

Edie looked up, pain in her eyes. "I can't bear it."

I have little knowledge of couples splitting up bar the obvious: good-natured people morphing into unreasonable, unhinged, irrational psychos. This either lasts for a short space of time or decades. At one of my friend's weddings, the mother of the bride forbade her ex-husband from walking his daughter down the aisle. I viewed Edie with sympathy, but I also thought she was bloody hard work.

"Might it be a good idea to give Chancer space?"

She recoiled. At a loss, I ran my finger over the grain of the table, trying to look wise and enlightened. "Maybe the time for fighting is over."

"I'm not the one doing it."

I looked up, caught her exasperation. She had the demeanour of a three-year-old told that she could have a present soon, but not quite yet. I gave a hoarse laugh. "I'm not the oracle, Edie."

She softened a bit. What else could she do? She hung her head, her shallow chest rising and falling, as if she were about to faint. "It's just—" Something was clearly bothering her.

"What, Edie?"

She looked up soulfully into my eyes. "What if he's met someone, someone he likes better?"

"That's not the impression I got."

"Honestly?"

"Would you like me to talk to him?"

She didn't answer straightaway. Her top teeth sank into her bottom lip. Chewing. Thinking.

"I'm seeing him this afternoon."

The corners of her eyes flickered, and she broke into a radiant smile. "Would you?"

I smiled back, racking my brains how best to steer the conversation. Before I had a chance, Edie drank up, stood up. "Hell, I have to go," she said, "I'm going to be late picking up the kids from Mum's."

Furious with myself for missing my chance, I said I'd see her out.

"Thanks for being a pal." She gave me a big hug, her scent enveloping me in spring flowers and neroli. "And, God, I'm so sorry," she said, wide-eyed. "Here's me blithering on about my relationship problems, completely forgetting you. How are things?"

"Oh, good days, bad days." Shit days, actually.

My hand hovered over the doorknob. Edie waited, the tap of her sandal against the polished wooden floorboard her only giveaway that she was impatient to leave. Time to go for it.

"Did Chancer ever meet a woman called Drea Temple?"

Edie put a hand to her chest, her porcelain features turning the colour of old cement. "Oh God, so there is someone. Where did he meet her? How long has it been going on? I knew it. I simply knew it."

Before she had a seizure, I said, "No, no, it's all right, Edie, I didn't mean. I meant —" My mind scrabbled for a rational explanation. I was horribly conscious that Edie was hanging on my every syllable. "Her name came up in a random conversation," I said clumsily. "You know how it is."

Breath seeped out between her lips like a slowly deflating balloon. "You completely had me there," she said, with a jittery laugh.

"So, the name doesn't ring a bell?"

She shook her head slowly; the way people do when asked for directions and they haven't a clue. "No. Why?"

"She was a friend of Zach's a long time ago. I wondered whether Chancer knew her too."

"Well, if he did, he never mentioned her to me."

Chapter 68

Chancer was unusually quiet as he drove, with no trace of his natural exuberance. The deep tan he'd acquired over the summer months made his eyes bluer than usual. Edie's claim that he'd thumped her sat heavily with me.

Like a croupier in a casino, I mentally arranged the cards in front of me. Was Chancer off his game due to divorce proceedings, the morning's argument he'd had with Edie or a recent conversation with my brother?

We were driving towards Welland, over the common, past old-fashioned tulip-styled lampposts. The way the sun caught the hills made them look like fire-breathing dragons. Then it was over Castlemorton Common where long-horned cattle flanked the road on both sides. Beyond: a narrow stretch and car park.

We climbed out of the Jag, put on our boots and set off at a cracking pace up a rutted path with spectacular views behind us. The sun powered down and I was glad I'd grabbed a wide-brimmed hat to protect me. Halfway up, we passed an abandoned car, and a scattering of cottages. I let Chancer go on ahead. We didn't speak much other than to comment on the weather and the scenery. I could tell by the way he walked, his shoulders rounded, that he was troubled. I was troubled too.

Eventually, the path forked left, and we trudged up a narrow rocky incline, up and up, to where a monument stood on our right and the Brecon Beacons in the distance. From here, the going was better, less steep, the way flattening out a little. Only then, when a couple of serious walkers overtook us, and it was just he and I, side by side, did we pause for water and speak of anything that mattered.

"I want to put the record straight about a couple of things."

I turned to him and smiled. "I'm listening."

He smiled back, grateful and nervous. "Edie didn't lie."

"About you wanting to split up?"

"About me hitting her."

"Oh," I said. Christ, I thought.

"I'm not going to dignify it by saying that she made me. It happened once and once only, and it shouldn't have done, and I was wrong."

"It's not me you need to tell," I said chippily. "It's her." And there was me thinking that she was an overdramatic fantasist.

"I know, and I have, but do you see that we simply can't go on together?"

"If Edie can forgive you, then why not?"

"Because I don't love her."

"You must have done once."

"I never have."

"Hell, Chancer, then why marry the woman?"

He looked across, enquiringly.

"Oh, please," I said, heat spreading across my face and neck, which had nothing to do with the route march.

He reached out, took my hand and drew me close. "Why didn't I choose you, instead of Edie?"

His body pressed against mine. It felt all so familiar. I looked up into his eyes, saw the Chancer I used to know before life had moulded and distorted him into something unrecognisable and quite different. I didn't know whether this was down to an overbearing father, a difficult, unfulfilled marriage, the pressures of working in a dog eat dog industry, or something dark and unspoken. If it was, my last vestige of belief in someone from my past was dead and buried. I repeated the mantra I'd repeated at the time. "I'm not from your world." Or the right set.

"That was all in your pretty little head."

I remembered how Chancer had been, for a short space of time, my guilty secret pleasure. Nobody knew, not even Zach. When it got serious between us, I'd got scared. I'd been hung up about being outside 'the in crowd', never quite fitting in, and money, or the absence of it in my case, and not being as smart or as well-educated as his friends. His family terrified me, particularly Stephen Chancellor. I'd gone travelling in a lame effort to help me straighten out my mind. As one month drifted into another, we lost touch and, when I came back, Edie was on the scene.

He leant in, dropped a single soft kiss upon my lips, not at all like Rocco who felt as if he were devouring me. Yet it still felt wrong. "We can't." I pulled away. "It's too late."

"Is this because I lost my temper once?"

"Because it's not fair on Edie."

"Fuck Edie."

"No," I said firmly. "I'm not in a good place." There's Scarlet and Rocco, and Zach and my dad who colluded to cover a crime, and my mother who kept her mouth shut, and a girl called Drea Temple.

"But with time?" He looked expectant and fearful. I opened my mouth, but no words came out. "Look, you don't have to make a decision," Chancer said with forced jollity. "Let's head up towards the quarry."

In reality, the way ahead to Gullet Quarry was barred and with good reason. A notorious spot for wild swimmers and skinny dippers, or people wanting to cool off in the mistaken belief that is was a safe environment, too many young men had lost their lives in its unfathomable depths. Steep-sided and with murderous drops, it wouldn't have been my first choice for a swim – not that I was much good at it in any case.

"Race you to the top," Chancer said. Unable to resist a challenge, I took to my heels. I was fitter but Chancer was stronger. We level-pegged it and then, in a final spurt, I nudged ahead. Chancer caught me and spun me off my feet, swinging me round. "Put me down," I giggled, my hands drumming his shoulders. It seemed so long since I'd last laughed like this. Carefree. Like the old days before things turned ugly. "See," he said, planting me down carefully. "What's not to like?"

I gave him a wry smile. Chancer had always been so persuasive, but I could be persuasive too. "Can I ask you something?"

"Fire away."

"Did you ever meet a woman called Drea Temple?"

I expected a strong and immediate reaction. Either an emphatic, "No," or silence followed by him dropping his arms, drawing back, with an expression of stunned numbness. I expected him to speak in an empty tone. Instead, his hold on me tightened and so did his voice. "Yes, but if you're asking me whether I had anything to do with her death, you're wrong. As importantly, why are you interested in a woman who disappeared a decade ago?"

Chapter 69

By mutual consent, we agreed to continue the conversation in the nearest pub. The walk down was as silent as the walk up. We took the only route along a path flanked with bramble and nettles and pitted with tree roots, rabbit holes and badger setts. The path briefly widened out to where someone had started a fire and the chalk-white sides of the quarry were visible. Impossible to evade the sense of danger only a few feet away, I stayed clear of the massive drop on the other side of the fence. Trees, so impossibly green, made your eyes squint.

My gaze eventually dropped, mesmerised by shifting shapes in the water below that had claimed so many. Some said there were hidden rocks and obstacles, but shock was the primary factor in almost every death. I knew that sudden immersion in water that never had a chance to heat up had a stunning effect on the human body. Rapid cooling, restricted blood flow followed by panic as muscles refused to respond and fatigue set in. Is this what befell Drea Temple after the smack to her head? Not a great way to go, although better than smashing yourself to bits in a car crash.

Finally, we arrived at the bottom. The sun beat down on a rocky shore and semblance of a beach, giving it a deceptively benign appearance. This is where the sun-worshippers had assembled and, from here, taken to waters of dubious quality. Despite the beautiful day and sunlight glinting off the surface, it bled with unknowable terrors.

I let out an involuntary shiver as we travelled past barbed wire and an easy to scale five-bar gate, police notices and signs warning, in no uncertain terms, of the dangers. At the end, where the land met the road, boulders like sentinels sat squat and immobile to prevent cars from driving through.

The short distance to the car park was down a narrow road piled high with bracken on either side. A kiosk open for teas and ice cream did a mean trade with those who were there for the eats rather than the walking.

Silently, I climbed into Chancer's Jag. In close confines, the air felt dense and heavy as if a storm were brewing. Chancer didn't particularly look like a man caught in a bind. He seemed capable, in charge, as if he had the drop on me.

He drove a little way to the nearest pub, a place that served home-cooked food and local craft ales. I wasn't driving and ordered vodka, Chancer a pint of beer. All sorts of things were burrowing through my mind, none of them nice.

Chancer took a gulp and eyed me. "So, what's this all about?"

I shook my head. "You first." He leant back expansively, legs apart, a gesture I knew so well. "Don't try and bullshit me."

He met the warning note in my voice with an amused smile. "What has Zach told you?"

His side of a sorry story. "I'm not interested in Zach," I said, with what I hoped was sincerity, "I want to hear how you knew her."

"Simple. Zach introduced me." Chancer scratched the side of his cheek. "If memory serves me correctly, we first met at The White Hart."

"You met her more than once?"

"Well, yeah."

"Two, or three times? More?"

"Jesus, Molly, you make it sound like a date. There was a group of us. I was going out with Edie, in case you'd forgotten."

Low blow. "I hadn't forgotten. Did Edie meet her?" Had Edie lied?

"No," Chancer said vehemently. "She hated the White Hart. More of a lad's boozer back then."

"What was Drea like?"

"Completely bonkers."

"In a good way?"

"A lovely way. I liked her a lot. Off the wall, a little bit alternative, she had bags of personality."

"Did you find her attractive?"

"Whoa," Chancer said, as if he'd spotted a trap an inch before he was about to step into it. "If you're trying to suggest something, don't."

"It's a simple enough question."

"Which you're blatantly pushing. Every red-blooded male in the room found her attractive."

"Sex-magnet?"

"Zach certainly thought so. He was embarrassing to be around." As I feared. "What is this, Molly? You seriously don't think Zach had anything to do with her disappearance?"

I narrowed my eyes. How much did Chancer actually know? "You knew Drea and Zach were drug buddies?"

Chancer took another drink, by way of an answer.

"Come on, you must have known."

"Yes, I did."

"So?"

"So what?"

"When was the last time you saw her?"

"I don't believe this." Any warmth in Chancer's voice had evaporated. A shiver passed through me. I was glad I was in a public place in a bar packed with people. I stood my ground.

"Were you with Zach on that New Year's Eve?"

His voice lifted in anger. "I was not. I was at my folks celebrating. I saw Drea a couple of days after Christmas and I never saw her again."

"On your own?"

"Like I said, it wasn't what you think."

Something in the back of my mind detonated. And like magic, it all made sense. I'd never questioned Chancer's bond with my brother. Others had but never me. I'd believed that their relationship was based on loyalty and friendship. How stupid I'd been. How naïve. 'Quality', Zach had said. And a high-end product requires someone to provide it, who moves in the right circles, is good at numbers, percentages, returns, someone connected who didn't necessarily sample it, although might if his deal worked out and he felt like celebrating.

I wanted to scream, and I wanted to run. And I was furious that he'd duped and let me down so badly.

"You supplied him. You supplied her too."

"Fuck this," Chancer said, snatching up his keys.

"I never took you for a fraud."

He stood up. Fuelled with anger, an ugly twist to his mouth, he seemed bigger and bulkier and more than capable of hitting a woman. The pub fell silent. Drinkers turned. Chancer threw me one last eviscerating stare and strode out. My face on fire, I watched him and then took out my phone and shakily ordered a cab.

Chapter 70

At ten in the morning, Moreton-in-Marsh, with its wide streets and independent cafes and delis, bubbled with shoppers, tourists, tractors and old-world charm.

Nerves shattered; I was out of sorts. On the passenger seat beside me, my bag contained the notebook with a litany of wrongdoing huddled inside.

Heeding Dusty's advice, I arrived early and found a space outside one of several estate agents in town. From there, I headed down the high street to The Manor Hotel where I used the loo and ordered coffee from the appropriately named Beagle Bar. I sat in a leather bucket chair in a tiny alcove between the bar and the main corridor, and with a serene view of the garden. Anonymity mattered. When someone smiled there was no edge, no false move, no sly intent, no tricks. Here I could pretend that the world was a sane and ordered place and that I fitted into it.

Afterwards, I drove to a newish development of modern houses made to look old. With homes of various sizes and configurations, it was more village than estate. Rachel Haran lived in a creamy stone double-fronted number. It had leaded casement windows. The brass knocker was traditional, no nonsense. Before I had chance to use it, the teal-coloured front door swung open. A smiling woman around Dad's age greeted me. Ultra-short grey hair framed a face that told stories. She had sharp, searching hazel-flecked eyes, giving the impression that lying to her would be a pointless waste of time. When she shook my hand there was warmth in her palm, strength in her fingers.

"Thanks for seeing me," I said.

"Please accept my condolences."

She ushered me into a 'living the Cotswold dream' sitting room, all greys and greens, stone and neutral fabrics, and asked if I'd like coffee. Despite already downing enough caffeine to power me to the moon and back, I accepted. While she was gone, I sat down on a two-seater sofa where my eyes fastened on a photograph of Rachel Haran as she was several years ago. Dressed in uniform, she was smiling broadly as she received a commendation from the then Metropolitan Police Commissioner.

Rachel returned with a tray on which a large cafetière took centre stage. There were no biscuits, simply two fine china mugs, a small jug of milk, and bowl of brown sugar. It was a million miles away from the flapjack fiasco in Jacqueline Bevan's home. She asked how I liked my coffee and I watched and waited as she poured for both of us.

"How do you know my aunt?" A standard social icebreaker seemed the best way to begin the conversation.

"We met at a fund-raising event many years ago and became friends."

A 'clean' talker, she wasn't the type to waste time on embellishments.

She took a sip of coffee, eyed me over the rim, smiled and placed the mug carefully on a side table. "What's this all about?" she said, taking charge.

Either I jumped one side of the moral divide to protect my family, as everyone involved wanted me to do, or I leapt the other way and gave them up wholesale. If I could have found another path, I would have done. There seemed no middle ground.

"I believe my father has covered up a murder."

Shock tightened her features. "That's a very serious and dangerous allegation."

It wasn't the great start I'd hoped for. "Which is why I don't make it lightly. I believe he wasn't acting alone but in association with a former police officer, Clive Mallis."

At the mention of Mallis, Rachel Haran's expression darkened. She didn't say, 'nasty man' but she might as well have done. I told her how Mallis had confronted me with a thinly veiled threat.

"You reported this?"

"I'm reporting it to you."

"But I'm no longer a serving police officer."

"I've nobody else to turn to. I don't trust the police, well, not the ones I've met recently."

She raised an eyebrow. "I'm not sure I understand what you're suggesting."

"Corruption and perverting the course of justice."

She leant forwards, touched her lips with an index finger. "You seem a sensible girl and I fully appreciate that this must be a rather emotionally charged time for you but—"

"Makes no difference."

Her gaze was steel-plated. I didn't budge. This was going to be the shortest conversation ever.

"Can we get something straight?" Her tone contained a warning edge and she didn't wait for a reply. "The vast majority of police officers are decent, dedicated individuals."

"Yes, but—"

The flat of Haran's hand shot up, silencing me.

"All right," she said, eyeing me in a way that made me feel very small. "Let's start calmly with your story. If I can help, I will. If not, I'll forget we ever had this conversation."

Chapter 71

I started at the beginning, told her everything as accurately and faithfully as possible about Scarlet's death, the names of the police officers involved, my discoveries about Richard Bowen, Rocco and the connection to Drea, and finally, the revelations about my father and Zach. Towards the end, my emotions got the better of me and I staggered to a halt.

Rachel reviewed what she'd written. Panic feathered through me. Was this going to be another of those 'no case to answer' situations? Was I good enough as a character witness? Would she simply say: 'Ta very much. Very interesting but I'm not a copper now so take it to someone who is.'?

"I suppose it's all so long ago," I said unhappily.

Rachel's expression was cut-throat. "Ten years is nothing, thanks to improved methods in profiling DNA. Cold cases are being solved thirty years after they occurred. However, an investigation cannot be revived on hearsay. The facts would need to be verified."

"Yes, of course." I felt more than a little stupid.

She studied me; sharp eyes slightly narrowed. I think she

registered my lack of self-belief. "Okay," she said crisply. "What do you expect?"

Taken aback, I burbled something about truth and justice. She looked at me sympathetically, but I couldn't help feeling that I had a lot to learn about the mechanics of the law.

"The police need evidence and statements, not theories. Let's start with the immediate issue. Whether or not Stanton or Childe made the wrong call with regard to failing to look more deeply into Richard Bowen's death and the circumstances of the accident, whether or not they later put pressure on Richard Bowen's widow, or your friend, Mr Noble, would be difficult to prove. Why would two police officers risk damaging their careers?"

"Yes, I see." Stupid of me.

"But what about Drea Temple?" I pressed. To hell with Stanton and Childe.

"I'm coming to that," Rachel said in a tone that told me she was not a woman to be rushed. "What makes you think that either Mallis could contrive to pick up the Temple case, or that your father could ensure he did? Any number of others could have been assigned."

In one sentence she'd destroyed my argument. Under her searching gaze, I buckled. There was more.

"As you know, moving a body and failing to lawfully bury it is a criminal offence. Do you know how Drea was transported?"

"My dad's car, I guess."

"And ten years' on—"

"He doesn't have it."

She asked about make and model, which I could tell her, and about registration, which I couldn't.

"You say the coroner recorded an open verdict?"

I nodded. "Neither one thing nor the other, I suppose."

"It's usually recorded in the absence of other evidence." She fell briefly silent. "What the police would need to establish is whether Drea's death was accident or murder."

"But the blow to her head——"

"Might not have killed her. Cause and manner can be two different things."

I swelled with disappointment. Naively, I thought this would be so much easier. Every time I came up with what I assumed were cast-iron facts, Rachel dismantled them. "I don't really understand."

"Cause of death could be drowning. Manner of death: now that's open to interpretation."

"So, it could still be murder?"

"Could be. Might not be. The head injury might have happened shortly before death but the primary and only cause of death was drowning. If, on the other hand, the victim was assaulted, resulting in her falling into water and drowning, the primary cause of death would be drowning, and the secondary cause the head injury." She tapped the tip of the pen on her notebook. I wondered how many times she'd done that during her career. "If what you say is true, your father took extreme action, which would indicate he wished to protect his son. It's a nasty question but do you believe that your brother was involved in Drea's death?"

375

"Zach is weak, vulnerable and easily led, but he's no murderer."

"Fuelled by drugs, even the weak can become killers."

She was right, but something niggled. "What would have been Zach's motive?"

"Any number. Who got the lion's share of the drugs they were taking, a spat about money, sex?"

Fear took another shot at me. Zach had fancied Drea. So had Chancer and every red-blooded male within spitting distance of her.

"Do either Zach or your father know you're here?"

I shook my head.

"You realise they'll be arrested, interviewed, questioned and required to give statements?"

One word bashed me over the head: destruction. "There is another possibility about how she died," I said. "Maybe there was a third party."

"You're suggesting a random assault?"

"The house is in a very secluded spot. If you'd been there, you'd understand that there was nothing chance about the attack."

Rachel scratched her chin, weighing me up. "Where is the house exactly?"

I described the road out of Winchcombe and the way the drive snaked into nowhere.

"I'll take a look this afternoon."

I thought my heart would explode with relief. "Thank you. Then what?"

"One step at a time." The wait and see approach sounded

too much like kicking the can down the road. I waited a beat. "There's something else." I bent down and took the notebook out of my bag and handed it to her. Haran said she wanted evidence, not theories. Well, this was the best I could do.

Chapter 72

She reached for a pair of reading glasses and, scouring the pages, ran an index finger down each list. I watched her face, saw the light of recognition in her eyes, the quiet satisfaction in her expression, like a woman who has spent years mastering a difficult language and suddenly finds she's fluent. She glanced up. "Where did you get this?"

I told her. "I know what it is. It belongs to Clive Mallis." Haran's top lip curled, and her eyes dulled to the colour of finely rolled steel. The notebook held significance for her all right.

I could have told her about Binns and how he was gunned down. If Haran was as intelligent as I thought, she'd make the connection and work it out for herself. All I cared about was justice for Drea and Scarlet.

"What do you know about policing in the 80s?"

"Only what my dad told me."

"Did he tell you that it's regarded as the heyday for police corruption?"

My throat tightened and there was a bitter taste in my mouth that was not attributable to the coffee.

"My job was to root out bent officers," Rachel explained. "You may not understand this but there are degrees of corruption. There are those officers who will turn a blind eye to irregularities. Their only interest is to do the shift, pay the mortgage, get their kids through education and pick up their pensions. Then there are others swinging dicks, if you'll pardon the expression, who don't play by the rules and are willing to cut corners in order, as they view it, to see justice done."

"But—"

"These are not intrinsically corrupt men and women. In other words, the number of bad apples is very few, but those that are, tend to be rotten to the proverbial core."

I couldn't help myself. "And my father was one of them?"

Her expression was cross, her words direct. "Capable, dependable, assiduous and respected, your father was an excellent police officer. Frankly, I'm struggling to believe your father would engage in anything of a criminal nature."

As character references went, it didn't come any better. Tina Vernon had already confirmed as much. Hearing it from the legal side of the fence packed greater punch. Most of me felt relief, a slim part confusion. "But not Mallis?"

"He was in a different category. I'm afraid I can't divulge details."

"I know my Dad worked with Mallis."

"They worked professionally, as they did with other officers. At the time, your father was a DCI and Clive Mallis a young DI."

"How do you explain the fact that they've remained in touch for so long?" My father had hung on to the notebook, long before more recent events. Despite Mum's explanation, I wasn't sure I bought it.

Rachel sat back, crossed her long legs. I pictured her doing this before charging a criminal after lengthy interrogation. Her expression remained closed. If she had an opinion, it wasn't one to share with me. "I do not believe that your father was on the take. It doesn't chime with the man I knew."

And that was the problem.

"You didn't find anything else?" Rachel said.

"Like what?"

"Files, photographs? Back then, we had a particular issue with information going walkabout or missing."

"I guess this was before computerised systems."

"Exactly. No digital footprints."

"I found a folder on my father's computer called 'Operation Jericho.'"

"Never heard of it. What was inside?"

"Day to day stuff about police activities."

"Not exactly dynamite," she said airily. "In any case, without a warrant it can't be accessed."

I glanced down at my hands. Bunched into fists, I'd dug my fingers into my palms so hard they'd left indentations. I slowly unclenched them. Rachel topped up our coffee.

"What happened to Mallis while he was at the MET?" I said.

"Nothing. He applied for a transfer. Although it pains me to say it, we were glad to see the back of him."

Rachel stood up. She clutched the notebook. "Are you happy to leave this with me?"

"If it helps," I said emptily.

She walked me to the door.

"Don't look so glum. I still have contacts but, as I've made plain, I need to be sure. If there's any truth in your allegations, the case is open and ripe for investigation, and we have luck on our side."

Luck, fortune, fate sounded great, I thought, perking up.

"Mallis did what he always did: he shipped out and moved on."

"He did more than that. He climbed a rank to Detective Chief Inspector."

"Unfortunately, it happens, but rest assured that any officer reviewing the case will be utterly impartial and do so with fresh eyes." This would be good. Not so good, I feared that my flaky brother would be required to give evidence and I might be required to testify. I asked Rachel.

She viewed me kindly. "Nobody is making accusations at this juncture but, if the evidence points that way and if it's there, Zach and your dad clearly have questions to answer. If they've broken the law, I don't need to explain the consequences, especially for your father."

Hollowed out, I glanced around the room with the nice furnishings that spoke of an ordered life. I'd not got what I'd come for and now Rachel wanted me to validate all those months or years of working on cases that had frustrated and taken her nowhere. I understood. I really did. Silly me for failing to think her angle through.

Rachel had one last question. "Rocco Noble, is he aware of your findings?"

"Not yet."

"I'd advise you to keep your own counsel."

"Doesn't he have a right to know?"

"Until the facts are established, it might be unwise."

I wasn't sure I could do as she asked and said so.

"This man is important to you?" She held my gaze. Fact was I hadn't fully grasped how much he mattered until now.

"Yes," I said.

"You trust him?"

I shouldn't after the way he'd behaved, but I did. "I do."

Her smile was full, exposing small white teeth. "Then you must act as you see fit."

She patted me on my shoulder and opened the door. "You've done well. The irony is that you'd make a fine detective."

I didn't know what to say to that.

Chapter 73

I left Rachel Haran's wishing I felt calmer. All she had was a battered notebook and hearsay. And my father had been a good man, a good police officer. Everyone said so.

I didn't drive home. I took the M5 and joined the M50. It took me almost two hours to drive the sixty miles to Hereford, the place that had a special spot in Rocco's heart. Timing was almost perfect too. A little over a week ago, we'd sat outside in a courtyard café on our first official date.

Where I'd ripped him to shreds.

I parked the car on a meter in Gaol Street and cut through towards the Castle Hotel and cathedral. Without a flicker of breeze, a sheet-metal sky bore down on crushed and dry earth. Only rain and storm would clear it.

With school out for summer, buildings and buses belonging to the cathedral school took a long siesta. Nothing stirred as I strolled past and into cathedral yard where a solitary stone-mason, sweat pouring off him, worked alone, sanding a column to precision smoothness.

I searched the faces of every person sitting on the grass in front of the ancient building, some stretched out to catch the sun at its deadliest, others ate picnics in the shade. Rocco was not among them.

Hoping he might be inside, I disappeared into the cool interior, the size and magnificence of the cathedral as powerful the second time around and confirmation that I was only a tiny player in the grand scheme of life.

Walking to one end of the cathedral, I crossed over and stopped before *Ascension*, the new art installation honouring the SAS and their families. Beneath windows of vibrant blue stained glass, in an abstract design that defied you to turn away, a striking piece of sculptured stone. Engraved at its base, the SAS regimental badge and motto, and the words 'Always A Little Further.' The message spoke of endurance and courage in adversity and, as far away as I was from the soldiers it celebrated, it chimed with me. Mesmerised, I got exactly what Rocco had seen and half expected him to walk out of the shadows and join me.

But Rocco didn't come.

Dispirited, I stole back outside and cut down Church Street to the café where we'd argued, or rather I'd argued. Every table in the garden was taken. Hopes sagging, I made my way back through. About to step into the street, a waitress I dimly recognised from our last visit stepped towards me.

"It's okay, I'm not stopping." I was only too keen to escape what was a fool's errand.

"Are you Molly Napier?" Her accent was French and her smile hesitant, as if she'd been handed a Photofit and wasn't sure whether the person she was accosting was really on the run or not.

I twisted round, suspicious. "Erm, who wants to know?"

"A man with a big smile."

Rocco. It couldn't be anyone else. "Yes," I said, "that's me." Delight shone out of her eyes. She couldn't look more pleased if she'd won the lottery. "This is for you." She handed me a piece of paper, with a number written on it in Rocco's unmistakeable handwriting. Before I had a chance to thank her, she turned to serve a customer who wanted to pay a bill.

*

"How did you know?"

I coursed with lust when I saw him. When he drew close and kissed my lips, I felt ridiculously happy, safe even.

We sat outside in the shade of a courtyard bar and restaurant, a hidden surprise off the High Street. With the lunchtime rush over, and two bottles of Fentiman's lemonade apiece, we were alone. Rocco looked good. A close-fitting T-shirt hugged his gym-fit physique, and his eyes were bright, shiny and rested, more than could be said for mine.

"I didn't know you'd come. I hoped."

"Hell of a long shot."

His face cracked into a big grin that made me laugh. "It was pretty much an act of faith. Sorry about the cloak and dagger."

"That's when I knew it had to be you rather than some random nutter. How did you persuade the waitress?"

"Charming, isn't she? I ate breakfast there every day for a week and I'm a generous tipper."

"You actually moved here?" Which was dumb of me because how else could Rocco be in the right place at the right time? "What about your grandma's house?"

Some of the shine faded from his eyes. "I feel bad about it but I'm going to sell up."

"Not because of me, surely?" I would have hated that.

"Because life is too short not to be where you really want to be."

I wondered what he was doing for money and asked him.

"Got a job in a bar in the new leisure development across town."

"Seems you have it all sorted."

"Seems," he said with a difficult smile.

I shifted position; acutely aware that I had things to say that would not come easy. Perhaps I should heed Rachel Haran's advice. Perhaps now was not the time. My eyes darted to the entrance of the bar. I could almost hear Scarlet's voice urging me not to change my mind now I'd come this far.

"Are you okay?" Rocco said, leaning towards me, his hand on top of mine.

"You'll think I'm crazy." *I thought I was crazy.*

"What makes you think I don't already?"

Suddenly afraid of revealing what I knew, I drew my hand away, wiping the frisky smile from his face. I'd spoken to Rachel Haran without much effort, but Rocco was different. Rocco mattered. I dreaded his reaction as if, by virtue of the fact it was my family who played a part in suppressing the truth, he would find me guilty too.

Gentle and expectant, he took my hand again, looked deeply into my eyes, turning my insides to mush, straining my resolve.

"Lies destroy, Molly. Honesty will only hurt for a short time."

I sat up a little straighter and, before I changed my mind, told him precisely what had happened to his sister.

From shock and fury to disappointment and pain, every emotional reaction was mapped in his expression. Not once did his grasp slacken or let go.

By the time I was done, my chest was tight. Sad-eyed, he didn't speak.

"And now you know why you were leant on." Whatever Haran said, I was certain Stanton and, possibly, Childe had bowed to pressure from my father. My dad might have been a good copper, but it didn't make him immune from bending and breaking the law to protect his family.

Hands tell you a lot about a person. They carry tension and grief, kindness and hate. Rocco's balled into fists.

"When I think of that bastard, Mallis, how he lied to my family, even told my mother to back off." Clipped and justifiably angry, Rocco's ire was visceral. Thankfully, it wasn't aimed at me. "Why would that snake protect your father?" he said, incredulous.

"Because my dad had dirt on him." I explained.

"And he threatened you? Why didn't you say?"

Because I didn't trust you. I gave a lame shrug.

He glanced away, thinking and raging. "If only your father had done the decent thing all those years ago." I knew this only too well. "You really believe Zach is innocent?"

I'd been so sure, but what if I were wrong? "He's not guilty," I said doggedly.

"Then if not him, who?"

I shrugged and quietly told Rocco about my visit to Rachel Haran. He didn't look thrilled when I mentioned that she was open to the idea that Drea's death was accidental. "Trust her?" he said, with a penetrating look. "Forgive my cynicism."

I smiled warmly, took his hand. "Rachel is not my father or Mallis. She didn't admit it, but I think she tried to investigate Mallis for corruption when she was a serving police officer at the MET. She'd like nothing more than to bring him to justice."

"And your dad?"

"I'm less certain how it will pan out. My father won't confess, but Zach might."

"Is that what you want?"

"I don't have a choice." Sitting there with Rocco only confirmed what I already knew to be true. I couldn't condemn myself to living the rest of my life with lies and duplicity.

Rocco absently rubbed his thumb against the top of my hand. "I'm sorry for me, but I'm sorry for you too."

His expression scorched me. I didn't want his pity. I'd never wanted that. To divert him, I asked a question that had bugged me since the night Rocco had broken into my house.

"You said your gran told you something when she was dying."

Rocco nodded. "She received an anonymous note, telling her to look into your brother."

Who from, I wondered. Couldn't be either Bowen or Scarlet. Bowen was too eager to exploit the situation and Scarlet was hell-bent on taking the secret to her grave. There was only one person I could think of, not that it mattered anymore because he too was dead, and that was Barry Bevan, Richard Bowen's biological father. It would have been one last hurrah and a finger up to the man who'd threatened him.

"So, what happens next?" he said, puncturing my thoughts.

"Next?"

"To us." He scrutinized me as if examining a rare piece of porcelain. Did he think I would break into pieces without him?

"Rocco," I said solemnly. "I'm not sure."

"I meant what I said the last time we spoke."

He watched every move on my face. Did he spot the inexplicable panic stuttering inside me? I'd always been bad at commitment, but what Rocco asked of me, in the circumstances, made me doubt my own judgement. I'd screwed up so many times. "That's lovely," I blurted out, "and I'm flattered, but this is so messed up."

"Then help me straighten it out."

My phone started to ring. Zach. Flickering with irritation, I cut the call.

"Stay," Rocco murmured, guaranteed to ensure I wouldn't resist. "Please," he said, leaning across, finding my mouth, slow kissing me until my heart jittered and my brain turned liquid.

As we drew apart, a beep from my phone alerted me to a text message. Zach again:

'URGENT. NEED TO SEE YOU NOW. ON MY WAY TO YOURS' xx

I let out a groan, texted him back, told him I couldn't reach him for at least forty minutes. It didn't take membership of MENSA to work out why Zach needed to see me. In his head he was on a damage limitation exercise or, put another way, out to save his own skin. I explained to Rocco who was incredulous.

"You're not going?"

"I have to." Somehow, I had to explain to Zach that the police would want to talk to him and our father.

"Then I'm coming with you."

I pressed a finger against his lips. "This is my mess to sort."

"It could be a trap."

"Zach couldn't trap a fly. Deep down, he's a coward. Always has been."

"But—"

"Tomorrow. I promise. Same time. Same place."

I put his new number into my phone and kissed him. As I walked away, Rocco's eye boring into my back, I knew I'd made the wrong call. I was simply too proud to admit it.

Chapter 74

"How did you get here?"

Zach, dressed in a brightly coloured Tropical shirt, sprawled languidly across my doorstep as if he were sunning it in Barbados. He angled his chin in the direction of a dirty camper van parked on the opposite side of the road. Looked like it was held together with baler twine and rust. "Saffron leant it to me." One of the women in the commune.

Springing to his bare feet, he seemed less twitchy and in control. Perversely, I found this disconcerting.

He followed me down the hall and into the kitchen. I opened the back door in a vain attempt to disperse the heat inside the house. Humid heavy air pushed in. It smelt peculiarly pungent, as if the sea were around the next corner. Dark and heavy clouds banked on the horizon and there was little or no sound. A storm was brewing and the temperature riding high. After the long period of extended hot weather, it would be a monster.

I dispensed soft drinks and we took them into the living room. Zach sat. I stood.

"You said it was urgent." I took a long deep swallow.

"It's all fucked up."

"You drove all this way to tell me that?"

"Molly, can you stop being angry for one second?" I didn't respond. "Got anything stronger?" he said, staring at his glass. Without a word, I went to the kitchen and, after a rummage, unearthed two dubious-looking bottles of Retsina, the remnants of a Greek holiday. I plonked them in front of Zach. He twisted off the screw top, helped himself and offered me a slug. I didn't really fancy it but what the hell? I nodded, screwing up my face as the first fiery swallow landed splat on an empty stomach. "God, it tastes like crushed Christmas trees."

"More like the contents of Tutankhamen's tomb. Have another glug. It gets better." For the briefest moment I caught sight of the brother I used to know.

"Do you miss it?" I said.

"What?"

"Drugs."

He looked at me quizzically, unsure why the conversation had taken an early turn in a direction he hadn't expected.

"Seriously."

A smile snuggled in the corners of his mouth. "Never feel more alive than when I'm jacked up."

I studied him for a moment: my brother, Zach, all loose-limbed and luminous. "You're talking in the present tense." I didn't think it was a Freudian slip.

Confusion scampered across his features. "Am I?" He scrubbed at his head, as if he had a fleabite. "Habit, I guess."

"I'm not dim, Zach."

He clicked his tongue. "Nobody could accuse you of that."

"You're using again, aren't you?"

Zach shifted in his seat, took another pull of his drink. Grabbing his elbows, he pitched forward, hugged himself tight.

"I'm not judging."

"Aren't you?"

"Chancer supplies you." My voice was so low I wondered whether Zach would hear. He heard all right.

"Regular Miss Marple, aren't you?" His nostrils flared, and his mouth was a grimace.

"When did you relapse?"

"Why ask when you already know?"

"Since Scarlet?"

He let out a mirthless laugh. "Since you." He looked at me through narrowed eyes, yet there was vulnerability too. Zach was terribly afraid, as well he might be. And terrified people, particularly drug addicts, are unpredictable.

I let out a deep sigh and sat down. "Think Chancer was there that night you were with Drea?"

He stuck out his chin, letting me know exactly what a piss-poor idea it was. "Why are you doing this?"

"I'm not doing anything."

"You're trying to rearrange the blame. Not much of a friend or sister, are you?"

"Friend or family, murder is murder."

"There you go again. Banging on. What was it Dad said? Making the evidence fit the crime."

"Let's leave Dad out of it for now. Chancer *could* have been there."

Zach bolted forward. "You're mad, know that? One hundred per cent tapped." To make the point he smacked his temple with the flat of his hand.

I took another swallow of booze. So did Zach. He was right. It did improve. Most likely right about my sanity too. Maybe I *was* cracked.

"Jesus, Molly, I keep telling you."

"Telling me what?"

"That it was an accident."

I shook my head, kept chipping away. "Someone else was at the house that night."

"No." His knee juddered. Sweat seeped through the fabric of his 'T-shirt', making a deep V.

Sudden fear zapped my spine as I leant forward. "Are you protecting him?"

"Chancer? Don't be stupid. Chancer can look after himself." He snatched at the bottle, twisting off the cap, and topped up his glass; three fast movements.

"Then if you're not protecting Chancer, who?"

A tick pulsed below his left eye. Zach's hand shot out, reaching for his glass. I closed my fingers over it, pinning it to the coffee table.

He looked up, met my gaze, rage in his eyes. "Dad," he said. "That's who I'm protecting. He came soon as I called him. He took me home and then did things that night he shouldn't have done. He did them for me. Me," he roared, thumping his chest. "The only person you ever think about is yourself. Your fucking self-righteousness kills me. We've all made sacrifices, Molly, Scarlet especially. That's why I wanted to see you. If he goes down, we all do, and Scarlet will have died for nothing. And that's on you," he said, pressing a dirty finger in the middle of my forehead.

I shook so hard I could barely speak. Zach sat, a mass of crystallised anger. As soon as I got it together, I let rip. "You think any of this has been easy for me? I love my family. I put Dad on the same pedestal Mum put Scarlet. And you're right: Scarlet paid the ultimate price but her desire to protect was entirely bonkers. God only knows what she was thinking. Right now, all I want is justice for her and for Drea Temple. It's what they deserve so don't you dare tell me that all I think about is what I want."

When my mobile rang neither of us moved until it cut out.

"Drink up and get out." Every blood vessel in my body thudded, draining from red to white. As far as I was concerned, the police could pick him up and do their worst. No way was I going to protect him. My phone rang again.

"For Chrissakes, answer it," Zach barked.

Staring him out, I tossed down the rest of my drink and snatched my mobile. "Yes."

"Molly, it's Rachel."

"Hello."

"I was too late. The house burnt down last night."

Chapter 75

My head swam and my pulse ran in quick time. "It's now the subject of an arson investigation," Rachel continued.

Scared, I glanced at Zach. Did his clothes and skin smell of smoke and fire? I didn't think so, but that was last night, hours ago. "Are you still there?" Rachel said.

I struggled to stay calm. "Could it be Mallis?"

At the mention of Mallis' name, Zach visibly bristled. I shook my head, listening hard for Rachel's answer.

"Too early to draw conclusions." She cleared her throat. "I shouldn't really be telling you this, but Mallis is part of a separate and active investigation."

"What sort of investigation?" A murder enquiry?

"I can't say. I'm going to make some calls and get back to you. In the meantime, take care."

I slipped my phone into my pocket, took a couple of deep breaths, another snatch of Retsina. Zach's eyes never left mine. "Who was that?" When I didn't answer, he stood up, hunched over, like he was freezing, and paced the room. "Fuck, Molly, you've gone to the cops."

I didn't correct him and say that Rachel was ex-police with the status of a civilian. I didn't say that any day now he'd be spoken to in connection with the death of Drea Temple. "What did you expect? Did you think this would all go away?" I spread my hands, tried to appeal to Zach's better nature because, deep down, I knew my brother had one. "Sit down, for God's sake." Amazingly, he did.

Every inch of him, limbs and skin and eyes, twitched. At the back of my mind, I wondered if I'd read him wrong. When he spoke next he dialled the tone right down. My brother could be a proper Jekyll and Hyde.

"How much have you told them?"

"Everything."

He listened intently, the tip of his tongue touching the corner of his mouth, as I described my visit to Rachel. After I'd finished, he said, "She has no hard evidence."

My words hadn't had the sobering effect I'd expected. "Not yet, Zach, but she will." No point in him running away with the idea that he was in the clear. I told him about the house burning down to see how he'd react. His features slackened in astonishment.

"You think Mallis is behind it?"

"Could be, could also be our father."

"Dad wouldn't."

"You sure?"

"He's a broken man, Molly."

I didn't know what I thought about that. Did I feel sorry for him? Hand on heart, not really. Must have been the booze because I was suddenly assailed with self-pity. "Why did you all have to keep it a secret?"

"Because you love Dad so much."

"Loved."

Zach's eyes turned down at the edges. "And you will again."

I shook my head.

"Is that a no, or you don't know?"

I couldn't answer. Zach looked away, feet tapping.

"What?" I said.

Zach chewed his lip, took an avid interest in the carpet. He didn't look up when he spoke next. "You really think Drea was murdered?"

"The blood wasn't from the fall."

More lip chewing. "And whoever it is," he said, looking up with a level stare, "is on to you." They'd been on to me from the very beginning. I was unnerved and bewildered back then. Now I was plain scared. Consumed by black thoughts, we gawped at each other. "Mind if I smoke?" Zach said in a shaky voice.

"Outside."

He stood up, patted down his pockets, fished out tobacco and matches. "We should call Dad."

"When will you get it through your thick head? NO."

"We have to call someone."

"I told you. I already have. It's under control."

He threw me an odd, spaced-out look and I watched as he ambled out, blank-eyed, into the garden. Draining my glass,

I poured another when a bleep bleep on my phone alerted me to a text.

Lenny: 'How did it go with Rachel?'

Me: 'Fine.'

L: 'Want us to come round?'

Me: 'Maybe. Not Sober. Zach is still with me.'

L: 'Zach?! F**k – you okay?'

Me: I attached an emoji of a face rocking with laughter.

L: 'You sound weird.'

Me: 'That's because I'm pissed.'

L: 'No argument. We're coming.'

Me: 'No, I'm good. Need to kick back.'

L: 'Really? You're certain?'

Me: 'Positive. Talk to you in the morning.'

I looked at the measure of booze in my glass and thought I should chuck it down the sink. Screw it, I thought, tossing the drink back in one. I ought to phone Rocco. Ought to tell him about the house and the fire and everything and—

"I'll stay," Zach announced, wandering in from outside. To stake his claim, he plumped down and placed his dirty feet up on my coffee table.

I peered at him through eyes that weren't focussing terribly well. "You don't have to go all big brother on me." Clearing the glasses and tidying up suddenly appeared to be a matter of life and death, a sign that I was fully in control of my faculties, that I could handle whatever threat came my way. As I stood up, the room swivelled. Listing to the left, I misjudged the doorway, connected heavily with the frame and bounced off. "Shit," I said, lurching sideways.

"You need a little sleep," Zach said with a laugh. Grabbing hold, he manhandled me upstairs.

"Don't you feel drunk?" My top jaw didn't seem to connect to my bottom. I had to concentrate really hard to make the right words come out of my mouth. I was fucked if I knew which order they should be in.

I didn't hear what Zach said in reply. I was way too far gone.

Chapter 76

A flash of lightning lit up the room. I woke with a start, my phone blaring and bouncing off my hangover headache in sickening waves. Enormously hot and sweaty, muzzy with sleep, I snatched up my mobile, took a look. "Fuck, fuck, fuck. Zach," I hollered, thick-tongued. With no response, I hurtled downstairs.

Zach was on his way out of the living room. He looked remarkably awake and bright-eyed, unusually so. If I weren't so rattled, I'd have quizzed him about what he'd taken. "Problem?" he said, with the kind of lucidity induced by a finely tuned dose of amphetamines.

"The alarm's gone on the shop." Cursing, I glanced outside. The wind had picked up and fat drops of rain slammed against the windows. "What time is it?"

Zach reached over and took my arm. "Your watch says midnight." Somehow, I'd lost several hours, exhaustion finally catching up with me. "Clock on the cooker says eleven."

I turned around to see the control flashing. With an electrical storm in prospect, a power outage had tripped the switch. "Damn it." Dry-mouthed, nauseous, I felt absolutely dreadful.

"You all right? Your face looks green."

"I shouldn't have drunk centuries' old Retsina on an empty stomach." As if in response, acid from my gut tunnelled up towards my throat. At any second, I'd throw up over my feet.

"Won't the police deal with the shop alarm?" Zach said.

"Gotta be joking." I cursed myself for not spending the money on a remote system. "Oh hell," diving into the cloakroom, I made it just in time to chuck up into the toilet bowl. Shakily, I flushed the loo, ran cold water and rinsed out my mouth. My head still banged, but there was no time to waste. Emerging shamefaced and sheepish, I rifled through the jackets hanging on the coat stand. "I've got a waterproof somewhere."

"Stop."

It had been a couple of decades since I'd heard my brother speak with such authority. I looked up.

"Go back to bed."

"I can't," I said rattily. "Sometimes burglars trip an alarm to see if the owner shows up. If I don't get there pronto, I could lose half my stock."

"Which is why I'll go. What's the code?"

"Zach, no."

"Why not. Don't you trust me?" His eyes bored into mine. I knew what he was thinking. Someone could have deliberately targeted the shop so that I'd turn up in the dark on my own.

"But what if someone's there, for fuck's sake?" I couldn't

bear the thought of him alone in the night, with God knew who. "What if —"

"Keys," he said, hand out. He burnt with a determination that I found concerning, yet also hard to resist. If it was important for Zach to prove himself, how could I deny him?

"If you're sure." I really did feel giddy and unable to drive.

"Positive."

I handed them over, rattled off the code and gave him instructions about how to disarm the alarm. "You'll come straight back, yeah?"

"See you in a bit." He stepped out as the first clap of thunder bellowed long and loud above our heads and spectacular drops of rain fell and bounced off the earth. Embarrassed, I slunk back to bed.

*

Wake up, wake up.

At the sound of Scarlet's voice in my dream, I opened my eyes. I called her name, but she didn't answer.

A thin blade of pain penetrated deep inside my brain. It was still dark. Howling wind and driving rain battered the Velux above my head. My phone, which I'd left downstairs, was the only thing silent.

I fumbled for the glass of water Zach must have put on my bedside table and took a long deep swallow. Zach, I thought, was he back?

I rubbed at my face, struggled to sit more upright and wished I hadn't. Nausea returned mob handed. I had a dry mouth, acid stomach and aching bones. Despite the sudden drop in room temperature, I boiled. Didn't help that I was still in my skirt and top. Every inch of my skin glistened with perspiration, ethanol stewing and leaking out of my pores.

I gaped into the darkness, expecting Scarlet to manifest in ghostly form. Would she appear with broken limbs and a smashed in face, like an extra from a Zombie movie?

One hand flew to my temple; the other pulled the sheet up over my head. Then I remembered Zach and glanced at my watch. "Dammit," I cursed through an expanse of Egyptian cotton. He'd been gone for over an hour. Where the hell was he?

Panic streaming through me, I sprang out of bed and lurched towards the door. Sly and tricky, the walls of the bedroom winked and shifted. Another bout of sickness threatened to derail me but fear for my brother won out. I slammed my feet into flip-flops and, grabbing my keys and the small torch Lenny had given me, hauled myself downstairs.

My phone was on the work surface in the kitchen, next to the microwave. Swooping it up, I called Zach. No reply. Went straight to his voicemail. I sent him a text and prised open the back door. A great gale of wind slapped me straight across the face. Rolling my collar up, head down, I crossed the garden. By the time I reached the carport, I was soaked through and my hair stuck to my scalp.

Over the limit, I shouldn't be driving. God help me. In desperation, I closed my ears to good sense and ignored the grumbling complaint of my conscience.

Windscreen wipers at full belt, front and back, the car slalomed down the street, across roads wet and oily from weeks of dry weather. The noisy banging in my heart was only matched by the sound of rain tattooing a beat against the roof of my little car.

The shop emerged out of a blur of streetlights. Several alarms had gone off along the row, although 'Flotsam' was obviously closed and curiously quiet. Craning my head, narrowing my eyes against driving wind and intermittent flashes of lightning, I could see no sign of Zach's camper van. Perhaps, he'd gone home. Vaguely comforted, the pressure in my heart abated.

I parked on double yellow lines and stepped out of the Fiat, straight into a puddle that splashed dirty water up the backs of my legs. Cursing, I let myself into the shop.

There's something spooky about an empty building at night, even one as familiar as this. Cruel illumination, that made my eyes hurt, told me that Zach had re-set the alarm like I told him to. Nothing was nicked, nothing moved, as far as I could tell.

"Zach," I cried out. "You there?"

Silence ticking, I was alone. But I couldn't shake off the thought that something was off.

Fear brewing inside me, I walked nervously through to the back office to check the shop's computer. It had an in-built camera for viewing each room. Empty space announced it had gone walkabout, which meant the security video was missing. Alarmed, I picked up the phone. Still working. I checked the till, which hadn't been forced, and went upstairs.

To be on the safe side, I liberated a vintage golf iron, a brass headed Hickory shafted putter, lethal if someone jumped me from the shadows.

But nobody did.

I prowled the upper storey, examined glass cabinets stuffed with jewellery and other people's ancient keepsakes, and then returned downstairs. About to lock up, my mobile rang. Adrenalin dumped its dirty great payload. Combined with a hangover, it almost did for me. Getting a grip, I realised that it was probably Zach informing me he'd gone back to mud and mess.

"Hello?"

The voice at the other end screamed my name so loud I jumped.

"Edie?" I said, in astonishment.

"Thank God you're there. You've got to get to the quarry. Now. Before it's too late."

"Edie, you're not making sense. It's—" I broke off and stared at my watch. "After two in the morning. What the hell are you on about?"

"Shut up. Shut up. Listen, for God's sake. It's Zach." Her voice was bent out of shape with hysteria.

"What about him?" I ignored the clammy sensation in my stomach.

"He sent me a text."

"You?" I couldn't get my head around that. Instantly, my bullshit detector sounded. No, not sounded, clanged. "Why?" I might as well have said *I don't believe you.*

"Zach sent it by mistake," she answered, raging with frus-

406

tration. "It was meant for Tris. He's at the quarry. He's in a real state."

"Tris is at which quarry?"

"No," Edie wailed, beside herself. "Zach is at Gullet quarry. I think he's going to do something stupid. He texted that it was all his fault and he was sorry, although I don't have a clue what he means."

Except I did. Oh God. Oh no. "Did you phone him?"

"He's not picking up."

"How long ago?" I stuttered.

"I don't know. Ten minutes, maybe less."

In one bound I was out of the shop, my phone welded to my ear. "Edie, call the emergency services. I'm on my way. Have you told Tris?"

"I phoned him straightaway. He might get there before you. Shall I come too? I could leave the kids with my folks."

"No, do exactly as I say and, for God's sake, hurry."

Chapter 77

Gullet Quarry: the one Chancer and me had walked beside only yesterday. With its steep-sided walls and deadly drop, it was the perfect place for suicide.

Suddenly Zach's upbeat mood made horrible sense. He'd made a decision, as had Scarlet before him. To his mind, the ultimate choice would set him free, liberating him from responsibility and consequences. I shuddered at the thought that either, by accident or design, Zach had killed Drea, and this was his way out. As weird as it was, I still loved my brother despite his faults because I expected so much less of him than I did from my dad. It seemed impossible to think of my life without him.

A burst of hail against the windscreen made me jump. Please, don't let me be too late, I shouted to the empty interior of my car, jamming my foot flat against the accelerator.

Aquaplaning around a bend, water gushing up on both sides of the tyres, I prayed. Prayed to reach him in time. Prayed to talk him out of what he had planned. Prayed for help. My mother's mental state was in doubt at the best of times. With

Scarlet's death, she was clinging on by the tips of her fingers. If Zach took his own life, it would be like stamping on her hands until she let go and plunged over the edge into insanity.

I drove into what felt the eye of the storm and it took forever to get to the lane that led up to the car park.

Lightning bursts lit up the sky on the second of every second. When a long-horned cow ambled across the road, I pulled on the steering wheel, losing control and the car skidded off onto the flat verge, tipping up on two wheels. Fear ripping through me, I leant away, arms juddering with strain as tyres scrabbled and squealed, desperate to find purchase. In slow motion, the Fiat pitched back down with a greasy thud and slid back onto the tarmac.

On I drove until another flash of lightning stabbed the night sky and illuminated Zach's campervan, side-on, like a barricade at a checkpoint. Slamming on the brakes, I screeched to a halt, jumped out and ran. Didn't even take the car keys with me.

Rain drilled the ground in angry bursts and stung my face. Wind lifted the hem of my skirt, buffeting it around my waist. I didn't care. Zach. I had to reach him. It was all that counted.

Flashing my torch around revealed that the camper was empty. Sodden and shivering, I slipped round to the front, pressed my hand against the metal. The engine ticked beneath a bonnet that remained warm despite the downpour. He couldn't have gone far.

Buoyed with hope I had no right to feel, I took to my heels, and battled against a formidable sky that pulsed with wind and rage. For every step, I was driven back several paces.

Battling around the metal barrier, I passed the ice-cream kiosk, desolate and intimidated by the storm's fury, until I drew level with a line of boulders and natural line of defence against vehicular access.

"Zach" I screamed. A marauding gust snatched and made off with my voice. The whole place seethed with dense dark shapes and skeleton trees, yawing and moaning.

Desperate, I ran towards the fence. Jamming the stubby end of the torch in my mouth, I shinned up and over the five-bar gate. Landing on the other side, my eyes struggled against the strobe effect of a lightning strike at mega voltage. Urgently, I raked the murderous walls of the quarry, scoping the peak for signs of my brother. At any second, I expected to see Zach teetering on the edge before tumbling into the night and oblivion.

By day, sluggish and inert, the stretch of water below roiled and boiled, spat and hissed; a living primal, vengeful thing, set to grab him. Surely, he hadn't already jumped? And where the fuck were the emergency services? Was Zach in a queue of countless others waiting fruitlessly for help? On a destructive night like this there would be plenty of takers, and what about Chancer? Where was he?

Startled by the thought, I flashed the torch around, eyes scanning the bushes and trees, half-expecting something or someone to step out. Why wasn't he here?

Swelling with fear, I recalled how furious he'd been the last time I saw him. I remembered his mouth twisting in disgust and anger. Chancer: a wife-beater. Chancer: a drug supplier. Chancer: oh my God, what if —?

My hand dropped, torchlight pooling on the ground closest to the edge. Bright colour flashed across my line of vision. I edged near, part of me in denial, the other sharp with panic. Squatting down, terror scythed straight though me for, on the ground, dumped in a heap, Zach's Tropical shirt.

I scooped it up, briefly held it to my face, a heady mix of tobacco, booze and weed flooding my senses.

In despair, I clambered to my feet, threw curses at the water, howled Zach's name into the depths. In films, he would step out of the shadows and it would all be okay and happy ever after, but this was no movie. This was real. This was ...

Burning pain blazed across my shoulders, sending tremors along my ribs and spine. My arms flew wide, the torch flung from my grasp. Lifted off my feet with the force of the blow, I launched up, my arms splayed, and then down, falling and falling. Unable to save myself, I pitched headlong with a scream, and the taker of so many lives, opened its jaws and swallowed me whole.

Chapter 78

S tunned.

In spite of the long dry summer, the quarry never heated up, and chill wind-whipped water clawed at my face. A force outside myself, as powerful as any assassin, sat on my chest. Disorientated, I flailed my arms, struggling to stay afloat, not sure in which direction to swim. All I saw was a vast expanse of wet and seething night.

"Help," I screamed. Gasping for air, my mouth filled with foul, rank-tasting filth, as if the combined body fluids of all those that had drowned before me had collected in this one stretch.

Panicked, I kicked out, my head bobbing briefly above the surface. Darkness had other ideas. It threw its funereal coat over my head, pushing me deeper so that hidden currents could drag me down and finally do away with me. The more I fought, the stronger they became. With the electrical storm gathering pace and energy, one strike upon the water would put an end to it all. Either way, I was doomed.

Night-blind and shivering, I cried out, yet my vocal cords

wouldn't work, and my words slurred. Cold penetrated so deeply its nails reached into every organ. My arms and legs failed to respond to the commands from my brain, and the blood in my veins slowed to a chug. Without energy, every cell in my body was in uproar. Cheats and liars and rebels, they didn't belong to me.

Soon, I would sink and that would be that. Any thoughts I had were unformed and flaky. If I imagined my life would flash before my eyes as my spirit drained away, if I believed I'd remember numerous happy times, I was wrong. I saw a man with a big smile and shining eyes. I heard his laughter crackling through the wind. I thought of him never knowing the truth about who killed his sister. I dreamt of all the places we would never visit together and the fun we'd miss, and closeness and intimacy—and—then— nothing.

Molly, don't give up.

I heard Scarlet's voice. Is this what happens when your body packs up? Does the dead clamour to greet you?

I can help you.

Go away. I don't want your help. I want to sleep.

No, Molly. Stay awake. Stay focused. If you don't, your body will shut down.

Stop nagging and leave me the hell alone.

You have to fight.

I can't. No more fight in me.

You're still floating, aren't you?

I want to be with you and Zach.

But Zach's not here.

What?

You heard. Now swim. It's this way.

With a supreme effort, I opened my stinging eyes. Across the water, a ribbon of illumination ran from me to dry land. If only I could follow it. Somehow, I took a slow breath in, tried to give a little kick, tried to scull the surface with hands that didn't belong and felt like arthritic claws.

"I can't do it." Each word slid out of my mouth painfully slow and disappeared into the icy depths. It was useless. I was sinking. Drowning. Dying.

Out of nowhere, I swear a force of energy reached out, scooped me up and lifted me high. Afloat, again, I'd stopped shivering and started tingling, neat adrenalin coursing through my bones. It felt like angel's wings carried me back to dry land and I remembered Rocco and white feathers and—

With a jolt, I found myself flat on my tummy, spluttering and wheezing, lungs on fire, and my face in the dirt. Dawn had taken its first tentative steps into a day still lashing with rain. Behind me, trees swayed, bent and snapped in a hissing roar. Wet-through, as cold and exhausted as I was, my body was firing again. Blood throbbed through my veins and to my extremities. Wiggling my toes and fingers, I bumped up against something small and solid. Miraculously, my torch had survived, and I closed my hand around it. That's when I realised that I was not alone.

Slowly, I tilted my head. I saw expensive trainers and jeans first, a yellow waterproof with the hood up next. Poised, like a knight in armour about to strike with a mace, the figure held something above me. What it was exactly, I couldn't make out.

"Stay right where you are."

And then I knew. I knew it all.

Chapter 79

Edie flicked her head and the hood peeled back to reveal her high cheekbones and pretty face. A thin smile briefly curved the edges of her mouth. It struck me that she was like a piece of fine art that only looks exquisite in a gallery. Out of its natural squillion pound environment, Edie was a cheap and tawdry fraud.

In both hands, she held a cricket bat. Now I understood how I'd launched into the water; she'd used it to strike me and she'd use it again.

"You killed Drea Temple."

"Nobody killed Drea Temple. She did it to herself. She was stoned. She fell. That's on her."

"You attacked her."

"What do you expect? She tried to take Tristram from me."

"Poor little Edie, you always were a jealous cow."

"Stop it." Her voice was a sly, defensive whine.

Good. I wanted to press her nerves. I wanted her to lose control. Face down on the ground, my situation could not be worse. Edie seemed ten foot tall. Despite having good upper body strength from shifting furniture, I was slight. Exhaustion consumed my body. Fighting to get out of the water had burnt every atom of reserve energy. Fundamentally, if you're on the floor, you're in the shit and my only chance was to goad her into making a mistake. If she came at me, at least I had the prospect of grabbing her legs – if I could find the strength. "Call yourself a wife and mother? You should be bloody ashamed."

"It wasn't my fault, do you hear?" Edie screeched. "I'm a good person. My children love me. I have responsibilities." Her arms trembled, and she let out a sob.

"You set out to kill Drea Temple."

"Shut up. Shut up. If you don't, I'll—"

"You'll what? Leave an animal carcass in my carport? Stick a blade in my kitchen table? Hit me like you hit Drea? You're nothing but a needy bitch."

I flinched as the bat wavered in the air. "Be quiet," she said in a trembling voice. "I'm not to blame. I'm a victim."

"For ten years you let Zach take the rap for your crime."

"That's not fair," she snivelled. "I told you. Why are you so horrible to me?"

"Because you're an evil eavesdropper." I imagined how on, one of her trips to pester Zach about Chancer, she'd overheard Scarlet's conversation.

"No, no, no."

I'd had enough. I was cold. I was furious. With a stupendous effort, I went to get up. One smart smack sent rivers of pain across my shoulders and knocked me back down into the dirt. "Fuck," I cursed.

417

"You stay where I say you stay. Face down." Her voice had lost its tremble. She was in charge, in control, back in the game.

"What have you done with my brother?" I mumbled into the earth. "Where's is he?"

"Somewhere safe."

I bobbed my head up. Mistake. Another crack across my back left me gasping with pain. Emboldened by my helplessness, Edie's voice changed up a gear. "He might pull through, might not. Doesn't matter because everyone will believe you attacked Zach after discovering he murdered Drea."

"Why are you doing this?" I howled through angry tears.

"You should stay out of other people's marriages."

"I'm not in your marriage. I'm not interested in your husband."

"But he's interested in you." The fabric of her waterproof crackled. I closed my eyes, braced for whatever would happen next.

"Look up." She spoke with sudden chilling composure.

I was too afraid. I didn't dare move.

"I said look up."

Slowly, I lifted my head, angled my chin, bewildered. Edie was squatting down, the cricket bat on the ground beside her. In her hands, she held a bottle of clear liquid and I didn't think it was water.

Tears seeped out of the corner of my eyes. I was so cold, so scared, so incapable of movement.

"Know what this is?"

Dull-eyed, I shook my head. Black chill settled in the small of my back and crawled along my spine.

"This," she said, "is why you are going to get up very slowly and walk back into the water." She gave the contents a shake and viewed me with an empty expression. "You will drown but, if you're a good girl, you won't be horribly disfigured before you do."

"Acid?" I gasped.

"Tris won't be so interested in you once the skin has melted right off your face."

With a malevolent grin, Edie sprang to her feet. "Neat, isn't it? Broken-hearted after the death of her big sis, Molly Napier takes her own life. Suicide runs in the family, it seems."

Terror shot through me as real and bright as any lightning strike. If I misjudged, even by a fraction, I could not begin to imagine the world of pain I'd encounter. But what choice did I have? Edie was bat-shit crazy.

I moved my left palm down and raised myself slowly up onto my knees. My right hand balled into a fist.

Edie jiggled the contents of the bottle. "No tricks."

Images of burnt hair and destroyed flesh flashed before me as our eyes locked. Breathing heavily, fear fizzing, I peeled myself from the ground. Almost upright, I tightened my grip, shifting my thumb to the base of the torch.

"Now turn around."

Like a suicide bomber depressing an explosive, I pushed the switch and swung my arm up. A full beam, powerful enough to wrench out retinas, shone directly into Edie's eyes.

An ear-shattering scream ripped through the sides of the quarry.

And it wasn't mine.

Edie staggered backwards, dropped the bottle, her hands flying to her face.

I launched straight at her and lumped her one. "You've fucking broken my nose," she howled, her voice taut with fear.

I couldn't swim, but I could run.

Darting forward, I bolted for the gate and vaulted over. I kept on running. I didn't stop, didn't look back. My joints and muscles screeched, and my bare feet slapped against the road. If they bled, I didn't notice. If my lungs screamed, I didn't pause. Behind me, Edie's thin voice was consumed by a mad as hell wind that battered the trees and yelled at the dawn.

Back in my car, I fired the ignition, slammed it into reverse and, stamping on the gas, drove.

At the end of the road, I snatched at the brakes, banged the heater up full belt, locked all the doors and called 999. With my teeth chattering and my arm shaking, I asked for police and ambulance. "I've been attacked by a woman at Gullet Quarry. She's armed with acid and she has my brother." If they assumed Edie had Zach at the quarry, I didn't care. I simply wanted them to arrive and quickly. When the man with the tired voice on the other end asked for more details, I hung up. Protocol and form filling didn't work at times like this. If Zach was to stand a chance, I needed big guns. Rachel answered after six rings.

I blurted out that Zach was in danger. "We have to find

him. Edie Chancellor murdered Drea Temple. She attacked Zach and won't say where he is. His life's hanging in the balance."

"Slow down, Molly. Who's Edie Chancellor?"

"She's married to my brother's best friend." A lot less lucid than when I'd spoken a few moments ago, I launched into a rambling explanation, finishing with my near-death experience.

Rachel's voice blistered with alarm.

"Are you all right?"

"I think so." Wet and frightened and cold to my core, I felt disconnected. My pulse felt staccato and erratic, but I took that to be a good sign; at least I had one. "I've called it in," I remembered to tell her.

"Good girl. Where are you now?"

"I'm at the end of the road near the quarry."

"And where is Mrs Chancellor?"

"Where I last left her, stumbling in the dark." I glanced nervously in the rear-view mirror to be certain she wasn't coming back for an encore.

"You'll need to give a formal statement to the police."

I blinked. As a witness, or what? At this rate, I'd be talking to Gloucestershire, Wiltshire and West Mercia. And Rocco, I needed to speak to him, tell him what's happened, yes, I should do that but, I found it hard to think, took so much effort, felt so tired, and mustn't forget my brother. "What about Zach?" I mumbled. "Last I knew he was at 'Flotsam,' my shop in town."

"Right, I'm on it. Do not go there. Wait for the ambulance."

I smiled. How could I go anywhere when all I wanted was to go home, get dry and warm, and sleep and sleep? At the sound of approaching police and ambulances, I reached for the door. I didn't remember much after that.

Chapter 80

I floated, light and carefree, and safe.

A police officer with a gentle voice got to me first and wrapped me in a blanket. Looking groggily into his eyes, I found it impossible to speak coherently. Afterwards, I was transferred to an ambulance where everything and everyone worked in slow motion. A paramedic said something about potential cardiac arrest, although my heart did not stop beating. I had too much to live for. When a stranger cut away my wet clothes, I didn't mind a bit. Careful and caring, quiet hands wrapped me in special blankets. Like an Egyptian Mummy, only my face peeped out. I silently thanked people.

Someone fed me a hot drink. Someone else put a warm compress against my chest. I didn't recall anyone measuring my vital signs, but I guess they must have done.

By the time, I got to hospital I could make out what was going on around me, although I was too tired to take part. Badly bruised, my bones ached, and my back killed. Maybe I had cracked ribs. All I wanted was sleep and, when I did, I dreamt of Scarlet. She was walking down a road with a ruck-sack on her back. I called after her and she turned, smiled and waved goodbye.

"Don't go," I cried, desolate as I woke up.

Nurses came and went. A doctor advised I should be kept in for observation. As my body reheated, my thoughts became more lucid. A nice D.I. called Tracey West popped her head around my door. She had a wide face with big open, and I liked to think, honest, features. "Are you well enough to give a statement?"

"My brother," I said, before she had time to sit down.

"He's been found."

I grabbed at the sheets. "Is he?"

"He's in ICU with a fractured skull. The medics will be able to tell you more. I think they're planning to transfer him to the QE in Birmingham."

Closing my eyes, I silently told Scarlet that he was still alive. Maybe she already knew. "Where was he found?" I said.

"In the cellar at your shop, which is now a crime scene." Rachel, I thought with relief, she'd come through for me.

"Can I see him?"

"You'll need to consult the nurses."

"Do my parents know?"

"We haven't been able to contact them."

I started. "Neither of them?"

"I'm sure we will," Tracey said smoothly. "Now can you tell me what happened? Take your time."

I started off with what occurred at the quarry. I kept it factual and unemotional.

"Mrs Chancellor is extremely distressed and claims that she only meant to scare you," West said.

I was flabbergasted. "With acid?"

"You've had a very narrow escape," Tracey admitted. "She'll be charged with possession of an offensive weapon."

"You should have charged her with attempted murder."

Before Tracey could launch into the niceties of British law, I did a re-run of my conversation with Rachel Haran. As tough as it was, I stuck to facts when talking about my father, as if I were discussing some bloke down the road. There was no escape from what I truly felt. Relief that my instincts were sound yet crushing disappointment that my father was not the person I thought he was. Dad had lived a lie for so long, he'd made me a co-conspirator. Did I still love him? At the moment I was too raw to be certain of anything. I wondered how long it would take for the police to make an arrest. They'd have to find him first.

Chapter 81

Ahospital porter helped me into a wheelchair. It made me feel like a two-year-old, but no way would they let me walk unaided to see Zach.

I'd seen my brother pale and lifeless before, after an overdose. At the time, doctors had packed his stomach with charcoal, infused him with saline and put him on a ventilator. They'd told Mum and Dad that the next twenty-four hours were critical.

I gazed at him now as I did then. Only this time, part of Zach's head was shaved. He'd lost half his dreads and his face was puffy and discoloured around one eye. Who knew how mashed up his brain would be beneath the dressing? If he pulled through, how would he be? Would he remember and what would happen to him?

I asked a doctor about his chances. "Too early to say," she replied with a sympathetic expression. "After the operation to reduce the swelling in his brain, we put him into an induced coma to give him the best chance of healing."

"He looks so vulnerable." His arms were stick thin, shrinking his tattoos.

426

"He's young. He'll receive the best care in Birmingham."

"He's an addict," I said gloomily.

"Even addicts pull through."

"You're not thinking of getting out of bed now, luvvie?"

The nurse, a big woman who, on every level defied NHS advice on obesity, tucked me in. I shook my head with a sheepish smile. "Do you need a bed pan?"

"I need to make a phone call."

She smiled, disappeared and, as good as her word, trundled in with a portable phone trolley.

I made a reverse charge call to Lenny. "Molly, thank God," she exclaimed. "Me and Dusty were about to come and see you." She waited a respectful beat. "Have you heard about Zach?"

"I've seen him. They took me up to the ward."

"How is he?"

"Hanging on in there." If I believed it enough, he'd be okay, wouldn't he?

"I thought he was dead," Lenny declared.

"Where exactly did they find him?"

"Two police officers rocked up and said that they'd searched the property. Frightened the life out of me. When they opened the cellar there he was. If it hadn't been for them turning up, God knows what would have happened. But, goodness, Molly, you're lucky to be alive."

I swallowed. I mentally added 'unhinged' to Edie's dismal list of attributes.

"Dusty's bought you PJ's and toiletries," Lenny continued.

I wouldn't need them but didn't tell Lenny this. "There's a key stuck to the underside of the window frame at the front of my house." Which, on reflection, wasn't very smart. "Could you go inside and bring me a pair of jeans, T-shirt and trainers?"

"Okay," Lenny said uncertainly. "You're not planning to discharge yourself, or do anything silly, are you?"

"'Course not," I said. "And, um, could you bring them straightaway?

I had so much to think about. West would be back to ask more questions I couldn't answer. Zach I could do nothing for apart from pray. My car was in dock and I needed wheels. Rocco remained an enigma. Way past the time we were due to meet, why hadn't he picked up my call? He'd be waiting, worrying and primed to hear from me, wouldn't he? That slow kiss said so. Then why did I nag with doubt? Why did I fear that he'd run out on me? Why did my eyes brim with tears at other possibilities?

Because the injuries to my body had messed with my head.

Because I couldn't trust anyone.

And most of all, because I missed my sister.

Chapter 82

"Darling." Dusty gushed, launching herself at me. "You look dreadful."

"That's the last thing Molly needs to hear," Lenny said protectively.

"Well it's true."

Lenny flashed an apologetic smile and parked a plastic bag next to the bed. "Your stuff's all there," she said. "And I slipped your purse and spare key inside."

"Can I borrow your phone?" I asked Lenny.

"Sure."

I phoned Rocco again. Same response: phone switched off.

"Something wrong?" Lenny said.

"It's nothing." In reality, it was everything. Dread expanded inside me.

"What's the news on Zach?"

"It's a waiting game."

"Would we be able to see him?"

"I'm sure that would be fine, but what about Mum and Dad? The police don't seem to be able to locate them."

429

Lenny cleared her throat. Dusty walked to the end of the bed and took an avid interest in my chart.

"What?" I said suspiciously.

Dusty exchanged an awkward glance with Lenny. "Now I don't want you getting all upset."

I spiked with fresh anxiety. "Tell me what's going on."

Dusty looked to Lenny who spoke. "When we went to your house, we found Mr Lee."

"He's perfectly fine," Dusty interrupted, in response to my dismayed expression. "Delighted to see us, in fact."

"What the hell is he doing at my house?" And then I tumbled to it. "They've gone, haven't they? They've scarpered. What a gutless pair of—"

"We went straight to your mum and dad's," Dusty explained, "but it's all shut up."

Agitated, I pushed back the sheets and swung my legs round.

"Molly," she said, attempting to placate me, "I understand but—"

"Their son's life is hanging in the balance. I've narrowly escaped death and they've fucked off because they can't bear to face a symphony's worth of music. How could you possibly understand?" My voice was outrageously loud, a cover for the pure devastation I felt inside. I'd so loved my father. Once, I'd have trusted him with my life. That he'd run out on me was too much to endure.

"Darling," she said, uncomfortable with my loss of volume control, "You need to rest. There is absolutely no point getting yourself into a state."

If there is one thing I cannot abide it's when being upset is somehow the fault of the upsetee rather than the person or set of events responsible. My face must have said it all because Lenny shot Dusty a warning look.

"Molly, I really think Dusty is—"

"I'm sick of everyone having a good view of my rear," I said indignantly. "The sooner I get some clothes on, the better."

Chapter 83

O n unsteady legs, I tottered out of the ward, found the
ladies and staggered into a cubicle. Clouting both my
elbows, I managed to get dressed. Emerging into the wash
area, I nodded at a cleaner. Catching my reflection in the
mirror, I concluded that Dusty was right. Like tracing the
scars on an old piece of furniture, I could map the emotional
trajectory of the last two weeks by the fresh lines on my
face.

I slipped out into the corridor and made my way through
two sets of double doors and took the stairs. So many people
coming and going in the main reception hall, it was easy to
mingle and sneak outside.

A white-bright sun took pole position. The air was cleaner
and fresher, apart from where a hardcore group of smokers
puffed away a short distance from a sign that announced;
'No Smoking.' When a taxi dropped off an elderly man right
outside the door, I snuck in and asked the cabbie to take me
home. There was no other place to go. Had to be done. If I'd
gone back to the ward, Dusty and Lenny would have put up

all kinds of reasons for me to stay put. I'd apologise and explain to them later.

"Bad storm, last night," the driver remarked.

"Uh huh."

He quickly gathered I wasn't much of a talker and the rest of the journey was silent. When we reached my place, I emptied my purse and paid him.

The second my key scraped the lock, Mr Lee let out a yap, stood up on the sofa on his hind legs, and threw himself at the front window. It was the first sign of normality in days. Seeing his soft, slobbery face cheered me.

I walked straight into the sitting room and scooped him up. Shiny-eyed, he licked my face and generally let me know he was pleased to see me. He adored my mother, but in lieu of her absence, he was prepared to transfer his affections. Stuck in that moment, I thought of the futility of a lifetime of trying to make her love me. I wondered where they were and how far they'd got. Knowing my father, they would be out of the country in a place where the extradition laws were flaky.

I put Mr Lee down, his claws skittering on the polished wooden floorboards, released the lock on the sash window and opened it wide to get rid of the doggie stink.

"Want to go out?" I said. Interpreting his dance around my legs as an affirmative, I followed him to the kitchen, opened the back door and watched as he trotted out into the garden.

Rocco, I thought, gazing across the lawn, where the hell are you?

A sudden movement behind and I felt a pair of hands slide

over my eyes, the body of another pressed close to my back. "Rocco," I laughed gently, "You're a dark horse."

Drawn back, I went with it, played along, and took a couple of steps away from the door. I giggled but, as the pressure on my eyes increased, I stopped finding it funny. Starbursts of light flew in front of me and I felt disorientated. "Hey, stop messing about." The heaviness slackened, fingers gliding down my cheeks, slipping to my neck, my throat. Big hands. Man's hands. Hands that wanted to kill me.

Fear as sharp as razor wire cut through me. My arms flung out wide and wild. My feet scrabbled for purchase. I was dragged backwards. The air in my lungs never made it to my throat, the scream that threatened to emerge summarily executed.

His sour breath was hot and close to my ear. I caught a bitter smell, a distillation of coffee, sweat and ruthlessness. I should twist and turn. I should bite and scratch. Determined to extract his DNA, I should take lumps out of him with my nails. I did none of these things. Maybe, if I pretended my hyoid bone had snapped, he'd let me go.

Pitiable and feeble, I stopped moving at all. I took a last look at freedom, the garden beyond, the dog pottering about, sniffing every bush, peeing on every blade of grass, oblivious to the chaos in my kitchen. I'd never envisaged life ending this way. Finally, I keened my ears for Scarlet's voice, but there was nothing there apart from my assailant's.

"You crazy bitch. You fucking ruined everything."

Compression increased. Veins in my cheeks careered to the surface. Blood vessels in my eyes bulged. Pressure built and expanded until my head was empty of thought, of belief and hope and love.

In the sickly silence, my thoughts grew faint, like I was calling from a faraway place and nobody could hear me.

The room slid. With a tremendous bump, I hit the deck. My chin banged on the tiles, splitting my lower lip and chipping a tooth. Greedy for air, I gulped and tasted blood in my mouth. My heart vibrated against my already battered ribcage.

Stumbling to my knees, I heard shouts and the dull thud of fists on flesh. On unsteady feet, I stood, swayed and turned around.

His face contorted with rage; Rocco sat astride Mallis. He had him by the collar of his shirt, smashing his head again and again against the floor. Mallis cursed but didn't resist. Weirdly, his snake-eyes smiled. And then I saw why.

Everything happened in slow-mo. I saw the gun first. My voice wheezed, "Rocco." He dived. My trainer connected with the side of Mallis's hand, unbalancing me, though I did not fall. A loud crack and flash and the pistol cartwheeled across the kitchen. Mallis rolled towards it, arm reaching. God alone knew how many shots he had left. Enough. That's all I knew.

My ears rang and I did not hear the sound of the front door battered off its hinges. I did not see eight firearms officers armed with MP5's storm the house. My eyes were only for Rocco.

"Get down, get down," a man's voice yelled. I dropped, lead-weight, to the ground, face pressed against the floor. I heard the noise of metal scraping across tiles, Mallis letting go of the firearm and a firearms officer, a stocky figure in black, kicking it away. Glancing up, I watched Mallis, bloodied and granite faced as two officers cuffed and arrested him.

Alive and unharmed, Rocco's gaze met mine. As surprised as me that we'd made it, he beamed a magical smile.

Chapter 84

It's a funny thing about the police. In the white heat of a 999, they turn out mob-handed, with vehicles and personnel all over the shop. At least four patrol cars will turn out for a minor prang at a road junction. But once the crisis is past, and the due process of law takes over, they are difficult to locate, let alone track down. Having given a statement, I'd phoned Tracey West and was told variously that she was on a rest day, on holiday, in a meeting, on a course, 'unavailable' and out on a call. Fortunately, my contact with Rachel Haran proved more fruitful. We sat in her garden, a modern concoction of gravel and potted plants.

"I owe you a very big apology. I was wrong."

So was I. For too long I'd pushed aside my instincts about my dad and followed my heart.

"It's been confirmed that an accelerant used to start the fire at the house at Winchcombe was directly linked to materials in your father's garage."

It came as no surprise. Last seen boarding a flight to Cuba, my parents were on the run.

"The police really need to speak to your brother."

"And that's not possible." Zach was still in critical care. Although the doctors were optimistic, it would be some time before he could give a statement or testify.

"So, what happens?"

"There will be two trials regarding Miss Temple. The first will try Edie Chancellor."

"She admitted attacking Drea?"

"After a night without her creature comforts, she broke down. I hear she wishes to plead diminished responsibility."

"Sounds about right."

Rachel's smile was north of chilly. "Not sure the courts will take a sympathetic view despite her excellent lawyer."

"And the second trial?"

"If your father were to magically set foot back in the UK, he'd be arrested and face a separate prosecution. Zach would be called as a witness."

"What would my father be looking at?"

"The holy trinity of charges: Preventing a Lawful and Decent Burial, Perverting the Course of Justice and Assisting an Offender. I don't need to flag up that the court would view these in a dim light. Your father's flight from justice doesn't help. I'm sorry," she said, looking pained. "Must be difficult for you."

Difficult didn't come close. "What about Edie's attack on Zach and me?"

"Separate trial."

"And Mallis?"

"Aside from his attack on you and Mr Noble, Mallis was

already under investigation for supplying reconditioned guns to the criminal underworld. Tools for reactivating weapons were found in his basement along with an eye-watering amount of ammunition. Ballistics experts were able to link his activities to numerous crime scenes, including the recent murder of a police informant."

It occurred to me that the police had not exactly knocked themselves out in nabbing Mallis on my behalf, but I kept that to myself. The good news was that he was in custody and a trial date set for the following year.

"How come Mallis escaped prosecution for so long?"

She flicked a cool smile. "The closest we ever got rested on a statement of an informer, who'd served time, and a restaurant owner who had a string of criminal convictions for fraud."

"Not the most credible on the witness stand."

"That was the view of the CPS. Despite the testimonies, statements and allegations, nothing ever stuck and then we received a major blow. Our informer suddenly withdrew his statement."

"He was got at?"

"Without a doubt."

She didn't say it, but she meant either by my father or Mallis. I asked her.

"Whatever I now think about your father, I believe it more likely that Mallis was the muscle." Which corroborated Tina Vernon's story. I wondered if I'd ever hear from Cecil Vernon.

Rachel cleared her throat. "Mallis is talking. How much of what he says is true remains to be seen. Corrupt officers will pretty much do anything to ensure that they stay out of prison."

Chapter 85

We decided not to stay in Hereford after all. I arranged to sell the business to Lenny and my house to Dusty. Rocco put his gran's old place on the market and gave notice on the rental in Worcester. It was a few months until Zach was well enough to give a full statement to the police. Around the same time, I received a phone call and, taking a trip to London with a thick roll of twenties, spent an afternoon in Room 73. On my return, there was one last thing to do before we left for the West Country.

"Hi."

I looked up, thought how terrible Nate looked, and pushed a pint of Greene King towards him.

We were in the garden of the Norwood Arms, on the busy corner of Leckhampton Road. Nate's hand shook when he lifted the glass to his lips. He looked older, more lived-in.

"Before you say anything, I'm not seeing her anymore. It's finished. Over."

After everything that had happened, Nate's affair no longer

ranked as the crime of the century. I made a sympathetic noise.

"What did you want to say? Not sure I can stand any more revelations." His smile was edgy.

"I want to put the record straight. For Scarlet."

He nodded uncertainly.

"Scarlet was perfect prey for a man like Richard Bowen." I didn't rub it in that, in the wake of Nate's affair, she probably felt lonely and unloved and was flattered by Bowen's attention. "Whatever she had with the man; I believe it was brief."

"I'm not exactly in a position to criticise," Nate said, dark-eyed.

"A few days ago, I met Cecil Vernon, a man who'd known Dad when he worked for the MET." I described what happened.

"You have to pay for secrets." Cecil sprawled in the only chair next to a window with a view of a brick wall. He was a short thickset man with a thin comb-over and seventies' style mous-tache that did not match the colour of his salt and pepper hair. I kept my distance, back to the door, prepared for a fast exit if necessary. There was no air-con in the room, but this was not the reason I was sweating. Vernon might be in his seventies but, to me, he was no less formidable; he could still hurt. The dead-ness behind his eyes told me so.

I nervously fanned out fifteen hundred pounds on the bed between us. "Is that enough?"

"It'll do for now." He made it vanish like a magician disap-pearing a dove. "You wearing a wire?"

E. V. Seymour

"Do I look like I am?" I wore a vest top and shorts.

The loose skin on Cecil's face tightened. "No need to be sarky." He ran his eyes over my body, from top to toe, then back up to my breasts. Instinctively, I crossed my arms over my chest, cupping my elbows.

He gestured with his chin. Light from the window caught a couple of stray grey hairs he'd missed when shaving. "Bag next." I chucked him my rucksack, watched as he turfed it upside down and ran stout fingers over my belongings. He checked my phone, scrolled down, switched it off. Satisfied, he piled my stuff back in and threw it all back. "Catch."

I caught hold of it by the strap.

"And before you get cocky, you breathe one word of our little chat to anyone, I'll deny we ever spoke and then I'll hunt you down." Calculated and deliberate, his voice didn't change in pitch or tone. He could have been ordering a range of dishes from a takeaway menu. Was I frightened? Yes.

"You spoke to my sister."

"I did. Pretty girl. Nervous but nice."

"What did she ask you?"

The corners of his mouth twitched into a smile. "You don't muck about, do you? That sister of yours was the same. Right eager beaver. Sorry to hear what happened," he said, as if suddenly remembering. "Tina told me."

I nodded. Couldn't bring myself to thank him.

"Must be a blow to you all. Bad job for your folks. Shakes you up."

I wasn't paying for a counselling session. "What did she want?"

442

"Hold up. Do me the courtesy of allowing me to pay my respects."

I had no choice but to suck up his rebuke. I bowed my head so that he wouldn't see how furious and frustrated I was.

The silence seemed to extend forever. Eventually, Vernon smoothed his sweaty palms down his shirt, took a breath in and, when he was good and ready, said, "Your sister wanted information about a man called Richard Bowen. I told her what I'm gonna to tell you. I never met him."

It came as a crushing surprise. Surely, it hadn't ended there. "What about your mate, Charlie Binns?"

"Some nosy git copper put the squeeze on poor old Charlie. Got him tied up in all sorts."

"Bowen?"

"Funnily enough," Cecil said, without a trace of humour, but plenty of sarcasm, "he didn't leave his name and address."

"What did this copper want?"

The sterile light behind his eyes didn't alter. "Information."

"What kind of information?" I doubted a skilled inquisitor with torture in his repertoire would easily make Cecil Vernon open up. "Charlie must have described the conversation."

Cecil paused, picking at a molar and dislodging a piece of food that he flicked away. "Said the man was snooping, digging up ancient history about a friend of ours. Clever with it. Tried to stitch Charlie up."

"Clive Mallis?"

"Mallis? Gotta be fucking joking. No friend of mind. Superglue wouldn't stick to that geezer. A right sort. Proper gangster.

Violence, the lot. Shouldn't wonder if he wasn't involved in offing Charlie."

"You'll be pleased to hear he's in custody."

A wondrous light entered Cecil's eyes. "That so? Fucking ace."

Before he got too carried away, I prompted him to continue.

"Ah, now we're getting to the nitty-gritty. Got that same hungry look in your eyes as your sister. Ravenous, she was."

I chewed my bottom lip until it bled, agonised by the thought of Scarlet's desperation. She'd have hated to come to a place like this to talk to a man like Vernon.

"Charlie calls his mate and his mate tells him to stay low. Says he'll sort things out and promises to protect Charlie's arse."

I felt as if I'd be driving for miles with the handbrake on. With it off, I careered forward, no gear changes, everything sharp and focused and speeding towards me. The 'sorting out' involved Mallis and one of his contacts, but the visitor was someone else.

"Was Charlie's mate Detective Chief Inspector Roderick Napier?" I felt like a child reading aloud.

Cecil frowned. The folds in his cheeks fell over the lines around his jaw. "Bit formal. Why don't you call him your dad?"

Because he doesn't feel like my dad anymore. I shrugged a whatever. Disdain gave form to the folds in Cecil's face. His mouth was one straight edge. How could a man like Napier breed such a disrespectful child?

"Your old man was a top bloke. I liked him a lot. So did loads of people. Old school. Proper gent. Reliable and all. Straight as a dye when it came to business. He—"

"I'm not looking for a character reference, or a stroll down

memory lane, Mr Vernon. I want to know what he did." *I want explanation. I need detail.*

Cecil shot me a look of pure contempt. "Your dad was a better source of knowledge than Google."

"You mean he gathered information?"

His hands clenched into fists. He looked thunderous. "What do you take me for, a fucking grass?"

"No. That's not what I meant."

"Should fucking think so."

I saw how my dad had made it his business to collect people: to recruit and exploit, to manipulate and to drain them of knowledge. "My father gave you information? Is that what you're saying?"

Cecil threw his head back and laughed. Tears sprang to his eyes and trickled down the lines on his face. It didn't make me feel any more secure. "Lord above. Don't they educate you kids these days? Mr N didn't give us nothing. He sold it."

I'd had to get my head around a lot of things in the past few weeks, most of it outside my comprehension, but I thought my heart might explode with shock. My father had fooled everyone, Rachel Haran included, for a very long time.

"My father sold details of active police investigations?" My breath came in shallow bursts and blood fled through my veins as if seeking an exit. Vernon clicked his tongue and cast his eyes across the empty bed. I slapped down another couple of hundred pounds, which he scooped up, counted and spirited away. "It will cost you more than that. Five hundred. Take it or leave it."

I gave him the rest of my cash. "This is all I have," I said, wobbly-voiced.

"Don't make my heart bleed." He took it, settled himself again. "We had a little name for it, Operation Jericho. Talk about bringing the walls of the Old Bill crashing down," Cecil said with a fat chuckle. "Mr N gave us tip offs about drugs raids, warnings about swoops on brothels and porn shops. Sometimes, drugs and cash were stolen. And there was bigger stuff going on, cuts from the profits of robberies and wotnot.

"Don't know why you're looking so fucked off," he said, reacting to my horrified expression. "That's how things were done back then. Straight business. No sodding about. You scratch my back and I'll scratch yours."

"And you told Scarlet?" I could barely get the words out, but speak I did. I wanted cold hard facts

"Of course, I told her. That's what she paid me for. Funny thing," he said, sucking in through his teeth, "I think she already knew."

"Christ," Nate said in dismay.

"It confirmed everything Bowen had threatened to disclose, that our dad was corrupt and not only capable of covering up murder, but complicit in instigating it."

"And Scarlet knew that if Bowen blabbed—"

"Everything would be destroyed."

Stunned, Nate ran his fingers along his face and jaw. "She meant to kill him."

"She did."

"Fuck. Fucking hell." Nate bowed his head. "She must have been out of her mind." I could only agree. It wasn't what I would have done.

He looked away, his eyes focusing beyond the railings, on

the road, houses and shops on the opposite side. "It's all my fault, isn't it?"

"No, Nate."

"How can you say that? "There was genuine anguish in his eyes.

"We all played a part. Me, included.'

Chapter 86

"That tap to your head was heaven sent," I teased.

"Ha-bloody-ha!"

It was true. The likelihood of Zach making a good recovery, kicking his addictions, and finding a purpose had seemed as remote as an Indie band playing at a State funeral – of which Zach no doubt would approve – but he'd done it.

In the autumn, when the stags were baying and sheep tupping, Rocco and I moved to Exmoor. We bought two small cottages, side by side, with land and outbuildings. Over time, we planned to convert and let them out for holiday rentals. Zach and Tanya came with us. Along with Mr Lee, this was our family now.

And yet; the search for answers had immunised me against the raw pain of bereavement. Now all I had was silence and loss.

"Fancy a walk?" Rocco said, as the sun drifted over the hillside. I nodded and he took my hand. We headed down through the orchard, over the gate and up into a neighbouring field. The sky seemed as wide and alive as Rocco's smile. When we reached a five-bar gate, Rocco drew me close. "You okay? You've been very quiet."

"Have I?"

"It's been a big move. No regrets?"

I shook my head. Maddeningly, a tear welled up and trickled down my cheek. "I miss Scarlet so much."

"I know."

"I'm sure her voice spoke to me when I was in the quarry and now it's gone. She's gone."

"Your mother might have Scarlet's human remains, but you carry her in your heart. She carries you with her too."

A lovely thought. I wasn't sure I bought it. Dead is dead, isn't it? Yet I so wanted to believe otherwise. "You really think so?"

He squeezed my shoulder and smiled. "I know so. Look." His voice sparked with wonder, "Over there in the orchard."

I followed his gaze. Nestling on the grass, were three of the whitest, purest feathers I'd ever seen.

Acknowledgements

This story, as with all my novels, would never have been written without extensive support and help from others. Broo Doherty, my agent at DHH Literary Agency, deserves very special thanks for being a fine editor, a good friend and, occasional 'shrink' for those crisis moments!

I'm naturally indebted to the entire team at Harper Collins, including Charlotte Ledger for her faith in me and enthusiasm for the story; Finn Cotton for reading early drafts, and not forgetting Emily Ruston for saving both my bacon and blushes, and for making the story so much stronger.

Graham Bartlett, former Chief Superintendent, is my new go-to guy for all things police procedural. Nothing was too much trouble and he answered my numerous queries with amazing patience and humour. Any mistakes are mine alone. 'Bent Coppers' by Graeme McLaglan proved an invaluable source of information regarding police corruption in the 1980's so many thanks to him. Thanks also to Oliver Goom for ensuring that Rocco's occupation in medical insurance, and the advice he gives to Molly, contains that ring of authenticity.

I'd love to thank the stranger who showed me how to find Gullet Quarry. Alas, I never discovered his name.

Malvern often gets a bad press from me because I hated my time at school there so I hope, in some way, this might redress the balance. Finally, Ian Seymour deserves more gratitude than he realises. My husband and first reader, he has the tough job of serving up constructive criticism while remaining happily married. Fortunately, he does it with style. Long may it continue.